SOMETHIN

MW01223874

A new thriller series by Dean Comyn

BOOK ONE: DROWNING

ACKNOWLEDGEMENT

This book series has been a long time in the making and would not have been possible without the undying support and encouragement of my mom (the Reader), my wife (the Scientist), my son (the Hockey Player), as well as Friends both Old and New. Special thanks to Tim Christison, who taught me a lot and coached me toward the final draft. And to my author friend Vince Stevenson, thanks for being my second pair of eyes.

Cover photo by Eric Zhu

PART ONE: FRIDAY NIGHT

23:41

"What do you mean he's gone, Dawson?" Detective Chief Inspector John C. Wayne had not been expecting a call from Detective Sergeant Michael Dawson, only a text message to confirm his subject was in bed. And he was not expecting that for at least another hour. Wayne had hoped to be asleep before it came.

"Gone. From the opera," Dawson panted. "Professor Veda, and Kaia. He— they're gone, sir."

Wayne could tell that Dawson wasn't his normal self but somewhere between confused and exasperated. Or drunk.

"All right, Dawson," said Wayne. He kept his voice low and even out of habit, as the calm voice of reason. "No need to panic. They probably left early, before the fat lady sang. Purcell isn't for everyone." *Or anyone, really*, he thought.

"All right, Dawson. What happened?"

Dawson sounded slow, but even. "I fell asleep, sir. I believe I was drugged."

"You believe?" Wayne caught his voice and offered an excuse. "It's Purcell, Dawson." He wanted to believe the easy explanations. But the worst-case scenario kept needling him.

"Yes, sir it was. But..."

Wayne let the silence hang as he walked back to his office, phone in hand. He put it on the desk next to his touch pad.

Wayne tapped the pad and dragged his finger diagonally to pull a 16x16 grid of camera feeds onto the left-hand screen. Each image had a small dialogue window below it with an abbreviated address and the camera's GPS coordinates. Wayne could see the last opera-goers still filing out of the Opera House.

He sent the link in a message to Special Analyst James Tully's phone as he continued to scan the viewers:

You up? Need you on this. More to follow. Show it to HOLMES.

Wayne knew Tully's expertise with the Home Office Large Major Enquiry System would come in handy one day. He hadn't expected it to be today. He drew a deep breath and let it out slowly as he continued to toggle round the camera feeds. Each highlighted image bulged out of the grid in a 3D effect as he zoomed in on his target.

Wayne saw the block of feeds from the car park off Drury Lane and highlighted and dragged it over to the right-hand screen. He watched as life played in three-second clips on each of the fourteen cameras in-and-around the three-storey car park.

He could see Dawson, dressed in a tuxedo standing next to the Peugeot assigned for ferrying Dr Veda and his date to the Royal Opera House. Wayne noticed the passenger door was slightly ajar.

"Did you open the door?"

"No sir. It was open just like this when I came up here."

This was a crime scene now, and Wayne went into management mode. The Home Secretary had given him Dr Veda exactly thirty-five days earlier when Veda had arrived in London from Oxford University. Wayne had no idea who Veda was before he got the call, and he said so. She explained that Dr Veda was doing important work for the Health Ministry, and his personal safety was of the highest importance.

The Home Secretary expressed concern that Veda might have difficulty adapting to life in London, so it was decided that he would have a plainclothes officer as his driver for an undetermined short-term transition period. Wayne accepted the Home Secretary's explanation before considering whether the professor had value to anyone or faced any threats.

Wayne had assigned Michael Dawson to the first official posting of the MCU2. Dawson's file was one of the first few dozen files Wayne had culled from his initial candidate search of the Met's personnel database. One phone call to Dawson's superior in the Intelligence Command had put him on Wayne's short list. Still in his twenties, Michael Dawson was one of the youngest officers to earn the rank of detective. But Wayne was most intrigued by Dawson's two failed attempts to join MI6. They met once, and Wayne revealed little about the task force he was creating before Dawson volunteered to request the transfer himself. He accepted his first assignment with few questions, and Wayne appreciated that. But it wasn't a babysitting job anymore.

"Well, you did look, right Dawson?" Wayne didn't wait for Dawson to reply. "What did you touch?"

"I pulled it open by the latch, but I didn't get in. Just looked. No contamination, sir," Dawson asserted.

"But you looked," Wayne repeated without reproach. He was curious. "Well? Anything?"

"Yes sir. Looks to be two small drops, on the inside of the door next to the lock button. Right here." Dawson held his phone at an angle and focused the camera on the pair of droplets.

"Looks like blood, sir."

He used his free hand to point at them from outside the window, flexing his index finger and bending his thumb to pinpoint the spots and the small gap between. Dawson held steady and waited for the inspector to respond to his find. Wayne glanced at the screen on his phone. His eyes were busy as he pulled up a map of Greater London on the main viewer on his desk.

"Have you got a photo of them?"

"The blood stains?" asked Dawson.

"No, Veda and…"

"Kaia? Yes sir. A few," said Dawson. "From tonight," he added. "Shall I share them, sir?"

"Well, yes. Ms Rebane," Wayne tapped his desk. "Send me the best one with both. Now," he said. "I'll send it out A-S-A-P." He always spelled it out, like Duke Wayne would have done in one of his classic war films. Wayne disliked the way too many people had made the acronym into a single word.

He had already dragged and dropped the file photo of Dr Veda onto the centre screen and was preparing to send it out with an alert, but a photo of both of them together would make more sense. Besides, Wayne realised he hadn't any photos of the girlfriend, despite her seeming to take up more and more space in Veda's world since they first met a few weeks earlier.

Dawson's message arrived and Wayne smiled at the attachment's title as he opened it, but didn't laugh at the irony until he saw the image of the couple standing in front of a phone box around the corner from the main entrance to the Royal Opera House.

"Dr Who, indeed," Wayne wondered aloud.

"Sir?" asked Dawson. "Didn't it come through?"

"It did, Dawson. I was referring to the caption you wrote. Dr Who?"

"Oh, that," Dawson breathed heavily. "It was a joke. The lady at the box office asked Dr Veda to repeat his name when we were picking up the tickets. I took the photo just after."

Wayne had a dossier on the young scientist. Now he regretted not performing due diligence on the woman when Dawson had first informed him about the budding romance in Veda's life. But he had no reason to be suspicious before tonight.

After all, according to the memo from the Home Office Dr Nicholas Veda was a relatively unknown scientist from Oxford, working on a cure for typhoid or some such disease, and of little interest to anyone outside the Health Ministry.

Wayne had read the good doctor's bio and was quietly happy to hear that spring had finally arrived for Veda when Ms Rebane entered his life.

But suspicion rang like a fire bell in Wayne's ear as soon as he saw the photo of the stunningly beautiful Ms Rebane standing next to the meek and humble scientist. He knew full well it didn't only happen in the movies.

"No, it's fine, Dawson." Wayne cornered his dubiety in the back of his mind and went on cordially, "Well, stand by, secure the scene, and I'll get a team over there."

"Yessir!" Dawson exclaimed, sounding relieved.

Wayne rang off, then opened his directory. He paused, his thumb hovering over the screen. His first instinct had been to request the Home Office to call in extra military, double or triple the street patrols in the vicinity of the Opera House and give them the order to detain Veda and his date on sight.

In a moment he could send out an alert to every level of the Metropolitan Police Service, have the photo in the phones of every uniform in the Greater London area, including transit and airports, through the Met's COMS system. And have thousands of eyes scanning the city for the well-dressed scientist and the knockout that must be accompanying him.

If he was sure there was foul play involved, he had to act. But he wasn't.

Wayne's unit had been officially active for almost three months but in fact had yet to engage in any official action. At the administrative level of the Met, all the commanding officers had received a directive to cooperate in any way requested if called upon by the Unit and DCI Wayne.

Despite being active, the unit was far from operational. No need had arisen to engage any other branch of the Metropolitan Police to date. Wayne had his core of First Officers in place but had deliberately kept the unit offline at the Met, and had remained on standby with the Home Office since St Valentine's Day, awaiting a direct order.

The directive to supply a security escort for the Health Ministry's virologist had appeared to be an excuse to be logging active hours until Major Crimes Unit 2 went operational. Wayne grimaced at his phone and scanned his directory for his contact in the HO. He read the time.

"Almost midnight." He put the phone down and sighed. But the grimace refused to loosen as his eyes roamed the map.

Wayne wasn't ready to call the Home Office until he was certain that the two young lovers hadn't simply slipped out of the Opera House for a little snogging. Even now they might be thinking about calling Dawson to pick them up. He was hoping the blood at the scene was somebody else's — preferably nobody's.

Either way, putting the Met Police ground forces and surveillance branches on it seemed prudent. He quickly typed a draft alert on his desktop.

Getting his team engaged and up to speed came first, he reasoned, if only by a few seconds. Wayne dragged their mobile numbers into the address box on the message pane. Then he paused to consider exactly who else needed to see the alert. *How high, and how wide do I wave this flag?*

His gut told him he was facing the Unit's Inaugural Event, but his head reminded him of the potential for political disaster.

After being introduced by the Home Secretary at her Easter Tea with the Superintendents, DCI Wayne had reached out to every commander in the Service to get a read on their reaction to the directive. Most reacted with the proper acceptance, all with varying degrees of reluctance. Wayne had restated the delicately worded article that described the position of his MCU2-cum-Task Force in the Met's hierarchy.

He had got a good read on many Commanders in the series of face-to-face meetings which he held after the Home Secretary announced Superintendent John Wayne's reassignment to the newly activated MCU2.

They were labelled meetings in his calendar but Wayne had tagged some as chat and some F2F discussion depending on how confrontational he anticipated them to be.

His assumptions had proved right in all cases. Most of the leadership within the Metropolitan Police Service understood and accepted that the new directive was about action not authority.

Wayne knew all of them well enough to know it would be difficult for some of these capital 'L' leaders to see it as anything but castration should the need arise for them to step aside and let Wayne take charge of and deploy their assets.

There were a few too many in high places with designs on climbing higher before they retired. If he had to pull rank to get things done, it would mean inaction until the Home Office reacted, leaving Wayne paralysed.

Worse yet if the two escaped lovebirds were to turn up getting it off in the bushes at Lincoln's Inn Park, a ten-minute walk from the Opera House...

He hadn't dismissed the public sex fantasy solution, but had to consider all eventualities, including activating Charles Burns, but only if the situation dictated.

He decided to send the notice directly to Dispatch, to engage the eyes of the Met—at street level only. IT Guy and Tully will have to find answers to the bigger questions. *As they arise*, he thought.

Wayne drew his hands back from the keyboard, leaving them hanging stiffly as he considered the next steps to follow the general alert. He opened another window on the left-hand viewer that displayed the location of each team member's phone on a smaller scale map.

He noted the locations and proximities to his primary points of interest. Wayne tapped on the touch pad to send the instant message—with the photo and details—to each unit member's phone, and also to an officer in Dispatch he knew well enough to trust to be discreet.

He watched his phone, waiting only a few moments before the message read confirmation appeared on all message tabs.

He knew that within minutes the alert would be sent out to a few thousand Met police patrols, constables and special constables across all the boroughs of London.

By Wayne's calculation, if the two young lovers had simply slipped away from Dawson, they would be spotted and quickly reported.

There was the real possibility that Dr Veda and Kaia Rebane were abducted from the car park, and the reality was that Wayne had no idea why, much less who.

An Albanian prostitution ring? Racists or terrorists? He fought off the impulse to call his contact in the HO and demand some answers about Dr Veda and his work.

Instead he opened the stream linking his computer display directly to Intelligence Specialist Analyst Tully and IT Specialist Inspector Guy Tellier and pinged them both for immediate response.

As a second thought, he sent Tellier another short message with Veda's telephone number and email address. He quickly typed in the subject line:

And their tweets etc., leaving the message blank.

Wayne closed the phone and checked his watch, then turned his attention to the maps on his monitors. He confirmed his time and distance estimates and contacted three members of his team, sending each a message with an address and a brief directive.

He sent Detective Sergeant Semi Riza to the car park on Drury Lane, informing him that a forensics team should follow his arrival. Then he sent the address and Riza's contact details in a second message to his ally in Dispatch requesting a forensics team and directing them to follow Riza.

In a separate message he requested dispatch of a wagon to take Dawson to the infirmary for toxicology tests and monitoring.

Wayne kept an eye on the message tab and shot glances up at the computer monitor as he typed and sent another message. He placed the phone on the desk and relaxed and flexed his digits, his arthritic index finger still slightly curved, as if reluctant to relinquish its grip on the phone.

The reply came in only a few seconds. He let out a long, satisfied breath and his grimace slowly turned upward, approaching a smile, as he read it.

Detective Sergeant Martin Blennerhassett confirmed he would take his car and meet up with a second patrol at Veda's residence in Kensington. Wayne dispatched Detective Sergeant John Aitkens directly from Scotland Yard to Veda's laboratory, as he was the only team member on duty. He determined that Aitkens and two uniformed officers would be arriving there before the others reached their destinations.

Wayne allowed himself a sigh of relief. The Incident Response had quickly become an investigation and his unit had it under control. His first steps had been sure. He felt confident that he had ticked all the required boxes if anyone in the Home Office asked to see the protocol.

The physical teams were in place or en route and the digital intelligence was being gathered and analysed. For the time being at least, he needn't involve any of the Higher Ups in the Met or the HO.

Either his team would find Veda and Ms Rebane in the next few hours or he would get a call from whoever snatched the professor and his girlfriend.

The possibilities swirled in his head. Violent abduction, a disappearance at least—planned or coerced? And Kaia Rebane. Wayne had to ask himself again *why no due diligence* when Dawson first mentioned the Estonian beauty in his daily reports. He cursed himself for not ordering Dawson to do a background check on her.

But Wayne didn't see a security threat when the details came down from the HO about this police escort assignment. The only potential conflict he could imagine would be in London traffic, and that was Dawson's business. He turned to the window and gazed at the endless flow of traffic on the Embankment below.

It was supposed to be…nothing.

Wayne sent another message to Tully:

Need to see everything on Veda and Kaia Rebane A.S.A.P.

Something told Wayne that adding Charles Burns to the receivers list would be advisable. His eyes wandered to the short, two-drawer mahogany filing cabinet to the right of his desk. He inherited it when he took over as Superintendent of The Specialist Branch in 2002, and it was the only furniture that had survived the move to his new office at MCU2.

He visualised the folder in the top drawer containing the transfer papers for Charles Burns. He had been holding off on signing the order to make it official.

But the current situation was expanding rapidly, and the former Major Charles Burns had front line experience in many extraction and hostage recovery missions — all with unqualified success — during his years with the Canadian Joint Task Force and British SBS.

Wayne hoped it never came to that. He reasoned that even if it didn't, he needed more boots on the ground, pronto.

Wayne located Burns' phone at the Alexandra Ice Palace. He pressed the dial button. Wayne knew Burns' experience in JTF2 could be valuable if the worst came to worst.

He rang off after he heard the first ring and stared at the number display. He calculated the distance to the Opera House and sent a text message directing Burns to call in A.S.A.P. then he set his phone down on the desk again.

Wayne arched his back and stretched, feeling the late hour.

"The night's just getting started," he mused aloud.

Then he made two direct calls. One, a logical choice and another, a gut reaction, centred somewhere near the throb of fear just behind his diaphragm.

He direct-dialled the security office at the housing complex in Kensington where Veda had been living since he began his work for the Health Ministry. After identifying himself, Wayne had a brief chat with the woman who had been on duty since 20:00. He asked if she had noticed any disruption to the video feeds.

"Not tonight, no sir."

Wayne asked if she had photos of the residents and if she knew Dr Veda. She answered, "Yes and yes, sir."

She reported no sighting of Veda, because he left for the opera before she came on duty.

"According to the key log," she said. "His key should be in the lock up." And it was. The guard explained how Veda, like many of the residents, took advantage of the services provided by the building management, but Wayne barely heard her. He was racing through the possible endings to the evening.

He asked if the guard had access to the recording of the video for the hours previous to her coming on shift. The guard kept it a little coy.

"Now, why might you be looking for video following one specific citizen, Mister Wayne?"

"Detective Chief Inspector Wayne." He politely took the guard's mobile number and sent her the general alert looking for Nicholas Veda and his date as persons of interest to Major Crimes Unit 2.

"See my message? That's why."

The guard apologised with a nod and went to work on her computer.

She typed a few commands and scanned through the images on a smaller viewer to her left.

"Nineteen-oh-seven. There he is. And his date." She paused slightly before she concluded, "Dressed to the nines."

Wayne imagined by her tone that the guard might be more jealous of Veda than of Kaia.

"And not been back."

"That's right sir. I've seen three exits and no entries in the last three hours."

"Almost four," said Wayne, trying to express appreciation. "Well, a team should be arriving soon to see if Dr Veda returns and will likely wait until he arrives."

Wayne got a little edgy when the guard balked at the idea of letting anyone in without a warrant.

"Will they have something... on paper, or something, sir?"

He rubbed his thumb and forefinger together, as if they held a worry stone or string of beads. "This alert status authorises the Metropolitan Police to immediate access anywhere, understood?"

"Yes, sir."

"Well, good. If you have a problem you can contact the Home Office directly," Wayne paused. "At nine am tomorrow."

Wayne poked his touch pad a few times with his stiff right index finger. "I just sent you the number," he said, and waited for the guard's reply.

"I understand, sir," she acknowledged. "I want to help in any way."

"Good. Meanwhile, keep a line free to call us if you see the good doctor, and detain any strangers until we get a good look at them, yes? We'll keep the link open on your video feed, so we'll be with you."

"Understood, sir."

Wayne knew she hadn't looked at the number he texted her. He wasn't sure if she needed to be reassured of all she had taken in, but he admired her for protesting and then capitulating. She obviously understood the situation and would act as directed.

"It was Purcell," he added, as consolation. "They were going to a Purcell opera. Do you know Purcell?"

When the guard explained with a grunt that she didn't, he added, "Well you're not missing anything. Detective Sergeant Blennerhassett and his team are en route and will arrive..." he checked the map and calculated the distance between Blennerhassett's phone signal and Veda's flat in Holland Park. "in about seven minutes. Do let us know if you see anything."

Wayne rang off, looking at his watch and calculating how long it would be before Aitkens and the uniforms got down to the lab, and wondering why he didn't ask the conscientious young security guard's name.

He flagged the number on his outgoing calls list, and next dialled the security desk at Dr Veda's newly constructed lab in Uxbridge Road, Shepherd's Bush. Any optimism he had left was slowly drowning.

Wayne panned his focus to the video feed from the cameras at the building where Veda's modest lab took up about two thousand square feet of the lower level.

The camera angle was fixed at the opposite end of the corridor beyond the lift and stairwell, directed toward the door, with the entry scanner taking up most of the foreground.

On the right side of the frame he could see only the corner of the security desk and what looked like a tall, empty rolling chair that was pushed to the corner behind the desk, its back turned as if it was being disciplined for some misbehaviour. Wayne was not able to remotely zoom or pan the camera.

Mech. fail, read the sidebar.

Wayne grumbled. He tried and failed to remember the last time he spoke to any of the three officers on duty at the lab in the sub level.

Wayne had received the contact details and a dossier on each man assigned to the detail by the Home Office. But he had only had perfunctory contact with them since the assignment began four weeks earlier, and only during office hours.

He dialled the number for the derelict HO man's phone and let it ring once, giving him the option to return his call, as he toggled through the viewer index to find the video feed from the main foyer. He zoomed in to the security station and entry gate.

A guard sat motionless, completely still for several seconds, behind the desk. Wayne wondered if the video was indeed live. He scrolled through his directory to the number for the building's reception desk in the foyer. A private contractor had handled the building's security since before Wayne had even heard of Uxbridge Commercial Plaza.

The man in the chair fit Wayne's idea of a night watchman—old and lonely. He watched as the man stirred and put his book down to answer the phone on the desk.

"Number Ten Uxbridge," said the guard in a Glaswegian accent.

"Right. Good evening. Detective Chief Inspector John Wayne here, Metropolitan Police, Major Crimes."

"Really?" The guard sounded unimpressed. Wayne let it go. He was relieved to have confirmed that the camera feeds were, live again, and so was the guard. He chose to assign the sarcastic response not to a man who was junior in rank, but rather credit it to a man senior in years.

"Yes," Wayne continued evenly. "Turn and look at the camera above your left shoulder and wave. Please."

The security guard complied despite his initial disbelief. Wayne gave a curt "Thank you" and went on to explain how his unit had "spotted some anomalies in the signal transfer" and how he hoped the guard would be able to help.

"It's because of this I need to ask you a few questions..." Wayne let his last word hang, making it sound like a question itself. He smiled out of one side of his mouth and waited until the security guard took the cue and gave his name and details.

Wayne asked if any visitors had come this evening, if and when any disruption in video occurred since the guard had started his shift, some five hours earlier. There had been no disruptions and no traffic in or out since 18:48, the time code of the last handprint-verified exit by an employee of one of the companies from the third floor.

"And I've had no contact with the officer on duty downstairs this evening," the guard added rather curtly.

Wayne let the guard know that a team was on its way and that they would need access to the lower level elevator. The guard asked Wayne to repeat his name and the names of the officers on the way over.

"Just covering me arse here," the guard explained. Wayne smiled at the phone and repeated the names of the men due to appear any minute at the guard's desk.

"And it's DCI Wayne here, of the Major Crimes Unit. You have the number. Yes?" He waited for the gruff Scot to read back the number before he rang off.

Wayne was never the kind of officer to wear his insignia as a reminder of his rank to anyone. He had risen to the rank of Major as a young man in the military and to the rank of Superintendent in the Met, starting there thirty years earlier as a sergeant. John C. Wayne shared the same build as his famous namesake, and he always carried himself with the same authority.

Now in his sixties, Wayne had officially stepped off the ladder, but not out of the chain of command. He had resigned his office with the former Specialist Command to assume the lower official rank of Detective Chief Inspector to lead the newly formed MCU2.

The unit had been set up to report directly to the Home Office and was not to be nested under any other unit in the Service, including the existing Major Crimes Unit. The full authority and autonomy granted by the HO fit with his own mandate to create a more direct response to national security threats than what the current levels of bureaucracy in the Met and the MI branches had been crippled by.

MCU2 was to become the more accurately titled Major Crimes Task Force before the current Home Secretary's term came to an end in a little over two years. Wayne had begun working on the germ of the idea over three years earlier with an officer and old mate from the military in the Home Office.

Now it was official. The new Home Secretary had writ large her dissatisfaction with the status quo and even hinted at her mistrust of the accountability of MI5 and MI6. Three months ago, she cut the ribbon without a ceremony, and told everybody to get on board.

Wayne had been tasked with assembling Major Crimes Unit 2, with the tacit approval to poach the other commands in the Met. Wayne had done so, to an extent, for several months before he formally accepted the command of MCU2. And Wayne had reached out through international channels to a few chosen candidates on many occasions, long before the previous Home Secretary departed.

It was only a matter of days after the announcement that Wayne had an Official Roster — the only way the Metropolitan Police Federation would approve any transfers.

Wayne had recruited three men internally: two he knew personally in the Specialist Branch and Dawson, whom he almost had to pluck out of MI5. Wayne approved three other transfer requests after conducting over twenty interviews.

Employment contracts were signed with Guy Tellier and the other non-MPS members of his IT team and Marty Blennerhassett, the 'Irish Import' as he had dubbed himself.

"If we ever get enough men for a side, Chief," was his joke. *If we ever get a game*, was what he inferred in the several weeks that had passed with no directive.

The unit had no open cases, no investigations. No orders.

Wayne's MCU2 was just getting started and any orders were expected to come from the HO.

His unit would work with any and all of the Met Commands, directing units from each and any branch as required. Wayne had been given the authority to engage any number necessary of available police, from any branch, including military and intelligence resources to create a task force instantly, and *ad hoc*.

Despite telling every new team member of the dynamic shift of the paradigm, some had suggested they were still sceptical of how self-directed the unit could be. In each case, the point had been carefully made that the Unit's autonomy was in question, not Wayne's authority. Their respect for him was unanimous.

Wayne had not given much thought to what a first operation for the unit might look like. But he had not imagined it would look like this night.

He returned his focus to the video feeds from the car park and the Royal Opera House. He highlighted four views from each and began toggling them all to play back in reverse real time. Each viewer showed people and autos moving in a backward dance. Wayne confirmed that he had opened links to allow Tully to see his desktop and then called him directly.

"Tully. Wayne here. Are you getting this? We need facial recognition."

"Yes sir," Tully yawned. "I've got it, and HOLMES and I are on it."

"So, you're asleep there," Wayne snorted.

"No sir. I'm in a handi-cab. Be there in ten. But we are on it, sir."

Tully may have yawned but he did not sound at all tired. He was engaged and already fired up. Suddenly his tone changed.

"Bollocks! Ah, sir it seems there's erm, an irregularity."

Wayne was looking at the screen with the eight views of the Opera House and the car park, still playing in reverse. They all went blue at the same time, 22:10, all looking like an old television that had been disconnected from its VCR but not turned off.

"I know," Wayne stared into the blue void facing him. "What is it?" He couldn't hide his shock at seeing his most crucial source of intel wiped clear before his eyes.

Tully sounded angry, and a little surprised. "We don't know yet, sir. I'm working remotely until I get in, but I'm online with HOLMES and I've just messaged IT. Guy's ahead of us and already has some major suspicions. It looks…"

"Like trouble," Wayne said with a grunt.

He watched the unchanging screen and the time code race backward as he first doubled, then accelerated to five times faster. The screens all stayed blue until 19:19 and magically, life was restored to them.

People and cars once again resumed their jerking, backward dance. Wayne and Tully both made a note about the time out and time in for the "Blue Out", as Wayne had named it.

"It's some kind of hack..."

"Hack? Are you telling me the London Metropolitan Police Service has been hacked?" Wayne worked his jaw as if he had chewing gum in his mouth for the few seconds before Tully continued.

"Yes sir. But no. Maybe a DoS, a denial of service but..." Tully trailed off. "Really unclear now. Guy can't say how big it is, or where it came from. Maybe he'll know how by the time we..." Tully stopped. "What's the plan, sir?"

"How big it is?" Wayne's baritone wavered. "You mean the range of the blackout? Was it more than just at the opera and car park?"

"Seems so, sir."

Wayne looked up at the screen and began selecting the camera feeds from a wider radius around the Opera House and the car park in Drury Lane. He dragged their images to the centre display and typed in the time code to check their playback. Grid by grid, it looked like half of London was blue. CCT cameras offline everywhere.

Wayne realised his fantasy of a tryst in the car park with a beautiful dancer was not how Veda's evening would end.

He straightened himself, as if he were giving an order to the assembled troops.

"The plan is to find Dr Veda and his date." Then he added, "I think we must assume an abduction has taken place."

Tully wanted to reassure himself more than Wayne. "Guy can't say where the disruption entered our communications network or where it originated. But nothing…" He trailed off again then hastily added, "Guy will have more answers. We haven't got any confirmed ground level reports yet, but IT is reaching out."

Tully was less surprised and more concerned now, as he repeated, "two hours."

Wayne was silent. His mind was racing through an ever-growing list of officially and unofficially recognised extremists.

Tully cleared his throat. Some of the anger was still there. "We'll all know more in ten minutes."

"Right," said Wayne. "In your office in fifteen?"

"I'll put the coffee on, sir."

"With your smartphone, right?" Wayne rang off before Tully could stop smiling and respond, "Yes, sir."

Wayne went back to his desktop and opened a search, but he paused to consider where to begin to set the parameters. He sent a copy to Tully with the caption: any ideas?

Wayne's hand hovered over the keypad as he debated a call to the Home Office.

Wayne checked his messages, then called Burns again but got voicemail. He dropped the call and sent Burns the general alert message, and waited with growing unease.

Charles Burns lined up on the right side of centre ice, waiting for the referee to drop the puck. The opposing team scored a goal and Burns was angry.

He poked the number stencilled on his opponent's right shoulder. "Number 87? Just like Sidney Crosby, eh?" Burns' tone was friendly, like a simple guy at a beer league hockey game. He was trying to get a rise out of his opponent.

"Hey, what's your name, 87?" The quiet question went ignored.

Burns looked at the name on the back of Number 87's jersey and leaned into Number 87's ear. "Oh, Dixon, eh?" He sniggered. "Fancy a bit of dick, son?"

Dixon had just scored his second goal of the game and tied the score at 4–4. With the second period winding down Burns' team, the Ravens, was facing elimination from the playoffs.

Burns figured it was time for a little gamesmanship. Dixon was smirking and pretending to ignore the taunts Burns was almost whispering in his ear.

"That was a fucking awesome move you put on our goalie, Dick."

Four players were within earshot and could tell by the way Burns said Dick what particular feature of the male anatomy he was referring to.

"You move like a dancer."

Number 87 stopped smirking, turned to Burns and hissed through his mouthguard.

"Just what the fuck are you on about, you fucking twat?"

Burns smiled at Number 87. "Tsk, tsk, tsk, language, Sidney." Then he turned his back toward the official and made an obscene gesture simulating fellatio at Number 87, then shrugged and grinned coyly.

Dixon was furious. He cursed and slashed Burns on his shin pads. Burns saw the referee's arm go up, signalling the penalty that Dixon was about to get.

Burns stopped moving his feet and coasted through centre, feigning a slight injury. They circled each other at centre ice, Dixon shoving Burns hard with his stick, so angry he was just making noises, not words. Burns protected himself but didn't engage. He looked over his shoulder at the referee again and saw his arm up, watching the play as it moved into the Raven's zone.

Burns puckered his lips for a sweet kiss and winked at Dixon. He absorbed another crosscheck from Dixon's stick then grabbed his opponent's arms as the armoured bodies came together. He taunted Dixon again, hoping to goad him into taking another penalty.

Burns whispered, "Ya wanna go? 'Cause I'll go ya!" He pushed off and shook his gloves as if he was about to drop them.

"We don't 'go' in this league..." Dixon held back. "Fucking...Yank!"

Burns got into Dixon's face. "You wanted to say 'dick', didn't you?" he laughed. "I'm a fucking Canadian, Ass Boy."

He had no idea how, but suddenly it had gone too far. Yet Burns felt no intention of stopping. He had always been competitive at sports, his physical abilities supported by mouth, and vice versa, and both were sometimes hard to stop.

The referee looked alarmed and blew his whistle repeatedly when he finally noticed Burns and his partner waltzing at centre ice.

The linesmen and the referee now had their hands full with the other players. Hilts and a few other players were already on their way to starting a fracas and had begun partnering up with a member of the enemy team as soon as they spotted Burns and Dixon grappling at centre ice.

After another hard crosscheck to the chest from his opponent, Burns grabbed Dixon's stick and got a gloved hand up into his face, giving him a "face wash" and popping the helmet off in one motion. Burns felt and heard the referees and the players closing in.

Before the two linesmen could reach the pair, Dixon dropped his stick and began swinging wildly at Burns. Burns got his hands up, protecting himself from the attack like a boxer as the wild blows rained down on his gloves, well-padded shoulders and the sides of his helmet.

"God, you even punch like a girl! Perfect! I'm in love!" Burns whispered loudly.

The referee blew his whistle again and again as players from both teams swarmed the pair. Pushing and shoving intensified as players from both teams were mixing it up in a chaotic waltz, where both partners were attempting to lead the dance.

Burns dropped his left glove and slipped a short, well-placed jab to the solar plexus and an uppercut to the jaw, then tied up Dixon's arms in his jersey as he slumped.

Burns had been careful not to knock Dixon out, but left him woozy enough to concede the fight. One of the linesmen tried to get between them to break up their altercation, but just then Hilts broke free of his dance partner and threw a half punch, half shove to Number 87 in the back of the head.

The other linesman came over and grabbed Hilts while the first linesman hauled Dixon to his side of the penalty box. The referee escorted Burns to the other penalty box. Burns pleaded his case with the referee as he was ushered to the open gate.

"Gotta give him five and a game, right ref? Plus the slashing and crosschecking? Using his stick as a weapon, ref. Not cool. You saw him. He went nuts. I tried to stop him." He gave a long hard look to Dixon, who still looked dizzy, and more than a little fearful.

The referee maintained his grasp on Burns' jersey and ushered him into the penalty box. "Two for roughing, two for unsportsmanlike conduct." He stole a look at Burns as he shouted the last sentence through the glass to the timekeeper.

Burns raised his arms in helpless protest as the referee returned to the altercation at centre ice. Hilts joined Burns a moment later.

The rest of the combatants looked less willing to continue the dance and skated back to their respective teams' benches, leaving Burns and Hilts in the home side penalty box and Dixon and another of his teammates, Number 8, in the other. The referee and the linesmen were at the glass porthole, sorting out the justice.

"That was fun,'" said Hilts. The Good Ol' Boy from Texas never hesitated to throw in when the game got rough. Burns scowled and turned toward his teammate. "Fuck, Hilts. Why'd you have to stick your big American ass in there? Look, I got him off the ice. Trying to get a power play, you—" Burns bit back on his anger. He knew Hilts had jumped in to defend a teammate, even though Burns didn't need any help. He explained to Hilts how he wanted to get 87 off his game and off the ice and the plan didn't include Hilts—and his deadly slapshot—sitting in the penalty box and thereby nullifying the Ravens' power play.

"Relax, Burnsy" said Hilts. "They still got the extra two." He pointed over Burns' shoulder at the second opponent who had joined Dixon. "Fuckwad over there got two for crosschecking Caver, too, so four-on-three for two minutes. And Percy's on fire. He'll get one back," Hilts reassured. "It's all good, buddy."

Burns stopped chiding Hilts when his phone beeped and buzzed from its concealment in his jockstrap, giving him a little thrill. The missed call was from DCI Wayne. It must have come when he was propping up Number 87, his dance partner.

Burns was torn. Tie game going into the third period, the Ravens needed to win the game to guarantee a berth in the playoffs, and a chance at the league championship. Sure, it was a "beer league", as he might have called it. He played on a League Champion Junior 'A' hockey team in Canada with a few players who had gone on to enjoy careers in professional hockey. It was one of his favourite *what if* possibilities. But that was a lifetime ago, and the Ravens were the closest Burns had got to that feeling of being part of a championship hockey team.

DCI Wayne's message could be a call to action, he reckoned. Maybe the transfer had finally been approved and he was about to join the team at MCU2, as Detective Sergeant Charles Burns.

Burns tucked his phone away and smiled. "Gotta go, Hiltsy."

Hilts knew it wasn't a joke, but he laughed anyway. "What? What do you mean, you gotta go?"

Burns hid his excitement—except for the grin that had stretched up to poke his dimpled right cheek.

"Called in by the boss. Task Force needs me," he shrugged. "I gotta go." He turned for a glance at Number 87 in the neighbouring penalty box then he smiled back at Hilts. "My work here is done. Sidney over there won't be a problem anymore." Burns laughed, then gave Hilts a serious look. "You better score a fucking goal, Hilts."

Hilts looked away and nodded, "You got 'er, buddy. Lemme know how it goes, and all."

"Will do, Cap'n."

"On your first day as a real cop."

Burns rose from the bench and called out to the referee who was preparing to drop the puck so the game could continue. Burns had twisted his grin into a pained grimace.

"Hey Ref! I gotta go to the room." Burns realised a second too late that a statement like that made by a grown man holding his crotch would get a reaction. Players on both sides were sniggering and laughing. Burns caught his own smirk and held his pained expression.

"Use your fucking water bottle, Ace," Dixon chirped from the other side the timekeeper and the low wall separating the penalised players.

Burns couldn't resist. "I'll be using your sweet mouth if I want to, Sidney." His stare said he wasn't being playful anymore. Dixon broke off and looked at the referee sullenly.

Hilts was outraged and tapped Burns with his stick, trying to pull his attention.

"What the fuck? Didn't you say you ain't even on the roster of that team til next week?"

Burns put a finger to his lips.

Hilts seemed certain as he went on without lowering his voice. "Definitely not something that can't wait until after we win this game. Right?"

Burns didn't respond.

"Who are you gonna train at this hour?"

Burns ignored the jab and returned Hilts' impassioned plea with his practised passive gaze.

Hilts asked, "One hour. We need you, buddy."

Burns leaned on the gate as if the pain in his groin had doubled him over as the referee skated to a halt, keeping about a metre away. Burns turned back to Hilts and winked.

"Sorry, Cap'n. Doody calls." Burns turned to the referee and pleaded, "Did you see where he got me with his stick?" Burns pointed at Dixon sitting in the penalty box and gestured to his lower abdomen. "I gotta get some ice on this. Let me go to the locker room. There's only three minutes left in the period, and you gave me four…"

The referee's eyes roved from Burns to Dixon to Hilts and the timekeeper. Burns finally caught and held the young man's doe-brown eyes.

"I hope I don't need medical attention."

Burns pulled up his jersey with one hand and reached down into his pants with the other. "I think I'm bleeding here, ref. Let me go look at it," he asked. "Somewhere else." Burns reached down with his right hand and pulled down on the front of his armoured trousers as if to allow his left hand to do a more thorough examination of his groin.

The referee had turned his focus to Dixon and was delivering as hard a glare as he could muster. But Dixon made it easy to be hard. He looked both guilty and beaten, staring at his skates. Burns raised his voice in pitch and volume and pleaded, "C'mon, Ref."

The referee signalled the gatekeeper to open up and nodded across the ice in the direction of the gate to the dressing rooms. "Go on," he ordered. Then he blew his whistle and pointed at the centre ice face-off circle.

Burns stepped out onto the ice and tapped the gate in front of Number 87 with his stick for one last shot.

"Ooooh I'm gonna miss you, Sidney," he said with a wink. "Maybe catch up after, huh? Good luck, and don't get hurt!"

Burns did one last turn on his way across the ice. If the referee had not been looking his way, Burns might have blown Dixon a kiss. Instead, he made a gesture of apology to his teammates.

Burns read their faces, and most seemed to believe he was injured, but he imagined they had no doubt the "Crazy Canuck" would return for the third period. He pumped his fist and raised his stick as he stepped off the ice.

"Git 'er done, boys," he said, in his best imitation of Captain Bryce Hilts. He gave a nod and a wave to Hilts on the far side of the rink and closed the gate behind him.

Burns strode on his blades down the rubber carpet on the floor between the seating galleries. He turned into the hall under the seating toward the dressing rooms. A young security guard sat in a folding chair next to a small square table, just big enough for two guys to play cards. The only thing on the table besides the deck of cards was a smartphone. The security guard picked it up and very deliberately checked the time. Burns twisted up a look of shock and anger.

"He kicked me out! Fucking ref," he said, thumbing in the direction of the ice.

The attendant stood up and stepped in front of Burns. Already a few inches shorter than average, the attendant seemed to shrink even smaller as Burns, an extra two inches taller in his skates, trod right up to his face, so close the guard could have kissed the grinning cartoon raven logo right on its beak.

Burns smiled at the young man's expanding forehead. It rolled into neat little lines as the attendant craned his neck to look Burns in the eye. He produced a set of keys and gestured toward the two doors on opposite sides of a narrow alley.

"Home or Away?"

"Home," Burns answered. He had dropped the resentful kid act. He was thinking about the call from Wayne, wondering if it was his first call to action.

"Well then, at least we know he's not a homer, eh?" said the man.

"No, but he is a bit of a Chief Wiggum, though," deadpanned Burns. It took the guard a moment, but he reacted like he got it, squawking out a single laugh that sounded like a tropical bird.

Burns decided to assume the guy was not mocking him and waited until the attendant had backed away from the door again before he stepped to it and pulled it open. He went in and crossed over to his stall on the opposite side of the dressing room. He sat down on the bench and took his skates off, taking care to clean the snow and packed ice off the blades. Then he set them down, almost delicately, under the bench before he got the rest of his hockey gear off and stacked it on the floor of the changing stall.

He decided to shower before he called Wayne, but by the time he towelled off another message had arrived with the subject line:

GENERAL ALERT.

This one wasn't from DCI Wayne directly but from a number identified as the Metropolitan Police Service.

Burns guessed it was related. He opened it and saw the message with info about two "persons of interest". Burns could see the photo had been taken outside the Royal Opera House, where he was being directed to go to in the text message from DCI Wayne.

The photo showed an attractive couple, dressed for a night at the Opera. At least, the woman was. The unassuming man looked too young for Purcell in his black tailored suit and bow tie, more like a teenager at a wedding. Tuxedoes have a way of making a timid man look like a kid at a grown-up party, thought Burns. He could see the man was of Asian descent, and he guessed at least a few years older than he looked this night. He figured the parents were from India, and Nicholas was between twenty-five and thirty years old.

The woman on Veda's left looked to be in her early thirties and of Russian extraction. Her dress was perfect for the arrival of spring in London, a sheer, lime green gown with a halter-top that was low and wide enough to reveal her strong neck and shoulder muscles.

A long slit from the hip to the floor revealed a toned thigh and sculpted calf. The front of the dress was open to the navel, her tanned and firm torso on full display. It flaunted her breasts separately, with the gossamer green fabric clinging to her nipples. She was posing, pausing on the red carpet for the paparazzi. She was beautiful and she knew it.

To say that Kaia Rebane photographed well would be an understatement akin to saying that Wayne Gretzky was good at ice hockey. Though she didn't appear to be wearing makeup, Burns imagined she would catch every eye in the room. Any room. She carried her tall frame delicately on a pair of short, kinky fuchsia boots, poised on incredibly thin high heels. A dancer, perhaps a model.

With a scientist.

Burns figured anybody in the Met seeing this photo, with the tag "persons of interest to Major Crimes Unit 2", would have a limited range of first impressions. A gangster and his moll, or maybe a Saudi prince and his escort?

Burns figured that at least a few good men and women of the Metropolitan Police had already imagined a few good conspiracy theories.

Burns hired on at the Met as a Specialist Training Contractor in November 2015, summarily upon retiring officially from his commission in the Joint Task Force of the Canadian military. He had been on loan to Her Majesty's Special Boat Service when his time came up. Burns had requested the permanent transfer after his last assignment with JTF2 in Afghanistan. The SBS accepted Burns' request and put him to work as a trainer for counter terror operations. He spent his last four years of service at bases in the UK and Europe, while completing his qualifications online.

The idea of becoming a police detective began to take shape long before he removed himself from active combat. Burns was determined to join the Met at the rank of detective sergeant. The Met's Commissioner had announced a policy of encouraging transfers between its branches, which was supposed to be a solution to staffing shortages in key areas. He figured his timing was perfect and made an appointment to see a counsellor at the Met's Human Resources department.

He remembered how he had met the initial deflection by the counsellor with a degree of directness that was not appreciated.

"I think your experience and expertise would serve us all better if you were to remain in your current role as a trainer, don't you?"

Burns stormed out, but not before suggesting she had spoken whilst doing something that would be difficult even for a contortionist to perform. She ignored his follow-up emails and hid behind her smartphone in her office when he came to speak in person a week later. Consequently, Burns went over her head and approached her superior directly. He had never been afraid to take that route, but he had rarely been successful in changing opinions in the chain of command.

There was another misunderstanding. The supervisor had already heard from the counsellor and accused Burns of being hostile, threatening to have Burns arrested, or at least reported to the union.

"Have me arrested?" Burns laughed. While the thought of escalating the situation had flickered briefly across his mind, even this overweight hippy saying such an asinine thing to him wasn't going to raise Burns' blood pressure.

He remembered a wiser man, his sensei, once told him:

"You must practice patience. Patience takes practice," Burns repeated, to himself, but loud enough and still directed at both the HR Supervisor and his assistant. Burns thanked them and left.

So, back at Union Jack's Pub, he typed up an email and sent it straight to the Director herself. He argued his years and final rank in the military, combined with his outstanding scores on every exam and level of training required made his application undeniable. Burns figured he may have fast-tracked it a little, but he could see no way for his petition to be refused. He stopped inches short of volunteering as Poster Boy for the Met's staffing initiative.

It was then that Burns had spoken loudly enough for John Wayne to hear about him. Burns heard that Wayne was setting up the new Major Crimes Task Force Unit at about the same time.

Tully informed him when Wayne had first asked for a background check on Burns. Tully admitted he told Wayne about their friendship at the time, and that he saw Burns' military records in the SBS and Canadian JTF2. Burns pondered what small amount of unclassified information about his missions might have spurred Wayne to call. Tully made Burns laugh when he said he couldn't figure if it was luck or balls that had got Burns there, and that he ought to be happy he had both.

Burns had a sense from the first meeting with Wayne that MCU2 would be a good fit for him. He also sensed that Wayne had a similar impression.

Wayne didn't brag that he knew the right people to ask for details about the clandestine operations Burns had been involved in. He let Burns know he had been filled in on what was redacted and what hadn't been reported. He stated that while he did not expect Burns to be in active combat situations with MCU2, he made it abundantly clear that it would not be off the table.

At the informal interview, Wayne discussed more details about the Unit and how it would evolve into a Task Force under the direction of the Home Office and outside the Metropolitan Police administrative structure. The way he described the function of his team sounded like Burns would find himself in a kind of mid-management position, one where he would not be the sharp end of the blade, but also not stuck behind-the-scenes. He saw himself leading investigations into organised crime and corruption, a long way away from armed conflict.

It was three weeks later, with no news of his rank being approved, before Wayne finally offered to get Burns into the unit as its Training Specialist until the approval came through.

That was three days ago. Burns was holding off on saying yes, stalling for the approval to come through. Or, if it had already, as Burns suspected, Wayne wasn't saying anything. Burns would say yes tonight. Even if Wayne didn't ask.

23:53

Burns replied to DCI Wayne's first message with a simple *"En route"*. He did not ask if he was being activated, as much as he wanted to do. He threw his equipment bag over his shoulder, grabbed his hockey stick, and headed for the exit. The horn sounded in the arena, signalling the end of the second period, as he pushed open the door and stepped into the night air. His teammates would be filing into the dressing room and he was gone. Captain Hilts would explain. He would have to.

Burns paused for a moment. He let his eyes drift upward above the horizon and into the parting clouds, visualising the game-winning goal he would not score tonight. The city lights seemed to be too distant to cause enough light pollution to filter his view of Polaris.

"This better be something," he grumbled.

Burns trotted to the car park and threw his hockey gear into the back of his Subaru Forester. He exited the car park onto Park Road and passed in front of the Alexandra Palace once more, imagining the ice surface being cleaned, before he turned south and headed toward the Royal Opera House. His phone rang. The call was from DCI Wayne. Burns felt the same chill he got every time he received the order to go, a lifetime ago. In a flash he relived the physical memory of skating on a fresh sheet of ice. He hoped his skates were still sharp.

Burns tapped his earpiece and answered quickly, "Detective Chief Inspector Wayne, yes sir. Sorry I missed your call, but I got your message and I'm on my way to the Opera House now."

"Right," said Wayne. "About that…"

Burns heard Wayne inhale and exhale. There was some tension there, Burns knew. He didn't think he was the source. *I fucking hope not.*

As far as Burns was concerned, Wayne had no right to expect him to be on call until he was officially assigned to MCU2. *Or is this it, and I'm in?* His anger ebbed under another rolling wave of excitement.

"It's Doctor Nicholas Veda, right sir?" Burns wondered if Veda's title had been deliberately left off the original alert. He had Googled Nicholas Veda before he got into his car and found enough information on the first page to start all kinds of conspiracy theories spinning in his head. At thirty-two years old, Veda was already a big name in virology and vaccine research at Oxford University.

"Yes, he's a former professor at Oxford, now with the Ministry," said Wayne.

"I see," answered Burns. Former professor? Burns guessed the doctor had been granted sabbatical leave. He reckoned no professor with tenure at Oxford would retire from the world of academia to join the civil service at thirty-two. But he couldn't catch Wayne's eye to see how much more there was to it.

Wayne stared at the window. He was trying to decide how much to say. He wondered why he felt so compelled to tell Charles Burns what little he really knew.

Wayne's phone chirped and drew him back from the swirling questions taking shape in his mind. The message came from DS Blennerhassett. Wayne read it and decided for the moment it wasn't good or bad news. Blennerhassett had arrived at Veda's unoccupied flat and described what he found:

no scene

Wayne replied with three words:

Secure and wait

He stared at the phone for a moment.

Wayne's list of questions was growing by the minute and he had too few answers to hide from anyone, so he started with those when he rejoined Burns on the call.

"Burns."

"Sir."

"Well, he's been commissioned by the Health Ministry. Here in London since..." Wayne paused. "Since the Ides of March." Then his phone beeped, signalling a new text message.

Wayne read it. Twice. Not because he didn't understand what it told him, but because he needed an extra few seconds to formulate a response.

"Hold the line, Burns."

Wayne fired off two quick messages, one to DS Riza and one to Inspector David Isaac, the Forensic Team Leader following Riza to the car park in Drury Lane. He gave the address of the lab to Inspector Isaac and labelled it the higher priority.

Riza confirmed he had a basic kit with him and would examine the car and report his findings, and bring any evidence in to MCU2, *asap*. Wayne tensed up. He stared at the map on the centre screen and found some relief when he tracked the distances between his teams and their target locations. He wondered if his teams would report in before he heard from Dr Veda's captors. His eyes keyed in on the red dot on the map of London that represented Burns' phone, which was about a half hour from the lab.

"Right," said Wayne. "Burns, I called you in because, well, I've got a bad feeling about this situation. We've been babysitting this professor for some time now. Higher-Ups whom shall remain nameless at this point, and hopefully in perpetuity, put a high value on his work. I assigned one of our men, under orders of the

HO, to be Dr Veda's security escort while..." Wayne paused, staring at his reflection in the window and the gap in his knowledge. "He's in London," he finished.

"I see," repeated Burns. So, Dr Veda was of high value to nameless government officials — and perhaps somebody else. Burns loved it.

"And what's my value in this, sir?"

Wayne knew where Burns was going, so he headed him off. "The situation is expanding. I need you..." Wayne stopped, searching hard for the word. "Engaged. Despite your uncertain status at the moment."

"I'm in."

"I can activate you as the unit's Training Officer, but that's the only official status I can declare. At the moment. Actually, not until Monday will anything be official." Wayne paused for a response that didn't't come. "Regardless."

Burns kept his sceptical sarcasm in check. He was being activated, in an undefined role to participate in...*what?*

"What do you need me to do, sir?"

Wayne wanted to, but decided he was not going to use the words hostage or extraction in any conversation with anyone for the moment. *Just boots on the ground.*

"You are to meet Detective Sergeant Aitkens at this address." DCI Wayne sent Burns a text with the street address and GPS coordinates for Veda's lab.

"It's understood that, technically, you can observe active operations in your capacity as Specialist Training Officer." Wayne was prepared to leave it there until he heard Burns' reply.

"Understood." Burns accepted the conditions of employment to speed his deployment. He asked the most sensible question.

"What do I need to know, sir?"

Wayne knew exactly how much Burns needed to know. Everything. They were of like minds. He'd sensed it when he first read Burns' file. From soldier to contractor and four years later to Met employee and full member of the MPF, he passed every exam to reach the rank of Detective Sergeant in less than a year. Wayne had got Tully to put the bug in Burns' ear about applying for the unit rather than recruiting him directly. He sensed that Burns was the kind of man that needed to know he had earned whatever opportunity he received. Wayne was ready to give Burns that opportunity tonight. His gut told him he had to.

Wayne cleared his throat. "Well, we have two missing persons."

"I see," said Burns. "Dr Nicholas Veda and Ms Kaia Rebane, missing from the opera, yes." He let it hang in the air as if he was jotting down notes and ready to continue. "And?"

"Unknown Asian male, deceased. Found at the address I just sent you."

"Right sir. Got it. On my way."

"Right," answered Wayne. Wayne kept his orders simple. "Observe, and assist if necessary. Then report to me when the forensics team signs off. Clear?"

"Understood, sir." Burns caught the emphasis on observe. "Hands off, sir."

"Right," confirmed Wayne. "And do play nice with the other fellows, Burns. You're on the same team now."

"Will do," Burns smiled and rang off. He was on the team. Unofficially…

Burns made a U-turn at Priory Road and slowed slightly as he passed the front of the Alexandra Ice Palace again, wondering if the game was on, then he headed up to Circular Road.

He set his car's navigation system for the address in Shepherd's Bush and pulled out his phone to resume his search for information about Veda. But he found little more than the basic bio on Oxford University's website and some links to publications with his name on them. The crosstown traffic was flowing smoothly but Burns forced himself to concentrate on the journey, rather than reading his phone in traffic and spinning more conspiracy theories.

Two missing persons, and one dead Asian male.

"Well, one missing person for sure," he mused. And one vixen.

Twenty-six minutes after he had tossed his gear in the back of his car, Burns turned in to Uxbridge Commercial Plaza and passed through the open gate. There were several buildings in a gated block about a square mile in size. Most of the old wartime factories had been remodelled and rebuilt as office and commercial space over and over in the last thirty years. The two with the frontage on Uxbridge Road were a large fitness centre on one side and a carpet wholesaler on the other. Number Ten was the rearmost of the three three-storey edifices situated on a cul-de-sac opposite the main entry. Burns idled past the cars parked adjacent to the gym and the shiny storefront windows. Three or four cyclists were pedalling stationary bikes and another two on treadmills were in various stages of fatigue and ecstasy, or so Burns imagined, while the lonely carpets looked on from their brightly lit showroom.

Burns parked in the visitors' space next to the two unmarked patrol cars and strode up the pavement to the glass entry. Burns had assumed the lab was a government facility and the lack of security or government signage was puzzling him. He stopped to read the names on the registry. All the nameplates in the glass case were reversed so they all read backwards, signalling they had vacated the premises, save one. It read 'Living Sciences'. He pulled out his phone and searched the web for information on the lab, but the nearest hit that came up on the first page was a homeopathic outlet store in Devon. That, and at least two links to articles about Tom Cruise and Scientology.

Unregistered name. Burns took in the two sides of the building he could see. Not exactly a secret location, but inconspicuous if not disguised. Living Sciences was the sole occupant of the building, out of sight on the

Lower Level. Now it's starting to look like a government deal, Burns mused. But not the kind he had assumed. He stepped up to the front entrance and a motion sensor triggered the tinted glass sliding doors. They parted to reveal a glass vestibule, large enough for four couples to slow-dance and not bump into each other, Burns estimated.

He could see the pass gates and the security desk at the far end of the foyer beyond the interior double doors. A guard stood up behind the reception counter, slowly rising up to a height of two metres. A lamp on the desk illuminated his long, drawn face from below, and Burns recalled all the classic horror films in his memory. He had become accustomed to the blurred flash that invariably followed an involuntary sensory recall event. As a teen, the blinding light seared a hole in his retinas and expanded to fill all perception of shadow and depth, as if the film he was watching had got caught in the projector and the hot bulb inside obliterated the last image. He called it a white out, not a black out. It never affected him physically, except that he had to stop whatever he was doing at the time until the colour returned to his vision and details became clear. The images became one face, a character that made Burns laugh.

"Lurch," said Burns.

He smiled and waved to the guard, holding his wallet up to the glass to display his Met ID. He heard a buzz and he reached for the door, pulled it open and Burns stepped into the foyer. Two steps up was the reception desk and security gates, one entry and one exit gate, both equipped with an optical pad that required handprint verification before unlocking. He held his smile firm and kept eye contact with the uniformed guard standing behind the desk.

"Evening," said Burns. He guessed the man was in his sixties, tall and lean but a bit stooped—not from age but more likely from being over two metres tall in Her Majesty's Infantry. The uniform was a private company but hair and the moustache, the squint and the insignia on the bars looked like an infantryman to Burns. Burns read the name on the silver pin as he approached the desk. Smiling, Burns held up his wallet showing his MET security ID, then faked a little clumsiness as he flipped it closed again and returned it to an inside pocket.

"Burns," he said with a smile as he extended his hand. "Major Charles." He held the older man's tired eyes. Then added with emphasis, "Ex." He hesitated to name his branch, just to be on the safe side. This guy was old enough to have rivalries going back to the Falklands. "Retired," he said, and left it at that. He smiled again and released his hand from the friendly grip. "Lloyd, is it? Ex-?"

Lloyd straightened himself up to his full height and stretched out his long arm.

"Paratrooper. Falklands."

"Right," said Burns.

"You there?" Lloyd asked.

"No, that was me dad," Burns replied in his father's voice as they shook hands.

Lloyd smiled. "Burns, eh? Think I knew him."

Charles Burns knew that his father was a legend to many more than those whom he led into battle. More importantly to the Commonwealth, he had also led them out. He always said he had retired with higher respect than rank, and that pleased him well enough. Burns allowed himself a moment of gratitude for the lessons his father had given, then smiled sheepishly. The Old Man had probably yelled at this lanky corporal to keep his head down.

"It's kind of a family tradition, yeah," Burns chuckled.

His thoughts lingered on his father and he embraced the moment as a shield against the memories of his own military career. Then he looked Lloyd in the eye. It only felt like a flash, but Burns could see the older man's eyes turn down in sympathy. Burns was ready for the question.

"Where were you, son?" asked Lloyd.

"Too many places," replied Burns. He killed the pause before it became awkward for both men. "Are you on alone here, Mister Lloyd?"

"Yes, indeed," Lloyd answered as he turned to the monitor screens displaying the camera feeds from various hallways and staircases in the building. He pointed to one image on the screen. "Except for the uniform downstairs," he said. "When there is one, that is." Lloyd turned to Burns again and added, "He's down there, I'm everywhere else."

Burns scanned Lloyd's security station and guessed that he was on autopilot most of the night, most every night. A computer monitor and keyboard sat idle on the desk next to the CCTV viewer, its blue ocean screensaver being only slightly more interesting than the dim infrared images of empty corridors on the viewer.

Burns looked at the monitor that Lloyd indicated with his flattened palm. He could see a wall a few metres to the left of the lift. A large chair on wheels stood facing into the corner behind a small desk just inside the open glass door in what appeared to be an otherwise empty reception area about three metres square.

"When was the last time you saw him, do you remember?" Burns hoped he didn't sound condescending. Lloyd didn't seem to be offended, but was eager to answer.

"Yesterday, well, Friday morning," he laughed. "They usually change shifts at sixteen hundred, two hours before I come in. "I'm on six till six." And they only do eights, I never saw the evening guy – the man who should be sitting in that chair," Lloyd shook his finger at the monitor. He glanced at the clock on the desk. "Of course, he's dead now, right?"

Burns thought it made sense and nodded. "His replacement ought to be here by now."

The two men stared at the empty foyer.

"Do you have their names, the downstairs security detail? Are they military?"

"No, and maybe," offered Lloyd. "Dress the part, to be sure. But they've been here since shortly after this Living Sciences moved in."

"I see," said Burns. "So..." Burns shrugged.

"Since February, right around Valentine's Day, as I recall."

"Who was the previous tenant?" Burns wondered aloud.

Lloyd gave Burns a knowing nod and went on. "The previous tenant was rumoured to be a sperm bank, but I can't really say. I was never invited to make a deposit," he chuckled. "Ah, they ended up closing down first."

"Before you could ask about opening an account?" joked Burns.

"Nah," laughed Lloyd. "I mean they were the first tenant out of the building last Christmas. The Ministry of Health came in and gave everyone the order to vacate." Lloyd looked bitter.

"Vermin and rot, so they said." Lloyd shook his head slowly. "They closed down the whole building, said they might have to demolish it."

Lloyd's expression sagged, his lips parting and closing slowly as if trying to draw the words out. After a long breath he set his jaw again. "Every tenant gone by the end of January. The only reason I still have a job was because half the offices on the second and third floors still haven't been emptied out. Some still have computers and everything. I guess movers are still coming and going during the day according to my colleague on the dayshift. But of course, not much after-hours traffic."

Burns could tell that he had won Lloyd's trust. He could be straightforward, ex-soldier to ex-soldier.

"What kind of traffic do you see downstairs on that monitor?"

"Three weeks ago, Living Sciences started moving in equipment and building materials, but that was through the loading dock." Lloyd pointed and nodded at the corner of the viewer where the feed from the loading area showed the metal barriers at its entrance. "The gate's down and the card lock is deactivated for entry after eighteen hundred."

He pointed a finger at the monitor with the view of the empty reception area and closed elevator several metres below their feet.

"Only thing on that monitor until last week has been your sometimes sleeping, sometimes absent guard. Since then I've seen three civilians, academic types, leaving together on a few occasions in the early evening."

"Really?" Burns asked. He pulled out his phone and showed the photo of Veda to Lloyd. "Was he one of them?"

Lloyd didn't hesitate. "Positively. Your Indian friend was here with a Chinese and a white foreigner Tuesday evening." A sudden shock straightened Lloyd. "Is he the…" he asked in a whisper.

"Probably not," answered Burns.

"He's not the killer," asked Lloyd.

"Probably not."

"The Chinese?"

"Probably not."

Lloyd seemed relieved. "Say... when do you suppose your circus will show up?"

Burns let out a long breath and a short laugh and confessed. "Well, Mister Lloyd, to be honest, I was playing hockey an hour ago and got called in and sent here, so I know nothing." Burns extended his hand in gratitude. "I've learned more from you in the last five minutes. Thank you, Mister Lloyd," he smiled.

Lloyd straightened to his full height again as he smiled and shook Burns' hand.

"Connor Lloyd. Glad to know it, Detective Sergeant Burns. Happy to be of service."

"Actually, it's Not Detective Sergeant Burns," said Burns. "Not Officially. Kind of just getting started with the Major Crimes Unit." Burns heard himself and felt as if he had stuck a pin in his credibility balloon. He instinctively squared himself and declared, "Officially, I'm still Training Specialist Charles Burns, until the paperwork clears on my transfer to the MCU2." Burns thought it best to leave the pin in until he made good on his exit. He gave a final squeeze and released his grip on Lloyd's hand. Lloyd nodded as Burns stepped away from the desk and toward the lift.

"Are the stairs just behind the elevator there?"

Lloyd nodded and stood for a moment, looking exactly like a man abandoned at his post. Burns found the door to the stairway and raised his hand in farewell. Without making eye contact, Major Charles Burns left Ex Corporal Connor Lloyd at his post and headed down the stairs to his first Major Crime scene.

Burns would have liked two or three more flights of stairs to trot down, but his legs still felt good. He pulled a half litre plastic bottle out of his pocket and swallowed its remnants, making a note to himself to refill it in the first sink he saw. He stepped through the door and scanned the corridor. The camera was positioned at a greater distance than it had appeared on the monitor upstairs and as a result Burns had a much-improved angle on the reception room. The high camera angle and the tall reception desk concealed all but the shoulders and headrest of the chair. He bent low and could see the chair wasn't empty. A pair of legs and feet in black combat boots stood flat below the front of the seat. Burns dropped his right arm and drew back his coat, sliding his hand round the holster on his hip and releasing the safety in one smooth motion. He was three steps into the room before he could make out the shape of a man's torso folded flat and face down on its lap. He made a quick visual scan round the room, coming to rest his focus on the open door in the far corner.

Voices trailed in on the low shaft of light coming through. He tuned his ears and convinced himself the loudest voice was Aitkens. They were newly introduced but Burns had heard Aitkens talking with the other members of the unit. He sounded like another guy from Guildford Burns had almost killed on an SAS training exercise in Finland. Burns knew he was going to have to put in a conscious effort to maintain objectivity if he was going to get off on the right foot with the men of MCU2.

Burns stepped around the L-shaped counter for a better look at the compacted corpse in the chair. He saw the circle of blood in the centre of the skull just above the neck, the sandy blond number two cut was just long enough to produce a matting effect. Burns recognised the damp hole as an exit wound and confirmed it with a quick glance at the headrest of the chair.

A tenpence-sized clump of bloody pulp clung to the black leather-look headrest, the filmy stain centred by a T-shaped tear in the soft vinyl. It looked like torn felt on a billiards table, a miscue. A thin line of darkening blood trailed down the centre of the backrest and stopped at a horizontal seam across the lumbar support.

Burns studied the area before stepping closer. The desktop surfaces were bare, save for a stack of three or four well-read magazines dating back to 2016. He guessed the waiting room reading material had been left behind by the previous tenant but was puzzled by the expensive chair. He mused over the idea that the dead soldier had somehow had a hand in choosing the place he died, albeit in his sleep.

Burns stepped back from the body and straightened himself. But the idea of a final salute seemed too comic for a man who fell asleep at his post, and he turned toward the door leading into the lab. He cleared his throat as he stepped over the threshold. His nonchalant nod of greeting was returned by the two men in uniform. Detective Sergeant John Aitkens rose and swelled like a maître d' greeting a regular customer.

"Mister Charlie Burns!" Aitkens called out. Then he quickly stepped forward to meet Burns, extending his hand over the yellow crime scene tape.

"Or rather, Specialist Training Officer Burns, innit." Aitkens' tone was syrupy contempt, he smirked like Lucy from the Peanuts gang. But he lacked her steely gaze. His eyes darted and drifted, never holding contact with Burns for more than brief glances. Aitkens puffed up his short and stocky frame.

"But that hasn't been made official, has it. You're actually more of a candidate Specialist Training Officer Burns," Aitkens finally dropped the false grin. "Innit?"

It was the first time Aitkens had made it sound like a question, but Burns refused to bite. He guessed that Aitkens had been told by Wayne what his official role was to be. He was struck with the hopeful idea that maybe Aitkens had thought it was a training op. Burns decided that would be useful to exploit the possibility in the present situation. He continued his detailed scan of the scene, glancing back at Aitkens from time to time, as if it were Aitkens that was under inspection but not worth talking to just yet.

"We've secured the scene," Aitkens asserted, becoming defensive in the silence. "And we were just discussing our first report. I'm due to call in to Chief Inspector Wayne in..." Aikens checked his watch and grinned to himself. "A couple of minutes. A forensics team is en route. We're just here to hold the fort but we think we have a good idea of what happened here."

On Aitkens' lead, he and the two uniformed officers exchanged short, stiff nods of affirmation. Burns imagined Aitkens had done most of the talking since they arrived at the scene and was using the Royal "We". He turned around to Burns and froze for a moment when he saw Burns had silently stepped closer. Burns recognised Aitkens reaction. He had crossed the threshold of Aitkens' domain, and for a moment he saw the conflict frozen on Aitkens' face. His brain was debating if Burns was a friend or foe. Burns kept scanning the room behind Aitkens, delaying eye contact but watching Aitkens.

"Since you're here," Aitkens finally conceded. He gestured hospitably at the violated yellow barrier behind Burns. "Care to 'have a boo', as you say?"

Burns wasn't sure when he used that expression in Aitkens' company, but he had, no doubt. It was a favourite. He returned the false warmth and mirrored Aitkens' smirking sincerity.

Burns had already scanned the visible area before Aitkens opened his arms in a gesture of invitation. Then he held his right arm in front of Burns, like it was a gate in a children's game. Burns frowned at the arm, staring at the points where he would grab, twist and dislocate the arm before using it to pull his opponent to the floor. He subdued the emotional reflex with a long breath, then he lifted his gaze to Aitkens' face. The eyes darted away and back and around the room before Aitkens settled his focus on Burns' hair.

"But you will remember not to touch anything, yes?"

Burns smiled at Aitkens until the arm was lowered. Burns glanced back at the door and around the reception room once more with only a slight pause on the back of the oversized chair where the folded corpse of the guard lay.

"Of course, Detective Sergeant Aitkens." He couldn't stop himself from saying, "This ain't my first rodeo," he lied, then quickly added, "But it is your show, Detective."

Aitkens seemed placated as he turned his focus to follow Burns' scan of the scene. Burns caught him glancing, still unwilling to initiate direct eye contact. Burns wondered how long it would be before Aitkens was tempted to repeat the first rodeo line, or if he even knew what it meant.

Every bank of overhead lighting was illuminating every corner of the large room. Burns absently wondered if Aitkens had switched on all the lights or if it had been the team that entered and killed two people before they removed the equipment. He could make out the square and rectangular shadows on the worktables and benches around the lab. He saw a fine dust, possibly gypsum particulates from a recent remodelling, that defined the spaces between the missing equipment and the half dozen machines that remained.

He wondered why some were left behind, whether it was by haste or selection. He kept his curiosity to himself, until he saw the body on the floor.

"So, what do you think happened here?" Burns asked the two uniformed policemen, but they were mute. The two men were standing, legs spread like gates on a pen, at opposite ends of an aisle between two workstations. They were holding captive a dead Asian male. He made a point of noting their name badges: S. Lennox and D. Klein. Then he returned his focus to the body.

The corpse was folded on itself too, but it looked more like a prayer pose and not like a man vomiting on his shoes in a chair, like the dead guard in the reception.

The hands were together as if in prayer. *Only missing the beads*, he thought.

Burns saw the blood matting the straight black hair that reached the collar of the white lab coat. The tiny entry wound was centred on the top of the skull. The blood that had flowed from the small hole was nearly dry around the wound but a stain soaked the man's chest and pooled in his lap. He guessed the man was shot as he bowed. *Begging or praying, or both?* Burns frowned.

"Cold."

He was addressing the living but looking at the victim's body. He caught the eyes of the uniformed officers again and offered them each another opportunity to play detective. Burns raised an eyebrow and grinned conspiratorially.

"So, how long have you been here?" he asked.

No one spoke. The two were surreptitiously glancing at each other and Aitkens, who almost grunted with satisfaction before he made a show of checking his watch. Burns remembered Inspector Wayne's insistent directive and gave Aitkens a benign smile.

"Thirty-seven minutes," said Aitkens. "We've been here thirty-seven minutes. Exactly."

"Uh-huh," Burns noted the time on his watch.

"Here for a good time, not a long time, eh?"

"Right," said Aitkens.

"Here, mostly?"

Aitkens bristled. "Here is most interesting."

"I see."

Burns scanned the scene. "Find the spent cartridges, Detective?"

"Afraid not, Burns. Looks like they cleaned up after themselves before making good on their escape. Out the back. And I believe you meant cartridge as in the singular. One shot to the head, fired from close range. Not sure what the weapon was yet but hopefully our friend Dr Lin has the answer in mind, hahaha." Aitkens grinned and nodded to Lennox and Klein.

"Yeah, more likely in his lung," said Burns. "And two shots were fired. One into the vic and one before that into the ceiling." Burns drew all their eyes in and gave the slightest upward glance, without pointing to a small black hole in the ceiling.

"There."

Everyone looked up and saw the neat little hole in the acoustic tile.

"Looks to me like he was warned or threatened first," said Burns.

Aitkens' jaw twitched as his maître' d smile deflated into a grimace. Burns continued. "And the gun was probably a Makarov PB. Looks like the powder burn pattern on the scalp came from a PB with the front part of the suppressor removed. Which means the head shot cartridge ejected here and got picked up." He gave a widening grin as he went on, "But the warning shot cartridge…" Burns stopped and swung his arm around, pointing like a game show host at the closed door next to the open lavatory. "Ejected somewhere over there."

"Learn that in your online university, did you Burns?" Aitkens snapped.

Burns ignored the jab and dropped his tone to a loud whisper. He raised an eyebrow and stared at Aitkens, who froze.

"Have you secured this place, Aitkens?" Burns shot a look at each of the two uniforms and back to Aitkens, getting blank stares in return. He raised the level of alarm and lowered his voice as he pointed at the door. "Anyone take a look in that room?" Without waiting for an answer, Burns reached inside his jacket and put his hand on his gun then advanced to the door.

Aitkens didn't lower his voice. "No, we didn't," he said to Burns' back. "It's not an office. According to the sign it's a WC. It was assumed that the thieves didn't value anything in there, since the door was locked and closed."

Burns wondered how hard it was for Aitkens to refrain from adding so there. He had seen the matching unisex symbols on the pair of doors, and he knew he would find nothing more than the shell casing. *If I'm even that lucky*, he thought. He had no idea why he was playing this little charade for Aitkens, but he felt he had to see it through to the end. Burns hoped a punch line would present itself, not only to spank Aitkens but also to provide some comic relief, for himself if no one else.

Aitkens let out a slight chuckle in the middle of an "ahem" and glanced round at the other men, smiling.

"The key is hanging right there." Aitkens pointed to a key on a short, curly plastic lead hanging from the door handle.

Burns nodded to all three men, accepting their silence as a tacit invitation to be their point man. With his chin held high, Burns drew his side arm and gripped it, and silently loaded a round into the chamber. He hoped he wasn't being too over-the-top as he crouched low and backed up to the wall next to the door. He didn't want to look like a clown, just a joker. *That shell casing better be in there.*

Standing on the hinge side of the door he checked back with all the men. One of the two uniformed officers seemed to recognise what Burns was up to, as he had a sly grin for Burns when their eyes met. But the other younger man and Aitkens seemed genuinely nervous, although Aitkens was doing a much better job of concealing his anxiety behind his sharpening contempt for Burns. All three had their hands on their weapons but not drawn. Burns called that a win.

He turned the handle without inserting the key in the lock. With one more scan of the men's eyes — and an expression of mock surprise for Aitkens as he slowly and deliberately turned the unlocked handle — Burns opened the door, revealing a mirror image of the small water closet next door, with the washbasin and toilet sharing the centre wall with their mates. The only difference was that the room on the right was being used as a storage closet for cleaning equipment and supplies. Burns made the game show host's face again, smiling at the unlucky but plucky contestants who had missed the big prize. He took a half a step inside the door and produced a pen from an inside pocket. He bent down and picked up a spent cartridge with the pointed end of the pen.

"I guess our perpetrators forgot about this one," he said.

Burns gave the casing a quick look as he twisted the pen between his thumb and fingers. "Makarov, nine-millimetre." He looked at Aitkens, who seemed to be getting testy.

"Do you have somewhere you can put this, Detective Sergeant Aitkens?" Burns grinned and let it hang long enough for Lennox to catch the inferred suggestion.

The fallen look on Aitkens' face told Burns that the detective sergeant had come ill prepared to collect any evidence. The inference would follow that he was only there to provide site security in the first place, until the forensic investigators arrived. Detective Sergeant Aitkens seemed to be squirming slightly under the weight of the embarrassment.

Burns knew Aitkens would be top dog on the crime scene, even after the forensics team arrived. Wayne had explained in some detail how his unit was under the direct authority of the Home Office, and as such its officers would be in command in every phase of an operation.

He was well aware that Wayne had earned the respect of every Superintendent in the Met's administration. But he especially admired what Wayne had described as the "unfettered authority" that he had, as head of MCU2. The universal order, signed by the Home Secretary herself, guaranteed the full cooperation of any other branch of the Metropolitan Police and define Wayne as its Acting Senior Commander, on a moment's notice if need be. Burns liked the idea of the unit being capable of acting quickly because of the skipped links in the bureaucratic chain.

Candidate Charles Burns had taken the time to study Detective Chief Inspector John C. Wayne, both by researching his records with the Met and Her Majesty's Army, and by reading every word and gesture his soon-to-be superior officer. Burns' observations and intuition told him that DCI Wayne was the man for job.

Detective Sergeant John Aitkens, however, did not fill Burns with the same level of confidence. Burns could see that Aitkens felt anxious, threatened. Granted, he had a limited time to observe Aitkens in person and had only engaged in small talk when they were introduced during one of Burns' visits to the unit in the previous weeks. Despite Aitkens' broad shoulders, Burns saw him as a man who never carried his responsibility without doubt. Burns had stood next to a few men who had the same look in their eyes, and too often they had put a mission in jeopardy. He wondered why Wayne would put Aitkens in charge of anything. In his role of trainer, Burns had given failing grades to recruits or trainees when his character evaluation had identified the candidate's lack of leadership potential. Burns guessed Aitkens could survive one of his training missions, but would not get a positive recommendation.

Despite knowing this, when Burns saw Aitkens letting his insecurities get the better of him, he maintained a neutral expression. He would observe without reacting as Aitkens slowly climbed back up to his place of authority. Burns had some difficulty assuring himself that it wasn't his own cruel humour compelling him to not only observe, but to offer his objective analysis. And watch him flail. If Aitkens assumed he was being observed, that served a purpose for the moment.

The moment had only lasted a few seconds but Burns enjoyed every breath of it.

Aitkens' eyes held a few shards of spite as he glanced at the two men, who both seemed unfazed and offered no response. He stared at the spent cartridge that Burns held on the tip of his pen. Then Aitkens turned his eyes upward but focused on the wall behind Burns' left shoulder.

"Secured, yes. Searched, no. Forensics, they do that. Under my supervision."

"Understood," Burns nodded. "So, no more bodies."

"Right."

Burns was having a hard time curbing his enthusiasm. He wanted to identify evidence. He wanted to investigate. His observations since arriving at the scene had set more questions, and he knew that the answers to most of them might be useful in the apprehending of the perpetrators.

The size of the operation was growing, and Burns was starting to make some alarming connections. He wanted to return to the unit and see what Tully and Wayne knew. But he had to follow orders, even if he wasn't officially on duty. His instincts told him there were no more answers to be found in the lab that would help to find Veda any faster.

"I'll just be observing then," Burns smiled, caught and held Aitkens' jerking, furtive gaze. "So, what about this?" He held the cartridge aloft, cavalierly waving the pen but keeping the cartridge perfectly motionless on the tip of it. Burns got the reaction he wanted. Not exactly a collective gasp, but a tangible surge of electricity in the men. He resisted the temptation to play it up for his captive audience and pointed toward the toilet. "Seriously, has this place been secured?"

Aitkens looked at him like a headmaster, as if Burns was a pimply student trying to look smart but always asking the wrong question.

Burns turned his face to avoid saying something he might have said in high school and went into the WC where he found and opened the first aid kit. He removed some small plasters from a plastic bag. He was about to slide the spent cartridge off of his pen cap and into the bag when Aitkens raised his voice.

"You can't put that in there, Burns. That goes into a proper plastic evidence bag, and when the crime scene people arrive, they'll take care of that. You shouldn't have touched it," Aitkens sniggered. "Now you gotta stand there with your finger up your... in the air until they arrive."

Burns stared blandly at Aitkens and replied, "Frankly, Detective Sergeant Aitkens, I'm a little surprised to see you don't have a crime scene kit here. But I guess I didn't realise how much delegating you have to do." Burns stared at Aitkens and dropped the cartridge into the plastic bag and resealed it.

"You arrogant bastard!" Aitkens' voice swallowed itself in a scowl. His eyes lowered slightly and settled on the left chest pocket of Burns' all-weather coat.

Burns shrugged and pointed. "This cartridge, that slug, it won't matter because the weapon won't be traceable. And there won't be any fingerprints." Burns had no doubt at least one of the thieves was a professional killer.

"You all saw the guard. He died peacefully. And Doctor Lin, here? Well not so much..." Burns allowed himself a moment of pity for the man who died pleading to somebody to spare his life.

"What guard?" Aitkens scoffed.

"The dead one in the reception area," said Burns. "He looks like he was shot in his sleep, at close range, too."

Burns caught the looks on the three men's faces. Each was genuinely surprised by Burns' statement as their gazes drifted past Burns to the entrance. They had missed the corpse in the reception. He fought off a smirk, unsuccessfully.

Charles Burns knew that he had been commonly perceived by his superiors as arrogant during his years in both the Canadian and British military. As a soldier, Burns had proved his superiority often, and in every theatre. Though he was not always humble about it, he felt less pride being "the pride of the regiment" than he showed. He saw himself as better than most, not everyone. But he was not an expert investigator yet. And, as Aitkens had said, the forensics team would conduct a proper investigation.

He studied the three faces. Lennox, his comrade-in-humour, knew this time he wasn't joking. Lennox was looking past Burns through the door at the reception area, the colour in his cheeks belied his embarrassment. The younger officer tried to mask his fear with a look of mistrust. Aitkens pretended to be distracted, keeping his eyes on his phone as he typed a short text message.

"What, you fellas missed the first corpse? Really?" Burns tried not to look incredulous, lest his sarcasm be mistaken for arrogance. The three men stood silent, the two junior officers looking to Aitkens for direction. He nodded to Klein, the younger one, and watched as he exited the lab toward the reception room. A moment later, Burns heard a quiet "Fuck me."

Aitkens seemed dumbstruck. He worked his jaw and wagged a finger at Burns and Lennox, then grunted a warning as he left them with the body of Lin. Three seconds later Burns heard the conversation. Aitkens was almost shouting, the young officer defensively explaining how the chair had been turned away and the folded body concealed from their view as they passed it and went straight to the lab, on his direction. Burns strained to resist the physical impulse to laugh when he heard the Klein's final defence:

"Easy to miss, that."

Burns smiled at Lennox, who was not smiling anymore. "Don't worry," he reassured. "This is on Aitkens. And nobody else has seen it yet. It'll just be our little secret." Burns winked. Until we get back to the MCU and I mention it to Detective Chief Inspector Wayne, he mused. He hoped he would not feel compelled to mention it, but if Aitkens didn't own up to his lack of awareness, Burns might feel obliged to force the issue. The thought vexed him. The only reconcile he found was in the fact that Aitkens' limited grasp of the circumstances was of little consequence to the case. Burns cleared the choler from his throat and stood silent. It was several moments before he realised he was staring at the body of Dr Lin and remembering a similar scene in a Balkan village half a world away. The sepia memories faded and were replaced by the image of Veda kneeling in prayer in Lin's place. Burns released himself from the reverie by wondering if Veda, the scientist, ever prayed for anything. The momentary distraction brought his focus back to his surroundings.

He decided to take the opportunity to have a look around and excused himself with a nod to Lennox. He walked around the bench that Lin had been kneeling in front of when he was shot, taking one more look at the body from every angle before he stepped into the adjacent office on the south side of the lab. A large metal desk stood against the far wall opposite the open door. A simple, low back chair occupied the space where Burns guessed the larger chair where the dead man slept had been sometime earlier. The desktop was bare, save for an older-looking blank computer monitor and its keyboard. Below the desk was a tangle of cables, some still connected to the power supply. A faint rectangle lay in the fine dust on the floor next to the snake's nest of cables. Burns guessed a hard drive had been stolen, or at least removed hastily. A small sheaf of papers in a wire wastepaper basket to the right of the desk caught Burns' eye. He crouched down over the bin and saw several pages of text fanned out against the opaque yellow plastic bag lining the basket. He recognised the page layout and knew by the few headings visible that they were part of an academic paper. Burns pulled out his phone to take a photo. He hesitated a moment, entertaining a fleeting thought about lifting the bag out of the bin and stuffing it under his coat...

He took three quick photos of the entire contents of the bin and quickly checked each one on his phone's display by zooming in on the text until he was able to read it clearly enough to scan a paragraph. He stopped himself from reading any more than a few sentences on the top page. A peculiar combination of curiosity and dread swirled in his chest. He carefully lifted the bin, hoping to see a few more pages from below through the thin plastic. A full page of text began with the heading 'Discussion'. Below the sheaf of pages, he saw a single, loosely crumpled page.

"Last page written, first page binned?" Burns wondered aloud. He angled the phone in his left hand to get three more good images of the Discussion and the snatches of text readable on the page. Then he set the bin down again and looked inside.

The temptation to lift out the pages and spread them on the desk to take a few more photographs was doused by the sound of Aitkens barking his name. Burns rose off his haunches and slid the phone into his pocket.

"In here, Detective Sergeant," answered Burns as he retraced his steps back to the office door. Burns caught Aitkens' reflection in the glass door, striding nearer. Aitkens had set his jaw with the determined look of a cricket batsman stepping up to face a heavy bowler. He stopped short a few feet away from Burns.

Burns' instinct was to dial down the tension. *Best give him something.* He lobbed an easy opener, hopeful that Aitkens would make contact and get in the game. "Looks like they had a hard drive or something here, but now it's gone."

Aitkens' gaze glanced off Burns, his eyes flitted around the room. Burns could see the anger — *anger borne of fear* — is his posture, but he had no idea if he could prove that he wasn't a threat to Aitkens. Because he wasn't sure of the truth.

"A hard drive, imagine that...Data theft, too, I guess, eh?" Burns pointed over his shoulder to the bin. "I wonder what the big stuff they took from the lab was for." Burns wore a mask of innocence, but Aitkens' expression remained anxious. *Not at all curious?*

"You're not here to wonder, Burns."

Burns held his breath for an instant to temper his reflexes, and smiled cooly. "Maybe you're not here to wonder, Detective Sergeant Aitkens," he said. Then the mask slipped. "But I sure as fuck am."

"No, Specialist Training Officer Burns. You're here as a..." Aitkens stopped and unconsciously turned slightly to his left, his eyes glancing back and then sweeping the floor. Burns wondered if Aitkens had received the same directive from DCI Wayne to "play nice" and had just felt DCI Wayne's presence over his shoulder, suggesting Aitkens bite his tongue.

Wayne's stern grimace flashed in Burns' memory. He knew it was in his own best interest to diffuse the situation, despite his impulse to escalate it. He told himself that his instincts about Detective Chief Inspector John Wayne as a leader of men were accurate.

Wayne had a reputation for being an excellent judge of character. He reassured himself that Wayne would see to it that he would have a greater role than security at a crime scene. *Whenever that becomes official.* He swallowed a small laugh.

"An observer," Burns said, holding the smile. He turned his focus to the window above the desk. He could see a wide metal sliding door across the hall, open half-way on its track. He peered through the gap but all he could see was what looked like a glass door reflecting light from the corridor. He turned back to face Aitkens, who seemed to be trying to make himself larger again. Burns chuckled to himself and reciprocated. He expanded himself with a deep breath, arched his back slightly and extended his arms, enjoying a good stretch through his upper back, shoulders and arms. Burns knew his all-weather jacket and combat trousers wouldn't serve to show off his hard and lean physique. But that didn't stop him from stretching and flexing until he could pull Aitkens' focus. He smiled with all the benevolence of a Buddhist monk as Aitkens' expression of grim determination hollowed into a look of confusion.

Burns opened his palms toward Aitkens and shrugged. "Just observing."

"Right," answered Aitkens.

Burns smiled and nodded in agreement. *Win-win,* he thought.

He held Aitkens eyes for a long moment. Burns could see that Aitkens' anger had come from embarrassment and guilt. He guessed at least a small part of the aggression stemmed from other inadequacies. Some guys always had to measure dicks, and Aitkens' was small. *You know that I've seen what you missed.* His smile flatten slightly.

Burns could let it go, or not. He could not state categorically that Aitkens was inept, but he had missed a body at a crime scene. As a younger man, Burns wouldn't have hesitated to bury another man — regardless of superior or subordinate rank — under a rockslide of vitriol in a situation like this, unrelenting until the man acknowledged his failure. The admission of guilt was not enough, and apologies must be followed by acts of redemption, in Burns' judgement. Whenever they crossed paths, nothing would save the guilty man from glacial salutes and sarcastic greetings and, depending on the occasion, sharply whispered reminders of his failure.

Burns had always had accurate instincts when it came to the people with whom he worked closely. He knew who to trust, and how much. He had made a point of removing men from his team if they did not prove worthy of his trust and respect.

Aitkens' fists opened and met on his belt, traced it round to his hips then drifted to rest at his sides. His eyes wandered the room, seemingly interested but jumping around too much to be taking anything in in detail. Burns waited for Aitkens to lift his focus back to eye level and steadied his gaze. *Just watching you*, he added silently. Aitkens broke off from Burns' icy scrutiny and checked his watch.

SATURDAY 00:24

"Detective Sergeant Aitkens," Lennox called out from the reception area. "Inspector Isaac is here, sir."

Aitkens smiled at Burns. "And you're not watching for much longer, I reckon."

Aitkens stepped away from Burns and returned to the reception area. Burns watched him leave and waited until he heard Aitkens' half of the conversation from the ante room. He stepped quickly to his left and glanced through the door to see Aitkens' back. No eyes were looking his way. He rounded the corner and walked past the office window where he had seen the heavy, rust-painted sliding metal door in the corridor, out of sight to Lennox and the cluster of police investigators in the outer room.

Burns eyed the lock hanging by its long shackle from the handle on the steel door. The body of the lock was turned away from its arms as if it was relinquishing their grasp, prepared to take the fall for its failure. Burns caught the impulse to draw his weapon as his thumb touched the heel of the grip. He understood the motivation. He was half-joking when he first questioned Aitkens' thoroughness securing the scene. But now the joker had to ask himself if the room beyond the sliding door was safe to enter.

Burns stood motionless a few steps away from the beckoning gap. With one slow, deep and silent breath he found the stillness and tuned his ears to the ambient sound around him. The silence of the open space made the lab seem larger than the hundred square metres that Burns had calculated it to be. He could hear a single, baritone voice speaking in the reception area. It droned monotonously, as if narrating a particularly uninteresting documentary. The tone became conversational when the man asked a question, which was answered frankly by another unknown voice. Burns chuckled to himself when he heard Aitkens loudly answer a question.

"That's for you to find out, Inspector," Burns repeated Aitkens' line to himself. "Hilarious."

Burns tuned out the conversation and focused his eyes and ears on the open glass door beyond the sliding door with the broken lock. He listened to the room for several seconds. Nothing moving but air in the ventilation ducts. And a faulty rheostat somewhere that chirped like a love-mad cricket. It gave Burns a sound to focus his eyes on beyond the half-open glass door. It was coming from a dimmer switch on the wall. A small keypad was mounted to its right. A green bar glowed above the numbers.

"Green means go," he said.

Burns stayed low and pushed the outer door aside with the back of his left hand until he felt it reach the stopper on its track. He held it there for a few seconds to see if the noise raised any attention among the others back in the lab. The door's grinding announcement went unnoticed and Burns stepped through the gap into a room much larger than he expected. He could see the far wall of the interior less than ten metres away from the entry. He could see that the glass door was part of a freestanding enclosure that had been constructed inside the locker. The enclosure's sliding glass door looked like it would provide an airtight seal. The glass and white panelled enclosure appeared to be made of vinyl with seamless, rounded corners. Burns stepped to the light switch next to the security keypad and pushed the fader up with his thumbnail, bringing the lights up to full. He lowered his weapon when he confirmed himself as the only occupant of the room.

Two identical large metal cabinets stood opposite each other a few metres apart in the otherwise bare room. Both doors were ajar, hanging open on their hinges at mirrored angles, like stainless steel shields in the arms of two charging soldiers. Each wore a small rectangular cooling unit for lack of a proper helmet, the German manufacturer's logo serving as the insignia. The floor was clean, dust free, with no trace of movement in the room. He stepped to his left and scanned the phone-sized keypad next to the open cabinet door. The small screen was black. A quick turn on his heel confirmed the other freezer was also without power.

He moved closer and examined the glass drawers mounted inside. He carefully extended his arm inside and immediately sensed a slight drop in temperature in the hairs on his wrist. He reached in a little further and used the back of his index finger to touch the centre drawer. He held it there long enough to confirm that it was colder than the outer surfaces of the cabinet. A small difference, maybe five degrees, he estimated. He couldn't see or smell any signs of condensation, but he supposed it could have been operating recently. His curiosity was curdled by a sudden fear. Veda's samples. *Here*?

Burns froze. He cursed himself for his recklessness then quickly reassured himself that if there was anything dangerous about Veda's vaccine, it left with the people who came to steal it. Burns puzzled a moment about who they might be but came up with nothing. Wayne must have an idea. Burns could trust that Wayne would act accordingly if he had sufficient evidence. He'd better know more than me, he thought.

Burns looked over at the empty cabinet against the opposite wall of the room, door-shield still at the ready. He stepped to it and, no less carefully if slightly quicker, inserted his arm into the gap of the door and touched the drawer's surface with the same fingernail. He compared the sensation in his other hand resting on its back against the outside of the cabinet. There was no appreciable difference.

Burns wanted to assume that the doors were open to ventilate the vacuum-sealed cabinets until the operating systems were functional, which meant they weren't operational or more importantly had never been storing bioweapons...

Or to keep small children playing hide-and-seek from being trapped inside. Burns laughed.

Burns slowly backed out of the vault. The thrilling charge he felt as the pieces of the story began to connect was quickly supplanted by a sharp alarm that raised every hair on his body. It was his body's response to the fear that had hit him in the gut so quickly. It wasn't the kind of energising fear he experienced in armed combat. Burns knew it really was true when someone repeated the line "You never feel more alive than the moment you know you could be killed". But what Burns felt now was a deeper, sickening dread.

There was no immediate threat to his personal survival, he assured himself. He believed that Veda's research held some lethal potential that somebody could create a threat with. But immediate? If he were to die due to the threat, that had not yet taken a visible form, Burns guessed that he would be only one of too many to count.

He remembered the photo of Veda and Kaia at the Opera House. He didn't see them as Bond and Bond Girl. And definitely not Blofeld and his mistress. It seemed likely that the scientist and the serum were of equal importance to someone.

He exited the vault before Aitkens' voice called him again, this time louder, nearer than Lin's body.

With two quick strides and a half turn he was able to meet Aitkens at the corner of the corridor. He stood with his back turned and looked over his shoulder at Aitkens, as if he had been waiting there for reinforcement.

"I guess the loading dock is out through those double doors," Burns pointed to the double doors at the far end of the corridor. Then he turned to Aitkens and watched for the reaction as he nodded coyly at the vault. "What do you suppose is in there?"

"Empty room," answered Aitkens. His eyes were fixed on the sliding door. Burns wondered if Aitkens noticed that it was open a little further now. Aitkens rolled his blank stare to rest on Burns' right shoulder. Burns studied Aitkens for a moment and decided it was ignorance and not disinterest that he saw in Aitkens' eyes. Burns felt some relief when a voiced approached asking, "Is there more to see there?" A tall, middle-aged Semitic man in a Macintosh followed the voice.

"The forensics team is here..." said Aitkens, looking just beyond Burns. He was stating the obvious, and it sounded to Burns like he stopped short of saying "and you have to go". But he was doubtlessly thinking it.

"Inspector David Isaac. At your service, as it were." Isaac's mouth opened into a wide grin and let out a friendly chuckle. Burns liked him instantly. He returned the smile over Aitkens' shoulder.

Aitkens waggled two disinterested fingers at Burns to introduce him.

"This is Burns. Charlie Burns."

"Ah. Detective Sergeant Charlie Barnes?" asked Isaac.

"No, it's Burns... Just Watching Burns," he offered. "Good to meet you." The two men reached around Aitkens and shook hands.

"Just leaving Burns," said Aitkens. He stared at the exit for a moment then turned and faced Burns. "Did you not look at the message from DCI Wayne telling you it's time to go home?" Burns shook his head no, pretending to pay more attention to his phone than to Aitkens.

"Did you not get the message from DCI Wayne about reporting to his office directly?" Aitkens repeated with more urgency. He addressed Burns but had turned to look at Isaac. Burns waited for Aitkens to swing his head round again.

"No." Burns recognised the hint of hostility in his own voice, but made the choice not to break eye contact all the same.

"Well I did," said Aitkens, as he wagged his phone with a hint more aggression. Then he turned his eyes to Inspector Isaac and Lennox, who had followed them.

Charles Burns knew he had received a text message while he was taking photos of the document in the bin, but he had been deliberately waiting to read it. He smirked at the idea of having a mock duel with Aitkens, who stood still holding his phone at arm's length aiming it face-forward at Burns. Burns straightened himself as he thumbed his phone and opened the message from DCI Wayne. Burns glared at the back of Aitkens' head. What disturbed him most was the difficulty he was finding to summon a reason to respect the Detective Sergeant.

Not off to a good start, thought Burns. Wayne was calling him back to the Met. He slackened his posture and turned to Isaac. He thought about giving the forensics specialist a summary of what he had seen so far. Then he remembered the spent cartridge in its ad hoc evidence bag on the countertop and thought better of it. As if on cue, Aitkens straightened and turned to face Burns with a practiced cordial smile.

"Well, I suppose you'll be off then, Mister Burns," grinned Aitkens.

"Yes, I suppose I will," said Burns, after only the slightest hesitation. He knew he was the bigger man, he just hoped he wouldn't have to prove it. He backed up, taking two long, deliberate strides away from the scene. He returned Isaac's smile and relayed one to his uniformed ally, Lennox. He deliberately excluded Aitkens from a parting acknowledgement then turned and strode toward the exit. He stopped at the open door to the reception area.

The fourth member of Isaac's team was taking photos of the hunched over guard in the reception room. He was taking his last photo from the periphery and was about to examine the body when he noticed Burns. He gave the man a wave before turning back to the lab for one last look around. He cleared his mind and began mentally retracing his path from one piece of evidence to the next. Burns handled his phone in his pocket, consciously scrolling through the images he had photographed. They were signposts in the stream of experiences he stored as memories.

He had taught himself how to use several techniques that enabled him to store and retrieve long-term photographic memories. A particularly bright day care worker had recognised that four-year-old Charles Burns was eidetic, and convinced his mother to visit a psychologist to confirm young Charles' photographic memory. Burns smiled as he recalled the three-way conversation between Miss Jenny and his parents. Miss Jenny seemed grateful when his father grudgingly agreed to make the appointment. His mother was proud when she told the Old Man she had already made the appointment. Charles remembered how Major Ken Burns tried to make his tall frame less conspicuous as he escorted his family out of the house full of waist-high children.

Burns was satisfied that the flashback had prevented his curiosity from taking over. He could step away from the crime scene and all the rambling theories that had flashed through his thoughts. For now.

He turned round in the door to watch the forensics officer as he examined the body more closely. *Rigor mortis* had begun to set in but hadn't reached the guard's lower extremities, and the legs uncrossed with a sudden thud as a size-twelve combat boot hit the floor. The young officer had shifted himself for a better angle and recoiled when the foot landed. Burns cast an empathetic nod, and the young man seemed relieved enough to continue his work. Burns wondered how much earlier the guard had died before Dr Lin was shot in the head.

Every answer he had found so far only raised questions. He wondered how much Wayne knew already. Burns wasn't sure how much information he would share about what he found and how he had found it. He probably wouldn't volunteer any information if Wayne didn't ask. Trust issues aside, Burns didn't want to be seen as some lone wolf or cowboy with no regard for protocol and procedures. At least not on his first assignment...

He'd better ask, reasoned Burns. He has to want to know what I know.

Burns reckoned Wayne had to make his official status "active", and not as Training Specialist Burns either. This thing was already huge and getting bigger by the minute. Hell, he's probably already had the Home Office call in the army. Burns had been trying to get a clear idea of the scope of the situation, only to find himself drawn to the impending threat at its core: Something was wrong with Veda's vaccine. Burns had read enough in his cursory examination of the pages in Veda's wastebasket to give shape to a fear.

The shape of the threat was unclear, but that didn't matter. His body was ready to fight. He had no idea if Wayne knew what they were up against or if either of them could expand their mutual trust enough to...

Wayne had been hard to read at times over the course of their previous meetings. Burns had felt there was mutual trust and respect immediately. But he wasn't convinced Wayne had been totally honest when he blamed the union for the delay in Burns' posting to MCU2, and that the only way to get Burns on the unit immediately was in the role of a trainer. He had made it sound like empathy: it was a concession for Burns and on his part, too. And Burns believed Wayne when he assured him it would be temporary. Now, worst of all, Burns had unintentionally invested himself in the case. His curiosity in Dr Nicholas Veda had revealed the scientist's greater cause, something the Home Office was equally aware of, and interested in protecting. Not well enough, apparently, Burns thought. Veda's disappearance, and the apparent disappearance of his research and work suggested another proactive cause was at work. What remained to be seen of course was exactly whose cause was being realised. Burns could only hope Wayne had more answers. Two men died during the theft at Veda's lab, leading Burns to believe someone was committed to Dr Veda continuing his work elsewhere. He also believed that whoever was responsible, they probably weren't trying to save South Asia from typhoid. Burns caught himself holding his breath as he recalled the empty vault. He let out a quiet sigh and closed his eyes and turned the pages of the picture book in his mind.

Burns was excited. Every fibre of his being was energised and ready to act. He had to remind himself that survival instincts, fight-or-flight responses had to be managed, controlled. And threats had to be neutralised.

"Mister Burns?" Aitkens' tone had lost its patience. The maître d' had become the twitchy vice-principal.

"Just taking it all in again," Burns offered lightly. Then he puffed himself up a little and added, "I guess Detective Chief Inspector Wayne wants my report, pronto, as it were." Burns held his focus on Aitkens, who had been staring at or near Burns' left shoulder for some time.

"Is there something else?" asked Aitkens with another deflected glance at Burns.

"Nope", answered Burns with a grin. He turned and strode to the exit. As he passed through, he suddenly wheeled around and thrust his head and shoulders through the door. He flexed his arms, forearms resting on the either side of doorframe and leaned in. Burns fired a wide grin at Aitkens and added, "I trust you'll make sure these fellows don't miss anything, won't you Detective Sergeant Aitkens." Burns gave a nod to Inspector Isaac and the other men, maintaining the grin until he turned and headed for the stairs.

By the time he had flexed and stretched his way back up the stairs to the main floor Burns felt his humour refreshed. He had tried to play nice, but he wondered if he could let the incompetence he witnessed go unpunished.

"Excuse me, Mister Lloyd," Burns called out to the security guard. Lloyd was standing in a shadow near the exit, looking even more like Christopher Lee in black and white. A closer look revealed at Lloyd's drawn face as a man slightly overwhelmed by the night's events. Or maybe just tired, Burns wished.

"What can I do for you, Detective?"

Burns smiled. "Where's the back door?"

"I was just going to make the rounds and could show you the loading dock if you'd like."

Burns spotted the views from two cameras covering the loading bay entry. "Any cameras out there?" asked Burns, pointing his thumb over his shoulder at the hallway behind the elevator. Lloyd indicated the images from a camera in the alley outside the entrance and the one inside overlooking the dock area.

"The gate keeps track of the entries, and some computer somewhere keeps track of that."

"Right," said Burns.

"I imagine they got tapes or what-have-you."

Good point, thought Burns. He checked his watch. Wayne probably had the meter running. "Yeah, maybe I'll skip the tour," said Burns. "Let the video guys find it."

He couldn't discuss what "it" was, or even if it mattered.

"Thanks for your help, Mister Lloyd." Burns extended his hand and Lloyd shook it firmly.

"Connor," he said.

"Right," said Burns. "Charles Burns. A pleasure."

"Anytime, Charles. Anytime," Lloyd smiled.

"Have a good shift, sir," said Burns. The two men nodded and went their separate ways. Burns got to his car and drained his water bottle. He wiped his lips and smiled as he slid behind the wheel and turned the engine over. In just a few minutes he would be back at New Scotland Yard, and he couldn't decide if he was more excited about Detective Chief Inspector Wayne getting his rank sorted or finding out how much intel Tully had gathered about the evening's events.

01:45

Nicholas Veda was paralysed, surrounded by complete and utter blackness. He had been dreaming. The faces of his family lingered, and he remembered Pondicherry. And Mary. Veda willed himself awake, not wishing to see how the dream ended. He had the sense that he was sitting upright, but couldn't move or even feel a muscle. He imagined he was bound to a chair, but his entire body was numb, lifeless and unresponsive. Except his face and ears. Every nerve on his face had stopped tingling and he could feel a wet hood plastered to his head. He realised his mouth hung open and was trying to draw breath through the heavy, wet material. A violent coughing fit made his head bob—he felt it in his ears—but he could not feel any other physical sensation. Veda knew his neck must be holding his head up as his body wracked with spasms, but his head seemed to be hanging in the bag, completely separate from his body. Through his coughing and gasping Veda heard a voice, maybe two voices or maybe an echo. He couldn't be sure. It was a language he didn't know. He coughed again and gagged as watery sputum pooled in the back of his mouth. Bile burned his nostrils and he smelled vomit. His stomach and lungs expelled the last of their contents, and Veda felt its warmth on his jaw as it spread out against the hood.

Veda became aware of his body when he felt the fear that was expanding in his chest. Fear became panic when Veda realised he couldn't tell if his eyes were open or closed.

A hand slapped his forehead and a foreign voice asked, "Are you awake?"

Veda's throat had been clamped by the terror that gripped him. The rest of his body was pins and needles, like a foot that had gone to sleep.

He managed only a guttural croak in response. He was trying to convince himself that he was dreaming when a fist suddenly struck him in the face. He couldn't feel his body's reaction to the blow as his head rocked back then snapped forward and down to his chest. The blow made his ears ring. Blood trickled from his nose and traced its way round his gaping mouth. Suddenly he felt his equilibrium shifted and the angle of his head tilted upward as if to look at the moon on a cloudless night. He wanted to ask what was going on. He wanted to ask why.

"Help," he managed.

The voice's laughter reverberated in the room. "Help?" he asked. "You don't need any help, friend. I will take good care of you."

Nicholas Veda knew he wasn't dreaming when the water hit him. He saw stars. It was like his head had been thrust into a fast-moving river. The cold shock made him gasp and he sucked the canvas into his mouth. But the reflex betrayed him, and he took in water instead of air. Gasping and gulping, his lungs and stomach filled and emptied themselves. He couldn't move his jaw to close his mouth against the deluge, so he tried to close his throat and draw a breath through his nose. The bag over his head seemed to fill with water in seconds. The adrenalin coursing through his body had set fire to his skin. Veda surprised himself when he felt relief—and gratitude—when he realised his body was attached to his head. But he was drowning. Blind, paralysed and drowning. He could hear the water splashing heavily on the floor behind his head, echoing on smooth tile walls, as the hood rubbed and scratched his ears and his heart pounded in his ears and it sounded like he was standing on top of a dam on a raging river and his lungs were going to burst. Then water filled his ears and all the sounds raging around him were muted—except for his pounding heart. It was beating so hard and so fast, echoing in his head. He could feel the frame of the chair against his arms and legs as the torrent of water pouring over his face and torso forced him down onto the chair. Veda had the sensation of falling head-first down a huge waterfall. But with the water rushing up. He was falling faster and faster against the current when a cough froze in his chest. A scream welled up in his throat and his lungs burned for oxygen. The scream drowned in the flood as Veda blacked out.

"It's almost 2 am," Burns cursed aloud in the stairwell at New Scotland Yard.

Burns took the stairs up to Tully's office, two at a time. He was taking full breaths and trying to get a burn in his legs or break a light sweat after last night's game. He had better steal an opportunity to work his muscles whenever it presented itself today, he thought, especially if he was going to be working a case.

The idea excited him, but he still didn't understand exactly what Wayne had in mind for him. What he had gleaned from the little snippets of Veda's story and the evening's violent crimes had the makings of a global event, and Burns instinctively wanted in.

The moment before he was about to open Tully's door he paused and drew a long, deep breath, remembering the day they met. It was his third day on the job at the Met as an employee—not a contractor. Burns had brought a small group of anti-terror candidates to the gun range when Tully caught his eye on the next range over. He was loudly cracking up with another officer in uniform. They had pulled the protective eyewear off but both men still had their earmuffs on and were almost shouting at each other, offering mundanely expressed excuses for missing a target, ribbing each other and making jokes about their prowess. Tully laughed last.

"Stats don't lie, my lad." He pointed at the scoreboard blew a breath across the rifle's muzzle as he leaned back into his wheelchair. Tully's last one was the best.

"You couldn't hit a barn door with your head!" And the unforgettable laugh.

Burns laughed and made a note to use that one someday.

A short while later, Burns stood near Tully when they were in the queue to record their results and check out on the range's computer. Tully was still ragging on his partner when Burns caught their attention with a polite cough.

Burns studied both men for a moment. He couldn't imagine the young officer would ever be in a life-or-death situation involving a gun. Tully looked like a man who would, and doubtless laugh out loud.

"Analyst?" Burns asked the loser. He turned to Tully "A nicer way to say desk jockey."

"We both are," Tully answered. "Analysts."

"Really?" said Burns. "I mean, I shouldn't be surprised, I suppose."

Tully stared, feigning bewilderment.

"No, I was going to say it's no surprise a guy like you can outscore…"

Burns hoped he didn't look as stupid as he sounded. He pointed at Tully's wheelchair and tried a wry smile.

"You're my first."

"Relax," answered Tully. "I was surprised, too," and they laughed.

By reflex Burns made a joke about it being especially surprising if he couldn't hit a barn driving that chair. He smiled benignly and hope his volley landed well.

"Bloody right," Tully lifted his torso and flexed his shoulders. "Pulled the guvner off the motor. And I could knock the bloody barn over with this head," Tully laughed. Tully waved his printout and challenged Burns to check his entry. "T'was the other fella there who couldn't hit water if he fell out of a boat. Me? I'm facking awesome at these VR ranges. Couldn't hit a giraffe's eye from fifty yards in the old days, but in here

I'm a…" his eyes sparkled and a broad grin split his wide face in two, baring his flawless teeth. "Legend."

Burns didn't hide his curiosity, but he framed it with a sly grin. "How long have you had your license for that thing?"

"For the chair or the MP5?" Tully laughed.

Later that evening over a pint they talked about how much they both loved hockey. Tully was a firm believer in the value of analytics and Burns called them "fancy stats". It was Tully who had got Burns a try-out with the Ravens.

Tully explained how he had broken his back in a shipwreck about eight years earlier. He rescued four people from a sinking vessel while on holiday in Cornwall. The storm blew his old fishing boat to shore. After it beached and Tully got the survivors ashore, he went back to the boat to drop anchor and secure his craft against the storm and the tide following it. He was replacing the life jackets in their stowage when he "just slipped and fell. Badly." Tully went on to describe how he pulled his limp body almost two hundred yards over the rocks to get to the shore using only his arms. Burns didn't doubt the story. He could see how Tully's powerful arms and shoulders filled his Chicago Black Hawks sweatshirt. His career in the motorised division ended but fortunately for Tully his transition to a permanent desk job went easy. He was a quick study using HOLMES, the Met's powerful data analysis system, and soon found himself on DCI Wayne's speed dialler list. Turned out he was a natural at memorising, correlating and analysing data. Burns had nicknamed him 'Stats Guy' after they'd watched a few satellite broadcasts of NHL hockey games from North America.

Burns considered Tully to be not only a good friend but also the most valuable connection he had at the Met. He knew what HOLMES knew, and a whole lot more.

He knocked and simultaneously swung the door open in an attempt to give Tully a jolt.

"So," he said loudly. Tully didn't react. He slowly turned in his wheelchair and smiled like a flight attendant trying to look perky on a large dose of Gravol.

"And good day to you, too, Not Detective Burns. Long day already, or another very short night?"

Burns pretended to be in a mood. "Uh huh. Answers, not questions, Ironside." "Ironside, the D.A..? Nice one, Burns."

"Dang, Tully!" Burns exclaimed. "Ironside? Really? Surprised a young lad like you would catch that reference. How would you know Raymond Burr? That show was on TV when your pappy was still in short pants. You must've stumbled across it on YouTube, right?"

"No, ya doddery old git. They remade it. Then they cancelled it. Had a black guy playing your old Perry Mason. Probably a bunch of racist old twats like you staged a demonstration in their wheelchairs. And yeah, of course I YouTubed it. Man, great theme song. Love that seventies shit."

"I am not a racist." Burns played indignant, then smiled. "I hate every race, colour and creed equally."

"W.C. Fields," said Tully, his dour face coldly unimpressed. "Profiler wannabe." He waved at the carafe on the side table next to his digital desktop. Burns stepped closer and sniffed in the direction of the carafe. He picked up and examined a small mug from the table next to the coffee. It was from the Hamburg Christmas Market, 2013. Burns took another whiff from the lid of the carafe and winced at Tully. "How old is this coffee, as old as *der Becher*?"

"Just made it 14 minutes ago," Tully laughed. "But no cream, I'm afraid. You'll have to settle for milk, lad."

"Yay," Burns mocked. "Nescafe made 14 minutes ago. And no sweetener, just good ol' refined white sugar. Lucky you're in that chair. You've got an excuse for being a little tubby, Tully."

"That's no fucking Nescafe, me Boyo. All the way from Sumatra, that is. Via Starbucks." Tully's grin gave way to a growl. "You be careful... You're lucky I'm in this chair, Johnny Canuck."

Burns helped himself to the coffee and milk in the mini fridge under the table, decided it was fresh and poured a cup. He took a sip and sat on the desk next to the wall opposite Tully's workstation.

"So?" Burns repeated. He left it open, letting Tully decide where the conversation went. He knew Tully would share whatever he felt appropriate for Burns to know before the briefing in ten minutes.

Tully turned in his chair back toward his computer's twin flat screen monitors and got down to business, pulling up pages of information as he spoke.

"Right," he said. "First things first: Dunno if this is good news or bad news, but the blood taken from the car isn't the Doctor's. Records indicate him as type AB but the bloodstain was type B. B negative, to be precise.

"Maybe the blood is the girlfriend's. A-type is more common in Asia. B-negative is old European blood." Burns had seen what Dawson had written in his description about her having a Russian accent. And he had memorised her features.

"Brilliant deduction, that" said Tully, affecting his best Holmesian accent.

Burns smirked. "You don't sound anything like him."

"Who?"

"Robert Downey Jr."

"What, Iron man? Get off," scoffed Tully.

"No, Sherlock Holmes, right?" Burns deadpanned. Tully was nonplussed.

"Jeremy Brett, you cretinous Canuck," said Tully, still affecting the British accent.

"Who?" Burns was genuinely at a loss. Tully sighed. "The real Sherlock, from the BBC."

"I thought that was Benedict What's-His-Pants."

Tully gave a sardonic smirk. "Anyhoo, I'm still trying to get some positive ID for the girlfriend, to cross check, but can't find any records for her. Bit of a mystery, she is. According to Dawson's reports, she enrolled in a Pilates class at "The Place" in Bloomsbury in March—the same fitness club Dawson goes to—I've got their registration records and can match the name and photo, but I can't even find a home address for her that checks out. The address she put on the registration form is the Anderson Hotel in Chelsea. They don't know her there, either," Tully grimaced at the screens. "No mobile phone, no email. She's not even on Facebook. Did manage to pull this image of her off the security cam at the lab. It was time stamped six days ago. Lucky they keep a digital copy of the feeds on the server for seven days."

"Nice one, Tully," said Burns. "Probably hasn't been in the country that long. Maybe search her last name and look for relatives in the London area?" Burns made it sound like question. Did Tully know what Burns was going to be in the unit? Burns still wasn't sure himself. Like Hilts had said, who was he going to train?

"Did find name matches. Problem is she's got two. Last names, that is, not relatives. Kaia Kass is the one she used when she registered at the London Contemporary Dance School in Kensington. Or, she's Kaia Rebane, the name she gave our man Dawson when she walked into Veda's life about four weeks ago and the one she signs on the register at the lab. And no listing for either name in greater London or anywhere else in the UK. Having trouble finding either name anywhere on HOLMES."

"It's pronounced Ray-bah-neh. It's Estonian. Means fox," said Burns.

"Accurate, judging from the screen cap... I could," Tully quipped.

"No, you couldn't," said Burns, tapping Tully's paralysed legs with an open-handed pat.

"Ha fucking ha," said Tully. "Sod you, Burns. Me John Thomas still works fine, thank you very much. Of course, I'd have to take her word for it." Tully laughed and patted his large round belly.

Burns smiled. "Seems simple, really. First thing you learn in Detective School. Follow the girl."

"In your case that's called stalking, mate." Tully scoffed.

"Follow the girl to the bad guys," said Burns.

The Metropolitan Police Service had access to London's massive concentration of thousands of surveillance cameras and should be able to spot this woman, whatever her name was. From what Tully had claimed about HOLMES' ability, Burns was disappointed that his friend hadn't more to go on.

"Let me know when, or if, your pal HOLMES' facial recognition finds any other names to match the face," said Burns. "Or you know, locates her." He got up off the desk and turned away, examining the stains on the table below the coffee maker.

"Roger Wilco, Not Yet Deputy Inspector Burns. I'll let you know," said Tully sharply as he saluted Burns' back. "I already did, wanker. Have something within the hour." Then he nodded at the door behind Burns. "At the briefing."

"Right," acknowledged Burns as he gazed at the door. He turned to face Tully and nodded humbly. As he was exiting, he turned and smiled, "You do have his looks though."

"Who, Iron Man?" asked Tully.

"No, W.C. Fields," smirked Burns. Tully shrugged and laughed.

Burns' smile dropped as the burning question formed on his lips.

"Who?"

"If you ask me," Tully lowered his voice to a conspiratorial level. "It's the fucking Russians. They were doing lots of chemical and biological warfare stuff before the Wall came down. Then it just stopped because why?"

Because their military was in shambles," Burns remembered.

"Exactly," Tully went on. "Surveillance in the early nineties reported zero activity in two of their largest experimental facilities in Siberia and what was rumoured to be a lab in St Petersburg. Satellites said the Siberian sites were vacant within weeks of the Fall. MI6, Interpol and even your pals in the CIA were unable to track any shipping of weapons of any kind, for some reason."

"What makes you think they're my pals?" Burns was a little offended.

"Apparently we— and when I say we I mean them, nudge-nudge," Tully winked. "We have some ideas of what they had, but nothing on what moved or where it went. It looked like a lot of 'grab what you can on the way out'."

"And Russian Capitalism was born," Burns agreed. "Everything was for sale. And sold."

"Next thing you know, private Russian enterprises started selling off inventory to nut jobs like Saddam, and worse."

"I know. I met some of them," said Burns absently. The stillness hung for a moment as the two men remembered how inauspicious the ending of the Cold War appeared at first. Then a smile split Tully's fleshy cheeks.

"Wouldn't it be funny if the two of them turn up in a video on Twitter humping like little bunnies behind the Opera House?" Tully joked. His mouth puckered and pulled in the rest of his face.

"Wouldn't it?" Burns agreed. There was another silence as the two men imagined a happy ending.

Tully's phone whistled and Burns' beeped almost simultaneously. It was a message from DCI Wayne. The message read: 'Meeting in 2b in 2'. Burns checked his watch and asked Tully," One fifty-two? What happened to oh-two-hundred?" Burns couldn't wait to get to the briefing and learn what the others knew, and of course share what he knew. His mind was racing, but he still hadn't a clue as to where.

Tully explained, "Detective Chief Inspector Wayne, in case you hadn't noticed, has a thing about punctuality. He'll mention it, I'm sure. He calls a meeting for an exact time but expects everyone to be there five minutes early." Tully began closing the open windows. "By his maths, we're almost late already." Then he turned and gave Burns a double take, as if he was surprised to see him still standing there. "Of course," Tully went on haltingly, "he could just be confirming the location. Meeting room 2b... with typos." Tully shrugged.

The two men looked at each other for a moment. Then at their phones. Both read 1:53.

"So," said Burns. "Five minutes early is on time. Fine." He put his cup on the tray next to the coffee maker and made his way to the door. Then he stopped. Burns still had a question — for now, not for later. How long would it be before this thing got to be too big for DCI Wayne's little Major Crimes start-up, and what other agencies would be swooping in to take over the operation? The pissing match to ensue would undoubtedly stall any action plan. He groused silently.

If indeed there was an action plan yet.

He couched his query as diplomatically as he could, pressed for time as he was.

"Tully, how broad is the search, I mean does it include any of our other friends in Europe, for example?"

"Detective Chief Inspector Wayne has got friends in the highest of places, my friend," said Tully, with a wink. "You on the other hand..." Tully took one more gaze at the photo of Kaia before shutting down the last monitor.

"Fox is right," said Tully with a whistled sigh. Burns didn't bite so Tully capitulated. "DCI Wayne has the full confidence of the HO. My understanding is the Home Secretary herself is one of those friends I mentioned. If he sees the need, all he has to do is call. He's already got a million ears and eyes out there." Tully caught his breath and whispered, "And very quietly."

Burns was satisfied for the time being. He stood still as Tully rolled past him through the door and into the corridor, then he called after Tully.

"Seriously. Who would want him?"

Tully stopped and turned back half-way and smirked, "What, DCI Wayne?"

"Nice one, but no," Burns insisted. "The professor. The immunology expert."

"Don't know that one yet." Tully lowered his voice to a conspiratorial level in the empty corridor and went on. "Terrorists... governments. Big Pharmaceutical... Greenpeace..."

They reached the lift at the end of the corridor and Tully gave Burns a curious look as the two men reached for the call button.

"Thanks," offered Tully. "But I ride alone. And no offence, Charles, but I'd rather not be showin' up late to the first briefing with the likes of you." Then he smiled as the doors opened and he rolled in and spun round.

"I'll take the stairs," said Burns. "Cheers, mate." He turned to his left and stepped into the alcove leading to the stairwell and scurried down to the next floor. He was five steps away from Meeting Room 2b when the clear baritone voice of Detective Chief Inspector Wayne stopped him.

"Burns," he called.

Burns turned to face Wayne and addressed him formally. "Chief Inspector Wayne, sir."

Wayne motioned for Burns to come nearer with a downward sweep of his arm. Fingers together, he stopped his hand in front of himself before relaxing the gesture and returning the arm to his side. Burns wondered if Wayne was a dog fancier.

Burns wasn't going to deny that he was really looking forward to being called 'Detective Sergeant Burns', but he had a feeling... the look on Wayne's face was not one of welcome. Not hostile, but all business, and at least a little angry.

"Right," said Wayne, almost standing at attention. He was tall enough to look down his nose at Burns, but instead he squared his stern visage to Burns and met him eye-to-eye. "Look, Burns. You'll be activated Monday morning as scheduled, but as the unit's Training Specialist, until we make your rank official."

Then with emphasis he added, "As agreed, Burns." His eyes weren't inviting a rebuttal, and Burns didn't offer one. Burns resolved to taking this learning experience at face value, hoping to be of some value to his new team. That's what he would say if anyone asked. Burns guessed that if Wayne didn't have him doing more than watching and learning during this operation it meant it already involved other agencies, likely Whitehall. Or he was waiting to hear from Veda's captors before doing anything. Either way, it was looking like Wayne was going to have to expand the scale of the operation, and Burns was likely going to be a very small cog in a big machine.

Wayne's expression softened. He cleared his throat and confessed, "I think I might need you Burns." He held Burns gaze. Burns knew he meant it.

Wayne stopped at the door but didn't reach for the handle. "Your status," he paused.

"It's not official until I say it's official," Wayne said finally. "We'll see Monday. For now, when I want your input, I'll ask for it."

Wayne had played the victim of bureaucracy last week when he explained to Burns the decision to activate him at the rank of detective sergeant was being delayed by either final review or an objection from a member of the MPF. Wayne had suggested he was doing him a favour by getting him activated earlier and that Burns should be rather grateful to be activated at all.

Burns was concerned that Detective Chief Inspector John Wayne was testing him for his suitability with the team, and he hadn't exactly got off on the right foot. Aitkens surely won't have anything nice to say about me, he thought. Maybe Wayne would let him work with Tully.

Wayne opened the door and strode into the briefing room. Burns tried to sweep away the confusion clouding his mind. His head felt like he was wading through a room full of conversations, each one trying to drag him in, each one pointless or a discord of unintelligible words. Burns stepped into the room just before the door closed with a click and a short, soft electric buzz.

02:00

The room wasn't large, about eight metres by six, and didn't look as though it was purpose built to be a private conference room. A glass wall ran from the door behind Burns round one corner and continued to the next, where it met the opposite wall. Thin flat panel blinds hung in the windows, open to the corridors outside. The opposite wall was bare, panelled from floor to ceiling with what looked like a mousy brown coloured indoor-outdoor carpet. The wall panels were joined by vertical black plastic strips and were fastened to the floor on a metal track. Burns thought the wall looked like the kind of soundproof divider used to split large auditoriums and conference halls into smaller rooms, and he wondered if another similar room lay on the other side of the divider.

All of the team members present looked up and straightened themselves when Wayne entered. He was acknowledged by the team with nods and formal greetings, but their eyes all hung on Burns as he made his tardy entrance. A long rectangular table with rounded corners occupied the centre of the room, with a number of rolling chairs set at the workstations, each consisting of a docking port and a flat screen display. Wayne directed Burns with his eyes to a seat at the near corner of the table. One vacant workstation lay between Charles Burns and Detective Sergeant John Aitkens, defended by the almost visible force field of contempt that he was shielding himself with.

Inspector Guy Tellier, or IT Guy, sat directly opposite Burns. He responded to Burns' cordial smile with a wide grin. Born to a French father and Vietnamese mother, Tellier had the most infectious smile of any man Burns had ever met, his face literally lit up. But Burns had only ever seen it twice, including this moment. IT Guy had a friendly enough ring to it, but the ex-Interpol communications analyst hadn't shown much of a sense of humour in the short time Burns had studied him. Burns spoke French the first time they met, and Inspector Guy Tellier beamed. Burns couldn't help grinning at the memory, proudly reminding himself he knew how to bond with teammates. He just needed to occasionally remind himself to make it a priority.

The others seemed cordial, if not smiling, as Burns turned from one man to the next. Burns recognised all of the men there, having met them all at least once during the last two weeks. He had done a bit of due diligence, looking up their names on the unit's roster and getting at least the basic personal data of each member, for his mental file. Here, at their first collective briefing, Burns was still forming first impressions. He recalled their personal data as he gave each man a quick scan and wondered how many of them had been hand-picked by Wayne and how many were transfer requests like him.

A smaller, similarly shaped table was at a perpendicular angle at the near end of the longer one but off set, disconnecting the 'T', to allow space for Tully to wheel in to his workstation between Tellier and Wayne, who stood at the head of the long table. He was gazing at the monitors above the far end of the table, ignoring the room full of eagerly waiting eyes. Tully's desk was slightly higher than the longer one, with five legs that could raise or lower the table to different working heights. The desk was equipped with three of its own monitors, and a docking station and other interface modules on the surface. From here Tully was organising the images on the three large screens at the opposite end of the long table.

Suddenly the blinds closed shut—quicker and tighter than Burns expected. They made a sound like a kid dragging a thin twig along an iron fence. With a final echoless clop the blinds sealed shut. Burns felt the air pressure change. He realised the room had been closed to more than just prying eyes and ears and wondered just how tightly the room was sealed. No one spoke, and it started to feel like a submarine to Burns.

Detective Chief Inspector Wayne tapped his touch pad, drew himself up and read the time and date aloud with a disdainful look. Wayne cleared his throat.

"Gentlemen. This is a closed-door briefing." He gestured to the windows. Anyone who hadn't switched off his phone did so, and Burns followed suit. He assumed that all the team members were more familiar with the protocol than he, since he knew nothing.

Wayne tapped his pad again and stated the time and date in a more monotone grumble.

"*Chag Sameach*," someone muttered.

"Case Number twenty nineteen, dash oh four dash two-four-zero-one," said Wayne. Almost to himself he added, "Missing persons." He went on with the names of everyone present and ended the record ident info with the tag, "First Briefing."

Wayne's eyes were fixed on the smaller screen in front of him, at a window not seen on the three large monitors or any other workstation. He was rereading the exchange between himself and Dispatch. The first order had been to call in to MCU2 if Veda and Kaia were seen, but Wayne had upgraded that to identify and detain. No sightings, nothing so far. There were still listed as persons of interest to MCU2, and Wayne was hopeful that would keep the interest of street level personnel without awakening those sleeping in higher offices at the Met. He managed a slight grin when he imagined the two naughty lovers caught *in flagrante delicto* by a Special Officer and being told to 'freeze'.

Wayne swallowed with a frown. "Not bloody likely," he grumbled. He straightened his back and squared himself, staring past the upturned faces at the monitors. Veda and Kaia Rebane smiled back, having the time of their lives at the Opera. The night was just beginning.

"Right," said Wayne, snapping himself out of his reverie. "Dr Nicholas Veda and Ms Kaia Rebane," he mispronounced, "have been missing since approximately twenty-thirteen, May twenty third, or six hours ago." He drew down his focus and met the eyes of the men as they turned back to face him. "First we see the big picture, then each of your smaller pictures in turn. I'm not promising a lot of time for questions or insight in this first briefing, so please stick to the facts first."

"Inspector Tellier will," Wayne paused. He grabbed a bottle of water from his desk and drew a deep breath. "Report on video and communications surveillance." He toyed with the plastic cap before opening the bottle to take a sip of water.

"Well, we have two missing persons, two crimes scenes and two corpses. Here is where we start to put the pieces together." Wayne took his seat, and after he received the thumbs up from Tully, he tapped a few commands on his keyboard. A set of small panes appeared on the left viewer at the end of the table. Each one represented the occupants of the workstations round the table with a small photo from the eye level cameras aimed at each person seated round the table. Burns noticed his picture was missing and promptly made a smirk at the lens. Wayne tapped his pad and announced, "Detective Sergeant Blennerhassett."

"Right, sir," said Blennerhassett. "Do you mean the flat or the airports, sir?"

"Just the flat," Wayne frowned.

"Right, sir. In that case, not much to report, and nothing you don't know, sir. We liased with security there, and then we investigated the flat. Nothing on his drive indicated he was going anywhere. Sir." Blennerhassett's smile suggested it was the obvious conclusion.

Burns wondered how long it took DS Blennerhassett to get into Veda's personal computer. That's spy shit, he mused. Marty Blennerhassett, formerly with MI5. Burns wondered if they had bothered to look in the closet for suitcases.

"This is the live feed from Veda's building security," Blennerhassett went on. "We're in contact. Looks like everybody but Veda has come home by now," he chuckled.

"Thank you, Blennerhassett," said Wayne. "Detective Sergeant Riza, would you kindly summarise the scene at the car park in Drury Lane?"

Detective Sergeant Semi Riza was the only team member that Burns had spoken to for more than five minutes, and he took an instant liking to the man. Tall and wiry, his greying and receding hairline was more than compensated for by a thick, black moustache. He had sparkling blue eyes and an easy, sympathetic smile. Burns imagined he was talking to a foreign film star or the leader of a coup in some Arab state when Riza opened up about his life over a coffee in the canteen. Semi Riza was about forty years old and a second-generation Turkish Londoner. His parents had immigrated to Germany after the military coup in Turkey in 1980. Both Semi and his brother had joined the Met, instead of going to university as their parents had dreamed. Semi was awarded a scholarship and attended London College, where he graduated with a degree in forensic sciences. He then re-joined the Met in the Crime Scene Unit and had become well known, both for his analytical approach to forensic evidence and his irrefutable performances in court on behalf of the Crown's prosecution.

He explained how the blood sample found was not Veda's, "because it looks to be a type 'B'. And probably not Ms... Rebane? Is that right?" Riza looked at Tully for confirmation on the pronunciation. Tully nodded to Riza, then stole a censuring look at Burns as Riza went on. "Unless she's at least ninety-nine per cent male." A light ripple of laughter rose and ebbed. Riza seemed humbled by the laughter, and a slight blush framed his charismatic smile.

Charles Burns returned the grin, but he didn't like the fact that he already knew so much that was going to be repeated in the briefing. He wanted answers to questions he didn't know yet, but he had a feeling there would be few, if any, that didn't support his assumptions.

Burns wanted to make the connection for everyone to see. He felt impelled to drop his knowledge of blood ancestry, and as the last wave of laughter dissolved in the sand-coloured window blinds he spoke out.

"Maybe the blood belonged to a friend of the woman." Burns hesitated long enough for half a breath, then he sallied forth at a measured trot. "1 mean it couldn't be Veda's, which is most likely AB with him being born in India, and it is more likely a male from Old European blood." Burns slowed to a canter, then a walk.

"Like Estonian, for example or, more likely Russian," he stopped. He'd tried and failed to be less emphatic. He realised his audience had judged him to be out-of-place. He tried to salvage the point with nonchalance, without an apology.

"Just saying, it could be someone she knows."

Burns imagined tumbleweeds drifting by. He looked over at Riza, checking to see if toes had been stepped on there. Riza, on the contrary, seemed impressed and offered an affirmative genuflection in Burns' direction. Then Burns caught Wayne's icy glare.

"And that will be all you'll be just saying," said Wayne.

A message appeared onscreen in DS Aitkens' dialogue box for all to see, asking if Burns had learned that online, too. A few coughs and a few shuffling chairs covered quiet chuckles around the room. Aitkens, was obviously surprised to see his text appear on the monitor, but quickly decided to drop his blind and gave Burns a challenging shrug of his shoulders and an expression of defiance, daring Burns to respond.

Burns declined the invitation, as tempting as it was, and straightened up in his chair. He was disappointed he couldn't at least send a silent, private retort to Aitkens because his iPad was locked out of the interface. Burns still hadn't received security clearance to use his electronic devices and wouldn't until Monday. If then, he winced.

"Moving on," said Riza. "The car and the scene at the parking garage were clean, as in probably wiped. Before Dawson was on-scene," Riza asserted. He halted, then added, "Only Dawson's print, singular, here..." Riza used his cursor and pointed to a spot on the inside of the door. Then, almost as an afterthought he added, "And the blood. That didn't get wiped. And Dawson spotted that."

A look went round the room. Burns figured the car would attract anyone's eye. Its slightly ajar passenger door was immediately visible from the nearest camera angle available.

Detective Sergeant Riza ended by saying, "The car is now downstairs, waiting for a complete bio mag scan." Riza paused for the question that didn't come and added, "We don't know when we will have results, but I do not anticipate anything of value to the investigation..." Riza trailed off.

"Right." The force of Wayne's voice was unsettling, to him. He squared himself again. "The main reason this has fallen to us first is because we had a man with Veda when he was — when he disappeared." Wayne gave Riza a nod before he closed Riza's pane on the viewer.

"Detective Sergeant Dawson was assigned as Dr Veda's..." Wayne stopped. He tried to weigh how much to say, how many excuses. He decided on, "police escort." Then in defence of Dawson he added, "He was drugged. Dr Veda and Ms Rebane were... they disappeared after that."

"How?" someone asked quietly. It was either a reasonable question about how Dawson was poisoned, or a stupid one. Either way, it wasn't asked. Burns watched Wayne take his time to decide to answer.

DCI Wayne's jaw tightened and relaxed. "Apparently, Dawson had a sip of a wine spritzer," answered Wayne. He cleared his throat loudly to suppress the sniggering.

Riza jumped in. "Blood alcohol levels were negligible but there was something else... thankfully not much of it made it into his bloodstream."

Wayne tried to lighten his tone. "Well, apparently, one sip of 'Barefoot Bubbly' in combination with the mystery toxin was enough to make him pass out for two hours," said Wayne finally.

"Full blood toxicology analysis will take some time," offered Riza.

Wayne stole a look at Riza before moving on. Riza looked apologetic. Wayne held his gaze on Riza, then gave him a curt nod.

"Thankfully, he didn't ingest more, and he'll be with us again in due course," said Wayne.

Not for at least another twenty or so hours, thought Burns. Dawson would be under observation at least that long. But why was Dawson with Veda and the Fox? Who decided Dr Veda needed security? Burns guessed that Detective Sergeant Riza had already begun to prepare his evidence for trial.

Burns couldn't imagine it going to court. If MI5 or the Met's Anti-Terror Unit or MI6 got called in, it would become somebody else's mission. Burns wanted badly to believe that Detective Chief Inspector Wayne would be able to quietly direct enough resources to successfully deal with a hostage situation, without the other branches. If they could find Dr Veda.

Wayne turned to IT Guy and said, "Inspector Tellier will give us the sit rep on communication and video surveillance... in a moment." Wayne acknowledged Riza 's raised hand with a nod.

"Sir, if I may," Riza spoke out. "Detective Sergeant Dawson's blood showed almost unreadable low levels of alcohol. But other toxins – "

Wayne cut him off. "Acknowledged, Detective Sergeant. On record." He stared at the photo of Veda and Kaia on the screen.

"It will be a few hours. We'll have a full blood and stomach contents analysis," Riza said finally.

Burns wondered how many opera-goers had missed the crime scene after the show, and how many ignored it. The car would attract anyone's eye, concerned citizens and thieves alike. Its slightly ajar passenger door was immediately visible from the nearest camera angle available, and likely from the lift and stairwell, too. There were only a few cars remaining on the same level where the Peugeot sat. Burns knew it was too late anyway, impossible to know how many were there when the blood was spilled until they find and replay the video.

"Right." The force of Wayne's voice was unsettling. "The main reason this has fallen to us is because we had a man with Veda when he was—when he disappeared." Wayne closed Riza's pane on the viewer and took another long pause.

"Detective Sergeant Dawson was..." Wayne stopped. Burns had wondered to whom it was important that Dawson be cleared of any trouble. That much was clear now. Plausible deniability. But why was Dawson with Veda and the Fox on their date?

Wayne pondered the display on his monitor and drew a continuous circle on his touch pad, following the curser as it trailed in an orbit on the screen.

Burns looked past Wayne over at Tully, trying to gauge his level of anticipation, but he was engaged in some activity on his phone. His lack of interest did nothing to dull Burns' growing excitement. London is the most watched city in the world, and the Met has access to thousands of camera feeds over all the Boroughs of Greater London. There had to be a large van or lorry at the lab to haul whatever equipment was lifted from the lab in Shepherd's Bush. And Tully's facial recognition program will have a lot to work with. Maybe even spot them at the car.

Burns finally let his breath go, almost panting until he could rein in his curiosity. He gave up trying to draw Tully's attention and turned to the diminutive Frenchman.

Wayne also turned to Inspector Tellier and said, "Inspector Tellier will give us the sit rep on communication and video surveillance as far as..." Wayne halted, then he gave Tellier a look, and crooked one-finger gesture, to indicate a pause before he handed the floor to him. Wayne drew a continuous circle on his touch pad, following the curser as it trailed in an orbit on the screen. Burns studied Wayne and wondered if he felt what Burns felt. Was he more disturbed by how little was known? Or was he deciding how much intel would be shared at the moment? Burns already had a sense that Chief Wayne liked to keep pretty strict control over information and its dissemination. But Burns' instincts told him that he could trust Wayne to judge the relevance of any evidence.

Detective Chief Inspector Wayne cleared his throat, making a sound like a short hum punctuated with a faint grunt. He took a deep breath, then let it go, almost whistling with exasperation.

"We have zero surveillance from the car park," Wayne confessed. "where Doctor Veda was snatched."

A shockwave sent a few heads swivelling back and forth from the monitor, where Inspector Tellier was laying out a map of London on the main viewer. Burns kept his disbelief to himself as the others reacted with varying grades of incredulity. Was it the shock of the idea that no surveillance had recorded the event, or was it Wayne's choice of wording? Snatched.

Wayne stepped on the murmur. "In fact, we have zero surveillance from... from a large number of reporting stations." Wayne left off, then gave a curt nod to Tellier.

"Inspector, please summarise what else we know so far. S'il vous plait."

And please tell us something we don't know, thought Burns.

Inspector Guy Tellier had been recruited out of Interpol by Wayne and had assembled a team of six Special Officers, all experts in information technology, cybercrime and electronic surveillance. The son of a Commandant in the French Sûreté Nationale, Tellier didn't immediately follow in his father's footsteps like Burns had done. Guy Tellier left home at seventeen, studied computer sciences and Chinese in Beijing and hired on with Interpol immediately after graduating. Tellier had made a name for himself by developing the organisation's electronic espionage division in his early twenties. Since then, he had forged an impeccable resumé, directing several high-profile investigations — and an equal number of clandestine operations — in the twenty-five years since. Wayne used his contacts in the Home Office to connect with Tellier, conveniently, as his early retirement age approached. A vibrant fifty-year-old, Guy Tellier accepted the offer to head the unit's IT team. He had given up correcting his colleagues when they mispronounced his name and had embraced the Anglicised nickname 'IT Guy' long before he came to MCU2.

Tellier rose from his place opposite Burns and stepped to the end of the conference table to stand beside the large viewer. As Tellier passed the men seated at the table, he seemed only slightly taller than them. He looked a bit fidgety at first, feeling inside the pockets of his jacket for something he apparently couldn't find. Burns smiled encouragingly. Wayne cleared his throat in an attempt to get Tellier started.

"Yes," Tellier returned Wayne's acknowledgement. His brown eyes darted around the faces before he smoothed his thinning hair and flashed a bright but nervous smile that disappeared when he began speaking.

"What we know so far: A disruption occurred between the hours of twenty-oh-seven and twenty-two-oh-seven." His voice rose a little, both in pitch and volume, as he blurted out, "A surveillance disruption." Tellier gazed at the tablet in his hands, ignoring the men seated round the table as he went on. "A large radius of cameras were..." he stopped. The room went quiet, and cold.

"Jammed?" offered Wayne.

"Non," replied Tellier, shaking his head vigorously. "Not possible. No signal disruptors were used locally. They may have used signal jammer at the lab... Probability... But not for the rest, *non*. That would be impossible. You would need literally hundreds of units to create the blackout they—not using short range signal jammers. Non. The perpetrators gained access..." Tellier caught himself and stole a look at DCI Wayne, whose stoic but non-censuring visage eased his nerves. He knew to keep his facts simple, without too many technical details, and his assumptions must be voiced as such.

"The Met's surveillance monitoring system has been attacked. Corrupted," he said flatly. His shoulders almost touched his ears in an exaggerated shrug.

"The concern here is that it appears that the signals were sent remotely but denied access to the Met's monitoring system." Tellier raised his head and glanced around at Wayne and the others before carrying on. With another slight nod from Wayne, he went on. "At the moment we can't say whether the signals were disrupted externally, between the camera feeds and operations centre, or if the system itself was disrupted by some kind of DoS, a denial of service. The radius, the area covered by the disruption..." Tellier paused. A light in Tellier's eyes seemed to be kindling wonderment.

"Not the entire city, only several hundred camera feeds." He tapped his iPad and a satellite map of the greater London area came up on the main viewer. He tapped it again and the map lit up with thousands of tiny white dots along the roadways and throughout the buildings, almost animating the image.

"This is the matrix of street level surveillance cameras across all the Boroughs," he explained. "And this," Tellier tapped his tablet again, "is the area of the blackout." The tiny lights in a large area in the centre of the map turned from white to red. Burns noted that both Heathrow and London City airports were within the red zone. Inspector Tellier paused a moment, quickly scanning the faces of the other men for their reaction. Burns saw it, and he knew Wayne saw it too, but he couldn't say if the others did. Tellier couldn't hide his admiration.

"Look at the pattern. The detail," he said, with that priceless Cheshire Cat grin.

At that moment, it was obvious to everyone. The blackout formed the shape of a giant hand giving the universal one-fingered salute.

"See how he used the areas of lower density for shading... the gap between the thumb and the forefinger..." Tellier trailed off until Wayne's gaze drew him back to the briefing. The look told him to leave it there, and he dropped his focus to his tablet and absently tapped at it and the giant finger disappeared.

Someone started to ask again, "How—" but Tellier cut them off.

"I don't know... At this point," he admitted. He and Wayne looked at each other for a moment. Wayne's look said that that was enough. Guy dropped his gaze to his iPad and tapped a few keys.

Aitkens grumbled, "He's flipping us the bird. You've got to be kidding. All this…" but he was lost for words. Burns could sense the collective bewilderment.

Detective Sergeant Mike Thornley half-mumbled, "Respectfully sir, who the fuck is Dr Nicholas Veda?"

"Typhoid," Burns said it first. "He wants to save the Third World from Typhoid. As far as we know…" Burns caught his use of the plural 'we', and left it there.

The question and Burns' answer were ignored momentarily, and Burns watched Wayne's colour go up as he clenched his jaw.

"You're out of turn, Burns. Again."

Wayne's nostrils flared slightly with an almost imperceptible snort. There was some shifting in chairs and a collective breath stopped short, awaiting the next word from Wayne. It was an outburst that didn't come. Tellier looked at Wayne for a long moment, waiting, wondering if he should proceed. His admiration for the skill of the blackout architect had been replaced by dejected frustration. He appeared to have nothing constructive to add.

Wayne stepped in and rattled the silence again with his deep voice. "Inspector Tellier and his team have been reaching out to all monitoring agencies and street level personnel trying to understand just exactly how — rather what happened, I suppose, first…" He gave a questioning look to Tellier, who shook his head and shrugged.

"We know Veda's phone was closed at the Opera House," Tellier offered at last. Then reluctantly added, "We are unable to identify or locate Ms Rebane's phone." With that, Inspector Tellier stuffed his hands into his pockets and shrugged dejectedly as he returned to his seat. Burns guessed that Guy Tellier was a man who was more accustomed to being the one who had the answers, and that he never felt as small as he was.

IT Guy had brought quite a reputation with him to MCU2, and Wayne had been restrained but not too subtle about his unmet expectations. And anyway, this was the biggest security breach that Burns had ever heard of. He caught himself on a question. He wondered if the Met Surveillance Command knew anything yet about how they got hacked, or by whom.

Wayne's humour seemed to improve as he acknowledged Tellier with a thankful smile. "Yes, and since the system's integrity seems to be restored, I'm sure I won't be waiting long for an update. Thank you, Inspector." After another curt nod to Tellier, he shifted to Aitkens and gave him the same forefinger gesture to stand by. Only this time it seemed more emphatic because it was Wayne's non-arthritic left hand. Burns watched as Wayne, in command of himself and the room, tapped his touchpad and the cleared the highlighted locations on the map, erasing the technical artiste's one-finger salute. Burns maintained his passive expression as Wayne's gaze finally came round to meet his. Burns let Wayne read his eyes, doing his best to meet the resolve, and the optimism, at least half-way.

Wayne opened his mouth to speak before turning his attention to the assembly. Placing his hands on the desk, he leaned forward.

"As I say, our surveillance is back online, yes?" he turned to Tellier, who nodded in the affirmative. "Right, and manpower is engaged at street level. Public transport has deeper coverage and…"

"Including the airports?" Burns couldn't stop himself. "Sir?" he added apologetically.

"Yes, we have direct contact." Wayne shot a warning glare at Burns then nodded in the direction of the monitors and the small pane with DS Gray typed under a small black window where a photo would be.

His smooth baritone continued without a shift in pitch or volume.

"Detective Sergeant Gray is with the airport authority at Heathrow and DS Dye is at City." The warning lifted and the storm passed over the sea green eyes. Wayne went on, "Obviously, we're not just looking for Dr Veda and Kaia. The evidence suggests this is not an ordinary missing persons case."

"A major crime, it is sir", piped Blennerhassett, releasing the tension in the room with a good chuckle.

"Indeed, Detective Blennerhassett," said Wayne. "A major crime that is receiving due diligence here in this unit," he added.

Burns smiled and imagined Wayne was taking a jab at Aitkens, but conceded it might be his own little private joke. If Aitkens didn't come clean about his flub at the lab, Burns would bring the jabs.

"Has anyone ever done anything like this before? I mean the finger thing."

"Inspector Tully is on that," Wayne cut him flat. "And we'll have more on that." he stopped and turned to Tully, who confirmed with a definitively raised thumb.

"Lastly," declared Wayne, "Detective Sergeant Klein is attending at the home of Dr Veda's father, Mr Soman Veda. And will report in... if necessary." Wayne paused long enough for Burns—or anyone—to chime in with a question, but no one said a word. Burns wondered if Wayne or anybody else was expecting a call to come from Nicholas Veda's captors. Burns was sure there wouldn't be one.

Wayne stifled a yawn and lifted himself up from the desktop, working his hands open and closed before he turned his focus to Aitkens.

"Which brings us to the... second crime scene at the lab on... Uxbridge Road," Wayne exhaled. He seemed to be struggling to keep his optimism afloat against the wave of fatigue that had washed over him. *Hang in there, old chap*, thought Burns, hoping the voice in his head was loud enough for Wayne to hear. Things were just getting started.

Wayne didn't introduce Aitkens, he simply indicated with an open palm that the floor was his. Aitkens responded by straightening to attention in his chair. Burns wondered if Aitkens might stand, to raise himself higher and lend more authority to his address. Aitkens remained seated, his focus rising and falling from the large monitors to his personal device, flashing glances that fluttered around Burns, darting skyward and flitting between his left arm and cheek.

Aitkens began by reading the time and date of his arrival at Number Ten Uxbridge Commercial Plaza and listing the names of himself and the two accompanying officers at the scene. Those were the only words that appeared on the overhead monitor, and easily read by all. Burns leaned forward casually, trying to get a look at Aitkens' face. He wanted to watch Aitkens' face as he gave his account of the crime scene investigation at the lab. But Burns couldn't see past Aitkens' ear. Because he chose to stare at the empty monitor at the far end of the table.

"I'll begin by saying Inspector Isaac and his small team were quick and thorough," said Aitkens. "He apologised for not being able to be present for this briefing but will have an electronic report available..." he paused to check his watch. "within the hour. I can summarise what we know so far, and show you a few pictures." He gave the last line to Wayne, eyebrows raised in an unspoken request for approval. Wayne consented and Aitkens went on, his confidence growing.

"A break-in occurred..." Aitkens had tried starting from memory, and failed. He searched his notes for a few seconds before conceding, "Sometime earlier in the day. And several pieces of laboratory equipment was stolen. We haven't got exact details of exactly what was taken, but I believe Inspector Tully has more on that." Aitkens needed a breath.

"I do," answered Tully. His tone and expression made it clear that it had been decided that the list was not to be included in Aitkens report. Aitkens accepted and moved on.

"I liased with building security, a Mister Lloyd Connors..." Aitkens was having difficulty with his interface. He checked and then disconnected it from its dock and reconnected. A small window closed and reopened on the viewer at the end of the table. "We found two bodies. The first identified as Corporal Wayne McDavid, part of the security detail assigned by the HO." Aitkens turned and mustered a smirk at Burns. "That's the Home Office, eh?" Aitkens exaggerated the last syllable, a jab at the only Canadian in the room. Burns calmly smiled and made a mental promise to continue to resist the impulse to spank Aitkens with the facts.

A photo of McDavid's folded corpse appeared on the viewer, followed by a tab showing his personal data. Aitkens cleared his throat. "Cause of death: gunshot to the head from close range. The second victim has been identified as Dr Tae Kwang Lin, COD another gunshot to the head..." Aitkens trailed off as everyone looked at the photo of the assassinated scientist. "We're not positive of his citizenship, but Tully seems to think he's originally from North Korea."

"Right again," confirmed Tully. He turned to Wayne and the two exchanged a look of unspoken agreement.

"And nothing else, for now. Right, Detective Sergeant?" said Wayne.

"Well, we're ninety-eight per cent sure of the murder weapon, and while the murdering thieves were prepared to face armed security, my guess is that Dr Lin picked the wrong Friday night to work late." He looked at his watch unconsciously. "Nothing else, sir," Aitkens finished.

"Thank you, Detective Sergeant Aitkens," said Wayne, "for your conjecture."

Burns squirmed and bit down but couldn't hold his tongue. "What about the stolen equipment?" Burns leaned in closer to Aitkens but asked Tully. He could see Aitkens right eye moving, nervously searching for the best place to land on the monitor in front of him. But his posture remained upright, confident as he turned to Wayne, who was giving Burns a searing, silent rebuke.

"Stolen property is not our primary concern," Wayne declared. Stolen people..." Wayne trailed off and curbed his temper. "You're out of turn, Burns." Said Wayne. "Again."

"Yes sir," Burns yielded. Then he turned to Aitkens. "My apologies, eh, Detective Sergeant Aitkens."

He hoped it sounded sincere enough to appease Wayne. Not to pet Aitkens' patchy ego. Burns had to care about a man before he would consider apologising for a criticism or accusation, since he never said anything that wasn't true. He could feel bad about taking an instant dislike to John Aitkens, because he'd already come to accept this disappointing surprise. He could count on one hand all the men who had earned his instant contempt. Senior officers, equals or subordinates, he was proud to say he almost never met a man he didn't like — at first.

Burns tried to pretend he didn't mind that Aitkens had left out the details about how the bodies were discovered. Can't put the credit or the blame on me, Burns thought. He wondered if Aitkens had already told Wayne everything. He hoped so. He saw no value in showing up—or calling out—a team member before he was officially on the team. He presented his passive-attentive stare to Wayne. Burns' frown lifted easily, by reflex, but his knitted brow took a little more effort to relax. He used his hand to smooth the creases on his forehead then he combed it slowly through his tousled hair.

"Right," said Wayne. His expression was serious but not grim. Then a smile rose.

"Well, safe to say the two murders are connected to our missing persons. I'll be speaking to you individually for any further debriefing. Your next courses of action are as follows." Wayne tapped his pad like an MC at a wedding checking the microphone.

"Detective Sergeant Aitkens, go to IT with Inspector Tellier and connect with Specialist..." He looked at Tellier for help.

"Specialist Roy," confirmed Tellier.

Wayne repeated the name, anglicised. "Sorry Guy, and apologies to Patrice," said Wayne. He frowned as his words appeared on the monitor as he spoke. "Delete last," he said flatly. He tapped his keyboard to halt the dictation. "My computer doesn't like my French pronunciation any more than you do. I have to say it like that, or it will come out looking like rhubarb."

"No problem," Tellier replied. "Specialist Roy has the contact info for everyone connected with the lab, and their current locations."

"Good," Wayne acknowledged.

"And the murder victims' phones," added Tellier.

"Indeed. But that is not your…" Wayne stopped then purposefully turned to Aitkens. "That is not a priority for Sergeant Aitkens." "We have electronic surveillance and uniforms at the residence off Australia Road in White City. The Ministry has been putting them up there until their paperwork clears. Reach out to the ranking officer on site," he told Aitkens. "His contact details are here." Wayne dragged his finger across the pad and a small tab slid into an expanded panel on the monitor.

"Maintain surveillance. Call them in for questioning. Report and track any movement," Wayne drew his focus on Aitkens, who seemed to feel it almost immediately and turned. "And notify me," Wayne ordered. "Interviews begin upstairs at oh-seven-hundred." He watched as the computer completed typing 07:00. "Be prepared for detention." Wayne sounded like he was telling his child not to forget to put a jacket on before going out to play.

"Detective Sergeant Riza," Wayne called out as Riza's pane on the monitor popped up.

"Sir," answered Riza.

"Speak to Inspector Isaac and push our evidence to the front of the pile, his scene and yours. We need to know if any matches are found on the blood from the Peugeot," Wayne caught Riza before he spoke and added, "and toxicology."

"Yes, sir," said Riza.

"Detective Sergeant Blennerhassett," Wayne said without looking up. Instantly, Blennerhassett's tab expanded on the view screen. The text rolled out in the dialog box as Wayne dictated the orders.

"Go to London City Airport and take over for Detective Sergeant Dye. You'll be in touch with Inspector Tully and…"

Wayne paused to send a nod to Tellier. "One of Inspector Tellier's team... I say take over meaning relieve, Blennerhassett. If necessary. Dye has been going over a lot of footage and AT control data. He may need to step off, but there's enough to look at, and two sets of eyes are better than one. Nobody is dismissed until I say so." Wayne paused. He seemed unsure for a moment, and Burns wondered if he was debating whether or not to command the computer to delete last, or if something else was causing this sudden discomposure.

"Keep me posted," he said, and it sounded almost threatening, as if he were expecting bad news.

"Will do, sir," Blennerhassett answered.

"Call me when you get there," answered Wayne. "In summary, gentlemen," Wayne's voice rumbled. "We have two major crimes and not a major coincidence. You have your orders. We'll meet next at oh-eight-hundred. Here."

"Sir? If I may," Tully interjected.

"What is it?" asked Wayne.

"There is the issue of our coms being, erm, compromised," said Tully. He looked over at Tellier who nodded vigorously at Tully, then Wayne. The three men exchanged looks until Wayne directed Tellier to speak.

"Yes, we can't be sure of our security here," said Tellier. "Phones stay off. No calls wis mobiles for now, and especially no internet—no whassapp, no tweets. SMS text messages only." Tellier looked at Tully and Wayne again. "Dat's all," he concluded.

Wayne lifted his chin and spoke. "This room is secure when closed, so you can use your devices in here. You all have access, however I expect you'll all be busy elsewhere for the next few hours. Hopefully things will be restored to normal..." Wayne trailed off and looked at Burns. "Except you, Burns. Your access is... not activated yet."

It didn't sound like an apology or an indictment to Burns. Just a fact, a reminder that he still wasn't on the team.

"We're not sure what we have here yet," said Wayne. "But you all have your orders. It's oh-two fifty-five. Report here at oh-eight-hundred, or directly to me, via text only, anytime between now and then. "You are dismissed, gentlemen," he closed the open files on his iPad then he stepped back from the desk and turned to Burns.

"You're with me, Mister Burns."

Yes sir," said Burns. He followed Wayne out of the room and down the hallway to the lift. They were stepping at a quick pace when Wayne suddenly stopped and turned over his shoulder to Burns.

"In ten minutes, at oh-three oh-five. In my office," he said and stepped into the lift quickly as the door split open. He stabbed at the button for his floor then pressed and held the button to close the doors, without a glance to Burns.

"Yes, sir," answered Burns, smiling. Burns' smile didn't land on DCI Wayne, who remained focused on the LED showing the floor number as the doors closed. Burns turned back and saw Tully rolling out of the briefing room. Burns met him halfway, Tully glowered and stopped.

"So, you're going to follow the girl, right?" said Burns.

"Fuck, Burns, I already am." Tully was a little testy. "I'm following a lot of tails, I mean trails," he insisted with a smirk. Burns smiled at the deliberate slip. Tully's expression soured. "Mind yours," he said as he wheeled past and tapped the call button.

Inspector Tellier passed them on his way to his office. *"Bon chance,"* he said. Burns guessed he had said it more for himself. *"Et toi,* Inspector," Burns replied.

"Good hunting," said Tully over his shoulder as he entered the lift. His cheerless expression was unchanged. He stared at Burns and rotated his chair around to align his body with his face. The door chime went off and Tully's face changed.

"Bon chance, mi amigo!" Tully grinned. Then he winked as the doors closed between them. Burns' own smile faded after a few lonely moments of standing in front of the closed elevator doors.

He had been caught off guard by Tully's lack of input at the briefing—nobody talked about the girl—but he was glad that nobody seemed to be expecting to hear from Veda's kidnappers about a ransom demand. He hadn't studied Veda's photo for long before he concluded that the young scientist was in danger and not part of the plot.

But Kaia definitely was part of it. He knew it. He could only hope that Tully or IT Guy could connect her to whoever was driving the bus. Veda's been kidnapped and his lab pilfered, he thought. Burns stopped himself from asking out loud the questions that were tumbling in his head. Burns checked his watch. Six minutes. Plenty of time to do the stairs down and back up to Wayne's office. He refilled his water bottle in the men's lavatory and headed for the stairs. He stepped through the fire door and paused on the landing. He arched and stretched his back before drawing his body down and reaching to touch his toes. Then he slowly curled upright and aligned his skeleton, preparing his muscles and joints for the coming physical stress. Burns stood and looked down the gap between the flights of stairs. He could see all the way to the ground floor. Maybe stairs down, elevator up.

Nicholas Veda knew he was dreaming.

"Nicholas!" his mother shouted. "You shouldn't be standing so close to the bars. That tiger can kill you in a moment." Then she was calm. "Come, let us go and look at the birds." Veda's mother sounded like a song from long ago.

"How can you be so young and worry so much?" Ravi laughed. Their mother seemed suddenly very young. Too young to be his mother. Nicholas walked with his mother and brother into the Marble Palace. It was overrun by jungle, with birds flapping and squawking everywhere. Suddenly, it was just Nicholas and his mother. "Where is Ravi?" he wondered aloud. He tried to remember how old he was and couldn't. He felt like a boy and a man and a shy teenager who couldn't talk to girls, all at once.

"Where is your father?" Mother seemed older again. And sickly, almost blue, like she was before she died. And Nicholas realised he was a child. And this was a dream. He took his elder sister's hand, she was so thin, and they ducked under a Semal tree as the rain pelted down on the promenade in Pondicherry.

"Father should be here. He loves the zoo. But he loves cricket more. He's watching Ravi play. It's not even a championship or anything. Ravi doesn't have to study every day! This is a dream. Why can't I control this?" He wondered, for a moment, if he had said that out loud.

Then Nicholas Veda was drowning.

He was standing under a waterfall with his mouth forced open and a heavy canvas bag over his head. Somebody was holding his arms down. He imagined he was trying to break Ravi's grasp. Then he remembered the chair. And the torture.

Veda coughed and wretched until the water filled his body. His eyes burned and tears dissolved in the raging river that was pouring over his face and into his open mouth.

"You won't die," his brother told him. And then the water stopped. He sucked the hood into his mouth. He snorted involuntarily but it cleared his nose, and, after a few seconds of gagging and gulping and swallowing the mucous and water, he was able to draw a few consecutive breaths without his lungs and stomach reflexively hurling fluids in defence.

Veda awoke with a start to the voice behind him.

"There he is!"

The voice was sing-songy, the accent foreign. He could tell he was hearing a man's voice but couldn't see who or where it was coming from. Every sound in the room echoed and vibrated like the tinny old transistor radio in the small water closet at the boys' school he had attended in Pondicherry.

Inside the hood it was hot from his own breath and still damp, and his head felt heavy. His neck was killing him, like it did when he had fallen asleep as a boy on the long bus ride between Chennai and Pondicherry. When he tried to move, he was completely paralysed. But he could feel his skin. All over his body. Some places wet, some aching where his flesh was being stretched by contusions. He felt a puddle of cold water trapped under his testicles. The skin on his wrists and ankles was stuck fast with tape and bound to a chair. He pulled at the heavy tape that held him fast and sensed the hairs on his arm being slowly pulled from his flesh as he strained. But soon he felt too weak to struggle and let his limbs go limp. In a rush, Veda felt joy and anguish. He could feel his limbs again, and tried to move them, but the effort exhausted him and he sagged into the chair, the heavy hood pulled his head down to his chest.

"That's it. You relax, professor. No problems here," the voice continued behind him.

Another voice to his left chuckled, and spoke in an almost flawless English accent, "Try not to move too much. It will take some time for your body to recover. The sedative we gave you also has paralytic properties. Dead weight is so much easier to transport, you see. But the hangover will be gone in no time. Remarkable little cocktail, really."

Veda flexed weakly against the bonds. His could feel something against the skin on his left forearm as he tried to twist his limbs free. He realised an IV was stuck into his arm. Panic squeezed his chest and confusion roared in his head. He couldn't understand why he could feel everything touching his skin-the tape, the IV, the heavy bag over his head—and yet his muscles would not respond to his brain's commands. "Where am I?" He croaked. "What do you want?"

The strong, fluid voice ignored the question and explained. "I asked Herr Noack to stop the water treatment for a time so I can introduce myself."

A long pause. A chair creaked. Footsteps. The voice continued calmly, very near to Veda's face.

"I know you are confused right now, disoriented. But soon your head will clear, and your vision will return, and we will have the chance to talk about..." the voice caught itself, then added wistfully, "The future." The voice had moved around to face Veda but was still some distance away as it continued. "The cocktail we prepared for you is a milder dose of a psychoactive agent I've used in different applications. I believe it may be compatible with..." the voice trailed off. After a breath the voice continued. "For now, you should sleep, and possibly enjoy some interesting dreams," said the voice. "Or not enjoy them. It depends on you, really. Do you have guilty feelings, Doctor Veda?" The other, meaner voice laughed.

"I have a few things to attend to," said the paternal voice, finally. Then, affecting a passable American drawl, he said, "Y'all just sit tight for now. All will be revealed in due course, Doctor." The voice changed to the foreign language again, and the two men had a brief conversation. The only words that Veda caught were 'Georgia peach'. They were uttered by a lower-status man, who was immediately scolded. Veda heard footsteps moving toward him. Then someone grabbed his arm firmly and twisted it a bit, holding the IV fast. He felt the chill of the fluid coursing out of the needle and into his vein. Then his arm was released, and the footsteps moved away behind him.

Veda was awake now and fear made his heart race to his throat. Panic! A second later his heartbeat dulled to the slow thud of a marching drum echoing down an empty hall. A moment later a door closed.

"Who..." Veda stopped himself from asking a stupid question. Or maybe he didn't want to know the answer. He wanted to shout but the noise he made felt more like a sob. A moment later he felt groggy, then happy. Then nothingness descended on him like a warm, wet blanket.

Burns bounded down the stairs, clearing his mind of the questions he hadn't answers for. In the lift going up he contended with the obvious. Wayne hadn't said anything about Burns at the briefing, hadn't even introduced him. And if Burns was in, Wayne surely would have said something. He could visualise himself rescuing Veda from his captors. A flash of guilt clouded the fleeting exhilaration he felt. Someone always had to be in a shitty situation before a soldier could become a hero.

Burns heard David Byrne sing "Same as it ever was, same as it ever was". Even if he had to sit this one out, Burns was going to tell Wayne what his suspicions were. Wayne seemed the type to keep tight control over information, so Burns might not get to know what Wayne knew, but he sure as hell was going to ask some questions.

The door to Detective Chief Inspector John Wayne's office opened before he could grasp the handle. He was surprised to see Wayne stepping into his face as the door swung open. Wayne straightened himself, filling the doorframe.

"Burns," said Wayne.

"Sir," Burns replied. He didn't have to check his watch to know he wasn't late. There was some surprise in Wayne's voice, but his face was drawn in an expression of consternation. "Look, Burns," Wayne started. "I haven't the time now. Put simply, you're on call. And your next call is oh-eight-hundred." He raised his chin slightly. "Now, if you'll excuse me, I have to be somewhere."

Burns took a step back and away from the doorway. He couldn't catch Wayne's eye as he passed.

"Sir," Burns called to Wayne's back.

"Eight AM," Wayne answered. He strode away like his famous namesake and disappeared around the corner at the end of the corridor.

"Oh-eight-hundred," repeated Burns. "Sir."

04:45

"I want to go back to Kolkata!"

It was Nicholas Veda's older sister Priya. She was crying. He held her hands in his. It was strange to see her as a child, yet she still seemed taller than he and his brother Ravi, who was one year younger than Nicholas and still the smallest of the three.

Nicholas tried to cheer his sister, "But we're here. Look. Can't you smell the river?" He gazed at the river, watching soap bubbles churn and froth in an eddy below their feet. He couldn't smell anything but pretended well. Then Nicholas knew he had to be a man—and then he was one, his older sister was now only slightly more than half his size. He bent down to his sister's eye level and hugged his arm around her and pulled her to his side. He could protect her now. He was big. Nicholas inhaled deeply, encouraging his now-younger sister to do the same. She sniffled a little and he dried her tears. She seemed fine again. He still couldn't smell anything.

They were in a taxi traveling from the Marble Palace Zoo to the cricket pitch. Once there, Nicholas and Ravi were soon hurling the ball back and forth, bouncing it harder and harder on the ground between them, trying to make each throw more difficult for the other to field.

It was Ravi who started throwing it harder and higher each time. He looked at Nicholas with growing anger and hatred each time as he prepared to hurl the ball at his older brother, now the smaller of the two. Ravi was a full-grown man. His right leg was a prosthetic and he had a brace on his left knee. Nicholas remembered the sound of his brother's knee breaking, it echoed like a gun going off in a water closet. It almost startled him awake.

Nicholas wanted to leave off fielding practice. Suddenly he was small, and batting. Someone was holding his wrists. They were the arms of a man who stood behind him. Ravi was preparing to deliver the ball. Nicholas readied for the throw but every time he tried to swing his arms, they were limp. The only reason his hands were on the bat handle was because the man's hands were holding them there, squeezing hard on his wrists. His movement went along with the man's hands as they swung and missed the ball. Nicholas was almost falling, almost hanging from the cricket bat and the man's hands. He tried to lift himself up and turn around to look over his shoulders to see who held him fast. He couldn't turn far enough to see but he knew it was his father. He gripped the bat in his hands and pulled himself up but couldn't get free or swing. Nicholas was dizzy, and furious.

The bowler was winding up for another delivery. It was Ravi as a teenager, growing into his lanky body but still slim, angular, with both legs intact, his brow knit in the stern concentration of a champion.

Nicholas pulled himself free and exploded at both of them, "I can't play this stupid fucking sport..." He glared at his father. "Because you didn't teach me! How fucking smart was that, eh? Now look at us. Ravi's a cripple and nobody wants to buy your stupid vegetables. And I'm so fucking clever my head hurts!" Ravi and his father both argued that nobody was crippled but Nicholas refused to accept it. He couldn't see Ravi's legs because he was kneeling, staring at the dirt. He couldn't raise his head.

Nicholas remembered the night he and Ravi were attacked walking home from the cricket pitch. Or was that a dream, he wondered. Ravi was gone when he opened his eyes. His father's morose expression bore the weight of his disappointment. Nicholas was certain his father would never forgive him, and would always see him as a coward. His head really did hurt now. The dizziness gave way to nausea.

Nicholas knew this must be a dream. He would never speak to his father that way. He must be drunk. The nausea was real.

"Forgive me, Baba."

Young Nicholas paused for a split second to read his father's nonplussed expression. Then he bolted, running out into the road and stepping straight in front of the taxi. His sister and mother silently screamed from the backseat as he hit the windscreen in slow motion. Nicholas saw the driver hit his head on the wheel when he slammed on the brakes. He looked unconscious, or maybe dead as he slumped over the wheel.

"Terrific. Another death I'll get blamed for." He seemed to be speaking out loud but to no one. He heard his voice in a short echo as he watched the big ships slowly moving up the Thames.

His eyes were open, and he was awake. He was sure he was awake now, and looking out a large window that was not so far away. His mind was truly clear—no more dreams or nightmares. It was a window overlooking the river. He wanted badly to rub his eyes, as if that would confirm everything was clear again. His hands were still bound, and he was still strapped to the chair in a small, glassed-in room... but he could see again!

The riverside scene outside the window on the far wall of the lab aroused him. He recognised the location. He was near the Chelsea market, looking across the Thames at Battersea Park and the shopping centre where old power station used to be. But he was sure he remembered looking out the same window and seeing somewhere tropical. How old is that memory? Years? He thought of home... No. It's not India. It's only been hours. How many hours ago that was, Veda had no idea. He felt a rush of adrenaline course through his veins as it all came into focus. He studied the view, blinking several times to confirm all that his eyes were taking in. He sighed and squeezed out the tears that flooded his eyes.

He was in London and someone would find him.

Veda tilted his head up and down, slowly back up again and down, saw his naked body strapped to the chair. A cold chill raced over his skin like he had stepped into a freezer. He willed his arms and legs to pull at the restraints, managing a weak tug against the nylon straps holding his limbs fast. He thought he remembered seeing heavy tape holding his wrists. Then he remembered he couldn't see at all before now. His muscles were coming alive! He heard a timid laugh escape his lips over the roar of the blood pulsing in his ears. Veda closed his eyes and said a prayer of gratitude. For being alive... and for not being paralysed, and worse off than Ravi.

Suddenly a body stepped between him and the Thames.

"Hello!" said someone. A second later a fist slammed into his nose and Veda blacked out.

Burns kicked off his shoes at the door and stepped into his flat. With a shuffling two-step he closed the door and hung his jacket on a chair in the entry. He went into the adjacent room and pulled off his street clothes, folded the trousers once and placed them on the well-made bed. Burns slipped on a white tee shirt and a pair of sweatpants with deliberately slow and exaggerated movements, catching the moment to take inventory of his joints and muscles. No nagging pains, no restrictions or strains. He felt pleased with himself for a moment, appreciative of his muscles' recuperative abilities. His gratitude was tempered by the glum memory of having missed the third period of the game.

Still, it was fair to be grateful. He had spent thirty years training his body, twenty training his mind, and Burns felt as physically and mentally sharp as he did at twenty-four.

It was his interest in ice hockey that kept him motivated to stay in shape. Hockey, and his teenage interest in girls, had led him to the gym when he was fourteen. It only took a few months of dedication for his training to give him any kind of an edge on the competition in hockey. The girls noticed, too. However, unlike in hockey, when it came to dating Burns was rarely the one to make the first move. Until he lost his virginity, at least. Burns chuckled to himself as he reflected.

He took a long swig from his water bottle and opened his phone to look at the photos of the pages in the wastebasket at the lab. He scanned each page and quickly got the gist of what little he saw. Of the pages he had photographed, one visible section proved to be the most compelling. It read more like a speech than a dry description of clinical research. Veda was talking about the 'realised possibility' of saving millions of lives by 'simply making it rain'. In another paragraph,

Veda mentioned that he first proposed mass vaccination in a previous paper. Burns made a mental note of the title for later reference. He stopped, caught up in his own curiosity. Why not just make it an oral dose, a couple of drops on the tongues of the masses? Another page read like Dr Veda was announcing a failed experiment, but with 'undaunted commitment' to...

Burns flipped to another visible passage but stopped cold when he read the words asymptomatic carrier. His curiosity curdled in his stomach. He couldn't see the rest of the sentence, and he couldn't decide if it mattered. He dropped his phone on the bed and sighed, half relief and half resignation. From where he stood, the disappearance of Dr Veda was suddenly huge. Despite his apparent recent failure, Veda was of value to someone, and not only the National Health Service.

Burns didn't have to think too hard before he concluded he had no idea who would want Veda. But the reason why was taking a dark shape. Dr Veda appeared to be some kind of genius.

Burns chuckled nervously. "Hopefully not the evil kind."

What seemed a little clearer to Burns was that Detective Chief Inspector Wayne and those above him in the Home Office had reason to believe somebody else might be interested in Veda and his work, too, given the armed escort since arriving in London.

And the girlfriend... It wasn't difficult for Burns to imagine Kaia Rebane could talk Veda or any other heterosexual man into just about anything. Especially in that dress. But they hadn't just disappeared for a little fun like a couple of teenagers, Burns was sure of that. His mind took an abrupt turn, back to Veda's speech. His breath stopped sharply as he allowed himself the possibility of being the only one who had read Veda's bad news. He laughed at the idea, resigning himself to the fact that it didn't matter anyway. Veda was gone.

Burns picked up his phone and took his stretching routine to the floor in front of the ancient study desk he inherited from the previous resident. With his feet planted, bending at the waist he reached out to the keyboard on the desk to type in his passcode and wake his computer. And stretch his legs and back. He synched his phone to his laptop and watched as the large monitor on the desk illuminated the still-darkened room. Burns was comfortable in the low light that shone in from the street through the bay window at the far end of the studio space he rented from an old mate from the SBS. Day or night, Burns rarely lit the room unless he was cooking or eating. He took most of his meals at the island that stood between the kitchen and studio, and the lamp above the ceramic range provided enough light for eating and washing up after. He spent most nights on the L-shaped sofa in the living room listening to his ancient hi fi stereo system. Falling asleep to music had been his preference since he was a teen. He had put a double bed into the small room near the entry, imagining he would share it with someone, someday. But the bed almost filled the room and it made almost claustrophobic when he laid on it alone. And the sound was better in the living room anyway.

Burns used his phone to reopen the search on his laptop. He pulled up a short stool he had cut to size for working at the antique desk.

He found little more than mentions of Veda's academic career at Oxford on the university's website, and links to Veda's Twitter and Facebook profiles on the first page of results. With a few more clicks he retrieved a list of Veda's publications and opened it. The page filled with a selection of intriguing, typically discursive titles like "Transdermal application of active protein NK75 (copyrighted) and *Salmonella enterica* as a conjugate vaccine against typhoid in India".

Burns knew typhoid killed millions every year, mostly in Asia. He guessed the number of cases in the UK was closer to zero. In terms of typhoid being a threat to the national health, it was hard to imagine what value the Ministry of Health might see in a cure for typhoid. Burns shook his head as he swiped through the pages.

"What brought you from Oxford to London, Professor?" Burns laughed out loud when he guessed the answer to be "a grey sedan".

He switched his search to Google Scholar so he could open the full documents, even though, he told himself, it might be enough to scan the titles, make some notes to further explore Dr Veda's research later. After some sleep. Burns flagged a few of Veda's publication titles, looking for a possible source of the full text he had found in the wastebasket at Veda's lab. The more titles he read, the more compelled he was to open the documents and read about Veda's research. He scanned a few abstracts and jumped to the conclusion pages of the two oldest papers with Veda's name as the First Author.

Veda had, at the young age of thirty, discovered what was being heralded as the first effective live vaccine against both typhoid and paratyphoid, an apparently antibiotic-resistant mutant of the original bacteria. Burns remembered a title that appeared in his first search of news stories and flipped back to it. It was an article in an American science journal; Vaccines that could change the world. Veda's name came up in the search because his vaccine was the latest in a series of cures the author described as licensed and approved, cheap and easy to make available to millions, but not being utilised due to the 'paralysis of governments'. Burns let himself ponder the odds of Big Pharma having a hand in there, somewhere. It was an easy connection to make to the story, but not so easy to Veda's disappearance, Burns reckoned. He gulped as he recalled the words asymptomatic carrier.

He turned away from the computer and looked out the window. It was only mornings like this, when he had been up late enough to see the glow of the next day that he cursed his flat's southern exposure. And not having installed curtains. He reached up with his arms, yawning as he stretched. At least there was enough cloud cover to prevent a direct blast from El Sol as he slept. *Soon*, he winced. He didn't have to look at his watch, the monitor told him the time when he turned back to his search. He clicked on Veda's Twitter and Facebook pages hoping to find a bedtime story, something that could replace the conspiracy theories billowing in the clouds over the streets of London beyond his window. A quick scan of Dr Nicholas Veda's Facebook page offered Burns some relief. Veda may be a genius, but he definitely didn't look like the evil kind. He looked young in his profile picture, maybe still in his twenties and standing in front of a Buddhist temple. Burns guessed it might be in Beijing. The photo file was locked — unless Burns wanted to send a friend request, and wait for it — so he clicked over to Twitter, only to find no form of Veda's name was registered to a user account and that it was available. Burns cursed and sighed. He was angry, disappointed to not find dull scientific videos or 140-character descriptions of food and parks, or Veda's girlfriend's choice for a honeymoon destination — anything about the girlfriend, or even science or politics... For some reason Burns was suddenly glad to know Dr Veda wasn't another tweeting twit. He might admire this man.

Burns stood up. He realised his brain was jumping around and reassured himself he was finally getting tired enough to sleep. He decided on one last task, one last test for his focusing abilities. He stood straight, faced the window and closed his eyes. With a few deep breaths he was able to stop the spinning wheel of emotions, but not the fatigue that was creeping into his limbs, moving outward from his chest. It hadn't reached his eyes. They were sharpened by his curiosity. A neighbour's light went on but he ignored it. He returned to the search results of Veda's scholarly publications. In his first paper Veda developed, and Oxford University patented, a new vaccine. Big money, thought Burns... He focused his photographic recall, but he couldn't remember any news headlines about typhoid vaccines, except the one decrying the fact that it hadn't been approved or licensed yet.

In Dr Veda's most recent publication, the one about the 'transdermal application of active protein NK75', he described how a newly synthesised protein enabled the vaccine to 'piggyback' water molecules, and a cloud seeding program had begun to show 'encouraging results'. There was a clear conviction that the "nano-vaccine" was efficacious. The protein compatibility, synthesis, effective transportation by water molecules, transdermal application. *Sus scrofa domesticus*. Burns was sure it was Latin for domestic pig, but he double-checked. He met a woman who was studying agricultural medicine when he was stationed in Germany in 1991. Burns chatted her up at an Oktoberfest party near the NATO base in Rammstein. He managed to ask her for her number, and she invited him to help her study for a biology exam. He thought it was a good line and was momentarily disappointed when he realised she meant it literally. He confessed on the second date, and she capitulated. He found a Latin dictionary in a second-hand bookstore and they played Q&A after breakfast. She passed the test, and so did he. The warm, glowing memory bubble of his time with Malin was suddenly deflated, slashed open by the look on her face when he told her it was their last night together. He shipped out to Kosovo the next morning and never saw her again.

Veda's three-year study had been published in Science Magazine almost two years ago. In the conclusion, Veda wrote that this new vaccine had proved 100% effective in *Sus scrofa domesticus*.

Nice, thought Burns. Someday all English pigs will be immune to typhoid. A memory jolted him away. He recalled the image of a headline with the clever rhyme about a Porcine Vaccine Queen.

Burns turned his search to periodicals and pulled up the recent news articles about the Biomedicine Faculty at Oxford. He used the keywords 'Dr Nicholas Veda' to search the archives of Oxford University, as well as the local daily papers.

He spotted a few articles, including one about a minor riot at Oxford in February and the subsequent disappearance of Veda's 'Porcine Vaccine Queen'. Several hundred students and residents in the village were involved in what was reported as 'a bizarre melee of violence and sex' that lasted much of the weekend.

The student paper's special edition had a more carnal lede. It began, "F#cking and Fighting", and likened the event to a Bacchanalian party, with conspiracy theories.

Apparently, the pig disappeared while several hundred students and local residents had engaged in a wild night of violence and public sex in the village after a rugby match. The article stirred up a social media storm with claims the pig had been liberated by an unnamed group of would-be activists who rescued the pig from its confines in the laboratory wing of the biosciences department, and had supposedly released it somewhere else on campus. The unnamed activist, despite being unnamed, gained a following in re-tweets expressing everything from curiosity to xenophobia in a matter of hours. However, according to police reports Mary was never found, or returned to the university, and no group took credit for the act. No charges were pending at the moment.

There were no details of Mary's purpose in Dr Veda's research, and there was no mention of danger to the public health, but Burns had read enough to guess she was more than a mascot.

Burns caught a yawn, then gave in and completed it by exhaling loudly. He sounded like an old door closing on its own. Another yawn, not out of disinterest, overtook him. Fatigue had finally set in his limbs and he seemed to double in weight as he exhaled. He allowed himself a long luxurious stretch and his deep breaths flooded his blood with oxygen and restored his muscles. But his brain was lagging. A swallow of warm water from the plastic bottle he had been clutching helped clear the cobwebs. He knew what he knew and what he did not. Burns couldn't decide which worried him more.

In his mind, he tried to picture Mary. *Queen Mary, or Typhoid Mary?* Burns wondered if it mattered where the pig was, and if there was any connection to the missing scientist.

Burns couldn't worry anymore. Not until he had answers or at least learned if any of his connections could be confirmed. He would have to wait until eight o'clock.

"Sleep now, or forever lose your peace," Burns said aloud.

He walked over to the sofa against the opposite wall and stood there, staring blankly at the monitor until it went into sleep mode.

"Easy for you," Burns chided the display.

He felt himself squinting as he set the alarm on his phone, then he yawned again suddenly, and his face muscles relaxed as he exhaled. His limbs felt loose, like a valve had just been opened. Sleep would come.

Burns flopped on the sofa then leaned over on his side to face the desk. He aimed his phone at the receiver on the shelf above his laptop, commanding it to open his iTunes to play some night music. He looked out the window and grimaced at the glow on the horizon. Burns bet himself he would be asleep before the sun broke the black horizon of brick houses across the road. "And awake in two hours and twenty minutes," he grumbled. He pulled his t-shirt off again, folded it lengthwise and draped it over his eyes. Then let his hands fall to his chest as he summoned sleep in supine submission. He had selected the Moondance album by Van Morrison to carry him off to sleep, but while the opening track was playing all he heard was Frank Zappa and The Mothers singing "It Can't Happen Here," over and over, as he tried to push the thoughts of a global pandemic out of his brain. At last, Van Morrison won out, Burns lay back in the "Caravan" and promptly slept.

05:00

Nicholas Veda woke to the sound of two men talking, but he couldn't understand anything they were saying. They were either far away or speaking in quiet tones, he couldn't tell. A thin echo seemed to circle the space around his head, he couldn't tell where the voices were coming from. He strained his ears to listen, but his mother's voice was drowning out the conversation. Over and over Veda heard her say, "It's not your fault." He didn't believe her. He had a hood over his head. The voices weren't speaking English, but one man seemed angry, the other apologetic. The conversation ended suddenly, and he was stranded in the cold, dark, echoing silence.

Veda flexed weakly against the bonds. He could feel something against the skin on his left forearm as he tried to twist his limbs free. He visualised an IV stuck into his arm. Was that a memory? Panic squeezed his chest and confusion roared in his head. He couldn't understand why he could feel everything touching his skin: the tape the IV, the straps, the heavy bag over his head — and yet his muscles would not respond to his brain's commands.

"Where am I?" Veda croaked. "What do you want?"

Veda was alone. He felt a cold pool of water trapped under his scrotum and he knew the iceberg was melting beneath him and soon he would drown, and he didn't care if it was 'global warming' or 'climate change' because he would freeze to death before he drowned, and his mum and his sister were already dead. The arctic silence suddenly crackled with the sound of voices. An angry voice was loud enough for him to hear.

"Dvadtsat' minut... Eto bylo by proshche, yesli by vy prosto vypolnili raspisaniye. Dvadtsat' minut ne vosem'desyat minut." *This would be easier if you just follow the schedule. Twenty minutes is not eighty minutes.*

When it switched to English, he understood the sounds but was confused by what he heard.

"You're not playing on your time, Gerhard. You're playing on my time, and that upsets me, I can't tell you..."

Gerhard remained silent.

"You've upset the rhythm, if not the entire programme."

"Letting his mind and body fall asleep and waking it again is part of the— *obrabotat*, here... not what you saw in the Stasi."

"I can give him another dose, General."

"No, you can't dose him yet. I want to talk to him. After."

There was a long pause. Veda heard nothing. Nothing except his heart. Now he could feel it, too.

But he wasn't breathing. He startled himself when a gasp exploded in his throat. It sounded like a frightened child. He was sure he had awakened when the air escaped his lungs and he drew another breath. And he heard it, the soft wind in his ears, the soft tone rising and falling with each breath, his chest marking the rhythm in time.

Suddenly, one of the voices was talking again, the angry voice. He was either arguing very quietly with himself nearby or loudly criticising someone far away. Or maybe the voice was speaking to Veda. Criticising me, he thought.

"Do it."

Veda understood. Sometime between the hood being cinched tighter round his neck and the first ice-cold blast of the raging river engulfing his head and body, for a split second, Veda felt his fear evaporate. This is it, he thought. Veda felt what he imagined must be relief. Peace? But before he could picture an afterlife, his body's survival instincts kicked in, and he inhaled deeply and clamped his mouth shut as the first small stream of water hit him squarely in the face. Then the dam burst. Veda resisted the urge to gulp for air when the freezing torrent came crashing down, roared over his head and pounded on his chest, freezing his lungs. Stopping his heart with a thud that shot electricity to his extremities. He held his breath against the cold shock. He wanted desperately to exhale but the fear of drowning as he drew his next breath paralysed him. He knew he'd black out soon.

If I could see. He was blind. Could he black out? He wanted to shout but he held his breath.

Before he could escape into unconsciousness his reflexes once again betrayed him. He had to breathe. He had barely parted his lips before they were peeled away by the force of the water, as if he was flying a rocket ship without a windscreen. The water forced the heavy hood into his mouth. As his tongue retreated, he gagged. The river poured into his body, filling his lungs and stomach to overflowing. It pried his clenched jaw open and he couldn't hold off the waterfall as it flowed into his throat. He was powerless to control the cycle of coughing and vomiting. His body convulsed in spasms as the two sensations became one spastic reflux.

He wanted to scream but he couldn't. *I should be dead*, he thought.

Then the water stopped. The two voices spoke again — more like one spoke and the other grunted... Veda thought it might be German until the Grunter grunted "Da."

A moment later the hood was loosened and pulled roughly off. Veda's first few reflexive efforts to draw breath were hampered by his body's attempts to expel the remaining water. His first few breaths sounded like an old violin being dragged across a bare wooden floor. But soon enough the gulps of air cooled and soothed his burning lungs and his breathing slowed and stabilised. The fire raging in his limbs and head was smothered by the cold chill that washed over his damp skin when Veda remembered where he was. *Or do I?* He panicked.

Veda pulled against the bonds. Panic squeezed his chest and confusion roared in his head. Blind.

"Where am I?" He croaked. "What do you want?"

No one answered. Veda was cold and clammy, his fingers like prunes. He knew his eyes were open, but everything was still shrouded in blackness. Veda blinked. Tiny dots began to form a grey and black matrix, as if he was wearing a fencing mask. Light began to filter through the spots in Veda's matrix. His chin was on his chest and he had some difficulty lifting his head. He succeeded finally by imagining he could see the face of the man who had just stepped in front of him. He drew his eyes up to meet his torturer. Veda pretended to be brave as he fixed his gaze on the imaginary face.

"There he is." The voice was sing-song-y, the accent foreign. And it came from slightly to the left of where Veda had guessed. He turned to face the voice, his courage fading under the effort.

"That's it. You relax, professor. No problems here." The voice that had been apologetic earlier was now jovial, even friendly.

"No problems here," Veda smiled. He wanted to raise his hands in surrender, and imagined he could see them pulling at the bands around his wrists. The smile died with a soft "Oh." Veda realised he didn't have the strength to break the bond between his damp skin and the cold metal chair.

"Try not to move too much." Another voice farther to his left chuckled. It was warm and resonant, and spoke in an almost flawless English accent that smiled at Veda.

"It will take some time for your body to recover." The wise, older voice went on methodically. "The sedative we gave you also had paralytic properties. Dead weight is so much easier to transport, you see. But the hangover will be gone in no—"

"Who are you and what do you want?" Veda pleaded. Veda's mind was roiling, as if his head was still underwater and his thoughts were the water rushing around. His eyes were beginning to see shapes in the grey. A grid formed and became the tiles on the wall of the Marina swimming pool in Chennai. He was underwater but close to the safety of the edge of the pool. The voice pulled him out of the water, speaking English again. "Apologies for the rude awakening, Dr Veda," the voice began. It had mellowed, and moved closer. It had shape. The grey form became a man, holding himself underwater as he lowered to Veda's eye level, smiling. Veda had imagined the man looked like Max von Sydow, to match the deep, gravelly voice. The angry voice was now calmly consoling him. Veda thought he saw flashes of light pass between them like the headlight of a scooter cutting through the middle of a conversation on a street corner.

"Your eyes will take some time to adjust," said the voice. The pool wall behind the man suddenly seemed a glaring white that hurt Veda's eyes. He winced. Tears squeezed out of his eyes. He blinked. The man had a face. It didn't appear to be as kind as it had sounded, more like Christopher Lee's Count Dooku, but at least wasn't hostile.

"What planet is this?" asked Veda. *That sounded stupid*, he thought.

"Delirium," the voice gently chuckled. "It will pass." Veda believed it.

Nicholas Veda knew where he was, or where he had been... it was a hospital.

"One of the more fortunate side effects of this little cocktail is the temporary blindness, really. Fortunate for you..." the Doctor trailed off, leaving Veda to wonder how he was fortunate. *Compared to whom*, he wondered.

"It's a lot like alcohol poisoning, Doctor Veda, but it will abate." The thick, warm voice was soothing, like the senior doctor in the emergency room at the Lister. The view of the Thames was from the eleventh floor of the Lister Hospital. That was a real memory!

"Can you see, Professor Veda?" The man was standing, the voice colder, impatient. Veda realised his eyes had been squeezed tightly closed until he heard the question. He blinked until he could focus on the space between the two men.

"Yes," said Veda quickly. Too quickly. It felt like a lie. "A little," he confessed. Veda looked down. The men were coming into focus. Something told him he didn't want to be able to recognise his captors. He didn't know if it mattered if he saw them or not, if he lived or died.

A hand took Veda by the jaw and turned his head to face the other man. The Grunter's face came into focus and it was clear to Veda that it must be the face of cruelty. Jet-black eyebrows rested on the edge of a thin ridge and the eyes seemed to be in deep sockets. The hollowed cheeks and bony jaw enhanced the demon's skeletal appearance. Veda shuddered to wonder if the dark eyes were still out of focus, or if there was nothing to see but darkness. He tried to crane his head away from the sinister grin that parted the demon skull's face, back to the calming voice, but the hand held his jaw firmly and Veda's muscles were weak. He closed his eyes, wishing he were somewhere else, despondent because he couldn't think of where.

"Humans have a great capacity to remember experiences and especially the faces." The Doctor-In-Charge continued in measured tones, like he was explaining to Nicholas' father what had happened to Ravi.

"Most people who have been punched hard in the nose can accurately recall the face of the person who struck them for years, regardless of how well they may have known them. They cannot forget the look on the person's face," the voice smiled. "This is Herr Gerhard Noack, and he probably is as angry as he looks. Not with you, Doctor Veda, but with himself. Isn't that right, Mister Noack?"

Noack remained silent, and out of focus.

A light flashed first in Veda's left eye then the right and the voice chimed, "Pupil response getting better." The Doctor laughed. "So, you can see. You see?" He laughed again as he released Veda's head.

"But you don't look at me, eh?" Gerhard Noack grunted.

"Sit tight for now, Professor Veda," The Doctor calmly rose as he spoke. "All will be revealed in due course." A prideful smile opened on the Doctor's grey granite face. "The cocktail we prepared for you is a milder dose of a psychoactive agent I've used in... different applications." The smile lingered for a moment, until the Doctor checked his watch. He said something sharply in Russian or German to Noack, who nodded.

"But we'll have the chance to talk chemistry and biology later," he promised.

"Now you can dose him," said the Doctor. Noack grabbed Veda's arm and twisted it a bit, checking the IV held fast. Veda watched, paralysed from the neck down, yet somehow still feeling everything.

"Who..." Veda wanted to shout but the noise he made felt more like a sob.

Noack inserted a needle into the shunt and in a flash, Veda felt the chill of the fluid coursing out of the needle and into his vein.

Veda's heart raced to his throat. He couldn't breathe. He strained to lift his head and focus his eyes on the Doctor.

"Are you a doctor?" Veda felt like it was a prayer.

Noack grunted a short laugh. Veda's pulse pounded its way to his temples.

"I was." It was the Doctor again. "In the military. An MD, in fact." The voice was soothing. Veda's heartbeat dropped back into his chest, and became the slow thud of a marching drum echoing down a long empty hall.

"I worked more with human subjects than you've had the chance to do, Dr Veda," said the Doctor, but his smooth voice was garbled. Veda wondered if he had imagined it when he heard the Doctor say, "So far."

"You have to forget about human trials!" Veda recoiled from the sound of his own voice. The room's tight echo stretched into a single sustained tone. It sounded like night in the garden of the first house he remembered from his childhood. Summer nights in Pondicherry... safe in his bed, a chorus of insects creating white noise outside his window.

Veda drew a quick, deep breath that almost became a yawn. He sighed, loud enough for his sleeping mother to hear. She opened her eyes and smiled. He felt groggy, and happy. He could sleep in peace.

PART TWO:
SATURDAY MORNING

07 :10

Burns felt surprisingly fit, after the long day and short night, and was grateful that his body would still respond to only a couple of sleep cycles and a bit of stretching. He had timed his alarm to allow for either a full breakfast and drive or a smoothie and a run to New Scotland Yard. The grey morning light that seeped through the clouds was holding the rain at bay, perhaps with even a chance of sunlight later. He opted for a smoothie in the shower, and a bottle of water for the road. His course took him through London's best greenery and scenery, with breaks at perfect intervals to break up the pace from walking to jogging to sprints. He warmed up walking past Knotting Hill and sprinted along the Serpentine in Hyde Park. He strolled through Piccadilly and past the Palace, then alternated sprints and trots through St. James Park. He slowed as he turned the corner past the Banqueting House, and watched the ferries and boats passing slowly on the Thames, whistling softly as he strode along Victoria Embankment at Westminster Pier. Burns found himself in a surprisingly optimistic mood. It started before the slight detour he made to pick up some doughnuts for Tully and the rest of the Team. His new Team. He planned to explain it as a Canadian tradition for the new guy to bring doughnuts. Besides, everybody loves doughnuts. It had been a while since he had been the new guy anywhere, and to make matters even less comfortable he still had no idea what exactly his function on this team would be.

The terrifying possibilities he considered last night had not gone away since he slept, and were no less terrifying in daylight. Yet Burns had a morning nod and a smile for every uniform he passed as he cruised up the stairs to Tully's office.

Burns was counting on Tully to have worked through the night to find some of the answers Burns was missing. He was one guy Burns had no trouble trusting. He had accepted him as a friend first, and Burns had few of those in London or at the Met. The other men in MCU2 were still unknowns as far as Burns was concerned, but he knew after their first pint together that Tully was the kind of man that was good at whatever he chose to do well. Burns could only hope that Tully had HOLMES working overtime on finding a pattern or a trace, some trail to follow.

Burns stopped at Tully's door and took a moment to appreciate the irony of the emotional table tennis match he was playing against himself. On the team, off the team. Detective Sergeant, Training Specialist. On call or on the case. Burns told himself he didn't even know if he wanted to be a part of Wayne's team, or if he thought he could solve the case himself. Sure, he did... part of him wanted to, but he had no idea of the size and scope of whatever the case was.

Worst case scenarios were always the first possibilities Burns considered. But he wasn't sure if he could imagine a worst-case scenario yet, concerning the disappearance of Dr Veda.

He knocked politely and opened the door, proffering the doughnuts before he set them next to Tully's coffee machine. Tully had just pulled up a new panel on the centre screen and immediately drew Burns' attention to it.

It was the front page of a daily tabloid. The headline read:

SOMETHING IN THE WATER?

"Did you hear this one?" Tully couldn't wait for a reply. "They went nuts all over Southwark last night." Tully grinned. "That's why... I mean, Met forces were on high alert. I heard they almost called in the army. Seems it started at a rugby match and spread."

"Rugby. A thug's game," said Burns.

"Played by gentlemen. Exactly!" Tully laughed heartily and continued. "But, W-T-fucking-F? Eh? Outdoor public sex okay, maybe that happens all the time but look at the hospital admissions. Three Fatalities." Tully stopped as Burns stepped to the desk and commandeered the touch pad to scroll to the story as it continued on page four.

"Do you mind?" said Tully. He gave Burns a look as he swung his legs round under the table and elbowed Burns away from his desk, reasserting his dominion. "Our dispatch reports back it up." Tully opened a few tiles on the left-hand screen including a spreadsheet with a breakdown of all the dispatch calls.

"Public sex. Public nudity," Tully marvelled.

"Nude public sex," offered Burns.

"Yeah, public beatings, too," said Tully. "Calls to the same locations on several occasions, multiple assaults, mobs... but no actual looting, so we're not calling it a riot." Tully's expression darkened. "Most group violence was toward peace officers."

"Uniforms," said Burns with a nod. "Any mob's common enemy." He looked at Tully. "Actual looting?" he asked.

"One shop owner may have done a little self-damage to his premises looking for a claim with his adjuster. Not much worth stealing in that part of town. Many reports of minors running amok in all this too." Tully shook his head. Burns guessed Tully had looked through all the reports out of morbid curiosity. He could scan pages of computer script faster than Burns could read The Sun.

"At any rate, the frenzy seems to have died down a few hours ago." Tully inhaled loudly and deeply to break the silence, then shook his head and sighed, "A lot of fuckin' and fightin'."

"Remind you of the good old days, does it?" Burns laughed before he checked Tully for a reaction. He was relieved when he saw he hadn't caused offence with his offhand punch line. Either way, Burns' mind had raced to the connection before Tully had unknowingly made it out loud. He needed a few seconds to decide how much to say about Oxford.

"That should have been the headline," said Burns as he leaned in to click the link to the full story on page four.

"You jumped past the Girl, you... commy bastard!" Tully pouted. Then he turned his chair, sweeping at Burns' legs again. "Do you mind?" He spared Burns a look as he craned in on his touch pad. He dropped a few tiles on the left-hand screen and pulled up a spreadsheet of the dispatch calls between 18:00 Friday and 06:00 Saturday.

Directing Burns attention with an exaggerated nod, Tully insisted, "Check it out."

Burns glanced at the spreadsheet, then angled himself around to face Tully. "Yeah," said Burns. "Numbers. I get it. But hang on a sec." Burns leaned over in an exaggerated effort, as if Tully was blocking his view in the cinema, and focused on the article.

The story continued below a smaller photo of a different confrontation between police and a crowd of naked and semi-clad revellers in Burgess Park. Burns laughed out loud. The visible faces were blurred, but the editors had applied less modesty when it came to the nude bodies. Two topless women served to capture Tully's attention and slow his patience. Burns scanned the reports and filed the short paragraphs and numbers and quotes in his memory, then reread the story a little slower.

It began in the early evening, shortly after a rugby match came to, as the writer had reported 'its wet climax in the rain' and continued into the night and early morning.

"Apparently, there's reports of everything from orgies to gang fights, sometimes both simultaneously," said Tully.

Burns scanned the information, storing it as images in his memory. Four dead in three different locations, of various violent causes. One hundred-thirty injured. One adult female was shot but not killed by a rubber bullet from the riot squad.

"None of them seemed really out of it or anything," Burns read the unnamed source's quote aloud. "Just another Friday night in the ER".

"Weird, eh?" said Tully, scratching his left shoulder absently. "Like they all drank the same cocktail."

"At the same bar. Right," said Burns. He was staring at the screen. So was Tully. Tully suddenly slapped Burns' arm.

"Do you think it really was something in the water?" Tully's question was sincere.

"Something in the air..." Burns let it hang but Tully wasn't seeing it. Burns swallowed, unsure of how much to say.

"Full moon maybe." Burns inhaled unconsciously and shuddered as he exhaled. He gestured toward the screen and waited for Tully to acknowledge. "May I?"

"No doubt," Tully replied. He rolled back from the desk and pretended to ponder the headline on the centre screen.

Burns looked at the map on the right-hand screen and loaded the addresses from the dispatch logs. He noted the locations of the two points at the widest distance from each other. To the northwest was

Geraldine Harmsworth Sports Facility, where the children brawled in the rain. Below that was Burgess Park, where the rugby match was held. Dozens of small dots denoting the other disturbances and arrests all fell at random locations between the two end points. If he drew a line around them all, it would form an elongated, inverted teardrop on the map, over an area of a couple of square miles, with the rugby grounds at the narrow point in the south and the playground near the rim of the bell. The tell-tale teardrop was stretching from southeast to northwest. Burns saw the dispersal pattern.

Whether it was by intuition or instinct, a question was forming in his head. It welled up and sparked the familiar, unsettling mix of dread and righteous fury he felt whenever he had recognised and acknowledged the hostile capabilities of his opponents in armed combat. Burns used his phone to check a map on a meteorology website to confirm his suspicion. He knew the prevailing winds of London to be south-westerly, however the wind the day before had been from the southeast, and not particularly strong. The mild spring temperatures had brought people out, despite the scattered showers throughout the area.

"Tell me you didn't just open a browser," Tully was nonplussed. His voice raised as he went on," On your phone. In here. You fuck."

Burns had forgotten the order to stay off the internet and cellular network at the Met. "Shit, I forgot." He looked sheepishly at Tully. "Guess I'll be getting a text about that, huh."

Tully's face was impassive. "Guess we both will," he grumbled.

"Sorry, Tully." He supposed it was true. Somebody down in Surveillance Command could see Burns phone and its location in the building — if they were looking. Burns hoped not. He closed the browser and pocketed the phone.

"Sorry, my friend."

Tully left Burns hanging guilty for a few long seconds before his round cheeks split into a grin. "I'm just fookin' wit ya, mate," he laughed. "The ban's lifted. Two hours ago. You couldn't get a signal if we were still in blackout." Tully laughed again, relishing the stunned look on Burns' face. Then he frowned. "Rookie. Now if you don't mind perhaps you could back the fuck off my computer and let me do my job." The grimaced faded into low smirk.

"Tully, my friend. Any chance you could pull up any reports of explosions yesterday around here?" Burns drew an invisible circle around the southern end of Burgess Park. "Maybe a little earlier than eighteen hundred?" he asked.

Tully gave him a curious look and began to scan the database.

"As a matter of fact, yeah," he said after a short search. "Here."

The two men read a report filed at 17:40 at Camberwell Police Station in Walworth. A veteran of the Falklands War had reported hearing what sounded like "a bazooka" in Surrey Linear Canal Park, and claimed he had seen two "suspicious characters" hurrying to a minivan and driving away shortly after, "like they had just robbed the Lloyd's Bank."

Tully said it first. "Chemical attack?"

Burns didn't answer immediately because he knew the 'why'. It was a distraction.

"Five weeks ago, in Oxford," Burns finally answered. He had tried to be subtle, reading Tully's reactions but Tully seemed unaware of the connection. Maybe the two really were chemical attacks, and connected. Burns was strangely calmed by the fact that whatever the toxin was, it had not been designed to be one hundred per cent lethal.

"Huh?" said Tully.

Burns pulled out his phone again. "Was it a rainy day, too, when Mary was kidnapped?" he pondered aloud. He checked to see if Tully was still with him. Tully's reaction told Burns he at least knew who Mary was.

Burns checked the weather records for Oxford for that fateful February night. It had rained off and on, the same scattered showers as felt across London in the past twenty-four hours.

"Mary disappeared on a night just like last night. Scattered showers, light winds, rugby, orgies and riots." Burns beamed at Tully. "If you showed HOLMES this, do you think he'd spot the pattern?" Before Tully could answer he added, "As fast as me?" then he laughed, "Burns one, HOLMES zero!" Burns stopped short of a victory dance, but for the final comic effect he extended his hand looking for a fist bump. Tully turned away.

"Sod you Burns, HOLMES has figured out more shit than you—"

"Easy, tiger," said Burns. "Just a joke, mate." he laughed.

Tully gave an uncertain nod of acceptance. But Burns was too pleased with himself and having too much fun to stop. He smiled and added compassionately, "I get it. Boundaries. You and HOLMES are... you have a special relationship. I get that. Say no more." He gently placed a hand on Tully's arm and added, "Everybody needs somebody, right?"

"Har facking har, Burns," retorted Tully without flinching under Burns' gentle grip. "The only special relationship I got is with Rosy here." He held up his right hand, making a circle with his fingers then closing it in a loose fist.

"Nice," deadpanned Burns, and he let go of Tully's arm and drew back his hand. "I hope you two wash up before you come back to work and play with HOLMES."

The two men shared a laugh that faded slowly as they both scanned the computer screens.

Burns was the first to break the silence. "The hospitals," he said. "I'm curious to know what kind of a hangover some of these folks have today. Could we get any blood analysis results from Guys Hospital and or St. Mary's? They would have at least tested some of the admitted for alcohol, wouldn't they?" Burns looked at Tully, who had seemed to grow uneasy.

"We should be able to get any data without any trouble, if they have something," Tully said. "But I don't know what they would test for unless they were looking for something. Like you say, maybe only alcohol. Hopefully somebody over there is as curious as you."

"Hopefully."

"Maybe there are some overnight guests, like under observation, you know? Or do they just catch and release?"

Tully furrowed his brow and grimaced. "I'll reach out and see what diagnostics they have, but I'm also not sure of their turnaround time for lab work."

"Right," said Burns. "Given it was the middle of the nightshift."

"Right," agreed Tully. Then he gave Burns a hard look.

"This doesn't come up in the briefing, Burns," said Tully.

"What, that bit about you and your hand?" said Burns, smiling coyly.

"No, you twat," Tully snapped as he typed a message on his phone. "Your suspicion about a chemical attack. Maybe it was a distraction."

"I never said that, either." Burns was adamant. "You were the one who said chemical attack, not me." Burns feigned innocence and went on. "I wanted to talk about the girl. And Veda's speech—"

Tully cut him off. "Yeah, well that probably won't come up either." Tully turned quickly and swept at Burns' legs again. Burns sidestepped and held up his cup, exaggerating the danger of him losing a few drops of coffee. Tully fixed a stern gaze on Burns.

"This doesn't come up in the briefing," he repeated.

Burns caught a look of contrition crossing Tully's face. The corners of his grin drooped and fell for a brief moment.

"Look, Charles. The Duke hears it first, then he decides what gets said and when and where, ok?" Tully reasoned. "I've just linked him into this and..." Tully spun round in his chair, turning away and added, "If you want to bring it up with Detective Chief Inspector Wayne before the briefing, you best head him off at the pass. Otherwise..." Tully waited for Burns.

"Shut the fuck up?"

"Sounds appropriate," Tully smiled.

"Fair enough," Burns agreed.

"But about your other question."

"You mean, my 'follow the fox' theory?"

"I mean, HOLMES hasn't found her yet, but I'm thinking we might find the mystery hottie before we're dismissed. Lot of cameras in this city. That face..." Tully trailed off.

"She is uncommonly beautiful," offered Burns, then he added with a nudge, "Planning an introduction between Kaia and Rosy, or have they already met?"

"After you," said Tully, eyeing the door behind Burns.

"What the fuck does that mean?" Burns had to bite, doing his best to look hurt. Tully stared back at him blankly.

"It means 'get the fuck out of my way' to me, but some people mistake it for the courtesy of an Irish gentleman." Tully paused, expressionless, staring at Burns. Then Burns caught the twinkle in his eye. He was leaving Burns room for a comeback. Burns smiled in acknowledgement as he stepped back and turned sideways to further open Tully's passage.

"Know any?" It was the best he could do.

Burns had nothing. Nothing but questions he hadn't figured out how to ask, or who might have the answers.

"I've got a briefing to attend," Tully said as he exhaled. With a self-important flourish he pulled at the sleeves and shoulders of his oversized Metropolitan Police Federation logo sweatshirt, smoothing his appearance before directing his chair to the door.

"Right," said Burns. He stepped in front of Tully as he was about to wheel past, forcing him to brake quickly to avoid crashing face-first into the seat of Burns' trousers, or at least end up with Burns in his lap.

"After me," Burns chuckled. Burns opened the door and held it for Tully, smiling smoothly enough for a tip at the Ritz, but still partially blocking Tully's path to the impending briefing at oh-eight-hundred.

"They should get you an automatic door, really," said Burns, as he reached for the handle. He turned back to Tully, mouth open, as if he suddenly remembered something. "I don't suppose you'll be taking the stairs with me," he said. "Although, it looks like you could go just about anywhere in that thing."

"Yeah," Tully grimaced. "Like up your chute, mate. Move." Burns made himself skinny against the open door. Tully smiled and rolled past Burns, who dodged and laughed. Burns let Tully get ahead, only to slip past him before they reached the end of the hall.

"See you down there." Burns gave Tully a nod and pointed down the stairs. Then he trotted down the first flight and disappeared as he rounded the landing.

"Hopefully not," Tully shouted after him.

08:00

At 7:55 Saturday morning, Charles Burns made sure he was in his seat at the briefing room table. He had put the box of doughnuts on the table next to the coffee and tea station and announced, "I brought some Tim Horton's doughnuts." He faked a shy smile. "It's a Canadian thing. New guy brings doughnuts," Burns shrugged. "They were closed last night, so..." Every man took notice and acknowledged Burns with a smile of gratitude. Tully and IT Guy were at their stations and Riza sat alone at the long table. Aitkens' chair was empty, and his tab on the viewer appeared to be deactivated, its blue borders were muted in comparison to those of the other members. Others were also absent, however their tabs on the screen were illuminated. Burns guessed Aitkens was on duty elsewhere, and not busted for incompetence. Yet.

A small Metropolitan Police Service insignia sat in the windows next to the names of each of the unit's active members, seven in total, minus Burns. He hadn't talked to Wayne—or anyone for that matter—about getting his iPad registered on the local network so he could participate in the briefing. He decided maybe he wasn't supposed to.

Detective Chief Inspector Wayne stepped through the door. His expression showed the same level of controlled tension Burns saw on his way out the door last night. Minus sleep. Wayne marched to his workstation before acknowledging the other men in the room. He turned to Tully and made a helicopter gesture with his left hand.

"Wrap us up, if you please."

Tully activated the room's shroud as the door pulled itself closed. The windows hummed softly as

Tully engaged the noise cancellation system. The windows and the hallway outside disappeared behind the unfolding blinds. They clapped shut almost noiselessly. Tully gave a nod and a surreptitious thumbs up to Burns that seemed to say, "Cool, huh." Burns wondered if he had missed the feature last night, or if Wayne had neglected or forgotten about it. Wayne glanced at Burns momentarily before turning and nodding to Tully.

Burns knew it would take an effort to avoid showing off what he had learned about Veda's work, and the answers he had already formulated to some of the questions he thought everyone should have been trying to answer. The last thing Charles Burns wanted to do was to look like the competitive new recruit. Just then he heard his father say, "Speak when spoken to, son." Always good advice, Pa, he concluded.

"Good morning, gentlemen. Can you all hear me?" Wayne was directing his voice to the large monitor at the far end of the table, addressing the tabs of the men not present. A ripple of affirmative replies passed round the table and ended with the voices of the absent members coming out of the small speakers in the centre of the table. Wayne reminded everyone of the closed-door status with an outstretched hand, purposefully gesturing toward the masked window and locked door.

Burns figured even if Wayne had serious trust issues, they seemed to be well justified by recent events. He wondered if Wayne upgraded the room's security from prying eyes and ears in New Scotland Yard or anybody who might be capable of disrupting the Met's communications server, like last night. He allowed himself a chuckle, wondering which threat Wayne had considered first. Loose lips or no, the Met got hacked, should have scared a lot of people in the building.

Wayne straightened and lowered himself to sit in his chair. He cleared his throat and raised his jaw as if he was speaking to an assembly, or into an overhead microphone. He began by repeating how Veda and Kaia were continuing to be described as persons of interest to Major Crimes.

"This was to invoke a little more due diligence on the part of the patrolling street personnel," said Wayne. "And to keep it otherwise quiet for the time being." Wayne's tone seemed grave.

"The two can't be officially treated as missing persons for a number of reasons, but for now let's say the fact they are both adults and the requisite twenty-four-hour time period hasn't passed." His expression lifted, his eyebrows raised in disbelief. "Well, we're not ruling out the possibility of anything," Wayne continued. "Meaning we haven't much evidence of foul play solid enough to act on, so we can't rule out a… tryst. Hope for the best, plan for the worst, I guess." No one spoke.

"But it seems most likely that Dr Veda has been… abducted," Wayne said finally.

He waited so long to say the word, and Burns knew why. It would be almost impossible to keep a kidnapping quiet for long, inside or outside the Met.

Wayne took a swallow from the cup on his desk and cleared his throat again. "I've seen all your preliminary reports and will now ask you to brief us with what has been highlighted for this briefing." Burns suspected this meant that Wayne had read, censored and returned each man's reports. The Duke seemed to like to control the tempo and the flow of information. Burns hoped it was for the sake of brevity, and not that he had been mistaken about his soon-to-be superior officer.

Wayne continued, "Special Analyst Tully and Inspector Therrien will also share some of the intel we've gathered a little later. The idea here is to put together the pieces we have and find our man, gentlemen. But we're going to keep it short and sweet in here so we can get to work on what we have. Very little room for questions. Clear?" Wayne paused as each of the men nodded in unison, even Burns. Burns felt the last question was directed at him. He acknowledged Wayne's grim warning by squaring himself with a curt nod. He figured Wayne didn't want to discuss chemical attacks or Dr Veda's "vaccine rain" and his stolen pig. Yet. Standing-to was the only thing to do.

Wayne began again. "Detective Sergeant Riza, a summary of where we are with the forensic evidence, please."

"I have very little to summarise." Riza, like many Turks that Burns had known, did nothing to hide his emotions when he spoke. His frustration had stretched his features. His jaw had drawn his mouth open and his thick black eyebrow rippled his forehead and pushed back his receding hairline. "Final analysis of the car samples found only traces of DNA on the seat covers. Enough hair to identify Detective Sergeant Dawson as the driver, as well as Dr Veda and the mystery blonde. They were in the backseat." Riza paused. Burns saw the helpless frustration give way to a swelling anger.

"The door handles were wiped clean," Riza grabbed his thumb as if he was beginning a count. "No complete fingerprints found in the back. The front compartment was wiped completely clean." Riza 's hand fluttered apart like a magician before falling to his sides. "And even less from toxicology analysis," Riza shrugged.

"And we've found no matches in our database, or Interpol, for the blood from the car, is that still true?" Wayne broke in.

"Yes, sir. No sir, no matches with Ministry records either," Riza's angry expression faded momentarily. "Never convicted and never used the NHS," he concluded.

"Thank you, Detective Riza," said Wayne. Then he bent his gaze to the monitor on his desk.

"About Dawson's toxicology results," Riza asserted. He tapped a few keys and pulled up a set of figures representing the lab results onto the centre screen. Burns saw a lot of zeros.

"We were unable to identify the agent used to intoxicate him—any agent—with our analysis downstairs. That is to say no traces from the major toxin groups. No known agents. Blood, swabs...We've done what we can with the contents of his stomach..."

"Oh, fuck." All the eyes in the room zoomed in on the small Tannoy in the centre of the table. It was Blennerhassett.

"Sorry?" asked Riza. He looked at Wayne, pleading confusion.

"Damn, is this thing on?" Blennerhassett blurted. "Sorry, sir, Sorry, Semi." There was a breathless moment of silence before he explained, "I just can't stand the sight of puke." Burns stifled a laugh, not as successfully as did the others in the room.

"Yes, fine Blennerhassett," Wayne exerted his authority, he saw the humour too, though his reaction was held to a quick flutter of his eyebrows. "And on that note, let's turn it over to you, Detective Blennerhassett." Wayne's smile dissolved before his teeth showed. "What have you learned at the airport?"

"Wait a minute, sir," Riza turned to face Chief Inspector Wayne. "I wasn't finished," he said. His posture was almost defiant, but Burns could see Riza's dark eyes were shimmering with uncertainty like the water at the bottom of a well.

"I'd like to suggest we send Dawson's blood and gastric samples to Salisbury for..."

"Duly noted, Detective Sergeant Riza," Wayne's tone was stern as he cut in. "Again."

Riza fell silent under Wayne's stony gaze. He nodded silently and looked round the room. Wayne turned his glare down and typed a few notes on his pad. The room fell still for a few moments and everyone seemed to fix their attention on their personal notepads. Except Burns. He was watching Wayne and Riza. He also didn't have any notes or his iPad, just the photos and links on his phone, which was switched off.

Burns knew Riza wanted to send the samples to Porton Down, the military's biochemical research facility in Salisbury. Burns wondered what Riza wanted to find, or if he was just looking for a second opinion. Why would Wayne put the kybosh on the idea? And what about Mary? Damn questions. Burns took a pull on his water bottle and swallowed hard. Then he tore a piece off his cruller and stuffed it in his mouth, licking the sticky icing from his fingers. He washed it all down with another swig, satisfied that he could still hold his curious tongue.

"Mmm, Timmy's," Burns sighed loudly. "Tim Horton's," he declared. He held the sweet treat aloft on its serviette, making eye contact with the men and gesturing toward the box. He made a humble, genuflecting invitation to the Chief last, which was rebuffed. There was a shuffle of movement as chairs rolled and their occupants shifted away from the table. Tully looked most likely to make a bee-line for the doughnuts but he too caught the surliness smouldering in Wayne's eyes. He checked with Burns, who was trying to guess what kind of doughnut he could get for his friend, to save him the trip.

"It isn't teatime just yet, people," Wayne's voiced rolled like a distant thunder. Burns realised too late what he had done. Nothing to do but apologise. Wayne fixed his steel blue eyes on Burns. Burns capitulated without hesitation.

"Sorry, sir," said Burns. Wayne seemed to acquiesce readily, his dour mood lightened slightly, and he called out to Blennerhassett on the monitor.

"Still there, Detective Blennerhassett?"

"Yessir, Chief," Blennerhassett answered cheerfully. Burns liked Blennerhassett's approach, his demeanour. He'd have to wait and see if he had a skill set, but Burns saw a lot of himself at thirty-two in the Irishman every time he spoke. As far as Burns was concerned, if a fellow had a sense of humour, that automatically made him easier to work with. As long as he had skills to match his wits. Burns knew he had to trust Wayne's judgement. But he had his own criteria, and so far, Aitkens stood out as a weak link—and not just for his lacking a sense of humour.

"And what have you learned at London City Airport?" Wayne spoke loudly, as if it was a long-distance call. "Have you resolved any of the tail number issues?"

"Well sir," Blennerhassett began. "As you know, we confirmed evidence of tampering with LCA's flight control comms, and our surveillance, I guess, right?"

He sounded like he was smiling at the irony. Burns checked Wayne for a reaction but saw only the stoic commander giving his full attention to the small speaker on the table.

"But not Heathrow," Blennerhassett raised his voice and paused for effect. "Their local server kept all their surveillance video. Tully and HOLMES were linked in as soon as Gray confirmed it. So far, no facial recognition for our missing persons of interest, I believe." Wayne turned to Tully who shook his head 'no', confirming Blennerhassett's assumption.

"LCA is our best guess for escape point," Blennerhassett declared. "But the audio from the tower at LCA has tail numbers conflicting with the flight plans, and the digital records of about a dozen planes between the hours of twenty-thirty and twenty- three-ten." Blennerhassett didn't sound disappointed by the silent response. "Anyway, I figured it would save time if I reached out to air traffic controllers across the network and see if their surveillance was recording, to see if we could find any matches in their arrivals. There were approximately forty flights departing LHR and LCA, to thirty different destinations, between the hours of twenty-ten and twenty-two thirty."

"Indeed, Detective Blennerhassett." Wayne raised his voice. His patience was straining but he held his tone even. "And where are we now?"

"Well, sir," Blennerhassett caught his breath in a sigh. "We've accessed the major carriers' databases and cleared most of their flights, except the long hauls, but we've still got questions about two private aircraft to Aberdeen—and so does Aberdeen. And also two more to Tallinn, Estonia and Brussels. We're waiting for them to confirm... anything... one of the Aberdeen charters with mysterious incongruent tail numbers was a patient transfer to the Royal Hospital." Blennerhassett seemed re-energised as he went on with the story. "The Ministry has nothing on the patient, but the manifest listed the patient as Sheik Moammar al Hadid, some rich Saudi Prince according to the passport. Makes sense to me, right? Arab sheik, Indian doctor... Close enough. Right?" Again, no response. Blennerhassett went on. "He and a medical team of four British subjects took off at 22:10, which we believe is in line with the travel time for the possible escape and subsequent departure of our persons of interest," Blennerhassett paused, then added," to points north, I suppose." It sounded like he wasn't convinced that Veda was a victim. "The hospital is resisting the release of info…"

"Yes, and Detective Sergeant Gray is due to touch down in Aberdeen in a few minutes and he'll report in then," Wayne punctuated the narrative gruffly, then seemed to relax after a glance at his watch. "Thank you, Detective Blennerhassett," Wayne addressed the Tannoy. "I expect you'll be calling in when you have confirmation on the other flights."

"Will do," Blennerhassett affirmed.

"Right," said Wayne. "Stay on the land line for the moment, Blennerhassett."

"Yessir."

Burns knew Detective Sergeant Martin 'Marty' Blennerhassett was following his hunch. Burns guessed he was hoping to spot Veda, and maybe the Fox, on CCTV in a queue at a passport control gate in some exotic locale. Detective Sean Gray jetted off to Aberdeen, after all.

Of course, Tallinn wouldn't be out of the question, thought Burns. Especially if Ms Rebane was Estonian. And it made sense to Burns, too. He had been convinced since he first saw the photo from the opera that Nicholas Veda was a victim of foul play. His research into Veda's life and work had only reconstituted his gut reaction. After hearing Blennerhassett's report, Burns had to consider the possibility of Veda somehow being a participant, willing or otherwise, if only for a moment. Suddenly, he was struck by a thought so hard it fell out of his mouth.

"Where did the stolen lab equipment go?" Burns asked anyone. No one answered.

"What about freight. You know, cargo planes, couriers and the like?" he asked.

"Blennerhassett has been focused on commercial and private passengers, so he can't answer that," Wayne grumbled. "But I can." He rose from his seat and turned to face Burns, squeezing the anger out through his curled fingers in fists and fans. "One UPS plane departed from London City at twenty-three-sixteen and its contents were verified. Nothing big enough to be our missing items."

"Yes sir!" Blennerhassett piped in. "According to the manifest, the transplant patient took some equipment listed as 'life support' with him—about three hundred kilos worth. Airside personnel we interviewed confirmed the plane was carrying passengers and cargo in the form of crates and boxes."

Wayne's anger had simmered and cooled by the time Burns sent him a look of contrition. Wayne accepted it with blithe indifference—good enough for Burns.

"Very good, Blennerhassett," said Wayne. "And I believe you can use your mobile phone next time you call in, isn't that so, Inspector Tellier?" Wayne returned Tellier's nod and went on. "So don't hesitate, will you."

"Roger that, sir. Will do," answered Blennerhassett.

"Now, Inspector Tellier," Wayne had to fight off a yawn as he took his seat again.

"It appears to be a very simple, very elegant DoS, a Denial of Service," Inspector Guy Tellier began. "According to our forensic analysis, only the Met's main communication network was affected. No disturbance in the database, no other localised security breaches detected. Only the comms, all digital video signals were...disappeared." Tellier couldn't hide his awe.

Wayne cut Inspector Tellier's reverie short. "However, the system has been restored and you have your people and Tully has HOLMES looking at every available surveillance camera, which is again every camera in the Boroughs, yes?"

"*Oui,*" answered Tellier. "We are looking for the proverbial WFT and physical matches for your persons of interest and Tully is using facial recognition. But we're talking about thousands of hours of recordings, and real time monitoring."

"Sorry, Inspector," said Wayne. "But, erm, WFT? WTF is a WFT?"

"Are you kidding me?" Tellier laughed in disbelief. "White Ford Transit, Chief. You gotta get out of your office more, get down to the street."

"I know, Guy," Wayne answered with a one-sided smile. "If only to feel the pavement, I know."

"Right on," affirmed Tellier. Then he added with a sly innocence, "What the fuck is a WTF?"

Wayne didn't bite at the set up but Burns caught the Chief biting at the corners of his mouth. He succeeded in folding the grin on itself and cleared his throat.

"Well, I understand your people are all caught up, so to speak, with the video since twenty-two-ten last night and will continue monitoring real time feeds," Wayne concluded.

"Right on again," said Tellier. "If they're in London, we shall see."

Burns wasn't sure if it was a language gap or not, but Tellier's words piqued him.

All the cameras in London could only spot faces in public places. But Wayne hadn't said anything about the possibility of Dr Veda being held somewhere in the greater London area. Burns figured Wayne was convinced that Veda had been whisked away, too. The map of the camera blackout had been the trigger. The sophisticated technology and one-finger salute aside, the fact that it was covering two of London's airports was enough for Burns to factor it into every worst-case scenario he could spin. Wayne saw it too, Burns decided.

"I'm going to need you to expand the video surveillance monitoring beyond our fair city, Inspector Tellier," Wayne ordered. "Tully and HOLMES have already gone international. Your authority extends to every roadway in the Kingdom. Reach out to the Ministry and get access. Try to think how far you might get in a WFT on a full tank, and start your circles there."

"We can do it," answered Tellier. He quickly tapped out a message on his phone. A moment later a reply came with a chirp. Tellier looked up at Wayne and read the message on his phone. "We have done it, sir." Another message followed. Tellier looked at Wayne again before he read it quickly.

"The feeds from Transport appear unaffected by the DoS. Suspicious vehicles have been flagged and tracked. We've collated and copied images for facial recognition. Tully's already got the links," said Tellier. He raised his eyes, and his shoulders came up in a shrug as he met Wayne's unemotional gaze. "Nothing so far, John, but it will take a few hours to—"

"All right, then." Wayne raised his baritone voice just enough to signal the conclusion. "Thank you, Inspector Tellier. Anything develops, you'll keep me informed," Wayne nodded. "Tully," he turned halfway round to face Tully. "Anything to show us?" Wayne turned his focus to the monitor screens.

"Well, sir," Tully said as he straightened in his chair and forced a smile. "No, sir. LFR is running everywhere now, as IT Guy mentioned," Tully paused. He smiled to bolster his optimism. "It will take some time." Tully turned to stare resentfully at the blank screens at the far end of the room. "We compiled a list of possible orgs or groups that could conceivably have an interest in Dr Veda. We had a hard time coming up with a top ten list," Tully said. He turned to face Wayne. "But to be frank sir, I can't imagine any of them having the capability to do..." Tully trailed off and looked down to his own screen.

"Fair enough, Tully," Wayne eased. "Well, cross them out, but don't delete anyone until we..."

"Of course, sir. We—I, I'm still making connections," Tully stammered. He stole a look at Burns before he concluded, "Nothing concrete, yet."

Burns took the hint and held his tongue. He knew Wayne wouldn't let the briefing go sideways, and fair enough. Burns knew 'Making connections' could easily turn into a spinning cloud of conspiracy theories, especially in a small group of curious minds.

Burns had to remind himself that the operation was a missing persons recovery. It seemed rational to conclude at this point that they were more likely to find Veda by looking for him, rather than waiting for a call that was likely to never come. He understood Wayne's focus on actionable intel. But if Veda had been snatched, he was snatched by someone, and they took him somewhere. Even if Veda was in on it, he was in with a group of professionals. Burns thought about it for a moment. The hack might be traceable to a known hacker, or even some amateur. But an armed and organised team had executed the theft at the lab. They left casualties behind and not much else. They were no doubt experienced. The way Burns saw it, maybe the only way to find out where Veda is would be to figure out who had him and find them. He hoped Wayne and Tully had a list.

Still, nobody was talking about the dark why. Burns promised himself he wouldn't be the first to do so.

Wayne suddenly clapped his hands, briefly fracturing the silence and drawing everyone's attention. The smallest of echoes bounced off his workstation and vanished in the low, humming stillness.

"Yes, well, Detective Sergeant Windeler is across the river working the list with an associate at JTAC now, so I'm sure between the two of you you'll have some answers soon." Wayne's words conveyed confidence, but Burns thought the tone was slightly condescending. Maybe it was his way of motivating Tully, trying to stir up a primitive competitive response.

Tully smirked as if he knew what Wayne was on about. Wayne wanted Tully to find Dr Veda before anyone else. Burns hadn't met Windeler but had seen the tab on the viewer labelled "B. Windeler". The man pictured was around Burns' age, maybe not quite forty yet, and premature baldness had convinced him to shave his head completely. Burns could see the five o'clock shadow circling Windeler's shiny pate. The glare of the camera's flash had left a small white flare just above Windeler's forehead. The hot spot didn't wash out the mischievous gleam or the easy smile. Burns presumed he was online but hadn't spoken, waiting his turn. A closer look at the tab confirmed Windeler's location to be Thames House, but the phone link icon below the photo was dark. Burns wondered if MI5 had been hacked too, and was maintaining radio silence, and Windeler couldn't get a line out. Still, Burns couldn't help but be impressed that Wayne had an ally at the Joint Terrorist Analyst Centre.

Burns was suddenly struck by the disturbing notion that the entire operation might be taken over by MI5 when Wayne and his MCU2 were just getting started. This looked to be a baptism by fire for Detective Chief Inspector Wayne, the first test for his Major Crimes Unit 2 and of the authority granted to him by the Home Secretary.

Wayne's features were being pulled at by the weariness that dragged his arms to his sides as he raised himself out of his chair, his flesh slow to catch up with his lanky frame as he brought himself upright. He straightened his arms and arched his back a little, extending his arms and tapping his fingers on the desk. Burns wondered if the old body might need a few minutes of shuteye after the briefing wrapped up. Wayne let his hands fall to his touch pad. After a few taps he looked up at the trio of screens at the far end of the room. He drew a long breath that seemed to re-energise him.

"Detective Sergeant Kaake, can you hear me?" Wayne spoke to the highlighted tab on the viewer. DS Kaake was at the car park in Parker Street and connected to the mobile network.

"Yes, sir. Loud and clear," answered Kaake. The voice coming from the Tannoy on the centre of the table matched the image on the monitor. The face was large and square, like a comic book hero from the fifties. Burns hadn't seen Kaake before, but his curiosity carried no suspicion, no instinctive distrust of an unknown. Burns judged Kaake's friendly, and fearless demeanour to be genuine. The confidence didn't come from a gym. Though the big man could have spent some time pumping iron, he looked like he was born big. *Big-boned*, as his Mum would say. Burns figured Kaake's heroic jaw line was his most chiselled feature. The uniformed shoulders expanded to somewhere beyond the photo's borders. Burns made a mental note to remember how to pronounce Kaake's name by association. *Beefcake*, Burns smiled.

"Do you read me, sir?" Kaake boomed, the bass tones causing the speaker to crackle a bit. "I'm on my mobile. I had to step out of the entry."

"I read you just fine, Detective," answered Wayne. "Do you have anything further to report from Drury Lane?"

"Yes sir," Kaake began. "Well, you know about the exits and entries, right sir?"

"Yes, of course," answered Wayne. "I read your last report."

"Right. Fifteen exits between the dark hours and only one entry. Ticket says the vehicle was in and out —"

"Yes," said Wayne. "Between 20:26 and 21:12. I know. I asked if you had anything further."

"The credit card used to pay on exit appears to be untraceable," added Kaake.

"So you wrote, Detective," Wayne snapped.

"Right, sir." The deep voice softened. "Sorry, sir," Kaake apologised quickly and went on. "Well, sir, I just talked to a witness who saw an ambulance try to enter the car park around the time of the blackout. A stagehand from the Royal Theatre around the corner was late for the show because he couldn't get into the car park. The ambulance tried to enter but it was too tall, had to back out onto the street but nobody would let him," Kaake let out a low chuckle. "I caught the stagehand coming out the door, on his way home at about oh-six-thirty."

Wayne and Tellier exchanged a look and Tellier immediately pulled out his phone. "There's your WTF, John," said Tellier.

"Indeed," answered Wayne with half a nod. He turned to the main viewer again. "Kaake, was your witness able to give you a description of the ambulance, by any chance a plate number?" Wayne asked.

"Only that it was white, he thinks with blue stripes and maybe a cross and lettering. Lights on top. No logo."

"All right, Detective," said Wayne. "Surveillance has been updated. See if you can get corroboration. I'll check back with you, if I haven't heard from you first."

"Yes, sir. Will do, sir." Kaake rang off.

"Right," said Wayne, staring at the monitors. Burns checked his watch and wondered if Wayne would call on the two remaining officers. Aitkens and Gray were both still offline, according to their darkened windows.

Wayne flexed his fingers and used the keyboard to type a brief note. He stared at the small screen on his desk for a few moments before tapping the return key with his bent finger. Then he pushed his chair back and stood up straight. He looked each of the men in the eye, silently asking if there was anything more to say. The question went unanswered, and Wayne gazed once more at the monitors across the room. The map and the vacant windows had nothing to tell. The original question was gone when Wayne's eyes finally fell to Burns, replaced by a look that told Burns to trust and be patient.

"Well gentlemen, that's all for now. You have your orders, and we'll maintain regular contact now that the comms ban has been lifted and the um, threat has been..." Wayne glanced over at Tellier. "Has disappeared."

Wayne stepped to his desk to shut down his workstation and gather his notes. He took a few sips of water before turning to Burns.

"You're with me," said Wayne. Then he looked at his watch. "In ten minutes, in my office."

Burns checked his own watch and answered, "Yes, sir. Nine-oh-five." He watched as Detective Chief Inspector Wayne nodded and left the room. Burns held back from saying anything, because everything he thought to say might not be received well.

Nothing came from Windeler at MI5, Klein at the family home or Gray in Aberdeen. Then Burns realised there was no tab for DS Thornley, whom he had met the night before. Surely Thornley must be on duty somewhere and hadn't been benched by Wayne for using the 'F' word in the first briefing.

The diminutive Frenchman was out the door behind Wayne in haste. Burns guessed IT Guy wasn't rushing to catch up with Wayne for a quick word, more likely he was pushing to get back to his team downstairs.

Riza was using his thumb to scroll through something on his phone and Tully's eyes were still scanning the smaller trio of monitors on his table in the corner of the room. Burns could see Tully was working on all three screens and, he guessed, at least three questions concurrently, judging by the way Tully's eyes darted and rolled over and down the screens. Burns bet himself Tully was following updates from LFR on at least one of the screens.

The Met had announced a trial of Live Facial Recognition in two or three boroughs in 2016 but there hadn't been much said about it in the media since. There hadn't been much public resistance to the idea of London's Metropolitan Police watching its citizens either. The police were, after all, using the technology to identify the criminals among them with the expectation of it eventually being a deterrent. The number of traffic and public security cameras deployed by the Met exploded in just a few short years, and soon every privately monitored camera became a part of the Met's vast surveillance network as well. The citizens have been under surveillance for years and used to seeing cameras everywhere. Nobody was quoting Orwell, but Burns couldn't help wondering what the reaction would be if people knew that they were now being actively watched and not just recorded.

For his part, Burns hoped they were using drones. And satellites. Give Big Brother a hug, he mused. It feels nice, even if crime rates haven't improved. Burns sat in his chair and waited to see who would leave last.

Riza left next, with a doughnut and a thank you nod to Burns.

"Good hunting," said Burns. It was all he could come up with. He wasn't optimistic that Riza's forensic work would satisfy any meaningful curiosity. At best, it would cover Dawson's ass for drinking on duty. If he was on duty.

Burns was searching for something to be optimistic about when he turned to the box of doughnuts on the sideboard. He turned his chair, rotating his body under his head, and sprang to his feet, stepping quickly to the brown box that beckoned him. After some deliberation he reached for a chocolate glazed doughnut. He smiled, relishing the first bite. He heard Tully's chair and turned, offering up the box.

"Doughnut?" Burns asked.

"No thanks, mate," Tully answered, obviously preoccupied as he rolled out the door. Burns thought about following him and asking a few questions on the way upstairs but decided against the idea. He didn't want to get either of them in trouble, if there was any trouble to get into. He stood at the coffee station and looked at his watch. Then he took another careful bite of the doughnut and savoured it slowly. He frowned at the kettle.

"Eight minutes," Burns mumbled. "What to do, what to do." He considered another stair run then declined his own offer. He didn't need it. He pulled out his water bottle and rinsed and swallowed. Maybe he could get a refill of Tully's Starbucks. Burns closed the doughnut box carefully and carried it out the door and up the stairs.

Burns gave Tully's door a few gentle taps and slowly opened it. Tully had a number of windows open on all three screens. With a tap on his pad they all vanished and were replaced by Tully's default desktop image, the Sports Illustrated Bikini Calendar.

"Hey there, Tully," Burns called from the door. "That 'my office, ten minutes' thing doesn't mean 'be there in five' because of Wayne's thing for punctuality, does it?"

Tully turned his chair round. "No, ten minutes means ten minutes," he smiled. He waved his arm and tilted his head in the direction of his coffee machine.

"You're good."

Burns grinned and placed the box of doughnuts on the sideboard and rubbed his hands together. "Nice," he said and lurched for his old cup next to the stack of serviettes on the corner of the table. The machine had just finished brewing another pot. Burns smiled when he imagined Tully had used his phone to start the machine. He stopped and faced Tully before pouring. He picked up the box of doughnuts and proffered them to Tully, who declined with a wave and a pat of his round belly.

"Are we good?" Burns had to ask. It was a question for Tully but also statement telling him that Burns wasn't holding any grudges.

"Yeah, we're good," answered Tully with a wink and a shrug. Then his expression changed. "But ten minutes is ten minutes, my friend."

Burns checked his watch. "Right," he said. He poured a cup quickly and filled it with condensed milk, draining the contents of the small carton. "Oh, crap."

Tully laughed. "No worries. I've got more. And thanks for the doughnuts," he said. "But really, piss off!"

"Cheers, mate!" said Burns. He raised his mug and toasted his friend before taking a mouthful. "Mmm, Sumatra," he said before exiting, closing the door behind himself.

09:05

In the twenty-or-so paces down the hall and around the corner to Wayne's office Burns had convinced himself showing up at exactly 9:05 served two purposes: to prove he followed orders, and to hear what the Chief wanted to say.

The black door to Detective Chief Inspector Wayne's office stood out in the wood-panelled corridor. The door was framed on one side by a glass panel of matching size. Inside, Burns could see a brown leather sofa and chair on opposite sides of a small walnut table. A glass pitcher of water and a small upside-down stack of paper cups stood on a ceramic service tray in the centre of the table. Beyond the waiting area, Burns could see part of a glass wall enclosing a small conference room. He looked at his watch and chuckled to himself.

"Thirty-five seconds, plus or minus," he shrugged to the nameplate next to the door. "We didn't synchronise." Burns quietly knocked on the door and turned the handle. It was locked. He waited a few seconds before reaching up and giving the steel plating a firmer, longer rapping. The door buzzed and clicked, Burns turned the handle and pushed it open. He was met by a vacant reception desk, its computer monitor dark and the chair tucked under the curved table. It looked out of place in the dark oakwood panelled room, too modern with its white laminated top and chrome legs. Another door stood on the rear wall of the room about four metres from the entry. Burns figured it was Wayne's private office. He stood still in front of the empty desk for a moment and stared at the closed door, unsure what to do. Wayne was talking to someone on the phone. He could hear Wayne's deep voice, but he was speaking too quietly for Burns to make out what he was saying.

Burns looked over at the empty seats in the waiting area of the office. They looked old and unused, like they might have been left under sheets since before the Met had moved in. The gloomy wood panelled walls were made more so by the total lack of photos or artwork adorning them. The morning light, grey as it was, illuminated the empty conference room beyond a glass wall, the long white table surrounded by its vacant chairs. The grey, shadow-less beam passed through the glass wall to serve as the only source of light in the waiting area. Burns wondered if Wayne hadn't got around to decorating his new office yet, or if it was bare and dim by choice. Neither would be out of the question. Burns smiled. He could appreciate a superior officer who preferred functional minimalism as he did.

As curious as he was to see the Duke's inner realm, Burns figured it would be best if he held his position near the entry until Wayne called for him.

"Come in, Burns," Wayne seemed to sigh from beyond the door, as if he was waiting. Burns straightened himself at the door and went in two steps, then stopped. He waited for Wayne to address him, but he was still typing a message on his phone.

Burns tried not to sound too curious, or impatient. "You wanted to see me, sir."

Wayne was on his forearms, leaning on his desk as he tapped a message in an uneven rhythm on his phone. When he finished, he put the phone on the desk and rose from his chair. It took some time for him to pull his attention from the phone. Wayne glanced at Burns, almost smiling.

"Yes," Wayne answered finally. He stepped to the window that ran the length of the wall to the left of his desk.

"And I gather you want to speak to me." He turned his gaze to the London Eye across the river.

Burns was caught off guard by the invitation. "I'm not sure I..." he managed.

"You looked like you were about ready to burst at least twice during the briefing," said Wayne. "I have to acknowledge your self-control."

Burns took the compliment with a grin. He knew the respect was mutual and felt the trust growing between them. He had a lot of questions about what was said, and more about what wasn't said at the briefing. He still felt ready to burst, but Burns could play it cool and humble as he stood waiting at the door.

"My dad would tell you I'm still learning when to talk and when to listen, sir." "Yes he would, Charles. I am sure," Wayne agreed. "As would others," he added.

Burns took it as a jibe, though he knew it to be true, and offered a light chuckle. Wayne seemed to have caught his second wind, and shaken off the commander's mantle in the process. He pointed at the door behind Burns. "Close that and come over here," he said.

Burns turned and pulled the door shut then he joined Wayne at the window.

"Questions?" asked Wayne.

"It just seems like there's a lot we—there's a lot I don't know..." Burns trailed off.

"First question," demanded Wayne.

Burns didn't hesitate. "Why," he said.

"That's not the first question I expected," Wayne confessed. "Before you say anything, if it's about your status, I am trying to find a training angle to justify putting you on the roster immediately and not waiting for Monday," said Wayne. "But I can't just..."

"Justify it?" Burns asked. "Can't you deputise me or something, Chief?"

"Burns, my hands are tied," answered Wayne. Then he added vaguely, "But it may be for the best."

"How so?" Burns asked.

Wayne ignored the question, and Burns let it go.

"Why?" Wayne echoed. "Not who, or even more pointedly where? Aren't those the questions we're trying to answer first, Burns?"

Burns hated it when anyone answered a question with a question, but agreed. "Of course," he said. "I guess I'm asking what do we know about the why. Why somebody would want to take him, and his laboratory, to... Aberdeen?"

"You want to know what I know," said Wayne, fixing his bloodshot eyes on Burns. "I understand." The look told Burns he was trusted.

"Ok," said Burns.

Ok," Wayne repeated. "Well, the Aberdeen Royal Infirmary has confirmed they received a patient last night, but we had some difficulty with their privacy policy." Wayne stepped over to his desk to check his phone. "Negative ID on the name," he read. He looked over at Burns, who was watching from the window. "Detective Sergeant Gray confirms a negative on visual," said Wayne. "It really is a rich Saudi prince getting a new liver." Wayne paused to check the text again. "Chubby fellow, says Gray."

It wasn't good news, but somehow not unexpected. "A red herring," said Burns.

"Indeed," answered Wayne. "Gray's gone back to the airport." He forced a smile.

"All right Burns, what do you want to know?" Wayne maintained his outwardly relaxed demeanour but there was a tension in his voice. Burns felt a rush of excitement at the idea of brainstorming with his boss. His brain began opening the files he had committed to memory during his late-night studies of Veda's publications.

"Right," said Wayne before Burns could begin. "The question is why. Well, his family doesn't have money, so unless the plan is to extort the government..." Wayne stopped himself. Burns could tell by the tone that the possibility existed, but the probability was considered low.

"At any rate," Wayne went on, "nobody's demanding a ransom or claiming responsibility at this point, but I do believe the Good Doctor has been kidnapped," said Wayne, putting a stamp on it.

"I meant why Veda, sir," said Burns. "He was studying ways to cure disease."

"Yes," Wayne raised his voice to close Burns' off, but he held the tension low. "He's been working on a mega vaccine of some sort. The government has been supporting his lab work since he had some sort of medical breakthrough at Oxford."

"Typhoid," injected Burns. "His mother and older sister died while he was away at boarding school when they were still in India. He's been working on a nano-vaccine for typhoid," Burns' mind's eye was playing like an old newsreel on fast-forward. He went on breathlessly. "But he may have developed a more broadly applicable answer to curing a lot more than just typhoid. It's a kind of packet of proteins that bonds his vaccine with water molecules to insinuate it into the bloodstream through the skin..."

Wayne turned to face Burns, without hiding his astonishment. "How did you..."

"I read, Inspector", said Burns. He heard himself and tried to walk it back. "I really read,' he said. "A lot."

Wayne could have taken it to be a slight, but he knew better. He had done his due diligence long before

Burns' first interview. Burns joined Anti-Terror when it was still called that, and Superintendent John Wayne was still its Commanding Officer.

There had been reports of Burns being an ass to a couple of the officers in the branch, or at least he spoke to them as if they were the ass. But DCI Wayne knew the offended officers, at least by reputation, and he could read between the lines. Truth be told, he saw Burns' arrogance for what it was. Burns simply believed he was always the smartest guy in the room. The problem for some people was that Burns usually was right. Wayne had seen and heard enough to believe it was true most of the time, too, and not resent it.

"I Googled him last night," offered Burns. "After I left the lab," he added.

"Right," said Wayne. He turned back to the window and spoke quietly to the drizzled city outside. "At any rate, nobody's demanding a ransom or claiming responsibility at this point."

Burns joined Wayne at the window and watched the raindrops do their slow motion race down the glass before scanning the road and the river below. The traffic moved at its usual crawl along the embankment road. The Coca-Cola London Eye was there, as it always was, dominating the London skyline.

Wayne went on, "It is also an assumption that Dr Veda did not disappear on his own."

"Meaning it's assumed that it wasn't his idea, or that it was with help?" Burns asked.

Wayne stood silently staring out the window, his hands clasped behind his back. He turned his head to face Burns long enough to admit he hadn't an answer.

"Regardless," Wayne continued. "He's valuable to someone."

"Exactly," Burns piped. "The who. And the way to the who is the why."

"Did you learn that one online, Burns?" Wayne jabbed his crooked finger in the air then withdrew it quickly. He looked out at the leaden sky and stopped half-way through a deep sigh. Burns cleared his throat and took a sip of water to fill the silence.

"I don't know how long your list is or where it starts and ends..." Burns paused, hoping to be interrupted. Wayne was giving nothing, so he went on. "I'm guessing the list of groups and organisations that would be interested, and willing and able to..." Burns knew he didn't have to say it.

He waited as the two men watched the rain falling.

"And you think this is an angle we haven't been considering as we compile our list?" asked Wayne.

"I would think it's a short list," answered Burns.

"Well actually we have been more focused on the 'willing and able' possibilities, yes..." Wayne answered.

"And considering 'ways and means', of course," Burns began easily, then cut to the point. "Even if they hadn't hacked the Met's surveillance server," he said with a dismissive wave of his hand. Then he raised a thumb and went on. "The abduction and the robbery were executed by organised, experienced professionals, likely ex-military." Burns dropped his tone and added, "Hopefully ex."

"All right, Burns," Wayne turned and cut Burns off. "You've made your most obvious point."

"Cloud seeding," said Burns. He studied Wayne, who was facing the rain outside, impervious. They were both close enough to the glass to see each other's reflection without turning their heads. Wayne's cold sea-green eyes seemed brighter reflected on the window. The sea was calm, accepting the rain with indifference. Wayne turned his gaze to Burns.

"Is there a question in there, Burns?" asked Wayne.

"What about Mary?" Burns asked without hesitation.

Wayne looked at him for a long moment.

"The truth is that the pig was probably stolen. By whom, it is unknown," Wayne stated.

"They can't have good intentions," said Burns.

"But that's not at issue, Burns." Wayne remained blunt. "And in fact, it's not our problem."

"Sir, the group that stole Mary did so with a similar distraction to the one in Southwark last night."

"Tully mentioned you put that out there, yes." The corners of Wayne's mouth fought off a smile. "A connection worth making," he admitted. "Inspector Tellier is working with Met Surveillance."

"How far outside MCU2 does this go, sir?" Burns asked, deliberately shifting gears as he plied for answers.

"As far as it needs to," Wayne hardened. "I'm dealing with everyone I need to, Burns."

"Yes, sir," Burns conceded. He knew he trusted Wayne as much as Wayne trusted him. Wayne seemed gratified. His eyes and mouth lifted, almost into a smile.

"The HO has been made aware of the operation," said Wayne. "Internationally, only Interpol so far, and strictly as a data source. But we have a wider network than you might imagine," Wayne cleared his throat for emphasis.

"Oh, I can imagine," Burns let out a nervous laugh. It lingered in his belly, tussling with the fearful notion that another agency in the network was working the other side of the operation.

"Yes, I'm sure you can," said Wayne. "But not right now." His baritone voice was serious again. "Right now, our mission is singular. We find Veda."

"And we're a singular unit?" Burns asked.

"Well, Doctor Nicholas Veda was under my watch, put bluntly, and I intend to be the one to retrieve him." Wayne straightened up and added, "If we find him, we'll find the bad guys," he added.

"You're going to need a hell of a lot more than MCU2 when you find the bad guys." Burns heard himself and stole a look at Wayne.

Wayne was surprisingly flippant with his reply. "We'll burn that bridge when we come to it," he said.

Two short, quiet peeps signalled an incoming message on Wayne's phone. He stepped around Burns to retrieve it from his desk and read the new message. Wayne gave a short grunt of disapproval. Then he turned back to Burns. "It's for you," he said. "I need you to go upstairs and relieve Aitkens while he, erm, relieves himself."

Burns stopped himself before his laugh became a guffaw. *Whatever I can do to help, sir*, he mused. He bit his tongue, and remembered he was speaking to his Commanding Officer. "Pee break?" he asked.

Wayne set his face against the wave, a smirk that was trying to become a smile.

"Number two, apparently," he smirked. "Actually, it's his second request. Just before you came in..." Wayne turned back to the view of the misty gardens along Victoria Embankment.

"Detective Sergeant Aitkens is with a potential witness," Wayne continued. "He's waiting for Thornley to return to duty and conduct the interview but..." Wayne caught himself, but not before his granite face flushed enough to warm his cheeks. "Mandatory off-duty hours, apparently, so..." he trailed off before his anger with the police union took hold of the conversation.

"Our guest is a walk-in," said Wayne. "We were unable to locate him on first contact, but he showed up downstairs about seventy-five minutes ago. Told the desk he worked with Dr Veda and he had information about his whereabouts. Said he wanted protection, but declined to say from whom or what." Wayne didn't seem as intrigued as Burns felt about the prospect of having a witness show up out of the blue.

"The attending officer put him in an interview room and Aitkens retrieved him there and brought him upstairs. Thornley should be here to take his statement," Wayne checked his watch and grumbled, "Directly."

"So, you want me to stay with the witness until Thornley gets here," said Burns.

"Yes," answered Wayne. "Or if Aitkens returns before. His name is Krutovskiy but he gave us a different name when he came in..." Wayne checked a file on his desktop. "Ivanov."

"Krutovskiy, Yessir," Burns repeated.

"Call him Ivanov, won't you Burns," Wayne insisted.

"And report back to you?" Burns hoped he would be able to rejoin his CO and pick up their conversation.

Wayne lifted his chin and answered curtly, "I'll call you or send a message."

"Understood," Burns straightened up but stopped just short of fully coming to attention. "I'll go upstairs and wait there until you send me a message." He couldn't avoid the goofy grin. "Or call," he nodded, remaining at attention. "Unless Aitkens comes back. Or shall I stay there until Thornley arrives?"

"Thank you, Monty Python," Wayne acknowledged. "Why is it every Canadian I've ever met quotes brutalises Monty Python at any opportunity?"

Burns smiled blithely. "Because it's our shared history?"

"The war of 1812 is our shared history," Wayne replied.

"And the Hudson's Bay Company," Burns grinned.

"Let's don't be cruel, Burns," said Wayne. He had no interest in playing along with Burns' fell humour. "We don't want Detective Sergeant Aitkens to have an accident."

Burns resisted making a declaration but smiled again at the thought of Aitkens pissing his pants. *Couldn't happen to a nicer guy.*

"First door on the left as you come up the stairs," said Wayne. "Please go now."

Detective Sergeant John Aitkens was waiting to open the door when Burns turned the handle.

"Hey there!" Burns exclaimed. He made a quick step to the left, deked around Aitkens and into the room. It looked like it had been a boardroom but was serving as an executive lounge—or the other way around—with its stuffed leather sofas and armchairs grouped in twos and threes around the large room, while the long narrow table and its high-backed chairs were shifted almost to the windowless wall on the far right. The window on the opposite wall looked like the open ocean at the far end of an archipelago, with the clusters of furniture dotting the flat brown sea between Burns and the horizon. A closer look revealed the Ministry of Defence building to the left and a view of Victoria Embankment all the way north to Whitehall Gardens. Some of the trees were in bloom, April's showers having done their job a little early. He was too far away from the window to see the lawns, but the muddy, brown Thames and the leaden sky framed the view on the right. The dull grey light that passed through the tinted glass backlit the silhouette of a slight man in a long coat.

"Nice," said Burns. He turned back to face Aitkens. "Looks like the rain has stopped."

Aitkens glanced over Burns' shoulder but didn't focus past the man standing with his back to the window. He pointed vaguely at the man but said nothing and half turned to leave. Burns watched Aitkens eyes as they searched left and right in the hall outside and darted back to meet his scrutiny.

"Got the runs, Detective?" Burns said quickly.

"What?" Aitkens' questioning eyes were able to hold contact with Burns for three or four seconds. Burns was impressed.

"I say, gotta run, Detective?" Burns grinned.

"I'll be right back, just…" said Aitkens through his teeth.

"I'll be right here," Burns grinned and pointed. "Men's WC is down and around to the left."

Aitkens stepped out and closed the door loudly.

Burns smiled at the door. He had couched his spite in humour, like with any man he knew who had failed a primary task on any mission and not admitted it. Mistakes get made, but Burns believed it to be far more dishonourable for a man to be guilty of not owning up to it.

Burns turned back to Dr Krutovskiy, who was trying to look patient. But he was having a hard time. Burns could see the man struggling to manage his emotions, turning his phone over and over in his hand.

"Good morning," Burns smiled and addressed the guest. "Charles Burns," he called across the room. Burns weaved slowly around the furniture and crossed the room to approach Krutovskiy. He stopped a few feet away, careful to keep the table and two chairs between himself and his frightened guest. Maybe we'll shake hands when we part, Burns chuckled inwardly.

"Good morning," Burns repeated. "Doctor Krutovskiy, is it?" Burns smiled at Krutovskiy, who obviously didn't know that Burns knew his real name.

"Are you…" Krutovskiy started to ask. He put his phone away in his pocket.

"No, I'm just here while Sergeant Aitkens takes a little um, break," replied Burns.

"Oh." Krutovskiy seemed at a loss. "But you're American."

"No, oh god no!" Burns laughed. "I'm Canadian."

"I see," said Krutovskiy, but Burns knew he didn't. He turned to look out the window.

"Can I see your phone?" Burns smiled. His friendly expression flattened. "I don't mean see it, I mean," Burns gestured with an open hand. "I'm going to have to take it."

Krutovskiy flinched and touched his jacket pocket before reaching inside and retrieving the phone. He looked at it for several seconds. Then he appeared to catch himself before forcing his gaze back to the window.

"You shouldn't have it on in here, actually." Burns pulled Krutovskiy back with his voice and extended his hand slowly, maintaining enough of a benign smile to keep his dimple creased. Krutovskiy didn't touch the screen with his fingers or thumb before he extended his arm over the chair he stood behind. Burns stepped around his chair and reached for Krutovskiy's hand.

"Sergeant Aitkens should have asked you but he..." Burns received the phone with a nod.

"Can I turn it off?" Burns held the phone aloft as he turned and walked over to the long table in the centre of the room. "It's kind of a security thing, actually," he added. He pointed out the phone's camera and microphone. "I guess they don't want anyone making any secret recordings or something," Burns offered a light laugh and shrugged as he placed the phone on the long table.

"No, please..." Krutovskiy surged upright but stopped short of rising from the edge of the armchair he seemed unable to recline in. He looked at the phone again. "Yes," he said. He waved his arm at the phone in dismissal. "No, it's fine."

Burns was trying to get a read on Krutovskiy when a flicker of red light caught his attention. He looked at the window behind Krutovskiy and saw a beam of red light refracted in the dense glass. Burns watched as it danced in tight, uneven circles on the pane behind Krutovskiy for one or two seconds and then vanished. Burns took a wide step towards Krutovskiy, maintaining a safe angle and distance.

"Have a seat," Burns barked. "Over here." It wasn't a request. He softened the tone after Krutovskiy jumped. "Please," he added, gesturing to the sofas grouped in a horseshoe a few feet away from the window. Krutovskiy complied.

Burns studied the glass, wondering about how many layers it had and how bulletproof it might be. He affected a casual air and angled himself to the window, scanning its exposure to sniper angles before leaning closer to the glass for a wider view. Across from the window stood the Ministry of Defence Headquarters at Whitehall. He recalled where Krutovskiy had been standing when the laser appeared and reckoned it had to have come from below. The only possibility would be a shot from ground level, and at a steep trajectory, somewhere north along Victoria Embankment.

Burns was convinced that it was unlikely a professional would take a low percentage shot in such a very public place, to say nothing for the trees. And maybe it was the unsteady quiver he saw when the laser first caught his eye that made him think it was either no threat or an amateur. Nonetheless, he had reacted instinctively and decisively, as he would have trained any soldier to do.

Burns wished he had imagined the flash of red light on the window that set his reflexes off. But Dr Krutovskiy's attention, and fearful look before they began chatting also suggested Burns should look down. If there was a sniper, he was at street level.

Burns recalled that Krutovskiy had got a message and probably read it while Burns was having a bit of sport with Aitkens on his way to the loo. Burns had heard the doorbell chime alert from Krutovskiy's phone but ignored it at the time because he had been putting too much energy into intimidating and harassing Aitkens. Burns felt no remorse. Life's little regrets hadn't added up to enough to keep Burns awake at night. Until Aitkens fessed up to his ineptitude, Burns felt he didn't owe the man any more respect than what he got from Mrs McKague, his curmudgeonly fifth grade teacher.

Burns took a few seconds to scan the wall, the ceiling and finally the pane of glass for the signs of the laser. Satisfied, he leaned in another step until he could see where he imagined Krutovskiy had been gazing. Ships were lethargically rolling past on the Thames, the road traffic moving at a slightly better pace.

Then he spotted the van. It was parked on the boulevard between the bus lane and the bicycle path. It was a Ford Transit, but it wasn't white. It was painted British Telecom yellow. It was parked in reverse, sitting in a gap between trees along the road, its open rear doors hanging above an open manhole. Burns instinctively pulled out his phone. He had to send a message to Wayne. He typed in all caps:

SUSPICIOUS WFT –PAINTED BT YELLOW- 100M N. FROM OUR GATE.

Burns decided to leave out the suspicious laser because of a lingering doubt. Some part of him refused to believe that anyone would attempt the shot. Possible, maybe. Probable? No. Burns shook his head and closed his message with

WTF?

Then he sent it to DCI Wayne.

Krutovskiy had been watching Burns with contained disquiet. Burns saw the frail hand touch the empty pocket then reached across to check a wristwatch that wasn't there. Burns checked his phone then raised it to show Krutovskiy the time display.

"Nine-thirty," said Burns. "In case you're wondering." He smiled a kind, one-dimpled smile. His mind was still on the van.

"Fine," replied Krutovskiy. It sounded like something he said whenever he didn't know what to say. Burns checked the glass again then stepped around a chair and back to the window. The interior of the van was in shadow and there was no activity around the van. No safety barrier around the manhole, either. Burns smiled as he caught himself hoping that whoever was in the van had something to do with the breach of the Met's digital security. He maintained his watch until he heard the door open behind him. He turned on cue and let out a huff and cleared his throat when Aitkens entered.

"Everything come out all right?" Burns asked. He pulled out his phone again, as if to check the time. Then he opened a browser and did a quick search for anything on 'Krutovskiy, Ivan. He committed the first two pages of results to memory, mentally stroking through the ubiquitous friend and ancestor finders. He closed his eyes and switched off the display then returned the phone to his jacket pocket. He turned to Aitkens, deliberately expressionless. Burns wanted Aitkens to think he had been writing something about him.

"Right," said Aitkens, the same way Krutovskiy had said "fine". Burns held flat and said nothing, forcing Aitkens to turn his focus to Krutovskiy, who was still seated on the edge of the sizeable sofa in the centre of the horseshoe. Aitkens seemed to be able to hold his gaze on the guest but was still at a loss for words. Krutovskiy, for his part, looked calm, like he had time to wait until someone else spoke.

"Still no Detective Sergeant Thornley?" Burns asked loudly enough to cause both men to snap their focus to where he stood at the window, watching the BT van.

"No," answered Aitkens. "And there's no need for you here anymore."

Burns caught the tone. Aitkens had to assert himself, and that was easier with Burns' back turned. Burns wanted to stay and hear what Krutovskiy had to say. But he also knew Tully would have more answers too, hopefully starting with the girl. As much as he relished the thought of getting further under Aitkens skin and into his head, Burns decided to agree emphatically instead.

"You are so right," Burns declared. He stepped away from his surveillance post at the window. Then he turned on his heel and started for the door. He stopped next to Aitkens and leaned in. Aitkens didn't flinch. "Keep him away from the window," Burns added quietly. He looked over Aitkens shoulder and caught Krutovskiy's eye. He wanted to give him a reassuring wink, but he was so struck by the serene look on Krutovskiy's face that he couldn't muster more than a sheepish grin. He saved the smile for Aitkens as he pulled away to leave. "TTFN," Burns sang. "Ta-ta for now!" He waved at the blissed-out Krutovskiy, who waved absently. Burns saluted Aitkens as he made his exit.

09:40

Burns was just about to turn the corner toward the WC to get a refill for his water bottle when he heard Aitkens call for help. It sounded as if he was trying to help a fallen passer-by in the High Street. Burns bet himself Aitkens didn't know CPR.

"Burns!" Aitkens exclaimed as he saw Burns stepping through the door. He looked straight at Burns, his eyes held firm as they delivered his plea. Aitkens was near the window, standing over the prone body of Dr Gregor Krutovskiy. "He got up suddenly and made a bee line for the window."

Burns checked the glass. No bullet holes. No squelch marks where Krutovskiy's face could have smashed. Aitkens' eyes darted from the corpse to the window and finally back to Burns, who caught and held his attention. Burns conjured up the image of his fifth-grade teacher, Mrs McKague, who could expose guilt in any ten-year-old, even if he didn't have any.

"What-did-you-do?" Burns scowled.

Aitkens followed the script. "Nothing," he said.

"Relax," said Burns. "Kidding." *Only half.* "Heart?"

"He seemed fine when I left," Aitkens said.

"Really Aitkens?" Burns stepped into Aitkens' comfort zone, stopping short of leaning into his face. "You wanna do that?" Burns smiled coolly. He relaxed his stance, dialling back his feistiness. "He was sweaty nervous. Look at his armpits. His hands were clammy. He couldn't sit down. You did ask him to sit down, didn't you?"

Aitkens shook his head no. "Like I said, I look over and he suddenly rushes toward the window."

"Looked over from where?" Burns asked, but he knew Aitkens had been at the table by watching his eyes.

"I was reading my text—" Aitkens stopped himself.

"Nice," Burns whispered. He side-stepped Aitkens and walked straight to the safe spot next to the pillar beside the window. He looked again at the unbroken glass then looked down. The telecom van was gone.

The traffic passed at a crawl in front of the gates to new Scotland Yard. A patrol car passed through the gate and entered the otherwise empty parking compound.

"I don't understand how smacking his face on the window can kill him," Aitkens complained. "He wasn't even moving that fast when he hit the—" Aitkens stopped.

Burns stepped past him and, surveyed the floor around the body then crouched next to it.

"You can't just touch a body!" Aitkens squawked. He remained where Burns had left him after the stare down. "It's not your department, Burns."

"I haven't touched it," Burns answered.

Krutovskiy was turned three quarters on his left side facing the glass, his back supported by the leather armchair with the best view. Burns saw no visible signs of trauma but Krutovskiy's face seemed flush, maybe a little fleshier, but undamaged. His body looked to be at rest, the legs were together and bent at a natural angle with the feet almost together, as if he had fallen asleep and slid out of the chair. The right hand had fallen across the forehead in the fall, Burns guessed, or maybe was shielding the eyes against the white light. Burns lifted the arm by the sleeve to get a better look at Krutovskiy's face.

Red eyes. Body swollen. Internal bleeding for sure. "Seriously, what did you say?" "Did he say anything?"

Aitkens stared at Krutovskiy and shook his head silently.

"We need to check his phone," said Burns. He stood up and took a step toward the table. Aitkens stepped to the right of the corpse and put his hand out to stop Burns.

"No, we don't!" Aitkens held his gaze on Burns, who welcomed another stare down. Aitkens was committed. Burns saw it in his eyes. He wasn't going to let Burns pass. No doubt about that. It was as if he suddenly remembered how he was physically bigger than Burns and he instinctively flexed his arms and expanded his chest like a bouncer at a strip club. "No, you're not touchin' that, mate."

"And you call yourself a detective," Burns mocked. He amused himself by imagining a half dozen ways he could immobilise Aitkens without killing him.

"He got a text message or a missed call on his phone over there," Aitkens teased. "I heard it ping. But he didn't check it."

Burns had heard the phone chime behind him as he closed the door and stepped into the hall. But it passed as an echo in his memory. He was recalling Krutovskiy's expression when they waved at each other, and the look on his face when Burns took the phone earlier, after the dead man had read the message.

Aitkens' phone buzzed and clicked softly. He smiled at the message and looked up in Burns direction. "I messaged the Chief Inspector. Forensics is on the way."

"Great," Burns smiled.

"Look, Burns, I appreciate you not saying anything at the briefing about us missing..." Aitkens eyes were moving again, looking past Burns shoulder and out the window at Whitehall or the sky, glancing back to Burns to make momentary contact. Burns waited him out, feigning ignorance.

Aitkens went on with a shrug. "About the guard at the lab... You didn't say anything."

"I wasn't the one speaking," said Burns. He held Aitkens' eyes with his frosty expression while trying to sound genial. "It's not up to me to say something, you see. It's up to you." Aitkens blanked. Burns resisted saying more. He shrugged and raised his hands in submission then smiled slyly.

"I don't know how this is gonna look," Burns joked, pointing at the dead witness laying between them. His grin widened. "But it certainly looks like you're... not responsible." Burns let out a stunted laugh as he continued to hold Aitkens in his glare. "If you catch my double meaning."

Aitkens didn't catch it, but luckily for Burns the door swung open and Detective Sergeant Mike Thornley strolled in, at the stroke of nine forty-seven.

Thornley was a big man, two metres tall and beefy. Burns had met him once, along with Gray and Blennerhassett, when Burns was petitioning Detective Chief Inspector Wayne to approve his transfer to MCU2. Thornley struck Burns as a gentle giant and it made him wonder what he was like as an interrogator.

Thornley raised his Starbucks cup in a toast. "Morning, gentlemen." He took a sip and mapped his route through the room. A split second later the jovial smile retreated under the bushy moustache as his eyes tracked to the chair that stood between Aitkens and Burns. He saw the partially concealed body of Gregor Krutovskiy. He stared at the legs for a moment then turned to Aitkens and Burns.

"Started without me, have you?" Thornley smiled. Burns laughed.

"Did you speak to Chief inspector Wayne?" asked Aitkens.

"Of course I did," Thornley answered with a shrug.

"Sergeant Aitkens is not responsible," Burns laughed. His phone pinged with a message from DCI Wayne. He read the short text and replaced the phone in his pocket.

"Forensics is on the way," Aitkens declared in his defence.

Thornley ignored Aitkens and looked at Burns. "What happened?" he asked.

"All they need to hear from anybody is what I know," Aitkens bawled. He turned to Burns. "I found this one so you can leave it to me," he barked.

"Righty-oh," Burns replied coolly. He would leave it all to Aitkens. Except Krutovskiy's phone, which he quickly pocketed while the other two men were staring at the dead body. "You're absolutely right."

Nicholas Veda awoke to a slap across his left cheek. The heat spread over his face and his eyes opened wide. A few tears dribbled out. He blinked until shapes formed in the grey and black cloud he found himself in.

"There he is," said the same spooky German children's show host Veda had heard somewhere before. The next moment the voice was coldly mocking, inches from Veda's nose.

"Where is your dick? Is it in there?" The voice came from a shadow, a silhouette of a man leaning close.

Gerhardt, Veda remembered...

Nicholas Veda saw the shape of a man in front of him but couldn't focus on the face. He guessed what Noack was grunting about as the man leaned lower and turned his head sideways as if he was looking under Veda's seat.

"It's hiding," Noack chortled. "In the jungle."

Veda braced himself for another probing invasion. Noack grabbed a handful of the hair on the back of Veda's head and leaned close enough that Veda could taste his hot breath. Veda didn't retch. He exhaled slowly as he swallowed the bile in his mouth. He blinked several times trying to focus and felt a tear escaping along the side of his nose. Veda's captor moved behind him and yanked the handful of hair, tilting his head back. Veda held his breath for a moment when he remembered he had regained muscle control of his neck and back. That's why it hurts now, he realised. He pulled against the hand with every fibre, feeling all his muscles engaged but enfeebled by the weight of his own skeleton and skin. The fist suddenly released his hair and Veda held his head steady. He tried to focus on his surroundings. He moved his eyes slowly to his left and back to the right, letting his head follow their lead. He was still in the same tiled room, looking across a lab to the window on the far wall. After a few scattered moments trying to understand his surroundings, Veda returned his gaze to the window several metres away. It was easier for his mind to focus on the world outside in the distance than the room where he was still bound to a chair. He was starting to recognise colours again—all greens and blues, far across the white wilderness of the unfinished laboratory. Veda stared at the vista. It's Pulicat Lake. I'm in India… No.

"Maybe Thailand," Veda suggested aloud.

"Ha!" Suddenly the thug was in front of Veda again. "You see this?" Noack held up his hands and pulled off the black leather gloves. Then he thrust his right hand into Veda's face, with the fingers spread and the thumb tucked under. "How many?"

"Four," Veda mumbled. Noack's sharp laugh made him wince, and he felt his arms pull against his restraints. His limbs felt heavy, but they were awake again.

"You feel this?" The thug pulled at Veda's pubic hair then grabbed his genitals and squeezed. Veda yelped. The short, flat echo that trailed after his scream slapped his eyes and rang in his ears. For a moment he wished he were still numb. Now he would feel everything, every torture. He turned his gaze to the window again. Then he sobbed a single bleat.

Noack's grip softened but didn't release Veda's genitals. "That yes?"

Without waiting for an answer, Noack withdrew his hand and raised it up to his face. His nose whistled as he inhaled deeply, as if he held an elegant rose. Then he clenched his fist. "See this?" he asked again, and slowly drew his hand back. Veda wriggled in the chair and turned his head from side to side, relieved he could move, but knowing he would not avoid the punch that was coming. He squeezed his eyes shut and braced with every muscle in his neck, hoping it would be able to keep his head on his body when the fist hit his face.

Noack struck Veda hard in the centre of his chest, striking with an open palm. The blow crushed the air out of Veda's lungs and sent a searing hot lightning bolt through his entire body. Fingernails dragged through the thin flesh on his ribs like a rake in a furrow. The hot hand dove between Veda's legs again, squeezing and pulling at him hard, until he felt sick.

Veda kept his eyes and mouth closed, and tried to breathe through his nose. His nostrils were full of mucous and his eyes full of tears, and he sputtered and gagged, fighting against the moaning sob in his throat. The hand gave one last twist before it slithered away.

Just as Veda recovered his breath a bright light flashed, blinding him again.

"One for the website," chuckled Noack. He produced a syringe and injected its contents into the shunt taped to Veda's left arm. "And one for the road." He slapped Veda's forearm above the injection site. Veda felt the hot sting on his skin and the cold fluid coursing its way to his heart.

"Then," Noack chortled, "we get you another drink. Ha!" Noack's laugh sounded like a shout of victory. Veda opened his eyes and turned to the window, wishing he were back in London. He knew if he looked at Noack he would not be able to hide his fear.

"Do you know what you're going to do? You're going to save the world. Ha!" Noack held Veda's face. Veda nodded weakly. Then Noack's voice said something about "sleep" and "timetable", but his lips didn't seem to move. Veda tried to understand whether he was dreaming or dead — or not. He was looking at a tropical paradise from an aquarium — no, a sample jar. Veda wondered if he would die in this jar. Of course, he would, if he couldn't fight the sleep overwhelming his neck muscles. His eyes were already asleep. But not blind, at least. He fought hard against the drugs, but the sun set, and Veda's world went dark.

Burns turned left to the men's WC to refill his water bottle. A row of three sinks were carved into a single marble slab that sat below a full-length mirror on the left wall. The antique fixtures and shallow basins wouldn't allow him to fill the bottle more than half-way, but the bottle fit easily under the tap of the disabled-accessible sink, which looked more like a janitor's sink mounted next to the wheelchair-accessible stall. Burns lifted the oversized lever and watched the water pouring out of the tap. He wondered if Krutovskiy had offed himself or had been offed. With what, cyanide capsule? Burns laughed, but not because it was impossible.

He stuck a finger into the stream of water and adjusted the temperature with the other hand. Burns looked at his finger, engulfed by the stream. Something made him think of Mary.

"What did that mean old sinister Dr Veda do to you, Mary?" Burns asked the poor little pig. "And where are you now?" Thinking out loud jarred Burns back to the chilling reality. Dr Veda's disappearance was only a part of something much bigger.

The water cooled in a few seconds and Burns pulled his finger out from under the stream, replacing it with the empty bottle. The water bubbled up inside the clear plastic bottle and he slapped the oversized lever down to stop the stream before it overflowed. He twisted the cap on and flicked his finger to shake off the last droplets of water that clung to his skin as he headed for the door.

Burns slowed his pace as he descended the last few stairs and Tully's door came into view. He was torn by the idea of stopping to visit Tully before reporting to Wayne. He wanted to see what patterns and connections Tully and HOLMES had identified. But DCI Wayne had called him back. The smartest thing would be to not piss off the commanding officer by being late again. Whether or not Wayne had a role for him, Burns felt like he knew too much, he had invested too much to be kept on the bench. He would make the case against waiting for his transfer to become official. If it came to an extraction, Wayne would no doubt find a way to activate Burns, pronto, as the Duke would say.

Unless it was out his hands by then. Burns fought the urge to ask if any other agencies were involved yet. There were other questions, and he hoped to be able to pick up where he left off brainstorming with Wayne. Burns figured whoever the Other Side was, they were a formidable foe, with skill sets and assets that put them in a league with a limited number of players and teams.

Burns had a better idea of who Wayne was and how he worked. He liked the idea of directing the action and solving a case without getting wet. Burns had left armed engagement, wet-work, behind ten years ago when he took himself off active field duty. He transferred to the newly formed Canadian Joint Incident Response Unit to lead their training department. Training soldiers to kill, and to survive, didn't satisfy his need to be an "impact player". The prospect of putting his intelligence to work solving crimes inspired him to petition for appointment as a detective. So, he studied for—and passed—the detective qualification. Now, here he was, a year later and still officially a Specialist Trainer. Not Yet Detective.

As he stood in the hall outside Wayne's door he wondered if it would ever matter.

10:00

Wayne was with Tully in the small glass meeting room when Burns walked in. The two men were looking at something on the table. Burns closed the door loudly enough to announce his presence. He caught Tully's eye, who said something to Wayne, who straightened and waved Burns in.

Burns decided to cut the bullshit and get straight to the latest connection.

"Did you get my message, Chief Inspector Wayne?" Burns began without saying hello.

"I did," Wayne answered. Burns phone had told him so, nonetheless he felt justified pointing out, "I didn't get a reply."

"No, you didn't," was the curt answer.

"About Dr Krutovskiy, sir," Burns began again. "It didn't look like he died of natural causes, sir." The two men looked at Burns and each other but said nothing.

"What about the suspicious WFT?" Burns asked. The window in Wayne's office couldn't provide a clear view of the Telecom van's location because the trees along the Embankment and its boulevard had exploded with bright green spring foliage. But if Burns bent down low enough, he could see the manhole. He watched a cyclist roll over the iron lid. Burns pointed to the spot.

"It was right there," he said.

"I called IT Guy as soon as I sent the message downstairs." Said Wayne. He nodded, as if he was assuring Burns of something. "He sent a team to look for evidence of any tampering. The van was gone but they did find the manhole. They managed to get the lid off, and back on, before Dispatch had a uniform on site." Wayne stopped. He flipped open the small notebook on the desk and made a note to speak to IT Guy about bomb safety protocols. He looked at it for a moment before scratching out the last two words. Then he turned to look at Burns.

"Turns out there was no telecom access at the manhole where your van was."

"Exactly, sir. A ten-year-old WFT painted to look like a telecom van sitting there. I..." Burns tried to gauge whether Wayne or Tully were convinced. He figured he had to go on, but Wayne held up a hand to stop him in mid breath.

"When they discovered that, they put in a call to the bomb squad," Wayne said. Burns hadn't considered that, but reckoned he couldn't be blamed for the Met's reaction. "Thank God they called me first," Wayne sighed.

"Sir, I sent you that message because I saw—" Burns caught himself sounding defensive. He knew he couldn't prove his first suspicion. He still hadn't convinced himself that a sniper would—then it hit him. He spoke quickly. "I saw a laser sight on the glass where Krutovskiy was standing," said Burns. "He was looking at his phone when I came in to, uh, relieve Aitkens. There was a BT van parked there, doors open."

"What, you think there was an assassin parked in a bright orange van on Victoria Embankment," Wayne's voice rolled low and slow, like distant thunder. "With a high-powered rifle?"

"No sir," Burns was emphatic. He looked over at Tully for support, but his eyes were fixed on his iPad. Burns hoped he was listening. He raised his voice.

"But I do think Krutovskiy got some kind of a signal..."

"A signal," Wayne echoed.

"A message," Burns insisted. "On his phone. He was dead three minutes later."

Wayne stooped briefly to look for the manhole. Then he rose and turned to his left, angling his view upward as if tracking the trajectory to the room one floor up. He glanced over at Tully, who was busily typing on his tablet, then turned back to Burns. The look of recrimination was gone. Burns saw the trust. He gulped down a long drink from the water bottle he had been twisting and turning on the windowsill. "Veda has been kidnapped but it's doubtful there'll be any ransom demands. They took what they needed from the lab, presumably to continue his work, then grabbed him, and his girlfriend..." Burns decided to leave out his suspicions about the girl.

"Krutovskiy," said Burns. "Who knows what Krutovskiy might have told us..." He paused for a deep breath. "This was all very well-orchestrated. I don't want to say with military precision, but..." Burns waited to be cut off, to be told to keep his conspiracy theories off the table, but neither man spoke. They either believed, like he did, or they knew. Burns stated the obvious. "Somebody has a lot more invested and a much bigger goal than political gain or wealth by extortion here."

"No shit, Sherlock," Tully chuckled without looking up. "There's still a lot to unpack, though." He looked at Wayne, silently asking for permission before returning to his work. He tapped a few keystrokes before swiping a finger across the screen. He repeated the motion several times, scrolling through several pages or images before looking up to Wayne, who seemed lost in thought.

"Sir, I just pulled the video footage from four cameras placed around the main gate of New Scotland Yard," said Tully. "The manhole appears to be in a blind spot."

"Perfect," answered Wayne.

The silence was Wayne's to command. He turned his gaze to the window, looking down at the Thames. The rain had stopped, but the sky showed no signs of change.

"We've got to get to the bottom of this before we get run over by our old chums in MI5." Wayne rumbled.

"They aren't interested already?" asked Burns.

"No," Wayne answered firmly. "And I have no intention of piquing their interest." Wayne looked at his phone for a moment. Burns couldn't tell if Wayne was reading a message or contemplating the one he might have to send. Wayne turned to face Burns.

"This is a missing persons case, and it has to stay in our house, Burns. The Higher Ups won't be having this blow up into... If the shit..." Wayne stopped himself.

"Who knew about the room upstairs?" Burns wondered aloud.

"I did," Wayne answered.

And Aitkens, Burns noted to himself. "So, a tracking device," he offered. "Did anybody search him before he came upstairs?"

"Of course," Wayne wasn't angry, but he was disturbed. His grimace had dragged his eyes down to the floor. "But we'll hear from Inspector Isaac if..." he trailed off.

Burns was excited. He had to step in. "He received a message as I was arriving, and possibly another, or a missed call, later but before he had his aneurysm..."

"Aneurysm?" Wayne asked. "Is that what it was, Doctor Burns?"

"Just a guess, sir," Burns answered. "Symptoms." He shrugged. "When will you know the results of the autopsy?"

"Autopsies are also not your business," was Wayne's cold reply. There was a silent moment while Burns and Tully and Wayne all exchanged looks round the oval table. Burns reached into his pocket and felt the two phones. They made a light clack as he gathered them in his grasp.

"I have his phone, sir. Krutovskiy's phone." He produced the late scientist's phone and displayed in on an open palm.

"Why do you have Krutovskiy's phone?" Wayne was incredulous, but somehow not angry.

"I took it from him," Burns answered. "I didn't think he would be allowed to have it in the building because..."

"I see," said Wayne.

"I was thinking you," waved the phone at Tully, "or Inspector Tellier could probably find out whoever..." Burns smiled sheepishly at Wayne. "Faster if we could just look at it right away, maybe learn something, instead of waiting for forensics to..." Burns concluded his defence and placed the phone on the table, then took a step back. He wasn't worried about the potential repercussions of his actions. Detective Chief Inspector Wayne had been hard to read at times but Burns knew he was a leader that listened and learned, then acted decisively.

Wayne picked up the phone and turned it over in his hand. He tapped the display, which remained black. He gave a look over at Tully, who was totally engrossed in whatever he was watching on his tablet.

"We're actually still more focused on finding Dr Veda," said Wayne flatly.

"I found her!" Tully exclaimed. "HOLMES found the Fox."

"Where?" Both men asked at once, causing Tully to do a double take. He decided to look at neither man before he went on.

"At LCA with a bunch of sales reps and girls in costume selling Estonian bear piss…"

"Really, Tully? Bear piss?" Wayne was nonplussed.

"Really, sir. Tried it at the Beer Fest," Tully made a face of exaggerated disgust. "Yeah, I was there…" he shrugged.

"To be sure, Tully," said Wayne. "Friday night," he nodded encouragingly.

"Check this out," Tully backed his chair away from the table and wheeled round the corner, holding the tablet in the air with his free hand.

He rolled into the space between the two men, tapped and dragged his finger across his iPad. After a short delay a video with sound played on the screen.

"This was posted on Instagram and YouTube around 4 am today." It was a short video clip that captured a group of models in barmaid outfits, most of them blonde, posing for the photographer. To say the costumes were sexy would be an understatement—the push up corsets and short skirts were standard beer-selling gear.

"Posted by one Dale Thomas of London, as in The City Of," Tully declared. "He's a known re-poster, but we can't talk to him. Until…"

Burns guessed why Tully didn't finish his sentence. He assumed it was because DCI Wayne hadn't brought The City of London Police into the investigation. Wayne's reasons didn't matter. There was no chance to find Dr Veda anywhere in The Square Mile. Veda was gone from London, Burns was certain. He wondered again how long it would be before the operation would exceed the capabilities of Wayne's fledgling MCU2.

"And..." Tully paused the video and manipulated the zoom, focusing in on one face. "There's our girl."

It was unmistakably Kaia.

Burns tried to imagine Dr Veda on a private jet, surrounded by Estonian beer hostesses, getting drunk with the bear mascot... But he couldn't. He knew Tully had though, and likely imagined himself in Veda's seat.

"So, is it your suggestion that Dr Veda was taken on board this charter to Tallinn? This beer company is somehow involved?" Wayne sounded like he didn't believe it possible. Burns had a flash recall of a headline about an Estonian Drug Cartel, but it was gone before he could remember the content.

"All we can say is that it appears that Kaia went to Estonia," Tully answered. "The Bear Beer charter was on its way back to Tallinn. It was one of the planes that the tower..." Tully stole a look at Wayne then concluded, "Blennerhassett had to go through the tower's audio to confirm tail numbers and departures. We now have the flight departure confirmed at twenty-three twelve."

"Do we have the passenger list yet?" Wayne asked.

"No sir," answered Tully with a frown. "Not from London City Airport, that we can confirm, and Tallinn's airport authority claims they don't have the authority to transfer electronically any information about Estonian businesses or individual citizens to anyone without getting it in writing from their Ministry of Transport."

"What about Interpol?" Burns asked. "Wouldn't they have access to the information?"

"They would," said Wayne to the window. "I thought Detective Blennerhassett was given access and..." He pulled out his phone and looked at the display for several seconds then started tapping and typing a message.

"He was, sir," answered Tully. "But it seems as though when they initiated the search it started a cascade…" Tully shrugged. "He completed a full search but when they went back into the database to cross reference, the forms were blank, just the empty templates…" he trailed off. "London City Airport has only just now been able to stop all its flight data files from…" Tully's heavy face sagged when he found the word. "Disintegrating." He shook his head in disbelief.

"Whoever disrupted the control tower's server let them have the information long enough to get planes off the ground but as soon as we…" Tully was running his finger around the edge of his iPad. Burns thought he looked edgy. Just then Tully looked up at Burns for a moment before turning to Wayne.

"The first query set off a chain reaction that started erasing all data for the departures, just departures, from twenty-twelve on. Until just now." Tully held his tablet up and angled it to show the display to Burns and Wayne. It looked like a page of code with the exception of two readable entries at the bottom of the page. The last line was the flight details for a charter that had departed ten minutes earlier.

"Wow," Burns muttered. His mind reeled at the level of sophistication that the Other Side seemed to possess. "Talk about covering your tracks. Booby traps and everything," Burns deadpanned. He had to mention it because suddenly it felt like a game. Deactivating the Met's security camera network of London and the scrambled flight information at airport were practical. But setting a trap and wiping the data? *Giving us the finger again*, thought Burns. He reckoned the faceless men on the Other Side were showing off, and it gave Burns all the excuse he needed to hate his opponent as much as he admired them. He quickly wiped the grimace off his face when he realised both men were looking at him.

Tully broke the silence. "IT Guy and his team are all over it but, to be honest, he doesn't sound optimistic." Wayne didn't sound optimistic either, even when he finished. "He did say that this auto-destruct thing gives him something to work with." Wayne did his best to look unimpressed, not intimidated.

"And we're quite certain this is our missing Kaia," Wayne looked out the window again. "This is an extraordinary situation," he said.

"So, we follow the girl?" Burns said it, but somehow he didn't believe it. The question died in the silence, which was cracked by the quiet 'tick-tock' of Burns' phone, telling him he had received a text message. It was from Hilts. The subject line exclaimed:

WE WON!

Burns was considering opening and reading the message when the stillness was suddenly fractured by a loud violin playing a dramatic theme on Tully's phone, which he fumbled a bit before silencing it with a swipe of his thumb. Burns looked at Tully, who was reading the message. For a second, Burns considered the absurd possibility of Hilts sending the same message to Tully. They knew each other, but Burns couldn't imagine Tully on a list of Ravens HC fans in Hilts' phone. He stole a look at Wayne, who was staring at Tully, dispassionately waiting for an explanation. Burns opened and read the message. He smirked at the deliberate misspelling, hearing Hilts' Texan drawl as he read.

Playoffs her we cum!

"OS updates?" Wayne asked both men.

"No, sir," replied Burns. His phone clicked and vibrated again but he ignored it. Tully's face told him he was reading a different message.

"No sir, It's HOLMES," said Tully. "We have more on Kaia." Tully was excited, but he waited for Wayne's approval before going on.

"Do tell," insisted Wayne.

"We found out who the Professor's girlfriend really is," boasted Tully.

Tully was looking at his tablet, opening, scanning, and closing several pages in rapid succession.

"Did HOLMES tell you she's a known terrorist yet?" asked Burns as he closed his phone and returned it to his pocket. Hilts' second message would wait.

Tully pursed his lips. "Pshaw", he mocked. "HOLMES' biometric facial recognition pulled up this as the best match we found so far for Dawson's photo file from last night at the opera, and caught her on the security cam eleven days ago..." Tully paused then added, "in Dr Nicholas Veda's lodgings. The last ten days are um, unavailable." He checked the text again. "She went to school in Estonia. See? Name used to be Vera Fedotenko."

Burns pointed at the photos. "Two schools, same year, two different surnames."

"It appears she attended two different High schools that year," said Tully. "One in a place called Narva when she was Vera Fedotenko and one in Tallinn, where she changed her name to Kaia Rebane." He stopped to read a few more lines, then added grudgingly, "Both private Russian schools."

"Russian? Really?" Burns teased.

"Anyway, this is... she." The first image showed a professional portrait of a young, attractive brunette girl of about fifteen or sixteen years of age in a school uniform. A very nineties hairstyle framed her high cheekbones and smooth, straight jaw line. She had cut her hair shorter and gone blonde in the second photo. It was her eyes, however which were truly striking. A mix of cobalt and ice with shards of turquoise, impossible to ignore. The images from the security camera and Dawson's snaps at the opera didn't capture the luminescence of her eyes, but the facial match was easy to see. Burns imagined Doctor Nicholas Veda fell hard and fast for those peepers. Tully spent some time looking at the photo.

"This was in oh-four," Tully's voice cracked. His attraction to the teenaged beauty was unconcealed. He blushed and muttered, "Wow."

"Just a teenager," said Burns, poking his friend.

"Put it away, Burns," Wayne scolded.

Tully continued. "The caption suggests she was in her last year of school, but we have no record of her graduating, or anything after that for that matter. But get this. Her father was a chemist." Tully's eyes were gliding over the pages as he scrolled through the information with a two-fingered swipe.

"Private schools. Very detailed records, lots in the social pages… but nothing else, no other images of her," Tully didn't hide his disdain. "I guess the internet didn't catch on early in Estonia."

"Chemical engineer? Like in weapons?" asked Burns.

"No, a chemist, you twat," Tully scoffed. "In your language I believe he'd be a pharmacist, like in a drugstore, cowboy. Har, har. He had a little apothecary in Narva, a small city —"

"Just across the river from Russia," Burns interjected.

Tully looked up at Burns. "Right. Two hundred kilometres east of Tallinn. But he may be the same Captain A. Fedotenko we cross-reffed to one who worked in St Pete's in the late eighties at the former Soviet lab run by... this guy." Tully clicked on another tab and opened a viewer with several photos of a sinister looking man of about forty in a Russian military uniform. He dragged one image over all the others so that it filled the screen. It was a digital scan of a photo, which had appeared originally in a former-Soviet military weekly propaganda newspaper. A man in uniform was receiving a medal from another man in uniform. Burns got the gist of the caption, something about recognising an unnamed achievement with pride. He saw the similarity in the eyes of the award-winning junior officer, like Kaia's but with more ice than cobalt. The eyes of the senior officer, Major General Ivanov, were as black as bullet holes at night. If you had to guess which one was the megalomaniac, it might be a saw-off, thought Burns.

"Do we have a name?" asked Wayne.

"That's Papa Fedotenko on the left," Tully answered. "Captain Dr Anton Fedotenko, born in fifty-nine in Murmansk, matches the photo on the Estonian business license from nineteen ninety-nine." Tully looked up at Wayne, who nodded.

"As far as we know, he's still alive and he still owns the apothecary..." Tully tapped the space bar for effect. "That's it so far." He pulled up another window on the left monitor, which set off a set of pop-ups on the far right-hand screen. Each tab had a photo in the top left corner, showing a young man becoming a Russian soldier, rising through the ranks.

"The other fella... Name's Vladimir Konstantin Ivanov," said Tully. "Born 1960. Officially retired as Major General Vladimir Ivanov." He read two more files. So did Burns, recording them in his memory. One was a criminal trespassing charge when Ivanov was a teenager. No conviction, but the record existed, despite

Ivanov's age at the time of the charge or his rank in the military when he retired. It seemed the young ne'er-do-well signed up right after the trial.

"Hmm..." Tully spoke up. "It seems Comrade Ivanov dropped the 'Konstantin' when he became a senior officer in Afghanistan."

"Didn't want his old White Russian roots showing," Burns added. Nobody bit on the historical note, so Burns let it go.

Tully said what they were all thinking. "This looks like a bad guy if I've ever seen one." He turned to Wayne. "Sir, I've got a lot to unpack here. HOLMES is on a roll. Do you want me to go on, or can I..."

"First, you'll send all this to me," said Wayne. "Why don't you take your search down the hall to your home base. You can interface with HOLMES directly," Wayne suggested. Burns caught a laugh in his throat, wondering if the Chief's word choice wasn't a jab at Tully. He stole a quick look at Wayne. It wasn't. Burns found it harder to wipe the smile off his face when he saw Tully's.

"Report..." Wayne stopped and looked at Burns. "Report anything." He waved at Burns. "Take him with you, please."

"Yes, Chief," answered Tully. He started to wheel away from the table then stopped before turning for the door. "Sir, nothing definite, but I don't remember seeing her there. Kaia. At the BeerFest. Not to say that I was looking at all the women but, y'know I wasn't..."

"Discriminating?" Burns offered.

"Yeah, I mean, not just the Estonian ones specifically, y'know? There was lots of interesting costumes..." Tully grinned at the memory.

"To be sure," said Wayne unmoved, ending the conversation with a glance at the glass door and an awkward smile.

"Don't remember seeing her there," said Tully.

Tully wheeled past Burns, who wanted to ask one more question.

"What about the girl?" he asked. "Estonia?" he added. "Okay, two questions," Burns smiled.

Tully stopped at the door. Chief Inspector John Wayne straightened to his full height, inhaling deeply as he rose.

"You've been to Tallinn, have you Burns?" asked Wayne, expecting confirmation.

"Yes sir," Burns blurted. "And Narva. Two summers ago."

"Good to know," was all Wayne said before he turned and stepped to the window.

10:10

Tully was halfway to his own door by the time Burns had stepped out of Wayne's office and closed the door behind him. Burns stood still and drew a deep breath, letting the adrenalin wave recede. The excitement he had felt when Wayne subtly suggested a trip to Estonia might be in his future vanished in the swash when Burns considered the reality of what it might mean to be activated in this particular mission. It meant an extraction. Another one, after all these years as a civilian.

Tully gave a low whistle, pulling Burns toward him with a beckoning wave.

"Coffee's on," Tully called out. Then he reversed his chair away from the door and stopped, as if he was challenging Burns to make a run for it. Tully leaned back casually, pausing to chuckle before engaging the chair forward. He threw his head back as if he were on a speeding motorcycle and slowly glided into his office. Burns sniffed the air. "I can smell it from here, buddy," he lied, smiling. He broke into a trot and reached the door in a few strides.

"Wow," Burns whistled as he entered the office. Tully not only had the coffee on but every square inch of his monitors was covered by files, photos, maps and web pages. Burns wondered how many pieces of the puzzle were on display... and if there were enough to solve it.

"HOLMES had all this on the breakfast table for you?" Burns joked.

"Not everything," Tully insisted. "I made the coffee." He poured himself a refill and gestured to Burns then he wheeled back to his desk. Burns tore his eyes away from the monitors and followed his nose to the fresh pot of coffee. He set his cup down beside the machine and poured the last of the condensed milk in before filling it with Tully's perfectly brewed Indonesian elixir. Burns frowned at Tully, who hadn't turned away from his search.

"Too bad HOLMES can't get you some cream for this," Burns sighed, gesturing with his cup. "Still, beats the hell out of Tim Horton's," Burns offered humbly. Then he quickly deflected. "What's that special ring tone you two have?" he asked. Tully pretended not to be listening as he typed in a few commands on his desktop keyboard and called up another file.

"It's cute that you have your phone set to alert you when HOLMES sends you a message. It's the TV theme song, right?" Tully grunted and Burns scanned the page. There was a list of banks and financial institutions on the left, the rest of the page was empty columns.

"What's his ring tone for you, U2's 'With or Without You'?"

"What?" Tully was reading a message on his phone.

"Sorry, that was the first Irish band I could think of," said Burns. "The Sherlock Theme for him, I get that..." Burns snapped his fingers. "No, wait... Sinead O'Connor, 'Nothing Compares to You!' Burns smiled as if he had made it to the bonus round. "Written by Prince, but..." Burns grinned.

"Fack off, Burns," Tully shrugged. Burns let it drop.

"She doesn't have a bank account," Tully announced. "Not in Europe, no financial trail. She seems to have never used electronic payment for the gym, the hotel, shopping...."

"Didn't take you long to learn that, eh?" said Burns. "And no criminal record?"

"Of course not," was the haughty reply.

"Anywhere?"

"We've just had a reply from Interpol, and yes, no record," Tully asserted.

"Okay," Burns sighed. "Well that's a relief, I guess." He really couldn't blame Tully for having a crush on Kaia, the adult version of Vera, but he decided the teasing would continue as long as Tully saw the humour. He wondered how close he was to that line. He was glad to see Tully had the photo of Kaia at the Royal Opera House, and not the yearbook picture, featured in the lower corner of the centre screen. Easy to recognise, hard to forget. Burns wondered if anyone ever asked her name twice... and how long she had been a ghost.

"Well, if I end up rescuing her, I'll put in a good word for you, my friend," Burns promised with a pat on the shoulder.

"You better," Tully chuckled. Then he turned to Burns and shrugged. "But I dunno, Charles. Been a while since you've done anything like that, isn't it?"

"Touché!" Burns winced and grinned.

Tully returned his focus to the three monitors over his desk. A single window emerged from the stack of open tabs on the left screen.

"So, there's Fedotenko," said Tully as he pointed at the open windows on the left. "Yeah," answered Burns. "Vera Fedotenko's father."

"Can we just keep calling her Kaia?" Tully asked. "It's just that it's more... y'know?"

"Sure thing. Kaia," Burns smiled. "Keepin' the fantasy alive for ya, buddy."

"Cheers," Tully nodded happily before striking up again. "But he seems to have disappeared from St Petersburg sometime in the spring of ninety-nine." Tully flipped the images back and forth between files.

"Seems to?" asked Burns.

"Seems to, meaning the Russian records are always ninety per cent classified — or wiped," Tully declared. "The same year he opened the apothecary in Narva." Tully shot a long, dull look at Burns and spoke slowly. "The-drug-store."

"Pharmacy, cowboy," quipped Burns.

"Right," Tully agreed. "Anyway, a few years later, there's his girl in high school, and that's it. Nothing more of her anywhere... Nice, huh?"

"Or him," answered Burns absently. He made the connection. A former Soviet officer leaves the military a few years after the wall comes down and starts a business. Licensed to dispense drugs.

"What about the other fella?" Burns asked.

"Him, we know less about," was Tully's short answer.

"Makes sense," said Burns. "Judging from his rank and authority... At Ivanov's level, the dirtier they are, the thinner the paper trail." Burns stared at the images HOLMES had found. None were surveillance photos, and only two weren't identification pictures. The photo together with Fedotenko at the award ceremony and a similarly official photo capturing a smiling General Ivanov at the opening of a health sciences facility in St Petersburg in June 1986. He was tall, almost Rasputin-tall, and well built. Not tall enough to have to duck his head in a doorway but wide enough to fill it.

"Au contraire," exclaimed Tully. "The non-conviction, as a teen?"

"Yeah, and nothing else," said Burns. "The lab — "

"Right," Tully cut in. "In most of the files I've seen, the details on the lab are also very sketchy. The press declared they were doing medical research, but the Intelligence guess is they were making chemical weapons. Can't be sure, of course. That ol' Iron Curtain, y'know..." Tully chuckled. "Of course, MI6 would know more..."

"Yeah," Burns agreed.

"Mostly chemical weapons, so there's that," Burns offered.

"Nice," said Tully.

"I mean, it's clear they were making chemical weapons," Burns insisted. "They used them. I saw..." Burns didn't need to see any memories of atrocities. He been told the ones that died did so unpleasantly. The survivors he had seen were dying horribly. He shifted his view to the blinds on the window across the room.

"But we don't know for sure if they were experimenting with biological agents."

"We don't know for sure, right," said Tully.

Burns felt his suspicion twitch.

"I mean, if Wayne knows any of this, the HO knows. Shouldn't MI5 or MI6 be in on this already?"

"He does. It does. And they're not." Tully spun his chair round to face Burns and declared, "Look, Wayne has the complete trust of the Home Office and the Secretary herself. The MI's don't."

"Bottom line..." Before Burns could ask, Tully cut him off. "If Wayne chooses to keep the rest of the Met's involvement at street level," Tully breathed, "there are reasons."

Burns fixed on the photos of the Russian military man with the coal black eyes. A memory flashed. Major General Vladimir Ivanov was on a list.

"Him, I know," said Burns.

"He looks knowable," observed Tully, glancing briefly at the St Petersburg photo before he returned to his searchlight scan across the trio of monitors.

"Hang on," said Tully. "It looks like Vera's dad may have died in that accident at the lab in St. Petersburg in 1999."

A tab on the left screen expanded. It was an obituary, of sorts, listing the brave comrades that died in the explosion or burned to death in the fire. Fourth from the top, Captain Fedotenko, Anton was listed as one of the casualties of the regrettable accident.

"The suspected Russian chemical weapons facility," Burns nodded. "Ivanov's lab."

"Indeed," Tully crooned. He pointed at the lack of current information accompanying the photos on the screen. "Either he died, or he didn't and moved to Estonia. Not a clue where he is." Tully looked hurt, frustrated by the confusion.

"And the rest," he announced, "is mystery."

"Unless..." Burns stopped. He wondered if Fedotenko was on a list anywhere.

"DCI Wayne has reached out," said Tully. "We have an—" He caught himself. "Access when we need it." Tully exhaled, exasperated, as if Burns was a child in the backseat and had been asking the same question every two minutes.

Burns stepped back. He took two sips of coffee, savouring the second before swallowing. He watched as Tully went back to the work of navigating a path. Burns smiled. He figured Wayne was right when he activated a search without raising alarms anywhere, within the Met or through public channels, even if it was for selfish reasons. The attack on the Met's communication system justified an embargo on the dispersal of information. Burns wondered if the Met really had got their breach contained, or if they were just too dependent on the integrity of the internet, of all things, and unable to function without it, so they were back online. "Oh, the irony," he mused aloud.

Here we go," Tully suddenly lit up. "Look at this!"

Burns saw it. Tully enlarged the brewery's webpage. The banner showed a polar bear on a brown plastic one-litre bottle.

"Plastic!'" Burns clicked his tongue. "Just when you thought the world was learning to use less plastic."

"Yeah, who's gonna save the beluga?" Tully was almost beside himself with exasperation. "Looks alright in a glass but…"

"You can't judge a beer by its bottle," offered Burns.

"Yes, Charles, yes you can." Tully sighed heavily. He shook his head then brightened again when he clicked the tab showing the Bear's latest tweet. It announced an event at the Conference Center Hotel and Spa. Tully beamed. "The Beer Girls will be there." He opened another window on the main viewer, scanning the hotel's homepage. After a few clicks he sighed again.

"Sixteen hundred," said Tully.

"Starting early," Burns added.

"It's Saturday," Answered Tully.

"Saturday Night in Estonia," Burns chuckled.

10:12

Nicholas Veda was doing his best not to panic.

He squeezed his eyes shut again and tried to force his way back into his last waking memories from before he had awakened here, wherever here was, trying to piece together what happened and why he and Kaia were being held here.

"Kaia," he said aloud. He felt a ripple of embarrassment swell into a wave of shame that pounded in his ears. Kaia. Nicholas hadn't even thought of her until just that moment. The same shame he felt when Ravi was crippled by the gang of football hooligans. And he watched, helplessly.

Veda felt sober. For the first time he knew that what his eyes saw was happening in real time. Outside the window on the far wall, it was another cloudy day in London. Veda could see ships moving past on the Thames.

He needed to recall the events prior to waking up in this place. He tried to slow his thoughts, one memory at a time, putting things into a sequence. Like tracing back through the steps of a failed experiment, he tried to make sense of the situation. It was a Friday. Gym Day. He remembered being back at his flat, getting ready to go to the opera. Kaia arrived quite early, having come straight from her dance rehearsal. She had brought her evening gown in a garment bag, said she wanted to shower in his bath since the hot water was so much more reliable. Nicholas remembered hopefully wondering how long it would be before they were living together. Kaia had convinced him to join her in the shower. First, she lathered up her own body, teasing her nipples with the sponge, then she squeezed the soap suds out of it between her breasts, letting the foam trickle slowly down her taut belly before turning to face the stream of water and rinsing her body clear. Then she turned her efforts to getting him lathered up. Suddenly Nicholas smashed back to his situation— bound to a chair somewhere. He felt guilty for a moment because of the stirring in his groin as he remembered how they had sex standing up, a first for him, beginning in the shower then climaxing against the cold tile wall in his en suite bath, the heat of her body crushing him joyously.

The sound of a door closing somewhere outside the room shook him from his reverie. Nicholas opened and closed his eyes. The sound was behind him, he couldn't guess how far away it might be. He wondered if he had been asleep and dreaming again. He listened intently, expecting to hear voices, footsteps, but none came in the silence. The small room he sat in seemed airtight and his view of the larger laboratory was limited to the narrow perspective provided by the half-frosted window. He closed his eyes, wishing he could hear the city outside…

It took him a few more deep breaths to refocus on his replay. Kaia looked stunning in her whispery gown with its open back and her long dancer's legs flashing, exposed to the hip with each stride.

Dawson had dropped them at the entrance and went to the car park. They snacked on hors d'oeuvres in the foyer before the curtain. They asked Dawson about the opera, Henry Purcell's "Dido and Aeneas". They joked and laughed about "famous English Operas". He remembered the night at the opera, but when was it?

Veda's body tensed and his adrenal glands fired a flash of electricity that coursed through his body. By reflex he pulled against the restraints. They seemed loose enough to offer some movement, but his muscles were almost instantly fatigued by the effort it took, and he sagged back into the chair. He tried to speak but only coughed out a single weak, dry hack. His mouth was parched, his tongue felt dry and heavy and thick. He listened to the sound of a single pair of footsteps as they approached in the hallway. Veda closed his eyes and counted the steps as they neared, passing through a door behind him and to his left—one, two, three, four, five, then they stopped. A pause, as he imagined the person was now standing beside Kaia. She didn't make a sound. Then the shoes shuffled three and a half steps and they were next to him. Nicholas heard the sound of what could have been a plastic IV bag being squeezed, then the small plastic ratchet being turned to open the flow. A moment later he became aware of a cold rush from the IV stuck into his left forearm. They must be dosing me again, he thought. He fought to keep his eyes closed, careful not to wince, breathing slowly. There was a silence, so heavy it was almost damp, and then the shoes were walking away in the vapour. The door opened and closed, only now it was as if this was all happening in a radio play being broadcast over a tiny transistor radio like the one his father kept on the shelf behind the cash register in his little shop. The final scene ended that way, footsteps fading out. Then they were listening to a cricket match, and how proud Nicholas' father was of his brother Ravi...

Suddenly, everything was clear. The halo of light that had circled his view of the world faded and disappeared. Everything in the periphery had shape. Veda recognised a crate standing between two long white tables and inhaled sharply. The only sounds in this vacuum were the ones he made. He was calm, his breathing relaxed and even. He opened his eyes. He was in London. In a new lab.

Nicholas Veda would not be a coward. He gripped the arms of the chair and tried to use his forearms as levers, pulling at the nylon straps. They pressed into his flesh but seemed to stretch before it became painful enough to stop. He wriggled his wrist, trying to slip his right hand free. His strength faded before the pain forced him again to stop. He decided to rest and try again until he freed himself.

"I'm not going to work here, and I'm not going to die here!" Veda shouted at the echo. Veda made a plan. With options. If... no, when he gets his hands free, he will tear himself free from the leg bonds and...and... run? What if Gerhardt Noack comes back? Fight? Subdue? Kill?

"He's coming."

There was a hint of pride in his voice.

"Who, The Duke?" Burns guessed.

"Yeah," Tully nodded. "Right." He smiled. "He's coming here."

"I take it the boss doesn't drop in often." Burns smiled. "Shouldn't you make more coffee?" Burns downed the last swallow in his cup, eyeing the dregs in the coffee pot. Tully was still too pleased with himself.

"I told him I couldn't leave," said Tully. "Said he could come round the corner if he —" Tully cut himself off as the door opened with a knock. Wayne entered with a waving salute, offering a serious smile and nod before he stepped to where Burns and Tully were pondering the tri-folded puzzle in front of them.

"Gentlemen," Wayne announced himself. His voice always seemed louder when he first spoke. Burns reckoned it was Wayne's deep tone as much as the forceful way he spoke. Wayne seemed relaxed as he went on evenly.

"Mr Tully. What have you gleaned from those files from our friends?"

Tully looked back at the monitors, then at his iPad, then his phone. Then he turned to Wayne. "Not a, uh, not a great deal of actionable intel, sir."

The Russian official information on Vladimir Ivanov had been enough to tweak Burns' suspicion, and Tully's too, he guessed. The link that Wayne had sent to Tully included intelligence reports from MI6 and Interpol confirming the manufacture and use of chemical weapons in the Eighties, but provided little more than speculation about the activities in Ivanov's lab in St Petersburg in the years since the collapse of the Soviet Union.

"Not only is it unclear..." Tully flipped through the tabs on the monitor, closing several. "Seems like we stopped looking when the Wall came down," he shook his head.

"Not everyone stopped looking," Burns half-mumbled.

"Bottom line, we don't know where he is," was Tully's final statement.

"Or if he's relevant," said Wayne.

"And no data for the time that passed between then and the explosion in ninety-nine..." Tully grumbled. "Wiped."

"What about Mary?" Burns lobbed the question at Tully, who let it roll by.

"The General retired three months after the explosion in St Petersburg," said Tully.

"And disappeared," added Burns wistfully.

The two men stared in silence, scanning the three screens. Tully's phone pinged a two-toned door chime. He read the text message and smiled.

"What about the pig, sir?" asked Burns.

"Do you think he's in Estonia?" asked Tully.

"Who, Veda, Ivanov or the pig?" Wayne asked.

"The pig was a she," answered Burns. "Mary."

"Tallinn Tower is still withholding," Wayne rumbled. "I've put in a call."

"Meanwhile?" Burns tried to make it sound like a question.

"Can we send someone to Estonia?" Wayne asked the question, knowing the two men both wanted the answer. He held their gazes until he turned away and stepped to the window. Then he split the vertical blinds wide enough to offer a view and stared out the window looking east, past the London Eye, toward Estonia.

"They refuse to release anything to us digitally," said Wayne heavily. "We need someone to get them to open up."

"That seems a bit..." Burns stopped short of saying *dickish*.

"They were told about the breach here when the request was made," Wayne looked at Tully. "I had to ask the HO to reach out to the Estonian authorities on our behalf, to insure their cooperation." Wayne sullenly remained at the window. "So, if we send someone to them, they'll hand over the passengers lists we asked for?" Burns asked. "Sounds simple."

"Can we, sir?" Tully asked. No one spoke for a time. Then Wayne closed the blinds and turned round to face the two men.

"Well, here's what we can do," said Wayne. "Burns, you're not officially activated yet."

"It is unfortunate. I know, sir," Burns replied. Wayne almost smiled again.

"What is unfortunate is that we're short of manpower here," Wayne admitted. Wayne's expression dropped, the corners of his mouth hung lower for a moment then flattened as he pursed his lips and swallowed the thought.

"They've been made aware of our request," said Wayne. "And your imminent arrival."

"My arrival?" Burns lifted his eyebrows, mouth open in surprise. "Does this mean my transfer and rank have been made official, sir?"

"Well, no, not in so many words, no." Wayne held up his hand, halting Burns' question. "You would be travelling to Tallinn as a tourist," Wayne insisted. "But on a mission."

"What about Detective Sergeant Blennerhassett. He is a Detective Sergeant, after all."

"He's following up on something else he spotted out of line at LHR."

"And we're looking for Veda on a beer company's corporate charter?"

"He may have travelled to Estonia," Burns allowed. "With Kaia Rebane or Fedotenko, but I can't see him pulling this..."

"Unless she totally flipped his lid," Tully offered.

"That seems even harder to picture than Veda being drugged and dragged aboard."

"By armed assailants," Burns smirked. "That wouldn't tweet well."

"Right," said Tully. "Guy with a bag over his head in handcuffs doesn't sell beer," He pointed at Kaia's image. "But she does."

"To you, maybe," Burns teased. Then he turned to Wayne and shifted gears. "Wouldn't we also be looking for the missing lab equipment?"

"Yes we would, Burns," was Wayne's cold reply. He didn't offer any more than a long look and a flat grin. "Thank you."

"What we're looking for, Mr Burns, is positive ID on Dr Veda and or Ms Rebane. Firstly."

Burns didn't care to ask about how Wayne expected to explain Burns' activation, on a mission abroad for Christ's sake. He had to believe that DCI Wayne didn't need to ask anyone for clearance.

Burns had already mapped out a reconnaissance plan. Customs first, then the charter company's hangar, or if Customs sent him that way, to the brokers' warehouses on the edge of the airport grounds, out near the lake. Daylight would hold, but making it there before the close of business on a Saturday? Burns gripped his phone, closed the map and checked the time. He hadn't realised until that moment that his plan was all about proving that Veda and his lab were not in

Estonia. Burns wanted to say it was a bad idea, that it wasn't worth it. Then he felt his eyes drawn over to the image of Vladimir Konstantin Ivanov on the far screen.

"Ryanair has a flight leaving Stansted at 13:35," said Wayne. "It's the only direct flight until tomorrow morning," he added. Even Wayne seemed to take a moment to "Why don't you take the weekend off, Burns?"

"And fly to Tallinn, maybe?" Burns played along.

"I can't very well send Tully here, can I?" Wayne answered. He shot a prickly look at Burns. Then he turned to Tully. Up came the serious smile again. "You can't leave right now," he said. "And I can't spare anyone else."

"So, I'd be..." Burns let it hang but Wayne said nothing. Tully offered an envious grin. "Free to look around," Burns concluded.

"One bit of official business to tend to," said Wayne. "A meeting with the airport authorities at Tallinn International," he shrugged. "Then a weekend free..."

"And of course, if we should come up with any ideas for sightseeing..." Tully piped in. He stole a look at Wayne, who seemed to concur.

"After all, I'm only on call, officially," Burns shrugged. "Sounds like fun."

"Look, Burns," said Wayne. He clasped his hands together then opened them at Burns. "Your choice, of course, Burns, but you can appreciate the situation. We need to see the passengers list from that flight. Estonian Immigration and passport control have refused to release the photos for identification of our missing persons, claiming internet security risks. All they've said is that all twenty-seven passengers were EU citizens and confirmed Estonian residents, and presented no red flags."

"Meaning no profiling."

"Huh," Tully scoffed. "Won't be so easy travelling to the EU for much longer."

"Hopefully they have a hard copy of your manifest, and cargo list," said Wayne.

"If there was any," added Burns. He turned to Wayne and changed his tone, trying to sound grateful. "I was hoping you wouldn't keep me on the side lines forever."

"My sincerest hope is that I don't need you for anything else," replied Wayne.

Burns was convinced Wayne wasn't trying to get rid of him, that he believed there were answers in Tallinn. Burns could only hope so. He also shared Wayne's hope for him not being needed for anything more than a little reconnoitring.

"We'll keep in touch," said Wayne. It was an order.

"Yes sir," answered Burns. "I'll call you. As soon as I touch down."

"I can wait until after you send the files," said Wayne.

Wayne's jaw muscles clenched. He shifted his glare from Burns to the window, watching the rain trailing down the pane. Finally, he turned back, almost smiled at Burns and nodded toward the door. Burns returned the nod in assent.

"Fabulous," said Wayne. "Enjoy your trip, happy trails, and all that. Don't forget to take some snaps to show us when you get back. On Monday, right?"

"Hopefully," answered Burns. He stood at the door and waved his phone. "Just read on Trip Advisor about two hundred and fifty-seven things to do in Tallinn, so…"

"Leave the comedy to the professionals, Burns," said Wayne. "And keep me in the loop." He tilted his gaze and gave Burns a quizzical look. "Where are you going to start?"

"The airport. I'll call you when I've got more," answered Burns. "Sir."

"Brilliant," said Wayne. "I've arranged a cruiser to get you home to pack your bag, but they'll not be taking you to the airport, being as it's an unofficial excursion. See the nice man at the desk downstairs."

"Thank you, sir," Burns grinned and left, waving a 'thumbs up' at Tully.

Burns used his time in the backseat of the patrol car to open his search for anything about Major General Vladimir Konstantin Ivanov that might put him in Tallinn, and connect him to Dr Veda, but to negative results. Frustrated, he turned his search to social commentary articles about crime in Estonia. A memory led him to refine the search to Estonian drug trade. He had seen the stories before. Manufactured pharmaceuticals—some patented, some not—had flooded the streets. They described increased distribution in Europe and worldwide, centred in Estonia, with possible Russian sources. But no names, not even a gang name or Russian Mafia reference... A new psychoactive cocktail was reported in a 2016 article in a science journal. The story told of a powerful stimulant with what was described to have 'varying levels of hallucinogenic effects among its users'.

"Viagra meets LSD," Burns mused aloud. He saved the page and closed his phone.

The plan was simple, with one possible problem, as far as Burns could see. Burns had got over the idea it might be an illegal action. He figured Wayne wouldn't involve the locals, or even Interpol, unless their cooperation was absolutely necessary. Burns was okay with that. He planned to avoid local law enforcement as much as possible, anyway. And it didn't matter that by volunteering for the unofficial assignment it meant he was unprotected in every way, if anything should hit the fan. Burns couldn't see that happening, at least not at the airport. He couldn't escape the feeling that Veda wouldn't show up in the database. It couldn't be that simple. Even if he'd used forged documents or an alias, his dark skin would stick out like a sore thumb in that part of Europe, someone would have ID'd him when the first photo of Dr Veda And the Model went round. Of course, Wayne had got the photo out quickly in London, however he couldn't say how far or how responsive the international outreach had been.

Burns stepped into his flat and switched on the kitchen light. It lit the studio softly from behind the partition wall between the entry and the kitchen. He kicked off his shoes and pulled the door shut, hung his jacket on the chair and stepped into the bedroom. He had to shuffle sideways around the queen-sized bed and reach the Swedish wardrobe that stood beside the small bay window. Burns made a note to put the bed on ebay and go back to a double, even if he only slept there half the time, and always alone.

He pulled the wardrobe's sliding door open, activating the small overhead lamp inside. A black metal cabinet had been squeezed into the closet, framed by a set of drawers on one side and a suspended rod holding Burns' thin collection of jackets and trousers on the other. Burns spun the dial on the lock, recalling the combination he had memorised a lifetime ago. The steel doors opened with a whine in fey protest. Burns pulled out the lock box he bought half that lifetime ago, when he left the military, and punched the code on the keypad. The red LED went green and Burns clicked open the hasp. He flipped the case on the bed, checked the contents and folded it closed. He had used the Glock last week at the range, along with Lil' Ruger, for an hour in the VR simulator. The Glock had performed with expected reliability despite its relative inactivity in recent years. It had been fired, disassembled, cleaned and re-assembled.

"One hundred per cent confidence," Burns declared as he replaced the weapons in the case.

He opened the drawer on the centre shelf inside the cabinet and retrieved his identification, all of it, and flipped open his oversized travel wallet. Then he slipped his passport under the clear plastic on the right and the Met and military ID cards into their slots on the left. Lastly, he tucked his firearms licenses and weapons permits under the passport. Burns had travelled commercially with weapons exactly four times before, but never when he was on a mission. Burns had always travelled in official vehicles — by land, air and sea — for every mission, official or unofficial. It was never better than coach, but always much simpler.

He knew enough to call ahead to the Airport Authority at Stansted and notify the firearms officer of his imminent departure. His first search for the Firearms Control Bureau on the Tallinn International Airport website gave the airport's street address, punctuated with E-22. It didn't appear on the map of the airport, but it wasn't a very big airport. Burns found the Oversized Baggage Claims Area in the 'E' sector of the terminal and guessed it would be nearby. He laughed at his impulse to pick up his guns on the way to meet the Security Manager, a Mr J. Koppel.

☐

Burns surrendered his gun to the control officer at Stansted and boarded the plane with his weathered, brown satchel as carry-on luggage. It was just big enough to hold three changes of socks and underwear, three t-shirts, a dark green wool pullover he had had since his last winter in Kosovo, and a pair of black cargo pants, all rolled in tight cylinders and laid out in neat layers, leaving plenty of space for his travel-sized toiletries pouch, and the gun box he would have to retrieve from the authorities in Tallinn.

He boarded the plane and saw he had lucked out. No other passenger chose a seat in the exit aisle. He pulled all the slack out of the seat belt and buckled it, then he stretched out and nestled his head against the bulkhead. For the better part of the next three hours Burns would wrestle himself to sleep, he knew, trying to clear his mind.

The flight was rather smooth and the droning engines served their purpose. Burns managed to meditate to a near-deep sleep, despite the hour. Somewhere in the open space Burns spoke to Tully through the ether, asking him to find more on Ivanov. When the captain switched off the seatbelt sign, Burns turned on his phone and started writing a message to Tully. He stopped when he realised he wasn't ready to send a quick query. He wanted to open a dialogue on more than one topic, and questions still seemed to outnumber answers. Burns decided that could wait until he had a few more answers of his own.

PART THREE:
SATURDAY AFTERNOON

17:00 (19:00 LOCAL)

The first answer Burns got in Tallinn was voicemail. The number Wayne gave him for the Security Directorship went straight to a brief message told in three languages: Estonian, Russian and English. Burns announced himself as Charles Burns, London Metropolitan Police.

"Mr Koppel, I've just arrived in Tallinn and I'm on my way to your office." Burns caught his tone. It would either sound simple and direct or be taken as a threat, depending on the health of the Security Manager's ego. Burns back-pedalled and closed with a friendly, "See you soon." *Friendly enough.*

Burns considered charming the younger flight attendant with a little broken Estonian, asking her where he could retrieve his gun. But he didn't even like the sound of it in English, so he left off the idea of asking the flight crew directions to anywhere except the Starbucks. Fresh coffee in hand, Burns headed for the terminal's main exit. He spotted a porter returning his trolley to the rack. He smiled as the older man turned round.

"*Tere,*" Burns glanced at the badge, "Jaanus."

Jaanus answered with a hint of Cambridge in his Estonian accent. "Hallo, sir. How can I help you?"

"Which way to Gun Control?"

"Ah!" The spry little senior somehow made the uniform look suave, his bearing almost regal. Jaanus gestured like a showman toward the northern end of the corridor. "You must enter from outside," he said with another grand sweep that ended with a bent hand, simulating the required exit and turn.

"*Tanan sind vaga,*" said Burns with a smile and nod of gratitude.

"You're most welcome, sir," answered Jaanus with a slight bow.

Burns phone rang as he stepped outside. It came up a local area code and no name. He answered on the third ring.

"Burns here."

"Hello, Officer Burns. This is Miss Eliise Oja calling from the office of the manager, Mr Koppel. You called earlier to say you were…"

"On my way, yes," Burns answered.

"Yes, we have a meeting time for you at nine-fifteen pm."

"Nine-fifteen?" Burns repeated.

"Yes, twenty-one fifteen, local time," she answered. "Does it suit you?"

Burns looked down the length of the glass wall to the car rental vendors at the near end of the terminal.

"Perfectly," Burns smiled and looked out at the administration building. It was maybe three hundred metres away as the crow flies, but the crow would have to fly over two fences and cross a lot of pavement airside.

"It looks like I'll need to rent a car just to get to your office from the terminal anyway," he chuckled lightly. He would have time to find the Customs office and maybe the charter company's hangar, if need be, before meeting Miss Oja and Mr Koppel. "Tell me, Miss Oja. Are your customs people holding anything from flight CR 1017?"

"That would be, um easy to check," she answered.

"Excellent," said Burns. He waited, trying to decide if Miss Oja's calling him "Officer Burns" was something that needed to be addressed.

"I'll… check that now," Eliise stuttered slightly. Burns heard her fingers tapping on a keyboard. A moment later the sweet voice returned. "No, Officer Burns," she said.

"Customs cleared CR 1017 at six o'clock this morning."

"That's fine," Burns answered smoothly. "You just saved me a trip. *Tanan sind vaga.*"

"*Sa oled väga teretulnud,* Officer Burns!" Eliise giggled.

"See you soon, then," said Burns.

"Yes," she answered.

"And it's just Burns," he mumbled.

"*Vabandust mind?*" Eliise asked apologetically.

"My name is Charles Burns," he offered humbly.

"Oh, I am Eliise Oja," she answered. "Cheers!"

"Cheers!" Burns answered heartily and rang off with a lingering smile. The curiosity fell over Burns' eyes and creased his forehead when he turned back to the entry marked Firearms Security in Estonian, Russian and English. The young man in uniform at the counter inside looked bored and angry. Burns had more Russian conversations stored in his memory than Estonian, but he would give it a go.

"*Kas teil on tore õhtu?*" Burns grinned, remembering the barista who had asked him twice. "Are you having a nice evening?" Burns grinned, setting it up.

"No," came the short retort.

Burns wondered if it was his pronunciation or simple habit whenever a local answered in English when Burns wanted to converse in the local language.

"Working overtime?" Burns sounded less optimistic and more familiar at once. Burns nodded at the clock on the wall and frowned sympathetically.

"My shift is over forty-eight minutes ago," the young man stated, his English thickly weighted with anger. Burns figured to displace it.

"*Kaua plaanite oodata...* How long do you plan to wait for...?"

"Lecky, the bastard," said the officer. "I have to wait," he complained. "There are twelve more landings that I might have paperwork for."

"If he doesn't show up soon," said Burns. Then he abruptly changed his demeanour and placed his paperwork on the counter and smiled.

"*Siin on minu.* Here's mine." Burns unfolded the stamped documents and turned them for the officer to read. Burns smiled, but with less sympathy. Back to business.

"Charles Burns," he confirmed by resting, not tapping a finger above the signature. "My ID?" He produced his wallet and placed it next to the paper.

The young officer responded and finally rose from his seat. Without giving Burns or the documents more than a brief glance, he stepped out of view behind a wall and returned a moment later with Burns' gun case.

"Would you like to open it here?" the young officer asked.

"What is your name?" Burns answered.

"Rebane, Mr Burns. Officer Robert Rebane." He offered his hand. Burns took it and smiled.

"Well, yes I will open it here, thank you, Officer Rebane." Burns knew it was a fairly common name, but he had to ask.

"Have you got a sister, Robert?" Burns tried not to sound too creepy.

"No. Four brothers. Me smallest," Robert shrugged.

Burns could see it was the truth. Burns had an unsettled moment where he allowed himself to mumble aloud, "That'd be weird" as he imagined Kaia as formerly one of Robert's brothers. He looked at Robert for a moment and concluded there was enough visible genetic evidence to suggest no relation. Robert was short and rather dumpy. Burns couldn't say how much was influenced by the government officer's lifestyle, but they couldn't be more physically different. And while Burns allowed it wouldn't be impossible for them to share a father, there were no obvious similarities facially speaking. Although Robert's eyes were also blue, they had none of the glow.

"You look tired," Burns offered sympathy again, in English. He opened the case and checked its contents quickly, thoroughly. He changed his tone again. "I'm not sure how long I'll be here, to be honest, Robert."

"Me, too," Robert answered hopelessly.

"Well, I hope I don't see you later," Burns smiled. "But I'm glad to hear you'll wait for me if Lecky doesn't show up." Burns made the expectation clear with the last line. Robert nodded obediently.

"We stay open. Until last plane."

Burns let out a small snicker and wondered what the young man would do if he were to load the Glock and strap it on before heading out the door.

The car hire companies occupied a long low building a few hundred metres away at the end the airport terminal. The first car rental agency was also the first alphabetically, Burns noticed. The logo was dimly lit above and behind a short, unmanned counter inside the otherwise darkened reception cubicle, but a light was on behind the door at the rear. Burns tried the door but it was locked. He shook the door to make it rattle rather than knock. No answer. Then he spotted the intercom and pressed the 'call' button. The sound of a phone ringing was interrupted by a static click and a female voice stated the agency hours of operation in Estonian. After the emergency numbers the woman switched to English announced herself as the company.

Then she laboured on, mechanically describing the customer's options.

"*If you are returning a car… Drop your kiss in the box to your right.*"

Burns took his thumb off the button and frowned up at the sign. "I remember when you used to try harder."

The next office was smaller, and so was the brand. Burns guessed they were local. That suited him fine, and the young man behind the counter inside seemed truly excited to see Burns approach the door. He reminded Burns of a dog, happy to see its owner and knowing it was "walkies time". This guy was a very big dog, built like a Rottweiler, with a number one cut that glistened with hair product, or sweat. A two-metre-tall Rottweiler, Burns mused. Hopefully just as smart.

The clip-on crimson necktie hung like a tongue on the charcoal shirt, barely reaching below the expansive ribcage. It seemed like the uniform was for a man closer to Burns' size, x-large, and not this young gym rat.

'Welcome to GoNow Rentals and Leasing," The clerk delivered the greeting with an accent that made Burns more curious. Just a few words, but Burns heard it. Fake accent, like an American doing Russian. Burns called him on it and asked him straight out.

"American?"

"Studied there," the Rottweiler answered with a smile, then quickly deflected. "You, too?"

Burns saw truth and lie. *Just making conversation?*

"Canada," said Burns, ignoring the surprised expression on the Rottweiler's face. Then he turned and looked out the window and asked quickly in Estonian if GoNow had anything bigger than his Nokija.

"I can get you into a Passat equivalent Skoda." *It was a guess.* Burns didn't let the mask slip, keeping his suspicions in check.

"A Passat Skoda will be fine," he smiled, feigning ignorance. The young man located the proper form and presented it to Burns, sliding it on the counter.

"You just need to fill this out."

Burns contemplated his instant distrust as he completed the registration form. He had always rationalised trusting his instincts easily, simply because they never let him down. Never. He had a knack for sensing imminent threat, and he knew there wasn't a risk present. The rental agent Rottweiler posed no danger. Whatever his reasons for being in Tallinn were, they couldn't involve Burns. Still, Burns maintained his distance, keeping the brute in front and outside his own kill zone as they walked across the parking lot to the car.

"You have the full coverage, so do we need to do an inspection?"

"Not necessary," Burns waved. "As long as the tyres are good and the tank's full."

"It's full," the agent answered and handed over the key. "Be sure to return it full, please."

"Will do,"' Burns answered. "*Tanan*."

"Enjoy your stay in Estonia!" The agent gave a wave as Burns closed the door, which Burns acknowledged with a blithe 'thumbs up'. The agent looked back once, as casually as he could, as he trotted back to the terminal entrance.

Burns opened the navigation panel on the dashboard display and typed in a search for the charter company's hangar. The pleasant Midlands female voice announced the destination as the route lit up.

"Regio Baltic Airways."

"Thank you, Dierdre," Burns replied.

He had called the voice Dierdre instead of *Dear*, ever since one night in Istanbul. He had been in the habit of answering the navigator's static directions with a "Thank you, Dear." that grew more sarcastic each time Istanbul's road system funnelled them into another labyrinth, prompting another pleasant suggestion to make a U-turn. Especially when she repeated herself.

His driver was local but not Turkish, as he remembered. Clio was from Romandy, Switzerland and worked for one of the world's largest tobacco companies. Burns had successfully petitioned her to drive him to his hotel because he had drunk too much raki. He liked the way she attacked him for using the word "dear" as a way of demeaning the woman who gave her voice to help us find our destination. So, the female navigator became Deirdre. Unfortunately, Clio enjoyed one of her company's more pungent European brands and couldn't manage to go more than an hour anywhere without lighting up. Burns only let her drive him home once.

Burns took another look at the map and tapped the screen to mute Dierdre. He took a moment to adjust himself and the controls in the cockpit then pulled out and headed for the exit.

17:40 (19:40 LOCAL)

Burns spotted the black Audi sedan exiting the rental lot as he checked his mirrors. While it could be a rental it was definitely luxury class. It also lacked the tell-tale branded license plate holder.

Then he saw the passenger point at him. The traffic passed, and there was no need for Burns to wait, but he held his position at the intersection. The driver's face was in shadow but Burns saw the passenger clearly, long enough to impress a memory. Aviator sunglasses and American hair, coiffed into a black ridge high above a broad forehead. Instinctively, Burns drove away from his original target, turning left instead of right toward the administration building and the charter carriers at the far eastern end of the airport. He went the long way around the metro station and out to the main thoroughfare back toward the terminal. He kept pace with the traffic for the brief dash to the south gate then drove into the "Kiss & Fly" lane and passed slowly through the airport. Burns watched as the black Audi turned into the circle behind him. But they didn't turn into the VIP parking. They turned left into the drop-off lane and out of sight. Burns decided to wait until he saw the Audi exit, hopefully with only the driver. He kept driving at the same speed, crawling along as if he was still figuring out the navigation and couldn't leave the airport. A moment later the Audi appeared and stopped suddenly. Burns knew it was because they saw him. He laughed at them, but he guessed they couldn't see it much less hear it. He had never been tailed before, that he knew of, but it never seemed like the guys following in the movies were this bad.

Still, Burns wasn't about to try and lose them in the city or on a high-speed chase out of town. Even if he did know his way around Tallinn, which he only knew from maps, he didn't have the time. Miss Oja was expecting him, and he hadn't been to customs to confirm that Veda and his lab didn't come to Estonia in boxes. Burns checked his watch, then he looked at the shopping centre that Deirdre had flagged as a Point Of Interest, less than two hundred metres away. It was a good thing he had muted Deirdre, with all Burns' deviations from her planned route, she would be saying nothing but "Make a U-turn" over and over.

"Chase me to the mall, boys!" Burns challenged. He would deal with them there, face to face. Or hand to hand, if necessary. That was something Burns had far more experience at than evasive driving.

Burns thought about reaching into the back for his gun. It made sense in some ways. After all, he reasoned, there's paranoia and there's due diligence. He had a sense a weapon might be necessary sooner than later.

He sped up to the main road, braking hard as he reached the intersection. Six lanes of light Friday evening traffic passed evenly in both directions, with a few more heavy trucks leaving the city and heading south, away from the water. Burns signalled left with the indicator and stopped at the signal. Burns scanned the oncoming traffic and watched the Audi, still stationary in his mirror. When he saw the traffic created a gap in the Audi's view he turned right and floored it, scooting along the shoulder that was narrower than the car until he squeezed the Skoda in front of an approaching cargo van, thankfully far enough in front to not elicit a blast from the trucker's horn. Not even a congratulatory honk. It didn't matter. The Audi driver didn't bite on the fake signal, or he saw Burns' weak manoeuvre. A part of him was glad to think his pursuers weren't slow enough to be fooled by a head fake.

Burns made it into fourth gear before the finish of his four-hundred metre dash to the Casino Entrance of the shopping centre, and didn't take his foot off the accelerator until he braked and dropped down into second to make a sharp right turn into the road that ran along the far side of the huge outdoor car park. Another quick right and he was the entrance to a covered car park and the loading dock. Burns drove up to the box and pulled a ticket to lift the gate. He noted the camera, angled to record each license and driver entering the car park, and wondered if there were more inside.

Burns zipped up to the second level, hoping there were a few cars parked to provide cover. Burns parked next to the only car in the first rank nearest the entrance, a late nineties version of his Skoda in surprisingly good shape. He got out of the car and scanned the lot for motion. And cameras. A single camera watched the mall doors. He spotted a vantage point between a Toyota sedan and a Volkswagen Transporter that would afford him cover and a view of the entry and the Skodas. He picked up his pace when he heard a vehicle accelerating through the gate on the ground level.

The Audi appeared at the ramp and stopped momentarily before turning into the parking area. Burns had left the Skoda in a spot easily seen from the entry.

Watching, the car passed his position slowly, the two men inside were focused on Burns' rental. As they passed right-to-left, Burns got a clear look at the driver. The memories struck him hard in the chest and stung the space behind his eyes.

"Pitsch!" Burns heard himself whisper. "What the fuck?"

17:55 (19:55 LOCAL)

Burns thought about how quickly he had arrived at this point. Violent intent. His first guess assumed they were CIA. Granted, that was a huge assumption. But that was the type of organisation that could pull off an operation like the one unfolding in England. And maybe Estonia. And if it was the CIA, it didn't matter which side they were on. Burns' survival instincts trumped all. He wouldn't ask until he had them subdued. In combat, it was always disarm and subdue. In the case of concealed carry, it went the other way around.

He had to get to them near the car. It should be easy to ask a few questions, have a conversation in a public place. *With minimal violence*, Burns mused.

The banks of fluorescent tubes on the ceiling of the car park were still in day mode. The shadows were short and low between parked vehicles. The sky was evening, not yet approaching dusk, but its warm glow spilled into the car park, bathing the concrete floor in golden amber light. Another spectacular sunset was on its way, but the viewpoint left a lot to be desired.

Burns had figured the American passenger to be the first target even before he recognised Pitsch. His action would be to neutralise the American first then figure out what to do with Pitsch.

He had no idea what he would do with them after that… maybe he was planning to teach them a lesson of sorts. He reminded himself this wasn't a training exercise.

And there was no way Pitsch was knowingly working with the CIA.

The Audi proceeded slowly down the last aisle and around the outside of the parking area. It came to a stop at the mall entrance. Pitsch was looking at Burns' car while the American peered through the glass doors to the mall. Burns tensed in his crouch, prepared to bolt should the American decide to go inside. He didn't, and Pitsch pulled the Audi around to park in the small group of cars at the far end of the floor. Burns guessed it to be staff parking. Pitsch backed into an open slot between a grey BMW estate wagon that looked to be pimped out on the cheap, and a little blue Nissan Micra, perfect for the young student working her way through college.

"Well you might be willing to wait an hour," Burns muttered. "But I'm not."

He visualised the attack. It couldn't happen with both men in the car. Burns checked his watch. *It might have to*. Then, if Burns had prayed, the Universe answered before he could say "amen". The passenger door opened and the American stepped out of the car. He scanned the lot, his eyes falling last on the mall entrance, before finally turning and stepping to the back of the car to urinate.

Burns charged into the American from behind, crushing him and his exposed penis into the concrete pillar behind the car. The American managed to brace himself enough to stop Burns from driving his head into the concrete, so Burns dropped him to the floor with a sharp stomp to the knee. Then he grabbed the bellowing American by his thick hair and delivered a hard blow to the base of the skull, enough to render unconsciousness but not kill. He felt the weight of the big American sag and let him drop to the floor. Burns removed the Beretta, with its ridiculously long suppressor, from under the prostrate American's arm then he aimed it through the rear window at the petrified Pitsch, who nodded slowly and reached up to put his hands on the steering wheel. The windows were tinted but the American had left the door ajar so the interior was filled with light. Burns imagined the glass between them a two-way mirror that had unexpectedly revealed the hidden observer to the subject being watched, turning the table. A still moment passed as the two men met on the opposite sides of a river of shared memories going back twenty-five years. Burns lowered the weapon and Pitsch turned to face forward. Their eyes met again in the rear-view mirror. Trust.

"Pitsch," said Burns.

"Charles," Pitsch answered. "Long time."

Burns asked Pitsch in German, *"Wer ist dein Freund?"* Who's your friend?

"You are, Charles," came the innocent answer.

Burns always thought German was the best language for sounding angry. Maybe that was because he had made a lot of Germans angry in his younger years. "Maybe you don't understand Hochdeutsch, Eastern Boy. I didn't ask who's your daddy."

Pitsch answered in German he didn't know it was Burns he was following.

"This guy was talking shit about you," Pitsch declared. "Said you might be a competition, a threat to his business with... my employer. The people I drive for. I'm just..." Pitsch stopped. The American groaned. He was coming around, and judging by the size of him Burns figured it would be advisable to reassert and maintain control. But he was also cognisant of the fact that somebody was going to walk out of the mall sooner or later. Having his opponent immobilised and prone in his own piss qualified as minimal violence. Asking questions in that situation might be crossing a line.

A phone rang in the man's pocket but he didn't react. Burns watched as the alert jangled twice more and stopped. The man stirred in the silence after, his limbs moving in small circles until each twist made a turn at their joints.

Burns slapped the man's left ear, hard.

"Can you hear me?" Burns asked the other ear. He kept his knee on the man's spine where it met the last four ribs, forcing air out of the lungs that carried a loud moan. Burns eased up and the lungs filled again. He stepped on the right hand as it moved toward the jacket pocket. The lungs pushed out a long, high-pitched whine until Burns let up on the hand. He stopped before breaking any bones then immobilised the arm with his heel on the wrist.

"Why, yes I can." The Kentucky accent spoke up with authority, despite being pinned to the ground by Burns. "I think there's been a misunderstanding," he drawled, and left it, as if that was all that needed to be said.

"There seems to be some confusion here, huh," Burns tapped the American's crown.

Do you know what this is?"

"A gun?"

"Yes," Burns answered. "Your gun." Burns showed his teeth. "What's your name, boy?"

"Peters," he said.

"Good," said Burns. "Now Peters, are you, or are you not CIA?"

The American turned his head, trying to raise it as he turned. Burns caught Peters' eye and held it, then he acknowledged the look with a nod. Peters was letting Burns know that Pitsch was a bad guy, or at least he didn't know Peters was CIA. Burns lifted himself out of his squat but kept pressure on the right wrist until he stood erect. He made sure Peters could see that Burns still had his gun trained on his head.

"I'm gonna need your gun too, Pitsch." Burns smiled through the window at Pitsch. He backed up, turning his weapon casually on Pitsch and eyeing Peters, who did his best to hide the shock of seeing Pitsch produce a weapon. Burns smiled and shrugged at Peters' stunned expression, faking innocence like an adorable sitcom actor playing a much younger character. He didn't have to repeat the gesture for Pitsch. Burns kept his elbow on his hip but had turned his arm flat, wrist up, aiming the black silencer at Pitsch's temple while keeping the weapon from public view. Both men knew what a mess the agent's gun would make at this range.

"Of course," Pitsch smiled. He released his grip on the wheel, wiggled his fingers and lifted his hands slowly, never taking his eyes off Burns and the long barrel of the gun. He seemed to breathe a sigh of relief when Burns turned his wrist to lower his aim from Pitsch's head to his hands, or his heart.

"Left hand," said Burns. He nodded as Pitsch handed over his handy little compact Sig. "Danke," Burns smiled. He touched his phone and thought of Wayne as he tucked the small gun into his pocket. And Eliise Oja. Then Veda.

Burns turned to Peters and shifted his weight and angle to look him in the eye. "I'm going to stand up, later I'll ask you to do the same. Bearing in mind that if you make any sudden moves, I'll put a very quiet bullet in your head. "Understood?"

"Understood."

"Then we'll get into the car, you in front, me in back."

Burns knew Pitsch wasn't a lethal threat to Peters but he sensed the agent felt otherwise. He saw the eyes shoot a fleeting glance at the car's open door. "Okay with you?"

"Sounds much more comfortable," Peters replied.

Burns stood up and backed away from Peters toward the front of the car. He stopped at the open passenger door, keeping his gun low, trained on Peters' hands as they fumbled to tuck himself in and get his wet trousers closed. Burns kept watch on Peters and the mall entrance. Peters couldn't use his left leg for support, the knee was far too painful to take any weight. He gave Burns a long hard look—not hostile, but not docile—as he pulled himself upright with his long, heavy limbs. Peters manufactured some dignity and limped past Burns, as tall as he could. He gripped the doorframe and slid down into the passenger seat. He let out that same quiet whine as he forcibly hauled his useless leg into the car. Burns closed the door and opened the rear door to slide in behind Peters.

Peters' phone rang again. He froze, staring at Burns.

"I should answer that," said Peters. It didn't sound like a threat. Burns shook his head. It didn't stop after three rings.

Burns phone announced a new text message. It was from DCI Wayne, with only a subject line, reading:
TAKE THE CALL

A little anger pricked at the base of Burns' skull. He ignored the order and read aloud as he typed a reply.

"Do you want to tell me why the CIA is following me?"

The look on the faces of the other two men in the car caused a mirrored reaction Burns couldn't stop. Agent Peter's guilt and Pitsch's shock became his own shock, and guilt.

"I am not CIA!" Pitsch howled.

"I know you're not," Burns apologised.

"I expect that's what the call is about," Peters offered.

"I'm just a driver," Pitsch pleaded.

"You were following me like you were still driving a tank," Burns chuckled.

"And you're still full of... surprises, Burns." Pitsch smiled.

Peters' phone jingled on. Wayne's reply came a few seconds later:

I'VE JUST HEARD.

Seconds later another message came in:

SHE'S NOT THERE

Burns took a moment to ponder whether DCI Wayne was shouting or if he was using ALL CAPS by accident. Maybe he misplaced his reading glasses. He also hoped Wayne wasn't fixated on finding the girl. Burns closed the phone and pocketed it.

"He's been sayin' that all day," Peters was aggravated. "I'm just a driver, I'm just a driver," he repeated it like a jealous sibling. He reached up with his left hand and began feeling the back of his head, searching for the bump that Burns hadn't left with his strike. Burns tapped the spot with the barrel of Peters' gun, drawing a compressed hiss from Peters as he inhaled sharply.

"Pretend you're driving, asshole." Burns commanded with a wave of the gun. It angered him every time he looked at it. The long suppressor screwed onto the gun's barrel made it look more like a dart gun than the deadly weapon it was.

Peters' phone jingle-jangled again. He looked at Burns, who shifted his position and reached between the seats.

"I'm going to take your phone, and you'll answer on speaker—"

Peters cut him off. "You need my thumb," said Peters, waving his swollen right hand like a Hawaiian surfer.

Burns screwed his face into a look of disgust. "I also didn't want you to put your pee-hands on it before I take it away from you." Burns stared hard at Peters. He guessed that scared Peters serious again. The jangling continued unabated. Burns turned to Pitsch and nodded at Peters' right jacket pocket. "But first Pitsch will take your phone and hold it for your thumbprint." He looked at Pitsch again, who seemed only too happy to comply. Peters pressed his thumb on the screen and the display lit up. Peters lifted his thumb and drew his hand back, waiting for permission to click, as the sleigh bells jingled on.

"And put it on speaker." Burns nodded again at Pitsch, who tapped the screen. The phone stopped the ringing.

"Hallo, Burnsy!"

The bad British accent set the hairs on his neck to prickling again. Hearing the nickname rattle him. He knew the voice.

"It's me, Hilts!" he declared. "This is your captain speaking."

"You've got to be..." Burns had no idea what to think. He had met Bryce Hilts in December and played hockey with him, once a week, every week since. They had a couple of beers a few times after a game with other teammates, but Burns hadn't socialised with the men regularly and only knew each of them by name when they were on the ice. Tully had introduced Burns to them one night after a Ravens game early in the season. It started as a challenge to Burns. Tully brought Burns to the game, claiming to know some of the guys and that he could put in a good word for Burns, teasing him to "get his ice hockey career back on track". They arrived midway through the first twenty-minute period and within five minutes Burns was talking like he should be out on the ice. Tully told Burns to "put his money where his mouth is" and another friendly wager was agreed. Tully had racked up quite a tab with Burns in the five months since, with Burns never failing to register at least a point in each game he played. He cursed himself for not knowing more about his teammates, particularly Captain Bryce Hilts.

"I ain't shittin' ya," said Hilts. "Turn the video on."

Peters flicked his left hand at Pitsch and wrested the phone from his hands.

"Like so," Peters insisted. He tapped the icon and Hilts appeared on the screen, smiling broadly as if he had just repeated the 1 – 800 number for the fifth time and was waiting for the camera to cut to the product. The smile broke into a laugh.

"Country music ain't country no more. It's what rock and roll used to be."

"You're preachin' to the choir, Reverend," Burns replied. Then only half joking he added, "But are you sure Hank done it this way?" The stilted laughter fell into silence.

"Well, Charles," Hilts' broad Texan accent roamed. "It's kind of uh, a good news, bad news thing."

"Really." Burns didn't know how long he would be able to play along but he held his passive expression and remained silent.

"I know, I know. It's all a little confusing right now," said Hilts. "I just talked to your boss. Detective Chief Inspector Wayne will be callin' you home soon."

Burns looked at his phone. He wondered how much had happened back at MCU2 in the five hours he been out of contact. And if it could get any weirder…

"Why?" Burns asked.

"Long story short, your guy ain't here. We're sure of that."

"My guy?" Burns repeated.

"Your guy. Dr Veda."

"Oh, that guy," deadpanned Burns. He knew there was more.

"Yeah," came the firm reply.

"And you're sure because…" Burns tilted his head as if to better hear the answer.

"And we're sure because we know where he is," said Hilts. "Our guy's got him."

Burns saw the pieces manoeuvring into place.

"Is your guy Russian?"

"Why yes he is, Charles."

"I see."

Burns let it hang. He could see Hilts' attention was split between his phone and something that drew his eyes upward and to his right.

"And big ol', good ol' Agent Peters here," Burns nodded at Peters, who was doing a good job of not verbalising the pain in his damaged head, wrist and knee. "He was following me because, what, he was going to deliver your message?"

"I did say long story short, Burns." Hilts tone was cold but his expression wasn't as serious. Burns stared. Hilts relented. "He's in Tallinn on unrelated business," Hilts shrugged. He looked over at Peters and his expression darkened. "Mr Peters will be going home soon now, too, I expect."

"Not right away, I'm thinking." Burns had no apology for either agent.

Peters was slowly melting under the cold scrutiny of three accusers, all three of which having found him guilty at three different times, of three different crimes.

"Not until he gets out of the hospital," Burns offered, with an obvious look toward Peters' knee. He looked back at Hilts and held up Peters' Beretta. "Does he always wear his weapon with a suppressor?"

"Apparently," Hilts answered as he stared questioningly at Peters. Then he looked at his watch.

"Agent Peters is there on unrelated business, he just ended up on your tail..." Hilts paused and turned away again. Burns could tell Hilts was pretending to be distracted this time to buy a little time for the explanation. "Let's just call it premature ejaculation for now," said Hilts. He chuckled and looked at Burns, who was laughing at the wet stain on Peters' trousers.

"I'll apologise over a pint when you get back."

Burns believed Hilts and let him know with a nod.

Hilts could have been smiling at Burns and gritting his teeth as he shifted his grin to Peters. The smile fell slowly but the lips remained parted. Burns had seen that look on the ice.

"And I assume I'll learn more about how your guy and our guy are connected," said Burns.

"Yes, like I said, when you get back," Hilts replied emphatically. "I'll be with your Chief Inspector when you get back to Scotland Yard."

Burns knew he didn't need any more details about Peters' mission. He knew he trusted Hilts. A hockey game is a battlefield, and they had been comrades in arms on the ice. That was enough for Burns to extend his trust into this arena, at least until he got back to London. He checked his watch and looked at his phone to confirm the time difference. He pushed away the idea of a video call with Wayne.

"Hey, what about the 'good news, bad news' thing?" Burns asked suddenly.

"Oh yeah!" Hilts was excited. "We won!"

"I know," answered Burns. "You told me."

"I also told you don't go anywhere," Hilts answered, then shifted quickly. "The bad news is we couldn't get any ice time for practice before next Friday's game."

"All right then," Burns smiled.

"Yeah," said Hilts. He let out a sigh of relief. "Gotta run," he said. "See you back in Jolly Ol' London, eh what?" Hilts rang off and Peters' phone returned to its default display.

After studying Peters for a few more seconds Burns ejected the Beretta's magazine and let it fall to the floor at his feet. He held his gaze on Peters as he pushed the clip under the seat with his foot. Then he shifted his grip on the weapon and presented it to Peters.

"There's still one in the chamber." Burns tried to sound nonchalant as he stepped out of the car, but his voice oozed contempt. "Should you decide to... do the right thing."

Peters took the gun and let his hand fall around it. Burns caught the furtive glance at Pitsch when Peters first had the gun in his hand. Burns instinctively put his hand on Pitsch's shoulder. The glass doors at the mall entrance parted and two women in their twenties appeared with handbags over one arm and shopping bags in the other. They spoke excitedly in Estonian and walked to the car parked next to Burns' rental, oblivious to the men in the Audi. Their voices echoed off the concrete, only muted after they jumped in and closed the doors of the more experienced Skoda. After the Skoda started up and rattled away, Burns opened the door behind Pitsch and stepped out of the Audi. He closed the door and draped his arm on the roof, leaning near the window to draw close enough to whisper to Pitsch in German.

"Drive tanks," said Burns. "Or play online poker... for fucksakes, Pitsch."

Pitsch nodded in agreement and was about to speak when Peters suddenly jammed his gun under Pitsch's chin and pulled the trigger. The report of the gun sounded like an echo of itself, popping like an overturned paper cup getting stomped on the floor. The bullet exploded out of the top of Pitsch's skull and passed through the roof of the car inches away from Burns' forearm, striking the concrete ceiling and falling on the bonnet of the BMW in the next stall.

"What the fuck?" Burns yelled. His right arm flashed in the window past Pitsch to take the gun out of Peters' hand in a move so quick Peters jumped, putting a strain on his knee.

"Jesus!" Peters wailed. "I thought you wanted me to."

"What?" Burns was incredulous. He couldn't read the look on Peters' face through the rage welling up in his eyes.

"Yeah, you know, you said do the right thing?" Peters looked like a scolded child who believed he was innocent.

"That was not the right thing, you fucking moron." Burns considered homicide. He tried to imagine what would have happened if he had given Pitsch his Sig before handing Peters his gun. No, there was no way Pitsch could have defended himself, even if he'd tried. Now he looked like a man who had fallen asleep at the wheel, waiting for his wife to come back with the shopping.

"Call Hilts back," he said. Peters seemed dazed.

Burns figured Pitsch never had time to feel the fear before Peters had splattered his brain on the header like marinara sauce on a taupe-coloured plate. The neat little hole under his jaw trickled blood that disappeared behind the loosely-tied necktie. Burns looked at the deformed slug resting on the flashy BMW and snatched it up. He showed it to Peters then put it in his pocket.

"You fucking idiot," Burns seethed.

"I did the right thing, like you said," Peters explained weakly.

"I meant blow your own fucking head off, you asshole!" Burns exploded through the open window and smashed Peters' nose with the hilt of the gun. Peters screamed and put his hands up to his face to stop the torrent of blood that gushed through his fingers. Burns twisted the suppressor a quarter turn and smashed the gun on the gearshift, snapping it off in the threads. Then he dropped the pieces in Peters' crotch and pulled himself out of the car over Pitsch's body. He stood outside the window for a few moments. Burns supposed Pitsch had died his friend. He re-holstered Pitsch's gun, offering a silent apology.

Burns checked himself for blood spatters and found none except on his fist. He looked at the hole in the roof of the car and remembered where his arm had been, only inches away.

"You almost shot me, you fuck!" Burns fought the homicidal urge again as he listened to Peters gurgle out an apology. The car park was otherwise still. Burns walked to his car, assuring himself with every step that Peters would not shoot him in the back. He got in and drove back to the airport, to carry out his orders. He thought about calling Wayne to see if he was still looking for Veda or the girl, or if he should just get on the next plane back to London. If he skipped the meeting with Eliise Oja, he might be able to catch the plane he arrived on before it turned around for London. Burns pulled out his phone and did a quick search on the airlines website where he booked his ticket and saw the turnaround flight number was scheduled to depart at 21:10 local time. He would have to blow off the chance to meet Miss Oja... and disobey Wayne's directive. The next flight was three hours after that. Fixing his ticket and getting his gun rerouted back to London plus customs... Burns put his phone away, wondering if he could bring himself to ask if Miss Oja could make a phone call, if they got to chatting...

There was a part of him that could justify taking his time reporting back to Wayne. But he had been given orders and they hadn't been changed.

PART FOUR:
SATURDAY NIGHT

18:55

Veda was awake. The IV fluids had flushed the drugs from his brain. He knew for certain he wasn't dreaming anymore. He had been reliving his brother Ravi's crippling beat-down by hoodlums as he stared blankly at the dark, shimmering Thames that flowed on through the night.

They were returning home from the cricket pitch about an hour after sunset when they were accosted by a group of five or six young men on their way to a football match. Ravi had been wearing a long muffler that must have been similar to the rival club's colour because the gang saw the two boys and ran across the street to surround them. The men shouted crude insults and tightened the circle. One of the older rowdies grabbed Ravi by the muffler and pulled him to the ground. He yanked the cricket bat out of Ravi's hand as he slammed him to the pavement. Two other men grabbed Nicholas by the arms and forced him to his knees. The racist taunts became cruder, dirtier, more sexual, and Ravi began to fight back. He struck two of the men, including his attacker, before they overpowered him and rained down with heavy fists and feet. Nicholas stared silently as he heard Ravi's bones breaking, frozen by the horror. He wondered what he would tell his father, and he began crying, trying to drown out Ravi's screams.

When the men holding him saw that Nicholas couldn't or wouldn't defend his brother Ravi's crumpled body, they turned their aggression on him. The rest of the gang closed in around Nicholas, some of them groping him and putting their fingers and fists in his mouth. He should have bit them. One of them urinated on Nicholas but he was unable to lift his stream up to Nicholas' face. Someone grabbed his hair from behind and held his head steady as the next two tried their aim. Nicholas was certain it was about to become a gang rape when a neighbour shouted out of her window at the gang, telling them "Go on, fuck off to yer football match. It's starting in twenty-seven minutes." The hoodlums decided that was a good idea and thanked her. Nicholas received one more kick to the chest as the last man departed with a threatening, "Be seein' ya, Mowgli."

It was the penultimate strike against pacifism. Veda wondered why he hadn't understood the irony of the nickname until he came to his senses and found himself strapped to a chair. He should have been inspired by Kipling's young hero and refused to fear evil.

Gerhardt Noack was no Shere Khan, but Nicholas Veda would be Mowgli.

He tensed and relaxed his limbs and pulled and worked his hands free. They were raw but not bleeding. They hurt, but Veda could use them to strike. Each breath filled his lungs with courage. His heart pounded like a steam engine on a steep grade. His skin was no longer cold. He looked down at the straps binding his legs. He poured his newfound power into the effort, but hadn't the strength or the leverage to work the nylon loose, much less break free.

Then he discovered he didn't need it. He almost fell out of the chair as he was bent overexerting his energy to break the impossible grip. The chair tipped and Veda saw one leg lift off the floor. He steadied himself on the chair and slowly lifted his body off the seat until he stood nearly straight. Then he planted his feet firmly in front of the chair legs, he pulled up on the arms of the chair. The nylon bands raked the thin flesh on Veda's shins and the metal chair was hot from the friction. Veda summoned his jungle strength and pulled hard. He lost his balance as the chair slipped away, freeing him from the bonds. Fortunately, he just sat back down on the chair. Veda closed his eyes and tried to imagine what he would do next. What he would have to do.

The air moved past Veda's face and every hair on his body as the door behind him opened. His breath stopped at the top of his lungs.

He knew it was Noack by the smell. Veda opened his eyes and waited. Seconds later Noack appeared, blocking his view of the London night.

'Enjoying the show, are we?" Noack sneered.

Veda said nothing. He stared at Noack, his dark eyes burning cold hate.

Noack didn't look at Veda's arms resting free on the chair, or his unbound legs and their nylon bracelets circling the chairs legs. Noack stood still in front of Veda, tapping his fingers together and looking like a headmaster who was trying to decide how to punish Veda's insolence.

Veda rushed at Noack and delivered a straight kick to the groin. Then he jumped to step around the crumbling Noack, bouncing off the near wall as he passed. Noack caught up Veda's foot between his legs and twisted, lifting Veda's feet from under him and sending him crashing back into the tiled shower wall. A mop and bucket broke his fall, stopping his head from hitting the wall. The bucket squirted free in the impact but the mop head had snapped off the shaft, leaving a metre-long pointed baton. Veda picked up the broken mop handle as Noack began to rise to his knees and delivered a two-handed strike to Noack's left ear, sending his low brimmed hat flying and dropping him to the floor. Veda stood for a moment, wondering if Noack was breathing, feeling the rage and letting it go.

He suddenly felt weak. He slumped down the cold wall and fell into a squat, resting on his haunches as he stared at the body of his tormentor, his enemy.

Noack was breathing. It didn't matter. Nicholas Veda was going to escape. If he was in a hospital, somebody will help him. If he was at the Chelsea Market, he could yell for help. The police. He wondered how far he would have to run before…

Noack stirred, making Veda bounce on his folded legs, which gave out and dropped him flat on the cold floor. His testicles hit the floor first and sent a shock wave through his nervous system. Noack suddenly sprang up and landed on all fours, like a terrier waking up from a dream. Veda's legs were heavy, he couldn't lift himself to flee or fight. He stared wide-eyed as Noack straightened to stand. Veda could see the homicidal look in Noack's eyes.

He wouldn't look at the eyes. He focused on the chest, and as Noack charged Veda raised the pike and held it steady to his hip. He watched as Noack impaled himself and fell to his knees between Veda's outstretched legs. Veda watched as Noack reached back with his right hand, but it fell before it reached the weapon on his hip. Noack hands twitched and waved at the spear that had pierced his heart. Then Noack fell limp and Veda felt the weight of his body. He felt his hands slip as the blood seeped out of Noack's chest. Veda raised his elbows to take the load and gripped the mop handle as tightly as he could. Noack wasn't a big man, even more like a ferret than a cat, but Veda struggled to hold the body away.

Veda felt Noack's last breath on his face, smelled it. He looked up into the pale grey eyes as they went blank, and the rage was extinguished. Veda unconsciously relaxed his arms and his grip on the spear. Noack's body fell forward, until Veda could see the gory tip stabbing the air above and behind Noack. Veda pulled himself from under Noack's lifeless body. He used the wall to pull himself upright and leaned against it until his blood stopped pounding in his limbs and his balance was restored. He stopped looking at Gerhardt Noack's dead body. He turned to the chair. He didn't fear it. He had to sit down. And he didn't want to sit on the floor next to the beast he had just killed.

"You will not find forgiveness," Veda mumbled.

Burns was on autopilot when he drove back to the terminal and returned the car. He didn't even engage the agent, who had dropped the thinly worn charade in exchange for a look of rational fear.

As soon as he stepped through the door the agent put his hand to his ear and whispered loudly enough for Burns to hear.

"He's here."

The agent stood behind the high counter, his hands out of sight. Burns didn't care if the agent had a gun. The young muscle-bound rookie didn't look the type to be able to make the split-second decision necessary to prevent Burns from either attacking or escaping at this range. Burns dangled the key fob then flung it sharply at the agent, hitting him squarely in the chest before the two big hands could react in defence.

"I'm trusting you to cancel the transaction on my card," said Burns. "And deleting my credit card from your database." Burns accepted Agent Rottweiler's nod and backed out to the pavement. He watched the agent as the glass door closed between them. He checked his watch before he turned and walked back to the Firearms Control Bureau, where he had the pleasure of meeting Lecky The Bastard.

He managed to scold the young officer in broken Estonian for being late, as well as asserting that what people had told Lecky about vodka being odourless was a lie.

Burns decided his angry Estonian sounded almost as good as his angry German. He knew verbalised anger and frustration as one of the ways he relieved intense stress. But he never took it out on someone who wasn't worthy.

Burns had walked through his rising rage between the Skoda and the GoNow Rental office. His instant reaction had been directed at Peters but the anger that still churned in his gut and crept upward was borne of unanswered questions, and distrust. He had no idea what had happened between Wayne and Hilts. Collaboration didn't seem to be a possibility for Chief Inspector Wayne. And Hilts was with the CIA. The whole scenario made Burns dizzy. He wasn't convinced the CIA was on his side and experienced doubt about Hilts, if only momentarily. But even good men end up playing for the wrong side. He knew better than some that the opposite was more often true.

Burns tried to laugh when he remembered his "candidate" status with the MCU2 team.

But he still had a mission. He had to follow orders. Whatever might have happened since he left London, Burns had to trust that Wayne was making connections and making progress. And that he still had a role to play.

20: 45

Burns found Eliise Oja on LinkedIn as he made the walk from the terminal to the administration building. Tallinn International Airport's Assistant Manager of Security wasn't blonde, as he imagined. At least not in her profile picture, where she appeared more strawberry blonde, if that was still a colour, and had it tied up in a tight bun. The sweetness was there, with friendly blue eyes and a warm smile. Burns was optimistic that Miss Oja would be helpful. Another part of him questioned whether it was animal attraction or a deeper connection he had felt when they spoke, and again when he saw her photo. It was a professional portrait, no doubt the same one that appeared on her ID badge. He had liked her before he saw her, and the attraction he felt served as a distraction from the freshly seared memories he would live with beyond tomorrow.

In person, Eliise Oja was almost irresistible. He saw her through the glass wall. She seemed to sense him there and turned his way.

"Officer Burns!" Eliise Oja's voice rose and lifted her out of her chair. She caught her excitement in a breathy smile. Burns felt it, a mutual attraction. She glanced at her watch, then again as if it was a distraction. She held his gaze for a moment. "You're early." The smile didn't break.

"Sorry, I didn't know how long it would take to..." Burns offered weakly. He lifted the plastic VISITOR badge as he took a step forward. "Yes, I'm Charles Burns."

"I saw you on the camera," Eliise smiled as she pointed to the monitors displaying the security cameras sector by sector. She stepped around the desk and extended her hand. "Eliise Oja. A pleasure to meet you," she smiled.

Burns advanced. Her perfume was fresh, and freshly applied he guessed. He felt a chill as he entered its atmosphere. Weightless, he reached for her hand across space. She held her warm grip on Burns' hand until he relaxed. The hands fell apart and they returned to rest momentarily in the air between them. Burns didn't know if he was falling or flying, or if Eliise was pulling him into orbit. Suddenly her eyes turned playful. Burns caught his breath and manufactured a sigh and a ready shrug, a reflex since puberty. He reckoned they both looked like teenagers now. The girl looking at the boy, seeing how long he'll wait to hear "yes".

Burns was a patient boy, even during those years, at least when it came to his relationships with women. He waited until the playful smile parted, not sure of what "yes" he wanted to hear: the "Yes, I'd like to have dinner with you" or the "Yes, I have your information here". After what seemed like a long time to Burns, she spoke.

"I thought you might have had some difficulty with your weapon."

Burns saw the twinkle of flirtatious humour in Eliise's eyes. He guessed that she was watching him when they first spoke on the phone. "You saw my gun." Burns pretended to blush. Eliise grinned mischievously and raised her tawny eyebrows.

"If you've seen one Glock, you've seen them all," she answered coolly.

Burns missed her already. She had correctly identified his gun, and she knew how to hit a punch line. But Burns needed to hit the road, soon.

"No, it was no problem," Burns chuckled. The possibilities hung between them like filmstrips in a darkroom.

Burns figured he would never get out of that room if he didn't get back to the mission, "pronto", as Wayne would say. He pulled his gaze from her blue sky eyes and scanned the glass walls three-quarters the way round the office before he could focus on the desk beyond Eliise.

"I came to request a copy of a Passenger's list." He kept it straight. "I believe my boss spoke with your boss."

"Your request finally came through Interpol," Eliise corrected. Burns guessed she had spent time in a British school, and had learnt the accent, and tone, from the headmistress.

"We..." Burns caught himself. "The flight data recording system at LCY was compromised."

"We heard about that, too," Eliise teased. "And the Metropolitan Police."

"We put out a missing persons alert," said Burns. "That's why you heard from Interpol."

"Actually, I'm not sure if we would deal with British Police directly were it not for Interpol's insistence."

"We might never have met," said Burns.

"Then where would we be?" Eliise returned the flirt again with a smile.

"I hope I don't have to speak to your boss, Mr Koppel."

"Why?" Eliise stammered and blushed a little.

Burns heard the double edge of his statement echo after it fell out of his mouth.

"I mean ever," He smiled quickly. "I'd much rather be here with you than with..."

"Well thank you," Eliise smiled coyly. "And I too wouldn't have it any other way."

"Good," said Burns. "Now that we've got that out of the way…"

A moment passed where the two seemed to be enjoying the same unseen sunset on the computer monitor. The digital clock ticked over. Personal time was over. They exchanged a nod like two co-workers working the same shift.

"Yes, the Bear Beer charter," Eliise sighed. "I would be happy to give you a digital copy of the passengers list."

"I have a pen drive," Burns said as he produced a small memory stick from an inside pocket.

"Please," Eliise raised her right hand to stop Burns as she pulled a similar disc out of a drawer next to the desk. "We will use this one."

Burns deferred, capping his USB stick and tucking it away in his shirt pocket.

"Do you think I could take a quick look at them now? I mean there are only twenty-nine passengers and four crew," Burns asked.

"Of course," Eliise answered. She sat down at her computer and soon produced a thumbnail file containing the passport photos of all on board Baltic's Bear Beer charter.

Veda wasn't there, nor was Kaia, or Vlad. One or two of the company reps and at least one of the male passengers looked guilty enough in their photos, but none that could pass for Dr Veda and Friends, and none Burns could see connected to the disappearance of a relatively unknown scientist. He was just about to pull out his phone when he stopped, remembering his personal checklist. Burns had to ask about the cargo.

"Would you have the manifest for this charter, both outbound and inbound?"

"You mean cargo?" Eliise asked. She seemed worried by the request. "As in your missing persons may have been cargo, or something else in the cargo?"

"Yes," Burns agreed, non-committal. "To compare the load both ways. I assume they left Tallinn sometime in the recent past." Eliise went to work on the keyboard and quickly pulled up the details for Baltic's departure four days earlier and the return flight sixteen hours ago. Burns scanned them both quickly. Same cargo, coolers, minus all but one of the boxes of merchandise and all the beer. Burns thought of Tully at the BeerFest and wondered if they had managed to give it all away or just abandoned the leftovers. Wasted beer, wasted time... Burns shook his head. He watched Eliise as she scanned the documents and thought about asking if she liked beer.

Burns sent a text to DCI Wayne requesting a call back. His phone rang a moment later. Burns excused himself to the hall and answered.

"Chief Inspector, I confirmed the passenger list, and the cargo. We were right."

"We were, were we?" Wayne asked.

"Well, right to confirm it, sir," Burns replied. He had been right.

"Well, we need you back here, Burns. I've been speaking with your American cousin, here. He has some insight into our missing persons case. How long will it take to get back to MCU2?"

Burns checked his watch. "Not sure," he spun to look at Eliise, who was watching through the glass. "Not yet. I'll have to see what I can do about my ticket."

"I understand. Well, do what you can. We haven't anything concrete to act on yet but..." Wayne stopped. "Just be sure to report directly to me when you have an ETA."

"Will do," Burns rang off first. He was already struggling with how to not say goodbye to Eliise. She was pretending to read something on her desk when Burns returned.

"So, I guess, I must be going," Burns smiled sheepishly.

"I understand," Eliise nodded. "Sorry you didn't find what you were looking for."

"Yeah, thanks," he answered. "I mean, thanks for all your help, not that I didn't find what I was looking for." He got her with that one, and he let her know he was serious. She responded by putting her card in his hand.

"I hope you return again, Officer Burns," she said. "Very soon."

"How's next weekend for you?" Burns said it without thinking. He made a quick deflection. "Where is Mr Koppel, by the way?"

"He went home at seventeen o'clock," Eliise grinned. She read Burns. "Like he always does."

Eliise smoothed and patted her card in his hand. "Now you won't lose this, now will you?"

"No, ma'am," Burns answered. Eliise made it easy with a polite smile, suitable for the close of a business conversation.

"Mornings are the best time to call me." Eliise offered her hand again and gave Burns a brisk, cordial shake.

"Mornings are good for me, too," Burns agreed easily. "I'll call you soon."

"I am looking forward," was the answer. Burns could see Eliise Oja meant it.

"Yes," Burns offered with a sigh. "Well, I have to get my ticket sorted out, so..." Burns waved his phone, defending his departure. He backed away, another step toward the door, still holding the phone like a semaphore mirror. She stopped him by taking a deep breath.

Eliise leaned toward Burns as if she was about to take a step. "What flight will you take back to London?"

"The next one, if I can make it," said Burns.

Eliise turned to her keyboard called up the departure schedule. "I am sure you can," said Eliise. She took a radio from its charging stand on the table behind her desk and spoke to the ticket agent and then the ground crew leader. Burns couldn't follow the second conversation but he liked her tone. It was a little harder than the warm, sweet song he had fallen for, but still ended with a laugh of camaraderie. Eliise knew how to give orders that people would follow.

"I made sure your weapon goes with you. It's at the plane now."

"Thanks a lot, Miss Oja," Burns extended his hand. Eliise held it firmly.

"Not at all, Officer Burns," she said.

"It's just Burns," he shrugged. "Charles Burns."

"Come!" Eliise shook his hand once more and dropped it. "I know a shortcut." Eliise smiled as she stepped past Burns and into the corridor. She took him to the boarding desk, where she spoke with the attendant. Burns produced his passport and the matronly woman scanned it into the computer. Eliise lead Burns and they passed through the gate and got in a waiting SUV that drove them about two hundred metres to the waiting jet. Eliise spoke into her radio and confirmed Burns' gun case was on board. She didn't say anything. She saw the smile on Burns' face and knew he understood.

The car stopped about ten metres away from the gangway, with the door on Burns' side lining up with the first step.

"Here we are," Eliise raised her voice over the jet engines idling nearby where the car stopped. She extended her hand again. "Have a safe trip home," Eliise sang.

Burns consciously told himself to be firm and gentle as he took her hand again.

"Thanks again."

He smiled at her as she rode away in the rear seat of the SUV. She took one look over her shoulder as the car pulled away. She timed it with the driver as he made a quick shoulder check, she managed to let the look linger long enough to let Burns catch the electric smile. She turned forward and he watched her through the glass until she was out of sight.

"Mr Burns!" The flight attendant was standing at the top of the stairs, waving. Burns trotted up the gangway. He didn't produce his boarding pass, only a broad smile as he reached the cabin door.

"We better get you into first class," The flight attendant smiled. "We wouldn't want to start something in economy!"

Distraction.

Burns sometimes used it to focus. Sometimes it provided an escape. Eliise Oja was much more than a distraction. She was an undeniable, irresistible force. He had to come down out of her blue sky before he was airborne again. Burns tried to distract himself with facts but the questions started swirling again. He thought about sending a message to Tully, but he didn't know where to start. Again.

Burns hadn't been on the ground long enough in Tallinn, and too much had happened in the last two hours, for him to be able to close his eyes and drift off during the flight. He could close his eyes, but he often couldn't keep them closed because every time he pushed back the circling questions about Veda and The Russians and MCU2 and the CIA, his mind's eye flashed with memories that splintered into more memories.

Burns met Pitsch in 1991 at the Canadian Army Trophy, a tank gunnery competition between NATO partners held every two years in Germany. Burns was an eighteen-year-old officer cadet with the Royal Canadian Dragoons. Pitsch was a tank driver from the former East Germany. At twenty-one years of age Pitsch was one of the youngest GDR non-com soldiers to be folded into the new *Bundeswehr* of the Germany Republic. He was also the only man in Grafenwöhr who knew that Burns was the one who had stolen the German flag from the canteen tent and replaced it with the Maple Leaf the night before the final trials. It nearly started a riot at breakfast. Pitsch took Burns aside and told him he knew where they would hang him if the rest of the German soldiers found out he stole their flag.

"Or we could sit back and watch the fun," Pitsch grinned. They did, and a friendship was born.

Burns never figured out how he knew, until Pitsch told him twenty years later, when they met by chance in a Berlin theatre. Pitsch was working in the theatre as stage rigger and he took Burns and his date out for drinks with his theatre friends. Burns told Pitsch he had left the military and was freelancing as a combat trainer with the Metropolitan Police in London.

"London?" Pitsch shook his head. "Oh, Canada!"

After a few more bottles of strong German beer, Pitsch's English improved and he finally admitted that he was passed out on a bench in the mess tent and Burns stirred him when he vandalised the bar in the wee hours of that Friday morning. Pitsch claimed he kept quiet because he didn't want Burns to get into trouble.

"Because you seemed like a nice young lad." And, since the flag was returned before lunch, and since Pitsch's team won, he "let it pass".

"You were covering your own ass for missing bed check!" Burns slapped him on the shoulder. He expressed his gratitude by buying the last round. The actors in Pitsch's group loudly declared him a hero.

"Retired hero," said Burns.

"Soldiers like us are retired not until we're old enough to retire," Pitsch said. "Ex-soldiers or soldiers out of work, but never retired."

"No," said Burns. "I'm really retired."

"Retired soldiers live in hospitals," Pitsch replied. "And cemeteries."

Burns knew it was right. His father, Colonel Charles James Burns was an exception. He didn't retire from the military until he was sixty-five, after a long and distinguished career as a leader in war and peacetime. He was a retired soldier, but not in a home yet.

Charles Edward Burns got out of the military as soon as he hit twenty years. Not before he had done many bad things that good men do for what they believe are good reasons.

Pitsch told him he left the German army for a woman. He fell in love with an actress. Burns knew her name but never met her. Lucky for Pitsch, she fell too. It had been almost eight years since that long night in Berlin. They swore a drunken promise they would keep in touch but Burns hadn't seen Pitsch once, until Tallinn. Pitsch had sent a few text messages the following year, lastly inviting Burns to Oktoberfest, but Burns never took him up on it.

Burns felt as drunk as he was that night in Berlin. He figured that some of the guilt he was feeling came from some part of him knowing that Pitsch had been a good man once, and maybe he died one, but he was into something bad. With bad men. And the CIA.

He spent the rest of the flight trying to picture how Detective Chief Inspector John C. Wayne of MCU2 met Captain Bryce Hilts of the Ravens Hockey Club Men's team, and apparently CIA agent. After a brief spin around imaginings of meetings and phone calls ranging from the sublime to the absurd, Burns' imagination mind wheel slowed and brought him back to the trust he felt, that he knew he shared with both men. It didn't matter what shape the mission or MCU2 had taken since he left London. Questions would be answered. Action would be taken. Burns would be part of it.

21:30

When he saw them together, he caught himself questioning how much he really knew about anything. They were standing over the table in the meeting room in Wayne's outer office. Burns told himself he was over the fact that Hilts was an American agent. He chastised himself for not knowing his teammate, at all. He surprised himself by not learning anything greater than trivial about the men he went into battle with on the ice.

Not that he could picture a conversation with Hilts on the bench, or even over a pint after a game where the captain would reveal his secret identity.

Hilts spotted Burns and told Wayne, who pulled his focus from the table. His expression didn't change as he waved Burns to the door.

"Burns," Wayne nodded. Stone faced but eyes glowing, he extended his hand across the table to Burns. The handshake felt more congratulatory than welcoming. Burns reflexively matched Wayne's firm grip and nodded in silent humility.

"I trust the flight went well," said Wayne. He almost smiled and his bushy grey eyebrows flickered, briefly threatening to migrate north and drag a grin with them.

"It did," answered Burns. He turned to Hilts, who was in closer range for a handshake. "Agent Hilts, is it?" Burns smirked as he held out his hand.

"As far as you know," Hilts answered. The two men clapped hands, stopping short of the shoulder bump they might do after a goal or a win.

"So..." Burns spoke calmly, but he was winding up, and he didn't hide it.

"We have a standing agreement," Wayne answered before Burns could start. "If they learn of anyone posing a threat to London, we hear about it."

"We have a standing agreement with MI6," Hilts corrected.

'Yes," said Wayne coolly. "And information trickles down, and at the end of the day here we are."

"MCU2 and the CIA," Burns kept it light. "Imagine that," he said, as if it wasn't hard to do.

"We have a person of interest in common," Wayne answered.

"Vladimir Konstantin Ivanov," said Burns.

"Right," said Wayne. "EE VAN off." He exaggerated Burns' pronunciation and shot a look at Hilts, who shrugged in concession. "General Ivanov," he said.

"Former General," Wayne corrected. He poked his arthritic index finger at the air then quickly withdrew it, opening the other fingers to conceal it. He turned his palm over and gestured toward Hilts with a cupped hand. "Mr Hilts, why don't you summarise what you've shown me for Burns here."

"Well sir, we have General Ivanov entering the UK at STN from TLL ten days ago, and leaving last night, from LCY," said Hilts. He shifted his eyes back to Wayne. "And when you opened your search on Ivanov, we flagged it," Hilts added.

"You knew he was here ten days ago. You were watching him," Burns said.

"We were watching him... and he was watching Dr Veda."

Burns turned hard on Wayne. "And you knew this?"

"Not exactly." Wayne didn't look like he had more to say as he turned his focus to the door behind Burns.

Tully was grinning like a lotto winner as he opened the door and manoeuvred his way through. Then, by reversing his chair, he nudged it closed. He caught Wayne's eye and flattened his smile and joined them at the table, wheeling quietly in next to Burns. After a brief nod to Burns and Hilts, Tully struggled to keep a straight face, silently asking Wayne for permission to burst. Wayne nodded.

"And," Tully paused for a breath. "We have a positive ID on Veda on your footage from London City Airport," piped Tully.

"And?" Wayne asked.

"And..." Tully smiled and winked. He pointed a finger at his iPad, then tapped it with finality and placed it on the narrow table. "Whatever I missed in the last two minutes coming down the hall, sir."

Wayne raised his hand. "Well, would you be so kind as to show it to me?"

Tully swiped and tapped the screen again then turned it around and pushed it across to Wayne. Burns passed quickly behind Hilts to stand next to Chief Wayne, to no objection.

The video, shot at night, showed a dark-skinned man with an oxygen mask over his face and an IV in his arm being wheeled out of an ambulance on a gurney to a waiting Antonov transport. Burns recognised its odd-looking engines and recalled it was manufactured in Ukraine. The last time he had seen one was in Kosovo. He squeezed his eyes shut against the memory, closing off the window on Pristina, and committed the tail number of the cargo plane to memory.

Kaia was walking beside, dressed demurely in light blue as the attending nurse and carrying a small black duffle over her shoulder. Two big-armed male attendants wheeled the gurney up the rear cargo ramp of the plane. The camera shakily zoomed in on a tall, greying man in a long dark coat at the top of the ramp. He turned as the gurney rolled past, signalling a crew member to close the gate as he followed Kaia into the dimly lit cargo hold. They disappeared into a pixelated soup as the gate retreated from the tarmac. Tully paused the video before the gate closed completely, and the light escaping from it left a white frown, frozen on the shadowy underside of the plane. Burns chuckled.

"And you got a positive for Veda from that?" Burns asked his friend.

"We enhanced it for facial recognition," Tully replied. "Ninety-five per cent certainty." That seemed good enough for everyone present.

"No sound?" Wayne asked. Burns had wondered but figured it didn't matter.

"Probably muted by our... eyes on the ground there," Hilts answered.

"Actually, I did that," Tully asserted. "Your boy had his thumb on the mic once or twice, but... His play-by-play is colourless." Tully smiled and shrugged. "Smartphone surveillance."

"Positively General Vladimir Konstantin Ivanov," Hilts drawled. He wagged his finger at the frowning cargo plane. "And that is one smart fuckin' phone, I'll tell ya." He unconsciously grabbed his belt and hiked up his trousers. Burns thought the Texan might spit.

"And his connection to Dr Veda?" Burns demanded.

"Um, didn't you see the movie, partner?" Hilts pointed and snorted.

"Before that you f—" Burns caught himself and stole a look at Wayne. "Did you have them under surveillance before this evening?" Burns smiled politely. Wayne cleared his throat and cut the tension with short glances at both men.

"They don't have the two men in the same room," said Wayne. "And neither do we." He looked down at his touchpad, idly swiping a finger across the display like he was flipping through a catalogue. "Phone records don't connect Veda to Ivanov," Wayne paused again and cleared his throat as he withdrew his hands and clasped them behind his back.

"In fact, IT Guy has been unable to connect a phone to Ivanov."

"But we have identified all of Veda's contacts," Tully insisted. "We know Veda hasn't been talking to any terrorists."

"Any known terrorists," said Burns.

"And exactly why haven't we got Mr Ivanov's phone records," Wayne scowled down at Tully. "Or do I have to ask Inspector Tellier that?"

Hilts jumped in. "You don't have any phone records and you won't find any because Ivanov uses a phone..." Hilts leaned over and put his hands on the table. He sagged for a moment, letting his arms support the weight of his heavy torso. Then he pushed off and stood up, spreading his arms in an expression of helplessness.

"Comrade Ivanov, like many Russians these days, has a phone that doesn't send or receive signals in any way we know of. Believe me."

"Sounds like one smart fucking phone, alright," said Burns.

"Currently know of," repeated Tully. He looked at Wayne and spoke directly to him. "It's been on the internet for a while," Tully shrugged. "It might be another Estonian connection."

"Tully," Wayne raised a crooked finger. His expression warned of danger.

"Don't go there," said Burns.

"Where, Estonia?" Tully asked. He didn't know. "Did you know they invented Skype?"

Burns squinted and shook his head once, slowly.

"The phone?" Tully asked Wayne, who ignored the question and returned to the window.

"And can you confirm Dr Veda's arrival at Reykjavik, Mr Hilts?" Wayne stayed at the window but twisted his head halfway round to hear the answer. Hilts stayed at the end of the table and addressed Burns and Tully.

"We followed the plane to KEF, and we have surveillance," Hilts had a look and tone of growing urgency. He looked at his watch and swallowed hard. "He's... going to be on the news. Shortly."

All eyes turned with Hilts to the darkened monitor on the desk. Both Wayne and Burns looked at Tully, the obvious choice, to find a news broadcast. He thumbed his phone.

"Look..." Hilts' almost shouted, then dropped his tone. "Two and a half hours ago security at the Center for Disease Control in Atlanta was compromised. We're just goin' public now."

"Sounds familiar," Tully quipped. "Not the delayed information, I mean."

"We know Ivanov," Hilts went on. "He sold Russian surplus to a number of buyers for many years," said Hilts. "Mostly chemical weapons, but also arms. Since the nineties."

"That long, eh," Burns shook his head.

"Your boys over at MI6 are the source for a lot of our Russian intel," Hilts shrugged.

"And he's responsible for this." Hilts tapped his phone and pulled up a live news broadcast. Then he waved Burns over to his side of the table, looking like a teenager desperate for an ally on the school bus.

The banner at the bottom of the screen shouted:

ACCIDENT AT CDC ATLANTA

A concerned-looking female reporter appeared in a window next to the angry-looking male host. She was standing in what looked like a small children's playground across the road from a large, curved glass building surrounded by emergency response vehicles. The reporter repeated what the anchor had told the viewers about no answers coming from authorities.

"Anyways," Hilts rolled on. "General Ivanov seems to be interested in biology now. Our intel has him acquiring..."

"Deadly diseases?" Burns interjected, angrily. "And by your intel you mean CNN?"

Hilts shook his head no. "We believe General Ivanov also kidnapped one of our scientists."

"You mean Dr Xiao Jin Cho, from China?" Tully corrected.

"American resident," Hilts stressed. "Dr So-and-So, yeah... Maybe," he shrugged. "Disappeared nine weeks ago. Last seen in Stockton, California."

"He's right, sir," Tully tapped his hands impatiently on the arms of his chair. "Holmes found a pattern. There—" Tully caught Wayne's expression shift and stopped. Burns saw the silent exchange between the two. He wanted to ask Hilts what the Americans had the Chinese scientist working on. He decided to shift it back to Wayne's singular mission to find Veda.

"Ninety-five per cent sure Dr Veda left London," Burns repeated. "With Kaia Rebane and presumably Vladimir Konstantin Ivanov." He recalled the video of Veda, Kaia and Ivanov as he spoke, and looked at Wayne.

"How did we miss the ambulance?" Burns tried to keep his tone casual. "Didn't Blennerhassett interview the ground personnel at LCY?" Wayne didn't react to Burns but nodded to Hilts instead.

"That video wasn't taken by airport personnel," Hilts admitted with an impish grin.

"Anyway," Hilts went on. "We know he did it and we know where he is. We tracked him back to Reykjavik."

"Back to Reykjavik?" asked Burns.

"Yes. It's a city in Iceland," Hilts answered, lightly mocking Burns. Burns held his breath to hold down a profane retort. He smiled at Wayne and spun it round to Hilts, whose innocent smile helped Burns to stay on his tack.

"You said 'back' to Reykjavik." Burns let it hang like a question.

"Yes," came the hesitant reply. "We believe he has a facility there, on the old NATO base. A spa." Hilts looked Burns in the eye with contrition. Burns knew he wouldn't say more.

"Really," said Burns. "And how did you hear about our missing persons?"

"Gee Burnsy, I dunno," Hilts replied. "Maybe the All Points Bulletin?"

"Regardless," Wayne's deep voice cut in. "Even if we call it a happy coincidence, we now have actionable intel."

"And we heard about Mary," Hilts mumbled.

"The pig?" Burns asked. He looked at Wayne and could see he was caught off guard.

"That's her," Hilts grinned.

Burns looked to Wayne, then Tully and back to Wayne, hoping either of them would jump in. Wayne finally spoke up.

"The pig is not our concern. We're trying to find Dr Veda."

"But sir," Burns blurted out. "Don't you think this is a little bigger than a missing persons case yet?"

Wayne stared at Burns long and hard. Burns didn't break contact.

"Our mission is to find Dr Veda," Wayne insisted. "The pig is MI5's problem."

"So are they going after Ivanov in Iceland?" Burns answered his own question. "No, they can't legally. MI6?"

Wayne ignored the question.

"Do you have video of Dr Veda on the ground in Reykjavik?" Wayne asked, his patience precariously balanced on each word.

"So, we got surveillance confirming the plane taxiing at KEF all the way to the hangar before anybody disembarks," Hilts said. "Now, we can only see ground level and up at the hotel spa or spa hotel or whatever." Hilts eyes widened and he looked like a big kid again. "We recorded no ground transfers, no moving vehicles confirmed since they parked that beast. But we have the population of the hotel growing by six, less than an hour later."

"How's that?" asked Tully.

Hilts raised his big shoulders, holding his breath before he spoke. "Can't get a camera inside, but we've done some nice work with sonar and thermal imaging." Hilts grinned. "The spa could be a cover. People come from all over to take the waters, as they say. And they all left yesterday on different departures."

"Before the Antonov landed."

"Right. Thirteen individuals left the spa in two groups via shuttle bus, we assume to the airport."

"But no visual confirmation of our missing person?" Wayne asked.

"Missing persons," Tully corrected.

"These were confirmed tourists, not our subjects," Hilts insisted. "And not your scientist. We believe they are still onsite."

"Passport photos?" Burns knew Hilts was telling the truth, but he had to ask. "Video from KEF? Have you confirmed IDs for all thirteen?"

"We got both. Apparently, Reykjavik wasn't, how'd you put it? Compromised." Hilts coughed. "No new check-ins at the spa since Friday. The only remaining guests are our targets."

"And they just appeared there, when?" Tully asked as he turned his focus from the BBC account of what had happened in Atlanta.

"There's a tunnel between the hangar and the spa," said Hilts.

"A tunnel. Of course..." Wayne's green eyes drifted from Hilts to Burns, then finally settled on Tully.

"Tully, have you been able to corroborate Agent Hilts' intel?" Wayne asked.

"Yes sir," Tully answered. "What there is of it on this side of things."

"Meaning?" Wayne demanded.

"Meaning it corroborates everything we know here," said Tully. He pointed at the broadcast. "And the BBC confirms the explosion at the CDC." He waited before repeating his earlier warning. "There is a deeper connection, sir."

"Yes, yes," Wayne was growing impatient. "And our focus remains on the connection that has led us to Reykjavik." He turned to Hilts. "To find Dr Veda."

"And then?" Burns asked.

"And I can get you there," said Hilts.

"Is Ivanov MI6's problem?" Burns asked Wayne. "Yet?"

"Don't know, haven't asked," was Wayne's flat reply. Then he added gravely, "Tonight we are MI6. And we have actionable intel."

"So, we're going to Iceland to get Dr Veda," Burns concluded. "And we're in with the CIA how?" Burns gave the question to all three men.

"Look, Burns," said Wayne, "MI5 has their mission. They're on the pig, for better or worse, because they, well they got it first." He gave a sideways glance to Hilts before going on. "MCU2 has its mission."

"And we have ours," added Hilts.

"Vladimir Ivanov," said Burns. He looked at Tully and wondered how many connections had been confirmed. Tully turned to Wayne and waited his turn.

"He's not been indicted anywhere, but there is a file on him," said Wayne to Tully, who remained silently simmering.

"There are files all over on him," Burns acknowledged. "The point is, the CIA knows where he is, right?"

Wayne turned slowly until he faced the window again. Burns knew he needed more.

"How many souls aboard the unmarked Antonov, tail number Romeo ten-Alpha-ninety when she left Stansted?" Burns asked. Nobody answered, so Burns did. "Okay, so let's say at least six. Your satellite images, did they see two large men and a gurney in the spa?"

Hilts shook his head and shrugged. "Two of the new bodies were in bed when our images clocked in, though."

"Together?" Tully asked. "Can I see that?" He checked with Burns first, the smile freezing and shattering when he turned to Wayne, whose immovable expression didn't change as he spoke.

"No, and yes," Wayne answered. "I asked."

"Oh," said Tully. "Good." He turned to Hilts. "So, like now would be good." He glanced at Wayne and the two turned on Hilts.

"I don't carry that shit around on my phone like y'all, okay?"

"But you've seen the images," Tully was leaning his bulky torso out of his chair, closing the gap between them.

"Yes."

"But you can't identify faces," said Wayne.

"'Also true," Hilts shrugged.

"Anyone carrying weapons?"

"Yes," Hilts answered slowly. "They have a total of four armed men at the hotel."

"Out of how many guests?"

"Looks like ten including the six from here," said Hilts. "And one night manager."

"Anyone sleeping under guard?" Burns asked.

"Not that we've seen, no." Hilts was almost apologetic, his hands coming to rest on the chair tucked under the table.

"Any hot nurses?" Tully queried casually. His expression changed, the calm hardening into concern. "Can you text me the coordinates?" He looked over at Wayne and nodded. "Now, please."

"Possibly," Hilts teased. Tully's courage held. His eyes narrowed and he managed to work his jolly cheeks into knots gritting his teeth in a cloaked sneer. Burns was a little surprised by how hot Tully had got, and so quickly.

"Kiddin'..." Hilts held up his hands in submission. "Of course you can have the address." He tapped and swiped his phone a few times and shrugged at Tully. "I was talkin' 'bout the hot nurse." Hilts gave his phone a final tap with his thumb. Tully's phone vibrated.

"Cheers," said Tully, calm again, once he read the message.

"One of the new bodies was female, yeah," Hilts smiled. "But sorry buddy, she weren't sleepin' last report. She was in the dining hall."

"How old is your intel, Agent Hilts?" Wayne asked. He looked as if he was asking the question but not listening for the answer, like he was keeping the conversation going until he knew what he wanted to say.

"We were sharing satellite space before, but we're live now," Hilts answered.

Burns jumped in. "And you don't have anyone on the ground 'live' there?"

Hilts shook his head no. Burns looked around the table at the three men.

"So your guy kidnaps our guy, Dr Veda, and flies to Reykjavik, then your guy jets off to Atlanta, blows up the CDC, and then what?" Burns pulled out his water bottle and took a long pull as he stared at Hilts.

"Like I said, this is an unexpected turn of events. Our intel told us Vlad was still in the R and D phase... resources haven't been assigned..."

"What?"

"Kidnapping scientists, buying and stealing tech..." Hilts sighed. "Until this morning we thought General Ivanov was just getting started."

"The new terrorist on the block," Tully chuckled.

"We can't say for sure it was a terrorist act," Hilts insisted. Then checked the time on his phone. "But we are saying it's a terrorist act." He wiggle-waved his phone. "In twenty-seven minutes."

"Why? Or is it why not?" Burns glared at Hilts.

"Because we can't blame the Russians right now."

"It's not the Russians," Wayne declared. "It's a Russian."

"That would be a best-case scenario, for sure," came the unconvinced reply from Hilts. Burns agreed with them both.

"It's going to take me eight hours to get a team there," Hilts declared. "The military will take approximately ten to twelve."

"And they'll take over," said Wayne. His face pinched a little. Burns guessed Wayne had no intention of involving any of Her Majesty's government or military, much less letting another Branch take control of his operation.

"But if we don't get in and out before the military, it'll turn into a cluster fuck..." Hilts stopped, his cheeks glowing brighter.

Burns saw himself in both men. Both were right-minded. Both seemed to reserve trust in any authority other than their own. Both were committed to action. Burns had thought when he retired from Operations and became a trainer that he had forever left the Front and would never be the sharp end of the knife again. But he felt it again. True, he hadn't really formed any expectations about MCU2 before he made the transfer request. He believed in the mandate but never imagined his role as detective or trainer would lead him to an extraction on foreign soil. Like it or not, the odds were good.

Burns pulled out his phone as the conversation hung empty in the room. He made a quick search for last minute flights and found a connecting flight.

"I can be there in five hours," Burns offered the image on his phone as proof. The look on Wayne's face told him that was the correct answer. He didn't ask if it was legal.

"Right," Wayne boomed without shouting. He had decided. "We're going on the intel from our American cousin here. With reasonable certainty that our missing persons are in a hotel spa in Reykjavik." He studied the aerial view of the spa, a little more than a kilometre away from the main terminal.

"Under light guard," Burns added. He wondered how much Hilts knew about his background in Special Operations. He knew they hadn't spoken of it.

"Recon would be ideal since the sat images and our limited local surveillance..." Hilts trailed off.

"Indeed," Wayne agreed. "And getting Dr Veda out would be our ideal, Mr Hilts."

"Understood," Hilts replied. "We would be happy to provide return transportation to London for Dr Veda," Hilts paused and smirked at Burns. "Plus one, or even two."

"And security?" said Wayne.

"You mean, back up?" Hilts asked.

"For the extraction," Burns answered.

"Only if you wait for us."

"I can't take my gun to Reykjavik," Burns remembered. "Too much paperwork, not enough time."

"I know a guy," said Hilts with a casual wave of his beefy hand. "Get you a gun and a car. But you gotta promise." The hand closed into a warning finger.

Wayne straightened and turned back to the two men. "Burns will go in advance of your unit to the spa and be in contact with your personnel when they arrive. I assume he'll have coms with your people?"

"Of course," Hilts agreed. "I'll set him up with a phone. He'll be in the loop before he leaves London."

"Good," Wayne nodded. "Before you go, Hilts, you'll give Burns here the contact information for the car and the weapon, right?"

"I didn't know I was leaving," said Hilts.

"Yes, you are." Wayne asserted. "Inspector Tully, could you escort Agent Hilts to the briefing room and meet with IT Guy there?"

"I… all right," Tully agreed with a frown.

"Agent Hilts has questions about our disruption here at the Met," said Wayne. "And clearance to ask them."

"I didn't really…" Hilts stammered.

"Yes, you do," Wayne's low tone dropped almost to a whisper. "Or your government does, or they will have. They'll want to know what we know. You can get out in front of this in the meantime." Wayne tilted his head at Hilts, glaring like a judge. He gave a slight nod and offered his most encouraging smile. Burns felt encouraged by Wayne's unsolicited gesture of quid pro quo. Whether or not it was of value to Hilts didn't matter.

Hilts' gaze turned to the window. He looked like he was trying to work out the timetable. That, or he was searching an imaginary calendar on the window to see which day his birthday fell on. Burns guessed it was a Thursday, judging by the measured enthusiasm that blushed Hilts' face when he finally stepped back from the window. He tossed his phone into his left hand, checked the time and the activity logs then put it away. He turned quickly to Tully and Burns then straightened to face Wayne.

"IT Gee, you say," Hilts was optimistic. "Sounds French."

"Inspector Tellier is from France, yes," Wayne confirmed patiently. "And he has information that your people may find useful to the CDC investigation." He is waiting." Wayne checked his watch. "I may join you there. If not, I'll see you on your way out." He looked at Tully and issued a causal request. "Update me, as per." Tully nodded and spun his chair round. He gave a look to Hilts and wheeled for the door.

"Burns, you're with me," said Wayne. "We'll get you to the airport straightway."

"Sir?" Burns spoke loudly enough to stop Tully and Hilts at the door. "Maybe Agent Hilts here could make the arrangements," Burns pointed at his phone and tilted it to show the time to Wayne. "Before he leaves?"

"That would be ideal, yes," Wayne answered.

Hilts took out his phone and tapped it a few times. Then he lifted it up in front of his mouth and spoke, flattening his Texas drawl into even syllables as if he was giving an order at the drive-thru.

"Kay-eee-eff. Guest package. One." Hilts held a finger up and waited a few seconds for the reply. Stephen Hawking's younger sister answered. Her electronic voice repeated his message then added, "Confirmed. Ninety-two minutes."

"Girlfriend?" Burns teased Hilts with a nudge.

"Be there when you get there, Burnsy," Hilts promised. He tapped his phone a few more times, then he aimed it at Burns, whose phone clicked a second after Hilts fired the message.

Burns smiled. It was none other than GoNow Rentals. The message gave Burns the details of his rental agreement, a phone number and a map showing the location of the pick-up.

"Thanks," Burns nodded to Hilts.

Tully and Hilts left the glass room and passed through the outer office and directly out to the hallway without a backward glance.

Burns watched Wayne as he returned to the window, studying his eyes as they stared down the unblinking London Eye across the river. Nothing had been said about Burns' status, and he figured there was no point in asking about it. Burns was in, no question, and he knew he was the best man, the only man Wayne had for the job, if it came to an extraction.

"And here we are," Burns mused aloud. He had to ask if he was being set up. "Tell me you just thought this up," he asked.

"It makes the most sense for us," Wayne answered duly.

"Us?" Burns asked. Apparently it wasn't enough of a question for Wayne to answer at that moment. "How many of 'us' are there sir?"

Wayne turned to look at Burns and smiled, almost surprised. "You're different, Burns. You seem to ask more questions you know the answers to than not."

Wayne's phone rang loudly inside his jacket, sounding like it could have been the first desk phone invented. He dug it out of his pocket and tapped it twice with his bent finger before the loud *ring-ring* was cut.

"Yes, Tully," Wayne answered. Burns couldn't hear what Tully was saying but he went on for some time, uninterrupted by Wayne, whose face was again turning to stone. "Right. How do I do that? Right." Wayne put down the phone and reached for his tablet. He grasped it in both hands and used his thumbs to navigate to whatever new information Tully had found. Burns saw the headline:

TYPHOID IN OXFORDSHIRE!

"That was quick," said Burns.

"If it's online, it's everywhere," Wayne shrugged. He addressed Tully on the phone. "It was one man," he insisted. "He was isolated almost immediately. He turned up to the agriculture centre ill, a week after the pig was snatched."

Burns laughed softly. Wayne glared at him as he went on. Wayne rang off and stared at Burns.

"He was a young man with… mental problems. A loner. I'll send you the file story."

"Most typhoid cases take two or three weeks to be diagnosed," Burns noted as he did the math.

"The young man died as a result of not being treated." Wayne had a brief, guilty flinch.

Burns saw it.

"They haven't disclosed which strain of typhoid it is, have they?" Burns asked.

"I can't answer that," was the answer.

Burns knew from what he had read it was likely to be the resistant strain.

"How he was infected is unknown... Safe to say it's not something in the water!"

Wayne's anger at the news story hung in the crags of his face. His eyes narrowed as he resumed his staring match with the Eye across the river.

"For sure," Burns agreed. "The Ministry should be able to calm any fears of an epidemic. They just need to show the water system is clean."

"Have you been to Oxford, Burns?"

"No, sir," he answered.

"They've had their issues, recently. But..."

"Typhoid is hard to transmit any other way," said Burns. "Except, close contact..."

Burns drifted his focus to the window as he recalled Veda's "rain". Thankfully, it wasn't raining at the moment.

Wayne cooled his anger, but Burns could see the simmering frustration. "The thinking was... was that the Ministry and MI5 had got ahead of it." Wayne scowled. "That is until now."

"This won't start an epidemic or a panic, sir," Burns asserted. "Yet."

"Agreed," Wayne answered. "We'll see how big it gets before we offer the whole story. If there is one to tell, that is. To be honest it's not in my hands either way."

"Still hard to picture," said Burns, shaking his head. "Snatching a two or three hundred kilo pig. It just is."

"I'll tell you what's hard to picture," said Wayne. "An unwell man who likes to… be intimate with farm animals."

Wayne stared at his hand as he worked the stiff fingers into a fist then loosened and stretched his hands open wide. "I would imagine they slaughtered poor Mary somewhere in Oxford. But, as you've said, he likely got infected before the pig went missing."

"'Do we know how or why he had access to the pig?" Burns asked.

"Unfortunately, no," Wayne grumbled. "I really can't say, Burns. As I've told you, the pig is MI5's business. We're…"

"Going to extract Dr Veda from a spa in Iceland." Burns confirmed it with a confident smile.

"It's in our best interest, in our citizen's best interest to make sure Dr Veda is returned to London." Wayne strode left and right at the window, facing forward like he was on parade, but deep in thought as he went on.

"If we assume the intel is accurate, and Hilts' has now given us the live surveillance…" Wayne stopped and turned to Burns. "I would understand if you had some trepidation. Not exactly like riding a bike, is it?"

"No, sir," Burns agreed. But he was more worried that it was exactly like riding a bike. He knew his body was up to it. Playing hockey had been his excuse for keeping in shape, and putting the pieces of the puzzle together had been exhilarating. He felt younger than he did when he retired from active operations, ten years ago.

Deadly force. Right cause. Extreme prejudice. As a soldier, those words were a way of life to Burns. The enemy had been identified and located.

Now the soldier in Burns was ready for action. More importantly, he knew it was a right cause. He hadn't expected to find himself at the sharp end of the knife again when he signed up for Wayne's MCU2, but he was more surprised by his readiness to engage. He realised that despite the angst that made him turn away from the violence of that hostile world, he would never hesitate to use deadly force.

"Recon the spa," said Burns. "And enter, sir?" He planned to do so, but he liked to have orders, on record, whenever possible. Burns had often acted in direct opposition to orders, but always with irrefutable justification, afterward. Ten years after leaving the field, ten years of not taking orders from incompetent commanders, Burns' reflex was to insist his CO "put it in writing".

Wayne had resumed his loping strides along the window, his green eyes searching, like a big cat in a glass cage. He stopped suddenly and nodded over his shoulder.

"I'm going to assume you and I have the same level of trust for our American cousins." Wayne squinted at the distance. Then he went back to the table and began tapping and swiping his tablet.

"Regardless, with Agent Hilts' help it's a quick action, and a quick solution."

"Means I only have to buy a one-way ticket to Reykjavik," Burns smiled cheerily. Then he thought about it. "Not that I like the sound of that."

Wayne cracked a smile. "You'll be reimbursed for your travel expenses, once we get everything online, as they say," he said. "Rest assured." He seemed to rest himself for a moment as he stared into Burns' eyes.

Burns was struck by the fact that he hadn't thought about his expenses until he heard Wayne's assurance.

"Thank you, sir," Burns acknowledged. "But I meant, you know, a one-way ticket..."

"I got it Burns," said Wayne. He gestured to the tablet. "Join me."

They studied the video in silence. Two streams shared the split screen: the thermal images from the satellite and a wide-angle live feed from a camera that had been placed outside but near enough to the spa to see through the glass wall that faced the road. One man was visible at the reception desk. Beyond that was the central hall, with a glassed-in exercise room on the left and a lounge area with a big screen television showing a football match to the right. The three men watching the football match were wearing matching shoulder–holstered side arms.

Two wings ran off from the foyer into darkness: one to the spa and pool, the other toward the guest rooms. A small lift was nestled into an alcove next to a stairwell that appeared to go up and down from the ground level.

On the left screen Burns saw the glowing images of two bodies relaxing in a hot tub, and a cooler-looking male and female standing in a guest room across the hall from the sleeper, whose body temperature was the lowest, if only by a couple degrees. Two more men were moving in the kitchen and dining room.

Burns had difficulty believing that Veda was one of the two unguarded, prone bodies in the CIA video streaming on the monitor. Almost on cue, one of the bodies rose and walked into the hall, as if being summoned, where he remained outside the door.

"Four-to-six armed guards. Handguns," Wayne repeated. "Our doctor is probably in the bed in room one-oh-eight."

"Bound," said Burns.

"Yes, no doubt. And possibly drugged."

"No need for guards standing by if he's tied up and unconscious, I guess," Burns conceded. That much made sense, but he had imagined the captors would be greater in number, if they were guarding a secret laboratory cooking up weapons of mass destruction. And a kidnap victim.

"Does Ivanov take Dr Veda and his lab equipment to Reykjavik?" Burns wondered aloud. "Or is the spa just a stopover?"

"Can't be sure about a lab if it's underground," Wayne answered. "And it could be. We know there's a tunnel."

"Right," said Burns. "A tunnel." He decided not to wonder what else was under the spa.

"Here's how I see it, Burns. If you see the opportunity to extract our target and remove to safe distance..." Wayne gave Burns that long hard look he had seen from so many CO's. They were never really looking for an answer. They were asking themselves the question. Burns silently affirmed Wayne's question.

"I know you've studied the area, and I know how you... see things," said Wayne. "I'm also guessing you've worked some of the angles, yes?"

"I have, sir," Burns answered. "It would stand to reason that if Dr Veda is there, he'd be the one still in bed." Burns pointed at the lone horizontal figure. "Maybe more will be in bed by the time I get there, or..."

"Or?" Wayne asked.

"Gone."

"Well, we'll have to ignore that possibility for now," said Wayne. He peered out the window. "But we'll keep an eye on it."

The two men stared silently at the screen for some time.

"It's not exactly a fortified position, is it?' said Burns. He checked his watch. "Depending on what it looks like in about five or six hours..."

"If it's a temporary location, our best hope is they wait at least that long."

"Can I get this on my phone, Sir?" Burns pointed at the video.

"I'll see to it," said Wayne. He picked up the tablet and worked his long thumbs over the display. "In fact," he added, "I think I can actually do that myself."

Burns looked out the window as Wayne navigated his touchpad. It wasn't raining, but nothing in the sky foretold the chances of it abating altogether. He didn't care. He would be in Reykjavik in a few hours, and he didn't care what the weather was there, either.

Burns phone announced the incoming message from Wayne.

"Right," said Wayne. "There's a link in that message," Wayne almost smiled again. "And we'll be in contact."

So there it was. Wayne wanted pre-emptive action, and Burns reckoned he knew at least two good reasons why. Dr Veda was a man of some importance, and Wayne, and his newly certified MCU2, had been charged with his security. How important Veda was to the Health Ministry or the Home Office didn't matter. Wayne wanted him back. Maybe to save face, or maybe to make a bold introduction for his new unit. It was personal, and Burns was ok with that. Burns had no doubt that other agencies would be involved before this was over. To Wayne, the Unit was responding to an abduction, and extraction was the solution. Burns figured they had enough intel to act on. And for now, it seemed that MCU2 didn't need to get any bigger. This was exactly where Burns knew he should be, as unexpected as it was.

"Understood."

"If it's not feasible to extract Veda, of course, keep cover and wait there until Hilts' cavalry rides in," Wayne was giving an order, in the next moment a suggestion.

"By my maths, you'll be onsite for the better part of two hours before his first team arrives." Wayne's eyebrows tilted upward, then folded and fell flat as he squinted at something in the rusty dusk spreading over the city. "He wants to be ahead of his own military," Wayne gestured at the door Hilts had passed out of. "We want to be ahead of—" Wayne stopped. "I trust you'll be able to assess the situation more accurately when you get there, and will act accordingly."

"Yes, sir," Burns answered. Detective Chief Inspector John Wayne was a commanding officer he could trust. Because he knew Wayne trusted him.

"Then you just have to get our man to the charter on time," Wayne added with a hopeful sigh.

"Back in time for breakfast!" Burns assured, with the appropriate bravado. He held the pose and confident grin long enough to reassure himself. Then he leaned in with a question. "What if I find Dr Veda," he inquired carefully, "and he doesn't want to leave?" It was another question he thought he knew the answer to.

"Then you would arrest him," Wayne replied.

"Do I need to have a badge for that, Sir?" Burns chuckled. Wayne checked his watch, unimpressed.

"You'll enter Iceland as an Official Transport Escort," Wayne answered. "I'm told your digital file will reflect that under inquiry."

Burns grinned. "Just picking up a VIP, popping in and out."

"Something like that, yes," said Wayne. "Let's hope so. I would also suggest that you return anything you borrow there beforehand. With your car hire, that is."

"Understood. And what do I do if I find Mary, or say, her blood?" Burns asked. Another question he had his own answer for.

"Well, I don't suppose you can arrest her," Wayne chuckled. "Don't try to bring anything else back, except for Dr Veda," said Wayne. "Leave her to the Americans."

"Pig roast, Mm-mm," said Burns. "With American barbecue sauce."

"What I'm saying is," Wayne took a deep breath. "Veda is the priority. And we don't think it's impossible to get Veda out before the Americans..." Wayne caught himself.

"We?" Burns asked again.

"Yes, we," Wayne affirmed. He raised his furry eyebrows and smiled, as if he was surprised Burns didn't know the obvious answer.

"You and I."

Burns made a deliberate detour on his trot down the stairs at the next floor, where Inspector Tellier would be briefing Hilts on the surveillance hack at the Met. His timing was perfect. Hilts and Tully had just left IT Guy and were about to step into the lift. Burns caught the door and slipped in behind Hilts, just as he turned to push the button. Hilts looked startled for a fleeting moment before defensive anger flared in his chestnut eyes. Burns smiled cordially and nodded as if he was going down too. He enjoyed giving Hilts a jolt, and the smile it brought helped to mask his own rage. He didn't want to escalate with Hilts in an elevator. He nodded at Tully, who backed his chair away from the doors. Burns pushed the button to close the doors.

"I'll just take the next one," said Tully. He grinned and gave a thumbs up as the doors closed.

"Tallinn," said Burns as he faced Hilts, cradling the grin and trying to keep the anger at bay. "Unrelated business?"

"Yes, Burns," Hilts snapped. Then the initial fear response dissipated, he caught his breath and went on. "Unrelated, as in... you know. Nothing to do with you. Or me, for that matter."

"So, your people in Tallinn," Burns asked, "Nothing to do with Ivanov, or Veda? Or is it just none of my business?"

"Or Kaia Rebane," Hilts held up both hands and drawled on. "None of our business. And they are not my people. Company men, yeah. But completely unrelated business, of a classified nature."

"I see," said Burns. "Fair enough."

"All right," said Hilts.

The doors opened and the two men stepped out together, as friends, and walked toward the door. Hilts handed in his pass and Burns accompanied him across the pavement to his car.

"So what the fuck was that spy commando shit in the parkade?" said Hilts strolling, still smiling.

"Your boy Peters?" Burns asked innocently.

"No," Hilts replied. "I mean, yeah... The whole evasive manoeuvres and stealth strike in the parkade..."

"I spotted two suspicious-looking men following me in a big black Audi," said Burns. "Self-preservation."

"Uh-huh," Hilts answered. "Anyhow, Peters will be in Tallinn for a few more days, at least 'til after he's had his nose put back on his face," Hilts grinned. "If anyone's askin'."

Burns seethed. "Anyone asking about Pitsch?"

"The driver? No," Hilts shook his head. Burns could tell Hilts hadn't asked. He wasn't sure if it mattered to anyone else.

"Should have put that asshole Peters on the next flight," said Burns.

"Yeah, broken nose, mild concussion in a pressurised cabin," said Hilts as he opened the car door. "Helluva job," He patted Burns on the shoulder.

"It would feel like his brains were being blown out on take off," said Burns. He stopped himself from picturing it in his head, but he couldn't shake the grim judgement that Peters deserved to suffer pain, if not death, for blowing Pitsche's brains out. *For no reason.* Burns stared at his reflection in the rear window of Hilts' big Dodge. No answer. Maybe *he would even bleed out,* he mused.

Hilts laughed until he saw Burns' face was serious. He shook his head and frowned as he got into his car. "Always that fine line," he said. "Between psychotic and whatever everyone else is." He turned over the engine and pressed the tab to roll down the window before closing the door. "Ain't that right, Burnsy?"

Burns found himself thinking beyond the mission again as he rode in the shuttle bus on its way to the commercial airliner waiting on the apron.

He was a fan of leaders who knew the value of 'keeping it small'. Burns had been part of many small-team operations in Europe and Asia, as few as himself and three others. But he had only ever been solo once, when he was the lone survivor of an IED attack on what had been officially called a reconnaissance mission in Afghanistan. He had been first down the hole and far enough ahead to be out of the blast. Trapped on the inside of the collapsed tunnel that crushed and killed his squad. He relived the emotional memory, and imagined seeing the look on his face the moment survival became the goal of the mission. Burns killed three hostiles in the tunnel before reaching an escape exit. He made his way to the extraction point the following night and waited…

Vladimir Ivanov had surprised the Americans and the British by successfully executing multiple complex operations with an apparently small, mobile and dedicated force. The organisation might be small, but it was sophisticated, and his actions swift and decisive. And well-funded. Burns remembered a line from an old noir film. "Crime is only a left-handed form of human endeavour."

He stopped himself as the bus came to a halt beside the plane. He couldn't wonder about how Ivanov would use Dr Veda, or his work, or why.

Burns would do his part and trust the others on the right-hand side to do theirs. Find Veda and get him out. Hilts and Wayne were swift and decisive. He chuckled, amusing himself with the new nicknames.

Swift and decisive. Two words he often heard but had never given lip service to describe the bureaucratic automatons that had made "military intelligence" an oxymoron.

He thanked the tall blonde female flight attendant for directing him to his seat. She responded to his graciousness with a flirty smile and a lingering touch to her plaited hair as she returned his ticket. Burns almost ignored her. He felt gratitude for the fact that he was exactly where he should be.

Burns didn't care if both men wanted to do nothing more than make amends for the duty in which they had failed. Wayne wanted Dr Veda and Hilts wanted Vladimir Ivanov, and both were acting independently, swiftly and decisively, presumably within their authority.

Burns had to believe they all saw that Ivanov presented a global threat. Hilts had Ivanov under surveillance before Atlanta for a reason. The CIA had been watching him in London, and was aware of Ivanov's presence in Iceland. If they weren't successful and couldn't stop the mad Russian from unleashing a bioweapon, there would be a whole hell of a lot more agencies involved worldwide.

Burns knew the way Wayne saw it, there wasn't the time or the need to engage any more personnel to ensure the safe return of Dr Veda. And he was certain the Americans would want to capture the international terrorist alive, in the hopes of getting intel about Ivanov's network and whatever he was up to, and what he had done with their stolen property. *A cache of diseases...*

Burns found himself strangely hopeful that he was going to help prevent a global catastrophe. The idea of saving the world sounded nice. But that also meant saving his own life. He didn't see himself as a hero. He realised he was being driven by his survival instinct, the part of him that was motivated to kill any threat to his survival.

As the plane touched down, Burns returned his focus to the mission. He sat up in his seat and stared out the window at the glowing horizon, visualising the stages between entry and exit. He had studied and memorised the map of Reykjavik International Airport and the commercialized former NATO base that bordered it and shared its airfield. If the resistance remained minimal, Burns figured he could eliminate the immediate threats with lethal force, if necessary. He would have surprise on his side, he was confident of that. He imagined rolling Veda out on his gurney, or maybe in a wheelchair, and waiting at the curb for Hilts' cavalry to arrive.

Burns grabbed his phone off the table at the inspection station and smiled and waved goodbye to the attending security personnel. He pulled up the surveillance video as soon as he was out of sight of the agents. The satellite image was unavailable, according to the typed message on the blue screen on the right. But the camera positioned at eye level was broadcasting. The spa appeared to be deserted. He didn't know if it was a signal problem or if the situation had changed dramatically. He waited until he was outside before he dialled Hilts. The call went directly to an automated operator, so Burns rang off and stared at the image of the spa's empty lobby on his phone.

It was three hundred metres along the service road to the group of low buildings surrounded by a car park that was shared by the worldwide car hire agencies, the familiar logos reflecting on the roofs and bonnets of dozens of shiny, late model vehicles. He spotted the smaller GoNow sign at the far end of the block. Burns trotted across the roadway to beat an approaching shuttle bus. He kept up the pace along the pavement as he strode away from the main terminal, breathing deeply and feeling the blood restore his limbs. He took the long way round the office block to satisfy his muscles, unsurprised to find the office dark and empty. He located the drop box and punched in the code Hilts had given him. A single key and fob hung on a hook. Burns grabbed the key, decided with a smirk against the idea of pressing the button to make the car locator chirp. Instead, he scanned the lot for the license plates that matched the number on the key chain and quickly spotted his target. The car was at the end of the first row, the only Ford in the lot. The American brand, of course. He suddenly wanted to hear Grand Funk Railroad. Burns chuckled to himself about how many times he had argued with a rental agent about what "or similar" meant. He opened the boot and used the same four-digit code on the brushed-steel case that held a black Beretta 9mm, two loaded magazine clips, and a small phone. He examined the weapon then emptied and reloaded both clips before a final scan of the case and its contents. His all-weather jacket was perfectly suited for carrying the tools he would need for this job, though he was never comfortable carrying a sidearm in a pocket. He took another look at the phone, which looked like an ordinary burner. He slipped it into an inside pocket, deciding to wait until he was in position to check in with Hilts. Then he closed the empty case and dropped it on the floor behind the driver's seat.

Burns spotted the spa's geodesic dome easily amongst the low buildings that occupied the former NATO base. The lobby was brightly lit, and Burns could see the night manager sitting at the reception desk, alone, looking at a computer monitor. He drove around a perimeter one street over, scanning for activity in and around the spa.

Burns circled back for a drive-by at the hangar. It looked deserted, no vehicles in the lot and only a few work lights burning inside. He figured the hangar was wide enough to house two planes the size of the Antonov cargo plane that had supposedly carried Veda, Kaia and Ivanov to Reykjavik. Burns stared at the high windows, too high to see any details of what might be inside. Burns thought about the stolen lab equipment and wondered if it might still be in the hangar, or if it had gone to the spa and was being set up in a sub level, beyond the eyes of the CIA's surveillance cameras. He decided to return to the hotel, as directed.

23:40

Burns pulled into the lot of the pizza restaurant across the road from the hotel. He backed into a stall near the restaurant's rear entrance, away from the two cars and a delivery scooter with an insulated box on the back. No diners were visible but the kitchen staff could be seen moving about beyond the service window inside. He thought about a pizza, and committed the delivery service number to memory.

Burns had a clear view of the Northern Lights Spa Hotel's main entrance. Suddenly he realised the angle was almost the same on the CIA surveillance camera. Burns threw off the idea that an agent was inside aiming his phone at the small window that faced toward the spa. The video feed was coming from a static position, almost in line with his position and zoomed in farther than Burns could see from his unobstructed view. He concluded it had to be on the lamppost at the front of the lot, and tried to imagine how inconspicuous the eye-level lens was. He studied his view of the spa's exterior and lobby. No shuttle van stood by, and the clerk at the desk looked bored. More importantly, he was alone. Burns checked the restaurant windows again and plotted his course from the car to the point of entry: the door at the end of the guest wing, away from the front entry and all the hostiles. He checked his phone again. Still no thermal images from the satellite feed, but the camera feed on the left was live. The night manager was hand-rolling a cigarette on the desk.

Burns pulled out the phone Hilts had left for him in the car and pressed the power button. The battery was dead. Perfect. He chuckled. It was a legitimate excuse for not keeping in touch.

He got out of the car and casually made his way across the road toward the empty lot next to the guest wing. He kept his hands in his pockets, the left one wrapped around the Beretta and the right fingering his lock pit wallet.

He saw the keypad entry and alarm on the fire exit and grimaced. Maybe Uncle Denis had updated his acumen since the nineties, but Burns knew he wasn't getting in through the back door. He turned around and scanned his surroundings then he checked his phone again. The night manager had stepped away from his desk and was standing just outside the main entry, enjoying his smoke. Burns watched him for a moment and determined by the way the young man was smoking, holding it between his thumb and forefinger, that the cigarette wasn't a legal, domestic brand. He was convinced the man was alone and not expecting any guests in the near future. Burns walked around the dome toward the main entry. He decided to use the element of surprise to give the young millennial a scare, stepping quickly behind the man before announcing himself.

"Good evening!" Burns exclaimed as if he was genuinely surprised to see the young man leaning against the wall next to the glass doorway. The young pothead coughed and sputtered so hard he spit the joint out of his mouth, sending it cartwheeling to the floor. He quickly darted down to retrieve the contraband then seemed to realise his guilt as he held it between his thumb and finger. He pinched the burning cherry off the end and stamped it out, then cupped the bent cigarette in his hand, blankly glancing up at Burns. Unsure what to do next, he tucked it into his pocket and straightened the tie that matched his navy blue jacket and trousers.

"Good evening, sir," he stammered as he wiped the spittle from his wispy blond moustache. Then he wiped his hand on his trousers and offered it. "Welcome to the Northern Lights Spa Hotel."

"Thank you," said Burns. He accepted the handshake cordially, without a glance at it. He dropped the smile and pointed at the young man's pocket. "Is that part of the spa's therapy program?"

After the nervous, spontaneous laughter subsided and was punctuated by a short cough, the young man replied. "Naw," he smiled. "They got some other miracle cure for everything, I guess."

Burns saw the light go off in the Night Manager's head. In a flash, he had guessed Burns was a cop. The pursed lips parted into a smile that revealed a mouth in terrible need of hygienic attention. Burns gave a smile of reassurance, letting the millennial miscreant know that he had no intention of causing trouble.

"I see," said Burns, as he nodded and smiled.

"Sorry sir," said the Night Manager. "But we don't have any rooms available. Renovations start soon."

"Any rooms occupied at the moment?"

The young man's face lit up as if the weed had sparked an exciting revelation. Then he looked hopefully at Burns, seeking confirmation.

"Are you police?" he asked innocently.

"Good guess," Burns replied. He pointed at the name tag hanging askew on the Night Manager's lapel. "What's your first name, Jonnson?"

"Bjartur, sir," Jonnson answered excitedly. Burns stared at the hipster's reddened eyes and watched as the excitement peaked and drained away in a moment, replaced by disappointment. Jonnson gave a nod of regret before giving Burns the bad news. "They're all gone."

"They?"

"All the guests," Jonnson answered duly. "And the others…"

"The others?" Burns repeated.

"I mean," Jonnson began shakily, "the ones that were not here for the cure. Cure People left, today afternoon and evening. Others left since twenty-two hour."

Burns understood the timeframe. Fear stung him like a spear, jabbing him just below his ribs. He guessed Ivanov had disrupted the CIA's surveillance prior to making his escape. He remained outwardly calm as the possibility that he had missed his target seared in his gut.

"Did you happen to see this man?" he showed his phone to Jonnson, who examined the photo of Veda and Kaia at the opera.

"No, sir. Never saw the man here at the spa."

"What about the girl?"

"Oh yeah," Jonnson almost whistled. "She was with… one of the guys."

"You mean with, as in…" Burns gave a sideways look and raised his eyebrows expectantly.

"Yeah, with him. Good-looking guy. Caught them snogging in the dining hall just before everybody leave in the shuttle," he shrugged. "Everybody's gone now."

"How many were they?"

"Five went in the shuttle, plus those two…"

"Did they look like soldiers?" Burns asked, studying Jonnson, who nodded, then suddenly remembered. "The couple might not have been in the bus."

"Did they have another car?" Burns asked. The night manager shook his head 'no'.

"I didn't see them leave but I know they're gone. I went round and locked up everywhere."

"I see," said Burns. He knew it was the truth. He closed his phone and put it away. His mind spun through the possibilities. Veda hadn't made it to the spa. Burns put away the questions about Ivanov and Kaia and her Other Man. And the Cure People.

"What's downstairs, Bjartur?" Burns pointed to the floor. He realised he was looking for negative confirmation and not an invitation. He felt some relief when Jonnson shrugged nonchalantly.

"The small storage under kitchen." Then Jonsson paused as a memory lit up in his eyes. "And the uh…" Jonnson searched for the word. "Tube?"

He thought about asking Jonnson to take him to the tunnel, then dismissed the idea. He would make his way above ground to the charter hangar. Veda was either somewhere under his feet or still in the hangar. He came back to the image of an underground lab, viruses growing in petri dishes.

But he still wasn't going underground before exploring the hangar.

"A tunnel," Burns grumbled.

"Yes!" Jonnson exclaimed. "Tunnel, yes," he nodded happily, repeating the familiar but forgotten word. "A tunnel. Very near the elevator. It goes… I don't know. Never seen," Jonnson confessed. "I don't like tunnels."

"I understand," said Burns. He turned to the west and stared through the wall, visualising the hangar two hundred metres away, and plotted his route.

"My boss says we're closed. They be the last guests for a while," Jonnson was trying to sound helpful. Burns heard the last bit in an echo that circled his skull, the implication spinning like a cyclone. Defeat. His mission was over before it began. And fear. Burns allowed it to churn in his gut. The idea of his enemy achieving success, and the devastating possibilities of what that meant welled up in his mind's eye.

That always worked. The sorrow was quickly replaced by anger. He had to recon the hangar before he could close the file in his mind. And he wouldn't wait for Hilts' team to arrive.

Burns became aware of Jonnson watching him. Looking curious and hopeful, the young man knew nothing, other than the police were interested in the last group who had passed through his lobby. Burns unclenched his jaw and forced a smile.

"Thank you for your help, Bjartur." Burns reached out to shake hands. Jonnson couldn't hide his disappointment as he weakly returned Burns' cordiality.

"Nice to meet you, too," he replied, his ice blue eyes turning sombre. Then hope returned in a flash. "I am here to eight hour. I can contact you if anything happens?"

"We'll be in touch," said Burns. Then he remembered the Americans and looked at his watch. "You might be visited by other agents," he paused. "Unless I can reach them first." He looked at Jonnson and decided he liked him. "Best for you to wait out here for an hour or so," he added. Burns watched as Jonnson's eyes flickered with excitement, and a weed smoker's paranoia. An unconscious hand went to the pocket where he had stashed the remnants of the joint he had been smoking when Burns arrived. Burns turned and left him with the dilemma of whether or not to finish it.

It was a clear, moonless night but the darkness didn't provide full cover at the two wide roadways Burns had to cross en route to the hangar. They were lit by lonely lampposts, usually in pairs near crossroads, but not close enough to each other for their pools of light to meet. The late hour meant the buildings and car parks were empty, the streets deserted. Burns crouched in the shadow of a small Quonset hut in the lot next to the Northern Lights Spa Hotel. He pulled out his phone and checked to see if the link to the satellite feed had been restored. It hadn't, but he could see Jonnson standing near the entrance, finishing his smoke. Burns laughed to himself. Then he hoped young Bjartur Jonnson followed his directive to stay outside, and not get caught in a CIA accident.

Burns thought about contacting Hilts then quickly punted the idea. Hilts hadn't sent a message or called since Burns arrived. He concluded it didn't matter if the CIA had been compromised or if Hilts had nothing to tell. Chief Inspector Wayne would tell Burns he still had his mission.

Burns scanned the immediate surroundings again before setting off. He chose speed over stealth or nonchalance. Not only because he was impatient for closure but also because he knew the physical stress would calm his quarrelsome thoughts. He kept the same trot-run through the shadows and open areas, focusing on his breathing. And his target.

He recalled the photo and easily replaced the tuxedo with a lab coat, and Veda holding a test tube that might hold the fate of millions. Burns wondered if Kaia was still wearing that dress. He hadn't given up on the possibility of seeing both. He tried to picture a laboratory set up in the hangar, with Veda and his stolen lab equipment. Burns saw no malice in the man. Whatever nefarious designs Ivanov may have involved Veda, but the young scientist wanted to save the world from disease. He wasn't a partner in any genocide scheme.

Burns' mouth dropped open, as if he had heard himself say the word for the first time. Genocide.

Fifty metres away from the hangar, Burns had reached the effective range limit of his only weapon, so he slipped into the shadow of a bus shelter and withdrew the M9. He opened and closed the safety with his right thumb then checked the clip and cocked it. His body confirmed its readiness with an exaggerated shrug.

Burns studied the large white building, cast grey in the shadow beyond the pale white streetlamp that stood near him. The wall he faced was three stories high and at least sixty metres long, and it ended airside. It had a curved roof, with a row of skylights at its apex. Dim light escaped from the high, narrow windows that ran along the wall just below the roof, but the interior wasn't bright enough to give the skylights more than a faint glow. Burns closed his eyes and listened. He heard a small diesel car shifting into second gear on the service road that circled back to the airport almost a kilometre away, and nothing else. He couldn't see the main entry from his position, only a corner of the parking lot where a small triangular billboard confirmed the charter company's name. Nevertheless, he determined the best option to be using the front door.

Burns skirted the pool of light at the bus stop and sprinted across the road, angling for the near end of the hangar wall. Crouching low, he peeked round the corner to find the car park empty. He had no idea if it was good news or bad. But he knew he still had to go in.

He spotted two cameras and estimated their range and focus. The nearest one was five metres directly above his head and focused away from the building onto the empty, striped macadam. The car park was big enough for eight or ten cars, with a space reserved for "Buses Only" painted in the corner of the lot nearest the building. A wheelchair-accessible ramp linked it to the walkway leading to the entrance. The other camera was mounted on the eaves overhanging the small vestibule that served as the main entry, twenty metres away from Burns' corner, and was aimed down at the pool of light in front of the entry. He worked the angles. He could see the steel door and the small square window next to it that would offer the only view inside. He wouldn't get the chance to try out the camera jammer that Hilts described as a "standard app" on the phone with the dead battery. He wasn't angry. Maybe he was relieved. He would have to gamble that his approach along the wall was concealed all the way to the door.

He had to breathe, to slow his thoughts. He was sure he could hear Michael Jackson coming from the building. The sound was faint but clear, coming from a portable music player.

Burns chose to ignore Michael's advice to "beat it". He kept his body a few inches away from the wall as he glided silently to the window and peeked inside. He could see a beam of light that was shining through the door, but no other light burned in the room nearest the window. In the shadows, Burns saw a small reception desk and a row of four chairs against the wall opposite the window. The entry to the hangar was in the far corner of the room, its oversized double doors pinned open by bolts in the floor. What he could see of the hangar was crisscrossed with light from the few lamps mounted high on the walls. He could see the tail of an executive jet, but the registration number was in deep shadow. He wondered if the jet was parked nose-out for a quick getaway. Either way, it wasn't the Antonov.

Just then a young, clean-cut man in a dark uniform passed through Burns' field of vision and disappeared behind the fuselage. Out of habit, Burns checked his watch. A quick recall of the man revealed a junior officer's flight uniform—not military. Just then one of the lights was dowsed, far away from the reception area, then a few seconds later another on the opposite side of the hangar. Looks like he's shutting it down for the night, thought Burns. He glanced over at the empty car park again.

No cars here. Just a tunnel...

Michael Jackson beat it and was replaced by a female singer he didn't recognise straightaway, but whomever she was singing to was "trouble". Burns knew he had to move inside, now. He pulled a small torch from a pocket on his jacket sleeve and used it to briefly illuminate the lock and handle on the door. Burns watched through the window and withdrew the small wallet containing lock pick tools that he hoped would be able to get him inside, and without too much noise. He had inherited the original set of lock picking tools from one of his father's mates who had died shortly after Officer Cadet Charles Burns became Lieutenant Charles Burns in the Dragoons. "Uncle" Denis was a neighbour and locksmith when Charles was in the military high school in West Calgary and had given the younger Burns his first real job, hiring him as an assistant when he had had bigger installation contracts. Charles was a quick study when it came to both mechanical and electronic security systems. He showed keen interest, he had presented articles and advertisements detailing the latest advances in electronic security, but Uncle Denis was still stuck in the Eighties. When young Charles left Calgary for deployment in Europe, Uncle Denis told him to keep the lock pick set.

"You never know when it might come in handy," he said. Burns never had much use for them in the past but was glad that he had taken them out now and then and practiced on different locks everywhere he had been based around the world. He even added a few master keys to the wallet along the way. Burns usually travelled with the lock picking case in the same lock box he used to transport his gun on civilian transport. Because of his credentials, the case had never been subject to more than a cursory inspection as he handed them in to the authorities. This time he had put it in his toiletries case for the hasty trip to Iceland and hoped for the best. It didn't raise suspicion when he passed through the security at the airport.

The first master key he tried was a fit.

The lock turned with two ticks, no louder than a mantle clock. Burns grasped the door and pulled steadily against the vacuum effect as he drew it open. He could see a little more of the hangar through the crack.

The young man in uniform passed through again. Burns guessed he must be the flight engineer, working alone. He hoped the man was just tidying up, working late not early.

Suddenly the music stopped.

Burns froze for a moment then assured himself he had not been discovered. The tension released its grip on his breath and a frustrated laugh escaped quietly. He returned the tools to his pocket.

He opened the door and entered, holding himself in a three-quarters crouch, and silently closed the door. Staying low, he moved to the edge of the shaft of light coming through the double doors. He could see the crewman rounding the plane about twenty metres away, carrying what looked like a medium-sized satchel or briefcase. Burns guessed it carried the flight report and logbook. He's going home for the night, he thought.

The Antonov stood tail-out, abandoned in the shadows on the opposite side of the hangar. Relief was replaced by urgency as Burns scanned the vast darkness for an exit sign or anything that might indicate an alternate path that would take his target out of contact range. The only other way out would be airside. The crewman walked about ten steps directly away from the plane toward a waist-high tubular metal fence standing in the open floor of the hangar. Burns straightened to his full height, remaining concealed in the door's shadow. He angled one eye to the edge of the door and could see the fence surrounded a grey metal plate, about two metres by four metres, on the floor. There was a hospital gurney with an IV pole attached parked in a corner of the deck. Burns watched the man grab a latch on the fence and step through the gate and onto the platform.

Burns was set to engage before the crewman had closed the gate. He knew it was a lift, and he decided that it would be best if he got to the crewman before he met whatever was at the end of the ride down, more preferably even before the lift moved. The crewman was still standing near the gate with his back to Burns, his attention fixed on his phone. Burns measured the gap. In two seconds, he visualised the nine steps and the leap over the railing. Sacrificing stealth for speed, Burns was in full flight as he vaulted over the rail. The crewman had half turned but Burns adjusted, driving his heel into the crewman's left knee, buckling it but not breaking it. Burns folded his legs as he landed, letting his victim's body absorb his full weight as they crashed to the metal floor. The crewman's first shriek escaped his lips before Burns could get a hand over his mouth. Burns' imagination amplified the echo rolling around in the hangar. He cursed himself for his noisy entrance. Too many years using a grenade to announce my arrival, he mused. If there were any hostiles around, they would now know he was here. Burns pulled out the Beretta and held it to the back of the crewman's blond head. After a short silence, he tapped the crewman's head with his gun.

"Where are you going?" he growled in a low, threatening Russian. He pressed a little harder with the gun and pulled his right hand away from the crewman's mouth.

The young man was panicked and in pain. He pointed to the floor. "Down. To sleep," he mumbled in Russian.

Burns had guessed right with the Russian, so he kept it up, asking, "Where? With who?" What the crewman told Burns he translated as "sleeping rooms in hospital. I have permission. Everybody sleeps in hotel but me." Burns could see how the irksome fact had spurred defiance in the thin young junior officer.

"Who are you?" he asked, in English.

Burns grabbed a handful of hair and turned the crewman's head harshly, then smiled and released his grip. "Was my accent that bad?"

"No," the young man yelped. "Just... not like guys around here. I speak good English." Burns gripped and held the thin, passive arms and squeezed. *A firm, tenacious yet non-bruising grip,* he remembered. It brought a smile to his face that tempered his patience.

The crewman pleaded. "Look, I don't know you, you don't know me." He made a show of averting his eyes. "I don't want no troubles. Just to sleep. Please —"

Burns cut the crewman off. "Look, I don't give a fuck about your life. You understand?" he twisted the crewman to face the abandoned gurney. "Tell me where the professor went and..." He left it there, not one to make promises he might not want to keep. "The hotel or the hospital?" For a second, Burns wondered if he had misread the stoner Jonnson.

The crewman had lost all his defiance. "I don't know no p-p-professor. Some darkie guy in a coma, I saw."

Burns pulled out his phone and showed the crewman the photo of Nicholas Veda. The crewman seemed relieved. "Yes! We dropped him down here but..." The crewman tried to affect a helpful tone. "Don't think he went to the hotel. Somebody said maybe he was too sick. I don't mind," then he corrected himself. "I don't know. Spa people don't look too sick." The crewman smiled weakly and paused. Burns was still listening for any signs of movement below the deck or around the hangar. Both planes were dark.

The crewman had convinced himself. "We fly him here two nights ago. He was not... eyes open. I think he is too sick. Haven't seen him since but, yes. Maybe he's in hospital too. I guess there, maybe."

Burns took it all in. The lift accessed the spa hotel and a "hospital", likely the lab where the plot to create a bioweapon would unfurl. It sounded like it was outfitted for humans. Maybe trials, maybe weapons, maybe...

"Show me," said Burns with a tilt of his gun toward the control toggle. It was attached to a heavy cable that lay coiled on the floor less than a metre away from the two men.

"Let me up, please."

"No," Burns answered calmly. "We'll stay down low for now." Burns reached over and dragged the controller close to the crewman's hand. Burns nodded again and the crewman squeezed the controller and pushed his thumb onto the red 'down' arrow on the toggle. The switch was fully manual, and only worked the lift when the crewman applied a constant pressure to the rubber button. But his hand was shaking, so Burns pushed the barrel of his gun into the crewman's ribs, forcing out a groan. Burns contemplated knocking the man out and taking his chances in the tunnels. He thought better of it and added his own force to the button. The gentle hiss of hydraulic pistons told Burns it was a repurposed man lift, likely used in exterior construction in its previous life. Hearing no motor sounds gave Burns a moment of calm before he braced again and tightened his grip on the crewman. He would use the young man as a human shield if it came to a firefight. A second later a band of light widened around them like a sunrise as the lift dropped below the floor and into a large room, finished in concrete decades earlier. A single bulb in a protective cage was hanging from the ceiling directly opposite Burns. He kept flat as the lift lowered out of its shaft and into the open space. When the lift came to rest, the nearest walls surrounding it were almost three metres tall in a space larger than the underground car park back at his flat in London. He squinted for a few seconds then scanned left and right. No reception. No hostiles. Not even a chair. One wall had been closed off by a floor-to-ceiling chain link fence that ran south, twenty or so metres into the shadows. Burns guessed it met a wall there but couldn't be sure because of the darkness. He couldn't see how deep the storage area was, but he could see that the width of it appeared to be spanned by racks and racks of what he assumed were plane parts. He could see what looked like a cowling for a jet engine on one of the stands. Russian recycling, thought Burns. He rolled off the crewman, keeping his man pinned with one arm as he scanned 360 degrees around and above to the hangar.

Five metres away, a converted golf cart sat on a black disc set into the floor. The car had seats for four or five people including the driver and a flat deck on the back, suitable for transporting equipment, or a patient on a gurney. The disc was met by two single-rail tracks, one heading east and one to the south. Burns knew the spa was east of the hangar and the crewman confirmed it. He pointed down the tunnel on the left and the one straight on.

"That way to hotel," he pointed. "This way I sleep, in *bol'nitsa.*"

"Hospital?"

"Yes!" He nodded excitedly then shook his head. "No, not hospital," The engineer gestured with his hands. "Smaller."

"Like a clinic?" Burns asked.

"Yes!" The engineer nodded happily. "But clinic empty now."

"Who's in the hotel?" asked Burns again, mustering some patience.

"Nobody now. Crew and tough guys left after dinner. Cure People left Friday. I mean I don't know who else stay but... but not the Cure People."

"Cure People?" repeated Burns. "What were they cured of?"

"Not cured. They cure. Cure People leave the spa and go to their home countries and cure every people's diseases." The crewman looked as if he just let the truth slip. "I don't know who say that, sorry. It's just a story." The crewman lapsed into Russian again and tried to explain. "I don't know how, everybody for real..." He trailed off. Burns could see the crewman wanted to believe that whomever he was working for was in the business of saving, not killing. But Burns knew more of the truth now, even if his hostage didn't. He felt the familiar flash in his gut that told him people were going to die. In the past it had also warned him that he would be killing, too.

We go to the *bol'nitsa,*" said Burns.

The crewman was relieved, and he reached for the controller to rotate the disc and turn the car back southward. "I go to sleep?" he said hopefully.

"Guards?" Burns asked as he gestured to get into the car.

"Yes," replied the crewman as he sat behind the wheel. "Two, or maybe one."

"How far?" he asked.

"Maybe four, five hundred metres. Not far."

Burns checked his watch and changed hands with his gun to keep it behind the crewman's head. The disc turned until the car centred on the track heading south. Burns felt like he was getting on a ride at the fair.

The crewman pressed his foot down on the accelerator and the car lurched up to its top speed. Maybe a little faster than a good run for Burns, at least tonight, he thought. He wasn't sure he could keep its pace for four hundred metres.

Burns looked over at the young man driving, guilelessly holding the wheel as if he were actually steering the vehicle. "How will we talk our way past?" asked the crewman.

Burns ignored the question. The young man was ready to switch sides and Burns couldn't blame him. Nobody is completely innocent, Burns reminded himself. The car continued south on a gently downward sloping track. Burns looked back and noted that they had dropped over a metre since leaving the roundabout. Suddenly the car passed a junction. Burns could see pools of light from a few bulbs angling lower in his view as the tunnel appeared to drop into darkness in the distance. Burns grabbed the crewman's skinny leg and pulled it off the accelerator and pressed it on the brake. The car stopped about three seconds later, just past the junction, but Burns got a good look before the car halted. This tunnel was older and narrower by a couple of metres, and the trackless floor ran eastward, the same general direction from where Burns had made his original approach to the hangar. No cameras, he noted with some satisfaction. In the general direction of Reykjavik at least, but nothing between here and there except the abandoned movie studio about four hundred metres or so from here. Beyond that was the Atlantic, as Burns recollected. Of course, the tunnel didn't have to go straight anywhere.

"Where does that one go?" he asked.

The crewman shook his head. "Never been," he said. "Never asked." At least fifty percent true, Burns mused.

Burns studied the junction again and noticed what could have been tyre tracks made by a vehicle similar to the one he was riding in at the moment. It had made the sharp right-turn approach from the lab side of the tunnel, and left traces of rubber behind, tiny rubber pebbles in two curved lines. But the marks were too faint to even guess how old they were. Burns momentarily considered the possibility of it being an escape route, then decided the lab had to be seen first. Not only to search for Veda, but also to see for himself what kind of weapon was being made. He looked at his watch again and calculated he would have a maximum of one hour before the CIA would have a tactical team on the ground at the airport. They would be at the spa minutes later. Burns did not want to be inside when that happened. He turned forward and gazed down the tunnel ahead. He could see the end point now, lit up by several tube lights on each side of the tunnel, perhaps another four hundred metres away. It wasn't possible to see any detail of the sides or walls or a room at the end of the line because of the forced perspective, ending in only a small square of light from this distance. Burns estimated they were halfway.

"Now we know why you're an engineer not a navigator," he said. He squeezed the crewman's leg again and turned forward. "Drive," he said. He had relaxed his left hand and let it fall to conceal his weapon behind the driver's seat. Leaning back, he told the crewman, "You're going to be cool, right?" The crewman lit up with an optimistic grin. He understood.

"Super chill," he repeated solemnly.

"How many of these cars?" Burns asked in Russian.

"Two," the crewman answered in Russian. "I only ever see two."

"Who else will be here?" said Burns looking forward and back as they left the pool of light at the junction. The crewman looked confused, so Burns asked in Russian.

"What about guards, soldiers?" Burns asked. "You know, tough guys. Ever see anyone like that in here?" Burns was trying to reconnect with the crewman, but he appeared to be in the passive stage of shock. Burns reached over and pulled the crewman's leg off the accelerator. Then he grabbed the crewman by the collar. "Hey, Super Chill. Who else will be down here?"

"One guard, maybe two," the crewman answered in English as he pointed at the end of the tunnel. He shuddered, as if struck by an unsettling memory, and went on in Russian. "Another creepy guy... I don't see him always. I only come to sleep. I go to bedroom," he said. "I guess only me. Maybe. I don't think. I don't... know your guy."

"Slow down a little," Burns commanded. He was having a little trouble with the crewman's regional dialect. He guessed there would be a guard waiting at the end of the tunnel. "Where would the other guard be?"

"Maybe sleeping, maybe checking." He tapped his watch. "My duty is in seven hours. My crew go to hotel, leave me. Other crew gone. Plane..." he paused wearily. "I sleep here. I don't think Eyes-Closed Guy..."

"You don't think," repeated Burns as he nudged the crewman's sacro-cranial joint with his gun. The crewman's foot slipped off the accelerator when he reacted.

"No, know! I don't know other guy! I only sleep here — two times... I have room." He proffered a small ring of keys on the lanyard round his neck and held forth a small round fob. "My room. Only twice. Three tonight... I don't see nobody. I have room. I sleep." The young man was almost sobbing.

"Take it easy," said Burns. He pointed at his driver's foot and waved down for him to step on it. Then he turned his focus to the terminal end of the tunnel. At two hundred metres away, Burns could see what looked like a small lobby beyond the roundabout at the end of the line. At the end of the platform where the car was to land was an empty space large enough to park another car. Behind it was a small desk and a glassed-in waiting room, built as an add-on to the tunnel, squaring off one side of the end of the line. One hostile was in view at the desk, but it was impossible to see yet if he was armed. Burns assumed he was. The man was easily a hundred kilos and almost two metres tall. He watched as the guard crossed and entered the waiting room where he turned to face the glass. Bending at the waist, he used the rail mounted on the wall to lower himself, stretching his back and limbs, the same way Burns would do. He wondered if the guard was getting ready for combat or if it was some other ritual. Burns tensed and released his own muscles, group by group, as he scanned the approaching landing site.

About ten metres before the end of the line the tunnel opened up into a wider space much like the one Burns and the crewman had departed minutes earlier, but with a lowered tile ceiling and finished white walls and glass instead of a wire fence.

The car arrived at the dock as the guard turned the corner, exiting the waiting room. He took a few steps then stopped, his arms hanging wide at his sides as if he just dropped a barbell after a successful dead lift. Burns stepped out of the car and the crewman did likewise, then he froze, except for his head which swivelled from Burns to the guard and back.

The guard looked at the crewman and asked in Russian., "*Kto tvoy drug*?" *Who's your friend*? The crewman tried hard not to stammer, "A friend."

"*On slishkom star dlya tebya*?" *He's too old for you, isn't he?* The question was for the crewman, but the guard was eyeing Burns' and his left arm held behind his back. The guard's right hand drifted in to his sidearm. His palm lighted on the hilt and a finger curled back to the clip holding the gun in its holster. He unfastened it silently but deliberately, and Burns knew this guard had had some training, and had seen action, too. The guard's grip found the hilt and trigger without completely drawing the weapon, and his eyes met Burns' with conviction. Without hesitation Burns charged, never his preferred tactic hand-to-hand, leading with a kick aimed at the larger man's knee and a hard strike to the throat. His crushed larynx stifled the guard's brutish scream, but he got off one shot before Burns could take him down and break the hand that held the gun. The crewman screamed, the echo lingering for a few seconds as it chased the report of the gun back down the tunnel. Burns broke the man's neck before he could suffocate to death. He turned to see the crewman writhing on the front of the car, trying to hold his right thigh with both hands. He couldn't stop himself from sliding to the floor. He was gripping the inside of his leg hard, almost at the crotch, to staunch the blood flow. Burns couldn't tell how much blood the crewman was losing, but he knew the wound was in a bad place. Burns took two strides around the front of the car to see the crewman's face, pulled long and pale in terror and shock. The crewman's left leg was much darker than the rest of his navy blue uniform, blood-soaked to the knee. He was bleeding to death, and Burns was relieved. He wouldn't have to turn his gun on the crewman and say "sorry", half to the crewman and half to himself, as he had imagined doing. Soon the young man would pass out and never wake up.

"*Teper' mozhno spat*," he whispered. *Now you can sleep.* The look on the crewman's face told Burns he knew he was dying. He kept still for several seconds, listening for approaching footsteps until the young man lost consciousness. He had screamed loud enough to be heard at the far end of the tunnel. Satisfied he hadn't been discovered, Burns fished through the crewman's pockets and retrieved a phone, wallet and the key ring. He slipped the keys into his jacket pocket then simultaneously checked the call log and scanned the wallet's contents. Three calls came from a St Petersburg number, and nothing else. He found a folded letter tucked in the wallet, which appeared to be the crewman's honourable discharge from the Russian air force in 2016. After twelve years of service at the rank of private, Anatoly Gagarin had retired. Burns folded it and replaced it in the wallet. He wondered what Gagarin's pension looked like and wondered if he was connected to the famous family, or if they would be notified. Burns replaced the wallet in the crewman's jacket.

Burns stood again and scanned the dock area and area just beyond it. The dock was two steps above the level of the roundabout and was also accessed by a long ramp. A small manual pallet jack was parked next to two rubbish bins at the far left end of the dock. An old black wall phone was at the corner where the dock met the entry area. Best of all, Burns saw no cameras. He spotted three mounting points: one on the end of the dock, another above the glass door inside the waiting room and the last just beyond the nurses' station desk beyond the glass, all missing a camera. He alternately thanked the stars and asked himself if he was glad no one was watching right now, or that nobody would be able to watch and rewatch anything that happened here tonight.

There was a handheld radio in its charging cradle on the small desk opposite the glass-walled waiting room where the guard had been doing his calisthenics. The walkie-talkie was switched off. Burns recalled how the guard hadn't even glanced toward the radio before or during their meeting, reinforcing the hopeful idea that perhaps there was no one else to talk to tonight. Burns advanced.

The slate-coloured linoleum floor near the entryway looked new but had strands of dust along the curved edges where it met the walls. A nursing station stood a few steps beyond the waiting room on the right side of the corridor. It was barren, no computers or files and only a similarly aged single line phone on the desk. Not even a chair at the desk. A few metres beyond the unmanned station Burns could see another set of glass doors on the far wall, and another sliding glass door in the wall behind it, creating another small vestibule. It reminded him of the entry at his old dorm on the CFB barracks in Calgary. The two sets of doors there were an effort to keep the cold Canadian winter at bay. Here they looked more like they might be used to control traffic. Burns wondered if it was to be a security post or a bio scan when completed.

Directly opposite the nursing station's gate another corridor ran perpendicular away from the desk and the main entry corridor. It was at least a metre narrower than the main corridor but still wide enough for moving people and equipment with ease. A wordless sign hung from the ceiling tiles over the hall's entrance. It had an image of a stick figure reclining on a tipped-over 'L'. The overhead lighting was switched off, the only light came from floor lights running down the left wall. Very hospital-ish, thought Burns. Enough light for a guest to find their way to the loo for a midnight calling. Burns stifled a yawn. He guessed he had got somewhere between two and four hours total sleep in the little naps he had managed since rising early Friday morning... a run in the park, played a little shinny that night... his status with MCU2 unclear. Then... all this. He let the yawn win out, drawing in the air sharply, holding it long enough to feel the oxygen feeding his brain, then letting it out slowly through the sides of his mouth. He found a moment of stillness long enough to extinguish his body's urge to sleep. He hadn't pushed himself yet, fatigue was not a factor. As long as he had air.

Burns looked back again to the clinical-looking entry beyond the nursing station. The inside door was frosted glass and the room beyond was also in night mode, so Burns couldn't make out any detail of the space beyond the glass cubicle.

He knew his first action had to be to find and eliminate Guard Number Two, if there was one. Burns decided a sleeping guard would be better to meet just now, and he advanced around the corner to where stickmen slept.

Burns could see eight pairs of doors and windows along the right wall. It reminded him of walking down the corridor of a Travel Lodge Motor Hotel anywhere, only with a bare wall on the left instead of a parking lot. The wall was painted in two shades of pale blue, the darker shade below blending into the floor's grey faux slate. There were curtains hanging in each of the windows but were all drawn open — except the third window.

Burns calculated five steps to the first window and door, and another ten more to the shaded window. The end of the hall was about twenty metres away. A chair and small table flanked a door on the end wall, sitting against the wall under the only working overhead light. It reminded Burns of an attendant's station in a public toilet in Istanbul, sans the change bowl and tissues. And the scented *kolonya* generously splashed on his hands… There was a small square sign on the door, but Burns couldn't quite make out the symbol in the dimness. He hoped it was a stick figure sitting on a toilet. After a final take to his right toward the glass entry to the clinic, or lab or whatever was in there, Burns took his first two silent steps. He edged his way along the wall toward the first window.

The curtains in the first window were drawn almost completely open, revealing a small single room measuring about three metres by four metres with a raised single bed that looked more Ikea than Infirmary, with a small grey bedside stand and matching wardrobe. Two blue vinyl and chrome chairs sat opposite the bed, looking more like they belonged in an airport boarding area than a private room in a hospital. The room had similar floor-level lighting, but most curious was the large picture window on the opposite wall. It was framed like another window, but it had a photographic print of a scene along the Thames. Just as he recognised the location, he realised that the image was moving. Burns could see two long barges moving in opposite directions and a lorry traversing the view on the near shore. It was night in the scene. The photo-realism and continuous play. He wondered if he was seeing it in real time.

The second room looked identical to the first and was also uninhabited. Burns felt his hackles rise as he turned his attention to Door Number Three. He took a quick look over his shoulder to the corridor behind him then tried to get a look through a small gap in the curtains. It only provided a partial view of one chair, which at least didn't have a pair of trousers or a gun belt hanging on it. Burns remembered the fob he had got from young Anatoly. Maybe this was his room. He froze and listened for a moment. Burns looked back at Door Numbers One and Two and thought to try the fob on one or both of them first but decided against it. He was already committed to Door Number Three. He cupped his ear against the wall next to the window. He couldn't hear any sounds of activity, but he had no idea how well insulated the wall was. Burns focused on the door and hoped that the mechanism wouldn't be loud enough to wake a sleeping man. He visualised the position of the bed in relation to the door, which would open inward and away from the main part of the room. Burns took a few long, slow breaths and mentally rehearsed his movements. Keeping low, with his gun in his left hand, he pressed the fob to the small black disc above the handle and heard a tumbler release the door from its frame. He paused, waiting for a sound inside, but none came. He eased the door open. It turned inward easily on its light hinges without a sound.

Still crouching, Burns brought his weapon up and aimed it through the gap in the direction of the bed, hesitated, then peered around the doorframe. Anatoly may have been the last one to sleep in the unmade bed, or it could have been the other guard that left the white sheet and taupe fleece blanket twisted like lovers on the narrow bed. Or maybe Veda... Burns was frustrated. Surprised that he was somehow more disappointed with not finding another hostile.

He stared at the picture window. It had a different image from the first two, a tropical forest stretching down to a secluded bay on an azure sea. Low waves rolled and curled gently onto the strand and disappeared under themselves again. Maybe Thailand, he thought.

He took another two steps to the next window, saw the room empty and the décor unchanged, then stepped quicker past the next and the next. All of the beds had been made, or hadn't been slept in. All the other picture windows shared the same view of the Thames, but when Burns reached the last room the two barges were gone from sight, replaced by a festively lit ferry crossing the river below Battersea Park. He stood upright, stretched a little, and padded the few remaining strides until he was standing at the table at the end of the hall. The sign on the door had male and female silhouettes standing next to a shower and the letters 'WC' below. Burns heard the faint sound of running water, not splashing on tile but more like the sound of water running in pipes. He pulled the handle down slowly and used his elbow to ease the door open a crack. He listened for a few seconds. It was water pouring into a sink or a toilet running on, not a shower. The room was brightly lit from overhead and the tiled walls and floor shone white. Keeping low, he opened the door a little more and saw the raised enclosure wall of a toilet. The door was closed but there were no feet showing under the stall, sitting or standing at the bowl. He listened again. The sound was water in pipes, but he was sure he could make out the gurgling noise of water going down an open drain. It wasn't coming from the toilet. Burns turned and shifted his weight to shoulder the door open a little farther. A white tiled wall next to the door of the toilet separated it from the shower stall. There was an open entry at the far end of the wall. The shower was empty, dry. Burns was now sure that water was flowing on the other side of the room, the side he couldn't see behind the door. The door had been open for several seconds now. If there was a guard there doing his washing up, he still hadn't heard Burns at the door, or at least that was how Burns preferred to see it. The question was to dive or swing. He switched his gun to his right hand and used his left to grip the door's lever to slow the swing and minimize the noise, should the door suddenly meet a wall behind it as he opened it to its full radius to view the rest of the room. Empty. A small sink hung bare from the wall, with a chrome-framed mirror above it, and a tandem of two porcelain urinals stood just beyond the sink. Burns could tell the flushing mechanism was stuck open on one of them. He clenched and unclenched his muscles, squeezing his hands into fists twice, letting out some tension before he turned and walked back down the hall. Burns asked himself if he was alone in the underground. He decided that even if he was, and Veda was somewhere else, he had to know what Vladimir Ivanov was doing in his secret facility.

Burns switched on his phone and saw a message from Hilts. It was a courtesy call, stating simply:

80 Min.

That was sixteen minutes ago. Burns appreciated the gesture and replied with a beer mug 'cheers' emoji. He had no idea what size of a crew Hilts would be bringing but he imagined their priority would be to secure any of the stolen viruses first, and no doubt, with a shoot-to-kill order. And they would start at the spa, so Burns would have some time to recon whatever lay beyond the glass doors in. But he was uncertain of their interest in Dr Veda. If they or anybody else knew about Typhoid Mary's potential for genocide, who wouldn't be?

"Where are you, Dr Veda?" Burns softly wondered aloud.

For good or bad, Burns still had to come down believing his side as being the only right side. His orders were clear: extract and return the British Subject to Her Majesty's care and protection. Burns believed he had to get in and out before Hilts' team arrived to guarantee that outcome. If he found Veda.

Burns glided along the bare wall back to the nursing station. He paused before he stepped into the main corridor, crouched low again and peeked round the corner to the glass vestibule at the end of the corridor. He focused his eyes and ears on the frosted glass on the other side of the double doors. The far wall beyond it looked to be tinted glass. Burns assumed he could be seen by anyone inside if he stood up in the corridor, so he stayed in a three-quarter crouch, taking two quick steps across the corridor to cover behind the nursing station.

No cameras or motion sensors-controlled entry through the first sliding glass door and it was open wide. No handle and no keypad on the second door inside, and it looked like an airtight seal from where Burns stood. He assumed there would be some kind of manual control at the station so he stepped through the gap in the divider that framed the nurses' station and scanned the underside of the countertop. In a moment his eyes found the two-button switch and he reached for it, pressing the green button without hesitation. He withdrew his hand and then froze as the sound of a soft chime rang out and echoed down the tunnel behind him. It was more of a welcome, like a doorbell and not an alarm. Even so, Burns couldn't wonder how far the sound carried on the other side of the door. The door was rolling open so he made his move. He sprinted fourteen steps full speed, angling to the side of sliding the door for as much concealment as possible. He stopped flat and low, and focused his listening on the other side of the opening. The sealed doors held Burns in total silence, alone with his breathing. He eased upward until his eye was level with the top of the frosting and peered over to see what lay beyond the door. It was a continuation of the corridor on his side, with the same floor level lighting. On the left Burns saw another hall, similar in width to the sleeping quarters hall. It ended much nearer, maybe three metres, at a wall that Burns could only see one corner of from his angle. The main corridor ended at another perpendicular corridor about twenty metres from where Burns crouched inside the glass holding chamber. The far wall of the crossing corridor was half glass, and Burns guessed if the lighting were better he could get a good look at the operation. But would he see Dr Veda? Some other mad scientist? Despite the negative results at the Travel Lodge, he was convinced Veda was too valuable to leave out in the open, and ex-General Ivanov probably would want to keep prisoner Veda's movement to a minimum. If he had something cooking in the lab, Ivanov would want Veda as near as possible. Burns slid the door open stepped across the threshold. He was thankful for the lack of sensors on the door, and no automatic return of the welcome chime as the door closed behind him. And no greeters...

Burns approached the short hallway first, which ended with a single door on the far wall. No light appeared from under the door. Unless it had a sealing strip that Burns couldn't see, the room beyond the door was dark. A small lightning bolt sticker on the upper left-hand corner of the door told Burns it was the location of the main power supply. He quickly considered it was worth a look. His first thought was old reflex. How many times had he located the power source and cut it upon incursion? Burns smiled inwardly at the thought. That didn't look necessary at the moment, and it wouldn't be advisable since he wasn't in possession of any night vision equipment, in the event of the shit hitting the fan and him needing to find the light switch in this underworld. Still, if he were to see any network access or servers, climate controls, fire suppression and any other automated systems, that were likely to be in this room, that would be valuable intel.

Burns checked his bearings again and found north. Then he took a moment to centre himself. No movement around him and no change in the low, ambient noise of the air exchange system that hung in empty corridors. He recalled the layout of the tunnels and their destinations as he visualised a larger map of the entire peninsula occupied by the airport, the old NATO base and surrounding area. The tunnels connected the hangar, the hotel spa and most likely the Russian embassy. He believed the story when told that the Russians had built a tunnel to a hangar with diplomatic transport status during the Cold War. They were rumoured to have used it to move spies and intelligence in and out of the west. He wondered when the last time anybody used it. Not tonight, he hoped. Burns didn't like the idea of another sortie down a dark tunnel, to who-knows-what kind of reception at the other end.

He would take the car, if he absolutely had to.

Burns made one last scan from the glass entry and turned toward the door at the end of the short hall. Still no visible light showing under the door. He had the feeling that Veda wasn't in there. But Burns believed he had survived every hostile action he had ever been involved in, from the Afghanistan to Kosovo to South America, in the Royal Canadian Dragoons and Canadian Joint Task Force and lastly for Her Majesty's Special Boat Service, because of his keen interest in staying alive. He also believed that meant knowing what was behind every door. He advanced with caution.

The lock was in the handle and looked about as secure as a bathroom door in a boarding house. It was too small for the handy master key in his kit but the old school tools would work. He knew it was a simple tumbler that Uncle Denis would have opened easily with one, maybe two picks. Burns gripped the handle and gave it a slight jiggle. He could feel the interior rod holding the two handles was slack in its seating, not disconnected but loose due to the age of the bearings and tumbler. He might be able to break it free with a hard twist. Burns visualised the locking disc and the taut springs that pulled and pushed the bolt and remembered the lavatory door in his barracks at CFB Cold Lake one summer. The soldier inside the WC had taken Burns' Walkman without permission, and killed the batteries to boot. The barricade didn't hold up to Burns' fury, nor did the thief's nose. Burns wondered if he was angry enough to twist open this lock. He tried his luck and gave it a slow turn counter-clockwise as he tightened his grip. Old but not rusty, thought Burns, just like me. And unlocked. He returned the tools to the wallet and slipped it into his jacket pocket.

He used his left hand to crank the door then let it swing open, extending his weapon at chest height. At a half turn the door gave a little squeak as one bushing ground against another inside the door. One hinge moaned, softly protesting the weight of the metal door as it swayed open. Burns released the door as it settled softly against the wall. The room was as wide as the hallway outside and twice as deep. He used his pocket torch to illuminate the room, scanning the floor first to the far end of the room where another door stood directly opposite Burns' entry point. The metal wall on the right was a row of locked fuse panels labelled MAIN, GEN 1 and GEN 2. Burns focus returned to the other door on the far wall. A thin, dim beam of light entered the room from under it. He reasoned if he turned on the lights in here, the beam wouldn't show on the other side of the door. He found the light switch and reached into his pocket trading his Maglite for his phone. He switched it on and shot a quick video of the room's layout, zooming in on the control panels and LED readouts on the various displays. He made a mental note that the network panel appeared to be active throughout the facility and wondered if he should deactivate his phone again. Burns paused a moment. Had he taken the video by habit, training or intuition? He settled on curiosity. He considered sending the video to Wayne or Tully, then he decided he had better include Hilts in the transmission, if only to say there was one friendly still inside the facility, should the CIA arrive before notifying him. He took the decision to keep the video to himself for the moment. He still had time to answer a question or two before reporting in, to anyone.

The door on the opposite wall opened into another tunnel, another corridor parallel to the main entry. The overhead lighting came from high single lamps spaced evenly on the walls running in both directions. The walls were bare rock, the ceiling lowered by water pipes and electrical conduit that joined from the power room. The floor was old concrete, smooth and a little glossy down the centre, as if it was polished by decades of leather shoes passing over it. To the left, the passage ended at a single small door set into a flat, finished wall. Burns calculated it to be the rear wall of the lavatory where the water was still running in the urinal. He judged the angle and concluded it would meet the other old tunnel he'd passed with Gagarin, if it continued on its line for another three hundred metres or so past the shower. Burns looked to the right and squinted. He couldn't decide if the end of the tunnel was less than a hundred metres away and dark at the end, or if it was much longer and he couldn't make out the distance. He looked up and followed the track of pipes running down the centre of the ceiling. They disappeared where the walls ended at the edge of the darkness.

Burns could never decide which was worse: a long, endless dark tunnel, or a shorter one with a blind corner up ahead. Or a junction. He was already well below six feet underground. The thought rattled him. Burns couldn't say when it began or where it came from, but that "six feet under" metaphor circled his brain whenever he had to go underground. Even in training exercises, in "friendly holes", he felt the heightening activity in his lizard brain and his survival instincts kicked in, way past overdrive. He was never panicked but always needed longer to decompress after the engagement was completed. Sometimes he was on edge for days. He had had to manage fear many times… mental exercises to calm and clear… then he remembered Iceland's seismic regularity and found himself awash in a wave of fear. "Fuck," he whispered. He hated tunnels.

Burns pulled his focus back to his immediate surroundings, the underground passage. Still no activity nearby and no change in the ambient noise. He took two steps before he looked over his shoulder and realised he hadn't closed the last door he used. He allowed himself one silent self-chastising remark about being rusty as he trotted back to close the door. Just before he did so, he peeked in to confirm he had closed the first door inside the electrical room. It was. He rationalised that a two-second pause did not constitute second-guessing himself. He knew he was out of practice. He decided not to remind himself anymore. Burns would complete the mission. He had to at least be sure that Dr Veda wasn't somewhere in the underground complex. He worked out his next advance.

Burns recalled the distance from the nursing station or reception desk to the tinted glass wall he had seen beyond the lab's entrance booth. He knew he could see that far in the parallel tunnel ahead. There was another door on the same wall a few metres just beyond the first. A few metres beyond the second door was blackness. He shook off the uneasy question about whether he was experiencing tunnel vision. His eyes weren't playing tricks on him. Older, not old, he decided.

Burns reckoned it was always better to go in the back door than the front, so he lifted himself up and quickly advanced to the first door with a series of long, light strides, remembering a time when he was skipping across a frozen stream trying to make himself lighter and avoid falling through the thin ice. The sound of his footfalls died a few metres down the tunnel, making less noise than wolf's paws on a game trail.

The first door was painted brown and looked as if it had been removed from a factory somewhere. The frame around it had been surrounded by a few sheets of unpainted plywood cut to fill the space on either side of the door. Punching through the wood would be easy if Burns couldn't work the door from his side. A small, framed glass sign above the door labelled it as a fire escape route. The direction of the running figure was toward the dark hole that the tunnel dropped into in the near distance. Burns chose to believe it was a mirror image on the inside and therefore directing the runner back to the main corridor, not toward the endless black tunnel. As much as he didn't like going in through the front door, he was much more comfortable with the idea of leaving that way.

Sliding up to the door he grasped the pull handle and squeezed down on the lever with his thumb. Opening it just wide enough for his left eye to see inside, Burns noted the wall and floor matched what he had seen in the first corridor, minus the dust kitties. He listened intently for several seconds before opening the door wide enough to pass through sideways. The only noise came from the air exchange, the low hum of fans moving air through pipes and vents in the tiled ceiling overhead. Burns allowed his mind to race over a myriad of reasons why he had encountered only a single armed hostile. He struggled to convince himself that Veda wasn't on another continent and not stuck underground between two in Iceland, like he was.

He crouched low again, keeping his head below heart level, expecting any first shot to be at least that high. He brought his pistol up as he duck-walked around the door. It was another empty corridor that ended at a corner about fifteen metres away.

This one was much narrower than the previous passage, barely wide enough for two men to pass shoulder-to-shoulder. The light was coming from windows on both walls, set about four metres from the door where Burns crouched. The windows on the left revealed a large open space, a laboratory. It was surrounded on two sides by glass walls that met at the corner where the passage he stood in turned to the left.

The wall on the right ended about four metres from the corner he occupied was a floor-to-ceiling projection of the same London scene Burns had seen earlier in the unoccupied sleeping rooms. The resolution was so high that even at this proximity Burns could swear he was looking out at the Thames from a window in the National Army Museum in Chelsea. It appeared the sun had already made its entrance from behind the grey curtain of cloud over London. Burns knew it would be hours before the actual sunrise arrived there. It would be sooner in Reykjavik. He checked his watch again. Burns imagined he would walk out of the hanger into the smouldering fire of "the magic hour", those long minutes before the sun breaks the horizon and forces the day upon a dreaming planet.

The photo screen was framed at the floor and just below the ceiling, and Burns could make out points every two-and-a half to three metres along the frame at the ceiling. The entire picture appeared to be one solid sheet held in place by an invisible frame. There appeared to be no projection equipment on Burns' side of the screen, and it was impossible to see any texture to it, as if the wall was made of matt finish photographic paper. He spread his fingers and pressed his hand to the wall, expecting to feel it give and to see an effect on the image. But the river traffic continued to roll along unperturbed. Pressing a little harder, he felt it give a little flex, like the Plexiglas surrounding a hockey rink. Hard but not solid like a wall. A little more pressure was all it took to meet the flexion limit of the panel.

His mental map told Burns that the other side of the image had to be the tinted glass wall he had seen from the first corridor. He imagined it to be the photo's shiny black backing, like an old Polaroid. He judged the central area of the view, the area between the power station and the running track at Battersea Park, to be about where the lab's main entrance lay on the other side.

The wall to Burns' left consisted of three long windows that offered a view of a laboratory, framed from waist high to just below the ceiling and running to the corner and around along the south wall. The lab was white and large, and lit for daylight. There was a rectangular booth made of glass or acrylic about three metres square in the middle of the open space, and what appeared to be several large crates and cases standing along and between the three worktables surrounding the booth. Some electronic equipment had been set up on some of the workbenches and tables, but Burns couldn't fathom what most of it was for. The lab looked like it was to be a permanent installation, and he wondered if it really had been abandoned so soon and so easily. Burns entertained the notion for a moment only, still somehow convinced that Veda was still inside. Somewhere. He was absolutely certain of that fact.

He couldn't explain—or admit—the fact that he knew, on some instinctive level, when targets were near. Somehow, through every stitch of information, every image, every page of every report stored in his infinite memory, his fear, his intuition had always guided him to the right conclusion. He had been asked but never explained how he knew the right course of action in every situation. But then Burns had a lot that he didn't share with anybody.

"Somebody's here," he assured himself, watching the boats on the Thames. "They left the TV on."

☐

Beyond the isolation booth and the work benches, in the far-right corner of the lab, Burns could see what he figured to be a corner office with half-frosted glass windows obscuring its interior. A light was on inside, but it was below the level of the clear glass. Occupying the far-left corner opposite the office was obviously the vault. It had the appearance of a large, freestanding walk-in refrigerator with its white enamelled exterior walls, perhaps slightly larger than the average mess hall food locker. The door looked as if it had been removed from a bank vault and rough-welded on, replete with a combination dial and a large wheel. It didn't look like the door or the frame had been fitted for any kind of functioning lock mechanism yet, and it stood slightly ajar. A line of light as wide as his arm shone from within the vault but the interior wasn't visible from Burns' position. From where he stood, he imagined it could serve as a good place to terrorise and torture a kidnap victim. The thought gave him pause. He scanned the room again, lingering on the office in the opposite corner. As his eyes continued to move counter-clockwise, he reflexively crouched down again when he saw another set of doors, directly opposite the lab's entry. There was a small square window at head height in each of the double doors. The glass was clear but only reflected the light of the corridor. If there was any light burning in the other room, it was very low-level.

"Or maybe he's in there," Burns mumbled to himself. Veda, or the other guard Anatoly had mentioned. He couldn't discount the office or the vault in the lab, but he knew he'd have to find out what was across the hall behind Door Number Three.

The double doors were equipped with panic bars and stainless-steel plates on the lower half of the doors, giving them the look of the entry to a hospital ward. Burns listened to the whispering hum of the ambient noise again for a few seconds, centred himself with his breathing, then he shifted low and quick along the wall to the corner. He angled in and took a quick one-eyed look from the wall's edge. Burns had correctly assumed the end of the south hall was on the same plane as the office inside the lab, about fifteen metres away.

Burns took a moment to envision the dimensions of his underground environment again. It was already larger than he had expected, and he had come at least a thousand metres down a tunnel to get here.

Burns was certain of his geographical location. The electric cart had taken him past the end of the airport taxiways to the open space beyond the runway, an undeveloped area that stretched to the end of the peninsula. Beyond that lay the cold North Atlantic.

There was nothing larger than the hangar where he had gone underground on the historical maps since the NATO base began spreading itself around the original airport in the last century. Nothing. He wasn't in the basement of another building. He was somewhere between the airport and the university campus, or under the cemetery.

He reckoned he wasn't deeper than five metres, but Burns had already been under ground longer than he liked to be. Not the longest, but the loneliest so far, as he recalled. He tried to distract himself from the memory by wondering if he could see his breath if he were topside at that moment. A chill raced from his core to his extremities as he visualised the span of solid rock between his lungs and the open air above. He recalled the smell of jet fuel lingering in the air as he had walked away from the terminal and allowed himself a moment of longing. He broke the feeling off in the scentless air. Burns had learned how the fear of loss could motivate some and demotivate others in deeper ways than any other fear. He became aware of his own constitution as a very young man when he realised he had never feared losing anything other than his life. Everything else was temporal, even family and friends. When Burns verbalised it, he felt blessed. His sensei had been impressed, but most people found his revelation cold.

Burns scampered low toward the hospital doors. He pressed down slowly on the bar of the right-hand door. Burns felt the slight vacuum resist as he eased the door open. As he broke the seal of the door, he heard a faint whistle as the air in the corridor pushed past him into the room. The only lamps burning inside were the same floor-level lights as in the sleeping area. Through the small gap between the doors Burns could see another half glass wall. Beyond the glass he saw what looked like a narrow aisle between two rows of small, empty animal cages, unlatched and unlocked. On the left the enclosures were open metal wire, those on the right seemed to be glass or acrylic. None of the dozen or so cells that he could see were big enough for anything bigger than mice, and maybe turtles on the aquarium side. Burns laughed inwardly. Ain't no pig in here. The room smelled like nothing had been in it for a long time. He listened for a few seconds again before he opened the door wider slowly, silently, with his gun trained forward.

The room that opened straight away from the door came exactly as advertised in Burns' first impression. It was a ward, like many triage rooms he had seen in military hospitals, divided into individual examination stations by cream coloured curtains. Although all the front panels were open, Burns couldn't see into any of the compartments. He marvelled again at Ivanov's ability to acquire resources. It looked to be accommodation for an even two-dozen patients, with twelve curtained rooms on either side. Burns felt relief when he saw the wall at the end of the room had no door. He stepped in and eased the door closed. The vacuum whistle reassured Burns that the air was off in this room. It was breathless and stale. He hoped it meant the ward was not in use, and he allowed himself a few extra breaths before he began the search for visual confirmation. He lowered himself and scanned the floor below the curtains, first on the left and then the right, and saw the wheels and lower frames of twenty-four hospital beds. But no shoes or other evidence of humans, hostile or otherwise. Burns tuned his ears to the sound of breathing. But there was none.

He advanced four steps, low-and-slow, head-on-a-swivel, careful to ensure each of his footfalls were only random whispers. He stopped near the centre of the ward to listen again. He could see there were twenty empty beds between the open partitions, the interior of last two pairs on each side still concealed from his angle by the dividing curtains.

Burns felt the stillness he first felt as the double doors closed—his ears had almost popped—he could only hear his own breathing and rustle of the heavy fabric of his black cargo pants. No breathing in the last four beds, he was sure. The air is off, and the beds are empty, he thought. But he had to have visual confirmation, so he crouched again and advanced to the end of the aisle, scanning each of the rooms between the hospital curtains. The last four beds were stripped bare. Burns wondered if they were unused, or if the sheets were in the laundry.

Again, he felt that strangely mixed reaction of relief and disappointment. He had to ask himself if even a not-breathing Dr Veda would be a good find.

Burns didn't rise to his full height until he reached the last pair of empty beds, where he paused, only momentarily, before quickly loping back to the double doors.

He stood in the corridor again and scanned the empty lab from outside, the corner office holding his focus as he crossed the corridor and entered the lab. Above the frosted glass, he could see the ceiling inside the office was not tiled like the lab but instead a seamless sheet of opaque, green-tinted mylar film stretched from wall to wall, with recessed lighting that looked like dark flowerpots resting upside down on a glass table. He believed he could make out the bare rock in the shadow above the mylar.

He scanned the lab again slowly, checking the vault door, which was still ajar, and again peering over the frosted glass into the smaller room. The three interior walls were covered by ceramic tile, and Burns knew his first assumption about this being an office was wrong. Nobody was working late under a desk lamp, nor were they taking a shower for that matter, but the light was bright enough that Burns had to look. He raised himself up to full height, his gun aimed at the window he faced. The light source was a high-watt work light on a yellow metal stand with its legs collapsed to their lowest height. Its beam was directed to the white tiled floor between its feet. But the light that bounced from the tight spotlight was enough to dimly illuminate the entire room, well enough for Burns to see the socket where the work light got its power, its ten-metre cable coiled neatly in front of the wall just below the power outlet. The room was otherwise bare, save for two folding chairs near the lamp. An ashtray had been left behind on one chair, as if the tiler had finished work for the day. An open shower enclosure spanned the far wall about five metres away.

There, sitting in what looked like an old barber's chair, he saw Veda.

That was his gut reaction, despite the black canvas hood concealing the man's face. He registered the man's dark umber skin pigment and ochre palms and placed them on a map in his mind's eye of all the racial origins of Man. *South Asia? Good bet*, he thought. Burns remained still and studied the figure, looking for signs of life. In the dim, reflected light he could see Veda was naked, except for the hood over his head. He was shivering in waves, definitely breathing. Burns wondered if Veda might even be sobbing softly. *Good*, thought Burns. Not that Veda was suffering, but rather he was alive and all of his body's survival systems were operating as they should.

Burns caught himself swirling in a tornado of mixed emotions. A part of him believed the world might just be a better place with one less scientist trying to fuck with Mother Nature. Men like Dr Veda who were trying to exploit her were playing with Pandora's Box, no matter what their intentions.

Burns mind was split again. The man. The vault. The man was the mission, but the slightly-ajar door to the vault could not be ignored. Burns didn't imagine he would find the errant guard inside but quickly reasoned that confirming it gave him reason enough to enter, if he had to mention it in a report. Searching the vault's contents for possible WMDs wasn't a part of his mission, just part of an idea that Burns had begun formulating when he learned the truth about Mary.

Veda's good intentions had drawn the attention of all the wrong people, or at least one bad guy. Burns didn't care if Dr Veda was trying to save millions of people by creating a super vaccine, just like he didn't care why Vladimir Ivanov wanted to use it to kill. To Burns, the men and their 'whys' mattered less than the weapon because it didn't matter who wanted it, it could become a lethal risk in any human hands.

Burns was a believer in the vast potential of human error, sometimes as the rule and not the exception. He also believed that anything with the potential to change the face of the earth drastically was never completely safe in human hands, or their machines or computers. He remembered a saying, that a researcher's mind was easily bent and there was no need to trust any scientist not to be mad. Altruism was an impossible ideal.

His mind spun back to the vault and all of its questions. Burns decided he didn't care why it was open, for the moment, and that made the other questions also irrelevant for the time being. He could ponder once he saw what was inside. Veda was alive and breathing, and alone. That was good enough for Burns, for the moment.

He scanned the windows and the lab once more. No longer looking for hostiles, or his man, he studied the layout of the lab with its three large, mostly bare worktables and the empty, freestanding isolation booth occupying the centre of the lab. Several metal-cased crates stood between the benches like road cases backstage in a concert hall. Burns assumed they had recently arrived from the lab on Uxbridge Road. Six tanks of compressed gas stood harnessed in a rack on the far wall inside the booth. He recognised their colour-coding and unconsciously squeezed the hand grip on his weapon. Nitrogen, hydrogen, ammonia, and oxygen on the highly flammable side, with carbon dioxide and chlorine on the poisonous side; all in hospital grade cylinders. The little glass room was definitely not the intended storage for the tanks, even if they were empty. He doubted they were empty.

The larger room seemed to be completely wired for electricity and two of the tables had water, but there were no cameras or even mounting points anywhere. "Just getting started", Burns murmured again. He paused a moment, gazing at the movie screen. He watched as the sunlight reflecting on the Thames was suddenly shaded by clouds passing overhead. Then he turned his focus to the vault and advanced toward it standing upright, his weapon trained on the opening.

The gap in the door was narrow and there was a small threshold to step over to enter the vault, but Burns could make out the floor and part of the left wall inside. He could see a large door resembling a walk-in refrigerator, with a small keypad and a digital read out showing 3°. Perfect temperature for storing fresh blood, as he recalled. He grasped the door just below the handle and slowly increased his pull until he felt it swing smoothly open. The interior wall opposite the refrigerator and the far wall were lined with glass cabinets standing like columns. In the middle of the room was a tall metal chair that would look less out-of-place in the lab, and beside it a small folding table with an open valise, waiting. Burns couldn't make out its contents from where he stood at the door, but he guessed torture devices and wondered if Veda's torture had begun in the vault before he had been subjected to the waterboarding in the shower. Burns rejected the idea, assured that Veda's captors would have no doubt started with the water, like any professional would do. So, who was this little setup for?

"The question answers itself," Burns whispered.

The cabinet on the far wall was lit from inside and Burns could see several rows of small containers. He registered a tremor of fight-or-flight instinct. He stood still and stared at the vials for several seconds before resuming his scan of the room. On his right were the same stainless-steel cases mirroring the one containing the potential bioweapons of mass-destruction on the left. These stood empty, expectantly. Just getting started but plans to expand, Burns mused silently. He returned his focus to the chair and table. The chair was lint free, hair free and stain-free, unremarkable, but the open case on the table next to it was irresistible enough to warrant a look on his way to the jackpot in the cabinet on the far side of the room.

Burns froze again, halted by the realisation that he knew why he wanted to get to the viruses, but he had no idea what he would do when he got there. He had come this far with little thought to any others: the CIA, the HO and Wayne. His mission had been clear at the start but Burns realised he had been harbouring other motives. He had been ordered to recover Dr Veda. But the viruses were a threat, and he wanted them dead as much as he wanted to kill Ivanov. Certainly, the others would prefer the former without the latter, he reckoned. He scanned the room once more and inspected the doorframe for sensors before he stepped over the threshold.

Burns had guessed right about the torture devices, but he was surprised when they looked more like they were made for recreational purposes. A pair of handcuffs and a ball gag were threatening enough, but a few clothespins on the table next to the case, the small cat o' nine tails and a large black vibrator in a faux suede sheath made Burns smirk. It only took a moment for him to imagine Kaia, willingly cuffed to the chair and Bad Daddy Vladi performing a little BDSM on her submissive, costumed body.

Burns caught his anger balling up in his chest. He wanted to find Ivanov and kill him. He drew in a deep breath and faked a shrug of nonchalance as he looked over at the cabinet full of sample jars and tubes, and back at the S&M gear.

"Why'd you leave all this behind?" he wondered aloud.

Burns reluctantly pulled out his phone and activated it. It was a good time to call in. He turned away from the cabinet and decided which number he would ring. He stopped when he saw the back of the tall stool where he had guessed Vlad and Kaia had played their sex games. He drew his thumb away from the touch screen as he cursed himself for missing the threat now in plain sight.

A small brick of Semtex H was plastered to the back of the chair, with a timer attached. It was only slightly bigger than a packet of cigarettes, but it was enough to destroy the contents of the vault. Burns doubted the blast would cause any damage to the lab outside. If the door had been left closed, for sure the explosion would be contained. A flash of icy fear lit up every nerve in his body. He pocketed his phone and advanced a step-and-a-half to study the device. It was professionally made but simple, a small electronic trigger with a green display that read:

1:23

He watched it for a sixty-second count and was relieved when it didn't tick down. The readout remained fixed at 1:23. No dramatic countdown telling him he had over an hour before detonation. Burns understood it was to go off at the hour on the display. He pushed the small tab next to the readout, changing it to the current hour and minute: 1:00. He checked his watch and started his own countdown. His watch chronometer ticked over to 01:00 just as he looked down and he started the countdown. He had less than twenty-three minutes to get Veda far enough away, ideally topside. He reckoned it would be easy in the golf car and could be done in a run if necessary. He could close the door and, even if it didn't seal, it would limit the concussion of the blast. If he left the door ajar there would also be a flash of fire, maybe enough to destroy the entire lab if the compressed gases came into play. The alternatives made him grind his teeth as he studied the device.

Burns was puzzled. He couldn't get past the idea that Vladimir Ivanov had planned to blow up another lab even though he was just getting started here. Burns wondered sarcastically what kind of self-respecting megalomaniac would set up its destruction before completing his evil lair.

The placement of the charge on the chair suggested to Burns it was there to destroy more than evidence. Burns guessed someone was supposed to be sitting in the chair when the timer beeped, making for a messy trip to oblivion.

He looked up at the small shelf of vials. Unless he departed in a panic, Vlad had left over two dozen samples behind, intending to destroy them. Burns didn't care what they were, the idea struck him that they would do no good to anyone anywhere anyway.

Disarming an explosive was one thing — Burns had received training during his time in Special Ops, everything from unexploded shells and anti-personnel mines to suicide vests. But he had never been faced with the task of disarming a device while engaged in an active mission.

But the idea of resetting the timer, even though this one looked to be without a booby trap...

Burns' thoughts raced, his action plan in reverse: he visualised waiting for the CIA team in the parking lot, the tunnel journey back to the hangar, the time to get Veda freed and back to the golf car. It would be quick with no hostiles, even if he had to carry Veda. *No Hostiles.*

Hilts' team would be arriving soon. It was time to call in.

Burns had deliberately left his phone inactive since he checked the feed after he cleared customs. He had convinced himself at the time that he was doing it to avoid detection by Ivanov's team, whom he guessed would be monitoring the local network traffic. He expected some level of surveillance at the hangar and imagined his foe would have a sophisticated set up. But despite the lack of cameras or sensors anywhere between the lab and the walk-in entry, Burns had consciously maintained his radio silence. Burns opened his phone and smiled when he saw the signal was good enough to send a text. He sent a short message to Hilts, asking for the ETA of his team. The immediate reply asked:

You@hotel?

Burns replied in the negative and repeated:

ETA?

He waited a few seconds longer for the second reply.

Giver take 16 min KEF, 01:20 @ SPA

So, the primary target was still the hotel. Good. Burns wouldn't give away his location yet, but he had to say something. His problem was that he knew the hangar was between the first team's landing point and the spa. If they dropped four men at the end of the runway to make the first ground assault, as Burns would do, those men would be on time for the blast. But they wouldn't be near the source if they went directly to the Northern Lights Spa first.

He typed another short text and sent it to Hilts, and to Wayne:

Hangar MT. No hostiles @ spa

He added ...*maybe* before hitting send, thinking it best to keep Hilts and the CIA team pointed away from the lab. Before Hilts could reply, Burns typed another message:

Am nearby. Tell your boys don't shoot me ;)

He left it at that, wondering if Hilts had his location yet. He calculated the SMS would leave a trail in just a few seconds that would end at the nearest tower, no doubt within a few hundred metres of his position. His phone's GPS might pinpoint him geographically to within the signal range. But even if he wasn't too far underground for the GPS to track, it would only be a dot on a map in Hilts' control room, wherever that might be. Burns knew he trusted Hilts. But he didn't have to trust the CIA assault team, and he instinctively knew it was best to keep them at arm's length for as long as possible. On the British side, so far he only had to trust Detective Chief Inspector Wayne. His commanding officer had authorised this solo mission, and, as far as Burns was concerned, there was no one above Wayne whom he had to worry about. Burns was gratified to have the trust. More importantly, he was thankful that he didn't have to trust anyone else, at least for the moment.

Burns quickly typed a short message and sent it to Hilts, and copied in Wayne:

Request ETA confirm

He had calculated that Hilts would read his use of the word "request" for more than the obvious meaning, but more to put it on the record for both agencies. If Hilts didn't catch on to that, he would hopefully see the message was cc'd to DCI Wayne and know.

With one hand on the chair, Burns leaned in and examined the device at eye level. It looked simple enough. All he had to do was pull the blasting cap from the C4 and the bomb would be disabled. But two small tabs below the timer display intrigued him, sending his thoughts beyond self-preservation. He checked the wires again and ran his fingers round the outside edges of the small plastic casing and found no protrusions, save the two small tabs aligned below the numbers on the display. He reached forward and slowly, smoothly grasped and pulled the lead out of its soft clay sheath, disarming the device. He held his breath and pressed the tab on the left of the clock and watched as the hour changed to 2, pressed it again and the 2 changed to 3. He glanced at his phone and saw that his message had already been marked read by DCI Wayne. Burns exhaled and pressed the tab again.

Hilts reply arrived as the timer ticked over to 4. The message read:

T- 31min +/-

need a ride home yet?

Burns didn't reply to Hilts' question. He had another question to answer for himself first. He needed to be sure that the timer was the trigger, and that the device wouldn't be activated by a phone call from above ground. His best guess was that Ivanov wouldn't risk remote detonation due to the possibility of signal failure. *Timer detonation is fail-proof*, he reasoned. Armed with this logic, Burns pocketed his weapon and knelt down. Of course, if he left the vault's door open, he would have to be sure they would be out of the blast range, if not out of the tunnel. He was confident there was enough C4 explosive to demolish the contents of the freestanding vault but not much more. But there would also be fire, likely enough to destroy the entire lab, if he left the door open.

The timer remained lit, still fixed on 1:23. His watch read 01:01. Burns wondered who might have earned this seat in Ivanov's eyes, and where they were now. He lifted the LED clock free with his right hand while holding the electrical lead between his left thumb and forefinger under the small blasting cap to avoid any incidental contact as he passed the timer to his left palm.

"T-minus thirty-one minutes," Burns repeated softly, affecting Hilts' West Texas drawl as he visualised the impending American assault. As long as they concentrated their numbers on the hotel and left the hangar out of the first strike, he ought to be able to get Veda topside and maybe even back to his car before the Cowboys came over the hill. It wasn't only a question of keeping Veda out of the hands of the CIA. Burns also had a strong aversion to being shot, even if by accident. He didn't want to imagine the scene at the spa when the black ops team crashed Jonnson's bliss. And he hoped he had been right before, when he told Hilts there were no hostiles on site at the hotel. More than that, Burns knew what to expect if Hilts had sent a team to the hangar. Sure, they would know of Burns' mission to extract Veda, but he knew what their orders would be. They weren't only here for the gear. The first strike would be to secure whatever and whomever they found before the bioweapons team arrived in their white spacesuits. If Hilts had been telling the truth, the first team wouldn't be here to handle WMD's if they were discovered. Their priority was to find Ivanov, and probably shoot-to-kill any armed force with him. They would be told to expect to see Burns, but most likely they were expecting him to be at the spa.

He recalled the cover and the conflict points between the hangar and his car. It was enough to force his mind to consider if he might be closer to the car — and safer from the Cowboys — if he were to exit through the dark tunnel. Burns checked his watch again and reworked the math.

Burns reset the timer to go off in twenty-one minutes. 1:18. It was early enough to precede the Yanks' assault on the spa, but an advance team that had rolled off the plane on the taxiway — as Burns had imagined — would be at the hangar in no more than fifteen minutes. And that was about how long he figured it was going to take to get Dr Veda out of the tunnel. Burns hoped the remaining ten minutes would be enough to make it back to the car, maybe even to the airport. He would decline Hilts' offer of a ride home. He would ask Wayne to clear a path through check-in and passport control for the Good Doctor and his escort, just as soon as he got Veda strapped into the back seat of the hired Ford.

As Burns rose and walked out of the vault, he left the door open. Whether the explosion did or didn't vaporise them, Burns could at least make sure the fire had air to breath and ensure the destruction of the viruses. He stepped out of the vault and turned his attention to the shower room where Dr Veda sat shivering.

Then he remembered the gas cylinders in the glass-walled isolation room. The compressed gases in the cylinders, mixed in almost any combination, were both explosive and toxic. If Ivanov was planning to torch this lab like his previous playrooms, they were a guarantee of total destruction of its contents and equipment, and anyone in the underground facility.

Burns froze at the door to the glass booth.

Another tab of Semtex plastic explosive, the twin of the one Burns had found in the vault, had been pressed onto the regulator and valve apparatus on the front of the rack holding the cylinders.

He cursed himself for not checking the unsecured room, considering Ivanov's proclivity for making explosive exits. Then he pictured Vlad seeing himself as a rock star, arms raised standing in front of the explosion saying, *"Thank you Reykjavik! Goodnight!"* as the underground lab went up in a cloud of flames behind him. Burns laughed to himself for a moment, imagining Ivanov's diabolical smile, before focusing on the explosive and the timer. It was identical to the set up on the chair in the vault, however its placement would generate a far greater range of destruction. Burns imagined the blast's energy would blow up the entire lab and blast a hole through the view of the Thames, dragging fire up the tunnel like a cannonball going out the barrel. Nothing worse than fire chasing your ass in a tunnel, thought Burns. He looked at his watch again, suddenly struck by the realisation that if he had gone to Veda first and taken him straight out, they might not have made it to the golf car without at least getting singed.

Burns opened the door and felt it stop as it struck something on the floor. He saw the body of a man, dressed in a very academic-looking blazer and turtleneck sweater, face down on the floor next to the wall behind the door. The room had been airtight until Burns cracked the seal. The body was the only thing he could smell. It hadn't begun to decompose yet, but the recently deceased had lost control of his bowels upon departure. The room was empty save for the body, the gas cylinders and the bomb. The victim looked like he had either died without trauma or had been placed there, as if rolled off a stretcher and allowed to die face down. Burns could see *rigor mortis* had set in. The man had been dead for several hours. Burns wondered what his connection was to Ivanov's plan for genocide. He carefully lifted a shoulder and rolled the body over a half turn, used his phone to get a photo of the expressionless face, then laid the man down again.

Burns allowed himself to wonder if Ivanov saw the man as unnecessary or collateral. If Burns' first impression of the former general had been on the money, the dead scientist had outlived his usefulness, apparently several hours before Veda would outlive his. Burns coughed out a short laugh, then he shuddered to think that maybe Ivanov wasn't "just getting started" after all.

Either way, the body was to be blasted into oblivion, as was Dr Veda. Burns realised he hadn't really looked at the face until he saw it on his mobile. He used the touch screen to zoom in and examine the face more closely. It was completely relaxed, as if the man had fallen asleep with his eyes open. The eyes were open and clear, save for one small hematoma in the left eye, and they looked as though they were still watching the horizon intently. The lips and nostrils were dry and there were no cuts or contusions or pooling of blood under the skin. Burns stifled his curiosity and put his phone away, then moved quickly across the floor to the ersatz rack where the gas cylinders stood like missiles ready to launch.

Burns scanned the device and the cylinders and plotted his actions. First, he used both hands to close all the valves, poisonous on the left and explosive on the right, and quickly repeated the procedure of removing the blasting cap and disconnecting the timer. He pondered the idea of resetting the charge, knowing it would level the whole lab and maybe even close the access tunnel. He checked his watch and decided against it. Destroying the viruses in the vault, if that's what they were, would have to be enough.

Burns had lost about two minutes. Not enough to worry about, yet. The golf car would be fast enough to put enough distance between him and the blast and fire. "Me and Dr Veda," Burns quietly reminded himself.

He visualised carrying Veda's limp, nine-stone body to the golf car in the exit tunnel and another four hundred metres after they escaped through the hangar. He imagined attempting to cross open space fast, and finding and holding cover between the hangar's car park and the lot next to the restaurant where Burns' borrowed car waited. He figured the hostiles were all long gone, the streets deserted. The only threat would be from the Americans. For sure they'll think I'm a Russian. He felt fit enough to run with Veda over his shoulder but wasn't sure they would be able to make it to the car before the cavalry arrived. He chuckled when he pictured himself strolling casually into the pizza restaurant with Veda hanging over his shoulder and ordering a pie "to go".

He wondered if he might say nothing at all about the bomb. The thought of Hilts' team reaching the vault and getting obliterated along with what Vlad had left behind frustrated Burns. He knew he couldn't let that happen.

Burns didn't feel like telling anybody anything, but knew he had to. He had to reach out to Hilts to confirm or deny any advance team was on its way to the hangar, and possibly prevent casualties. He knew he had to at least stall their arrival until after the explosion. He didn't plan on waiting around for them at the end of the tunnel. He looked at his watch again and breathed easily. If he made it topside before any agents showed up, he would call Hilts and say he was on his way out and by which route, to avoid any conflict with armed agents. If he met the Yanks on the way out, he would identify himself and turn them around before they got past him and down the tunnel.

"Just gotta hope the Cowboys don't arrive until after everything goes boom."

Burns stepped out of the booth and weaved his way through the tables and crates in the lab to Veda's shower room. As he opened the door, he got a full view of Veda sitting in his chair at the other end of the room. He stopped dead when he saw another body, face down like the scientist in the other room. This one was wearing military issue trousers and a black turtleneck pullover, lying in a pool of his own blood. A nine-millimetre Glock remained in its holster under the left flank. There was a small dark circle of blood between the shoulder blades and something protruded under the sweater, just below where the shoulder holster crisscrossed. Stabbed, not shot, he thought. And the weapon was still inside the body. He touched the coin-sized bump with the back of his hand and felt the point of whatever had pierced the man's torso. Instinctively he checked for a pulse on the neck.

Burns looked up at Veda sitting in the chair. His body was mostly still but the hands were moving, rolling over each other as though they were being held under a cleansing stream of water. He realised how much he had missed on his first too-brief look at his primary target. The body had been out of his field when he scanned the room and he felt justified assuming Veda was alone. But what he couldn't justify was overlooking the fact that Veda hadn't been bound to the chair at all. He also had failed to notice the IV bag and stand toppled near Veda's chair. Burns focused his gaze on the hood. Veda seemed to be looking at him.

"I killed him," said a small, submissive voice from inside the heavy bag.

Yes, indeed you did, thought Burns. "Plenty of time to feel guilty later," said Burns only half to himself.

He took a moment to centre himself and scanned the room again with fresh eyes.

Burns couldn't decide if the room was intended to be a shower, an operating theatre, or maybe a room for conducting autopsies.

He had to ask, "Why do you still have the hood on?"

"I killed him," Veda repeated a little louder, but still contrite, and Burns understood.

He feels guilty of a sin and wants to die.

Burns moved swiftly to stand facing Veda, pulling the hood off his head as his last footfall landed with a slap on the tiled floor. Satisfied with the fearful shudder he had elicited from Veda, Burns put his hand on Veda's shoulder and smiled into his eyes.

"Hello Dr Veda. My name is Burns. I came from London. And we have to go now. Can you walk?"

"I killed him with a fucking mop handle," was the dull response.

Burns was stuck for words. He had seen the broken bottom half of the mop lying next to the shower and tried to imagine how skinny little Nicholas Veda had managed to do it: not only making and concealing the weapon but then delivering the fatal strike. Burns didn't know if it had been instinct or training, anger or fear or luck that Veda had channelled when he drove the stake through the heart of the sinister looking man. He knew why Veda hadn't fled afterward. Veda had violently killed a man and now he wanted to die.

Burns had no trouble resisting the impulse to offer any sympathy. Less easy was the urge to comply with the unspoken request. He knew he would have to harness his contempt for Veda if he wanted an easy trip back to London.

Burns lowered himself to face Veda. He gazed into Veda's eyes, trying to pull him back to the present. And then he saw it. The red glow of an LED display reflecting on the tile floor, just behind Veda's chair. He grasped both Veda's shoulders and gave a short, sharp shake. Not hard enough to hurt him but hard enough to make his teeth clack and snap him out of his daze.

"Dr Veda," Burns patted Veda's shoulders gently. "Please don't move for a minute, ok?"

Veda nodded in compliance. Burns stepped around the chair and found the device, placed exactly as the one on the chair in the vault. It didn't take more than a few seconds to examine the bomb and disarm it. Burns had his internal clock running but he checked his watch to confirm he still had enough time to escape. He reckoned he still had enough time to drag Veda back and forth to the car twice.

"I killed him," Veda bleated.

Lovely, thought Burns. Shock and guilt together.

"Look, Dr Veda, I've got to get you out of here," Burns insisted. "I'm taking you back to London," he said, as he pointed at the image of the Thames and Battersea Park. "Now." He didn't know if Veda had seen the movie or even knew if it wasn't real, but he didn't care. He hoped that the image of London would trigger Veda's homing instincts and he would make their exit easy. But the look on Veda's face told Burns that his rescuee had expected that Burns was there to kill him. Veda's eyes were not disappointed but more hopeless or demoralised, as if Veda had been waiting for Burns to dispatch him so that he might face his final judgment. Definitely not a practicing Hindu, thought Burns. Only a Christian would believe something that fucked up.

"1 killed him."

"And I'm sure he had it coming," said Burns. He recognised his own conflict as the words left his mouth. He had pushed aside his personal convictions about the morality of Dr Veda's work in order to focus on the mission. Veda felt guilt for the death of one man, no doubt in defence of his own life. Was it irony? Burns wondered if the guilt went deeper. He hoped that whatever drugs had been in Veda's system would wear off sometime later and Veda's memory of the night would be lost in the ether, sometime after they escaped.

"Ok," Burns breathed as he dropped the timer to the floor. "We can go now." Burns took Veda by one arm, preparing to lift him to his feet. Veda flinched at Burns grasp and tried to pull himself free. He swayed, pulling weakly against Burns' grasp.

"No, no, no!" Veda sobbed through dry lips, looking like a character in a painting by Munch.

Burns became impatient but resisted the temptation to use physical force to get Veda off his chair, and all the way to the plane back to London.

"Look," he said as he took Veda's face in his hands. "Look at me," he commanded. "I'm going to show you something." He turned Veda's head to face the body a few feet away. "Look. There's more blood now. His heart's still pumping, ok?" He didn't tell Veda that his torturer had been alive, but just barely, when Burns found him. Now Burns needed Veda to see that his captor's body had been clinging to life. Burns easily swallowed his own fleeting guilt for leaving the man to bleed out.

"You defended yourself, your life," Burns fought against the anger swelling in his throat. Veda stopped swaying and his head tilted to one side like a dog that heard a sound it didn't recognise.

Burns relaxed his grip and stepped backward then turned and knelt down to the body, careful not to step in the growing pool of rusty crimson blood. He caught and held Veda's gaze again and turned the body over. The corpse gave the expected sigh as the small amount of air trapped in the lungs escaped. Burns hoped that it would release Veda from his guilt. Then he took five steps away from the body and angled his weapon at the head. After a quick glance to Veda, he fired. The head kicked back from the impact of the bullet, but the body remained still.

"There," Burns asserted. "You didn't kill him. I did."

Burns wasn't looking for gratitude. He just wanted to get on with getting out. Even passive cooperation would be enough. But Veda still hadn't snapped out of it. Burns holstered his weapon and was suddenly struck by a question. He wondered if Veda had seen the explosives stuck to the chair.

Burns felt a surge of anger that turned his saliva to acid. A tightening in his gut that happened every time he had had his life threatened by the actions of another human — malicious or not. Anger focused on an enemy came easy, and logically.

He decided to save his question for later, in case the answer made him want to scrub the mission. Then it struck him that Veda's hands were free, yet the heavy bag was still over his head when Burns had arrived on the scene. He almost laughed aloud as he tried to visualise the gangly scientist in a successful fight for his life with a hood over his head. He must have put it back on after he killed his torturer, thought Burns. He gave himself a moment to quell his anger, checked his watch and repeated calmly, "Dr Veda, we're going home now."

Burns put a hand on Veda's arm again, firm but not forceful. Veda rose from the chair, obedient and a little wobbly, but without support from Burns. He could see that Veda had absorbed a few blows to the face and chest, but nothing appeared to be broken or out of place as Veda steadied himself upright. Burns led him past the body and released his hold on Veda's arm as he reached for the door.

Burns heard and felt the thud of the explosion simultaneously. It sounded like a cannonball dropped on a kettledrum, with a long, soft decay. It felt more like a tremor underfoot than the shockwave of an explosive blast. Burns wasn't sure how far away or how big the charge was, but he knew it had come from his right at about two o'clock. He checked his watch and wasn't surprised to see it read 1:19. His internal clock had already told him it was about four minutes early, ahead of the other charges, but he was puzzled as to why.

Burns put his hand on Veda's chest to hold him back as he stepped past and through the open door into the lab. He smelled the gypsum dust in the air and understood that the explosion had been on the other side of the wall in the short alcove between the vault and the shower room. He guessed it wasn't any bigger than the charges in the vault and lab.

He took a quick look to the door and the main entrance beyond the glass, listening intently for sounds of movement. No doors opening or closing, no footsteps approaching, only the low hum of air moving through the vents in the ceiling. The bomb hadn't attracted the attention of any immediate threat to Burns, or his charge. The stillness calmed Burns, and with a few long breaths the tension in his muscles eased. His gaze drifted to the scene playing on the video wall. All the river buses were moored at the Battersea docks and a lone, low barge was making its way upriver. He let his body revert to a state of rest for several moments. His jaw was the last to unclench, still somehow gripping the fear, the survival instinct that powered the will to kill. Burns had learned, had come to understand the "lizard brain", as he called it, that he shared with nearly every species. He had trained for most of his adult life as a soldier, beginning as a youth, and had explored the teachings of the masters as he developed his skills in the martial arts. He knew the fear wasn't an emotional response, and it wasn't diminishing. Burns turned back to Dr Veda, raised his hand and sold a confident smile before approaching the hole.

The blast had blown a fan-shaped hole through the plasterboard at the foot of the wall, small enough that it could be hidden by a well-placed loveseat. A thin wisp of smoke trailed up from the opening, but no flames were visible yet. Burns could see the shape of a machine, possibly a generator, through the hole. Then he saw the fuel tank. He couldn't guess its capacity because he wasn't able to see it full dimensions, but the corner he could see was clearly that of a large industrial grade flammables container. He pulled out his Maglite and shone its beam under the slowly thickening smoke wafting out of the hole in the wall. The beam found the widening stream of liquid making its way through the gap and into the lab. Burns frowned as he smelled it. More like kerosene than gasoline. Jet A, not avgas.

"A bit of overkill, don't you think?" he asked anyone. Burns didn't know whether to find it comical or admirable. The bomber must have placed a charge small enough to blow a hole in the tank but not ignite the fuel, knowing Jet A to be less likely to catch until the C4 went off, which was why its timer had to go off a few minutes early. The flash from the compressed gas explosion would be enough to ignite the liquid fuel and keep the fire burning until everything was incinerated.

Burns decided that the best psychopathic maniacs were thorough, real sticklers for detail, and he tried to imagine how much of an obsessive character Ivanov must be.

The smoke from the hole expanded into a small cloud, and as it rose gently toward the tiled ceiling

Burns caught his breath. He remembered the halon fire suppression panel he had seen in the power room. He scanned the ceiling for sensors and found three, along with eight gas-dispensing discs spanning the main lab area. Burns had been assigned to work in a Joint Task Force surveillance set-up in Kosovo when Yugoslavia was pulling itself apart. He was instructed to "run like hell" if he ever heard the alarm go off because the halon would be released in thirty seconds and would capture all the oxygen in the room. And, he was told, "humans need oxygen". A few years later he learned that halon was actually not so bad for humans, just bad for the ozone. But he never lost that flight instinct whenever he imagined suffocating to death. He thought it less preferable than being cremated alive, or killed even slower by a lethal viral infection.

He hoped the single small black dots on each of the sensors were unlit power indicators, and the fire would burn unchecked. But his body had already shifted into flight mode. He checked his watch again.

"One-twenty-one," he announced. The river of fuel flowed increasingly faster into the lab.

Burns looked at Veda and asked, "You ready?" without making it sound like a question.

Veda moved slowly toward Burns' extended hand but didn't take it. The flowing fuel had made its way to the floor in front Veda's feet. Burns turned to Veda.

"Step carefully." said Burns. "Try not to splash."

He turned for the exit without a second glance at Veda. After a few steps he stopped to look back and see Veda take his first few undaunted steps in the river of fuel. Physically he seemed fine, and Veda no longer looked like he wanted to die. Burns was relieved. He decided that his compassion had not yet reached the level of feeling sorry for Veda, but he imagined he might one day feel pity for the young scientist. One day, he thought. For the moment, he satisfied himself with the relief that he wouldn't have to carry an incapacitated Dr Veda to the car and somehow get him on a plane. Burns led Veda, demonstrating how to carefully place and lift each stride until he reached the point where the stream turned toward the centre of the lab and away from the exit. As he turned back to Veda, he saw a low band of blue and yellow flame rolling out of the hole in the wall on the surface of the stream Veda was still padding through barefoot.

"Shit," said Burns softly. Something must have caught fire in the generator room and ignited the fuel. The pooling stream was only a few millimetres deep, Burns recognised it as a minimal threat, but Veda reacted by skip-jumping his way toward the dry floor where Burns stood. He slipped and fell just out of Burns' reach. Burns stepped over Veda and hoisted him out of the fuel before the flames could singe a hair on Veda's dark, furry legs.

"Close your eyes and mouth," he commanded. Then he used his sleeve to wipe Veda's face, who coughed and sputtered all over Burns.

The smoke was getting thicker and was flowing outward along the ceiling into the lab. The fuel began to pool in a low area of the floor near the centre of the lab, the flames flickering low on its surface. He looked up at the halon units and relaxed. He wouldn't suffocate, the jet fuel wasn't going to cause an explosion, and as long as another charge didn't go off in the next minute or so, he would be out of danger. Burns used both arms to wipe down Veda's body, then took off his jacket and slipped out of his black wool sweater. Without a word, he pulled the sweater over Veda's head and helped him feed his arms into the sleeves. Gratified to see it was long enough to afford Veda some modesty, Burns smiled his best cordial smile and shook the droplets of diesel from his jacket and wiped his hands on his trousers before pulling the jacket on over his black t-shirt. He slipped his hands into the pockets, reflexively gripping and releasing his phone and weapon.

"Let's go home," Burns shrugged nonchalantly, as if there was nothing left to do but leave.

"Okay," Veda nodded meekly.

Burns had decided to go back through the service tunnel and not through the main exit, partly to avoid a direct blast if there were any more charges he hadn't seen, but also to avoid any confrontation with hostiles—CIA or otherwise. The two men walked out of the lab side-by-side, and Burns watched Veda as they passed the scene along the Thames, trying to gauge his reaction. Burns squeezed Veda's shoulder and nodded.

"Soon be back in London, for real," Burns smiled cheerily. "Soon enough."

Burns smelled the smoke as soon as he opened the door to the service tunnel, only the whiff of carbon at first. He had Veda wait again as he trotted down the tunnel to confirm that it ended at the access door to the generator room where the bomb went off. No ladder or stairs to fresh air, no long tunnel. Burns was glad to see the dead end. There was no safety exit at the end of a dark tunnel. He wouldn't be using any unfamiliar tunnels to escape this time.

"Scratch one more shitty idea off the list," he said.

The gap in the wooden frame around the door was aglow from the fire behind, but the smoke in the tunnel wasn't thick enough for the fire to be out of control. Burns guessed the ventilation system was drawing the smoke elsewhere, likely sending up a signal that should set off a few alarms at the airport, at least.

"We're going to pick up the pace a bit," Burns declared. He pulled Veda's arm and dragged him until he could sustain a trot. He released his grip and Veda followed him as they went past the door to the electrical room and directly to the door at the end of the tunnel, the door to what Burns had presumed to be the toilet and shower room.

He was right about the room but hadn't guessed it might be locked. He decided to shoot the lock and pull the door open rather than use help from Uncle Denis. The report spun down the tunnel to the fire and back, the thin echo ringing in their ears. Veda jumped up and fell backwards to the floor.

That turned out to be fortunate. Just as Burns pulled the door open a large body in black came crashing through it like a fullback ploughing through a tackler. His pause to deliver his death cry had given Burns enough time to shove Dr Veda to the side with a hip check and deflect most of the energy the big man was bringing. Burns struck the guard in the chest with his fist but caught a knee to the jaw and went down, slightly dazed, as his attacker tumbled past and crashed to the floor. He shook his thoughts clear of the haze. Good news, bad news, he thought. Found the missing guard. He reckoned he would have met this guard first if he had entered the tunnel from the spa, and no doubt would have had to kill him there. Burns picked Veda up by the armpits and dragged him through the open door, then he threw Veda into the toilet stall and with a finger gesture told him simply to "Stay put."

He stepped back into the tunnel, closing the door behind, to greet the guard as he rose from his crash landing. Shaken but only slightly stirred, the behemoth rose up with his firearm drawn. He glowered hard at Burns, seeing the weapon in Burns' hand clearly for the first time. Burns wondered why the guard hadn't fired. Then he saw the pride behind the anger in the eyes.

Burns looked at his watch. It was 1:23. No other bombs had gone off. Burns smiled. Here was a chance to work his muscles.

He addressed the man in Russian, "If you put that away, you might live. If you don't, you won't."

The guard laughed and answered in English, "You want fight?"

"Not necessarily," Burns smiled coyly. "Not if you don't, that's for sure."

The big man smiled and held up his gun, then slowly removed the clip then ejected the round in the chamber and placed them on the floor at his feet. Burns frowned. The guard disassembled the weapon and placed the pieces next to the ammunition.

"You could have just kicked it over here."

"No. I keep here, for later. "I was to clean it tonight anyways," the guard answered in Russian. Then he added in English, "Also for later, for Justin," he shrugged. "Justin Case!" The guard laughed. "You know, the last dessert."

"The last resort."

"Da, the last resort. In case we get tired of fighting," the big Russian bear smiled. "You can do it too," he added, pointing at Burns' weapon. "Last resort. Final count down."

Burns laughed to himself. This guy was nuts. Maybe he played rugby.

"Showdown, Thug." said Burns. "Final showdown. Do I look like a fucking cowboy?"

"Maybe not, but you American, damn right."

This guy was a riot. Burns decided he really didn't want to kill the guard, but he owed it to him to set the man straight about his mistaken assumption before he disabled him.

"I'm Canadian, eh," Burns smirked. He released the trigger and displayed his weapon, pinching it between his thumb and forefinger. "I'm going to put this down here," he said as he bent down to place the weapon easily on the floor. "I'm not going to dismantle it, and you can try to get it if you want to." Burns gave his opponent a hard stare. "Not advisable. But I promise I won't use it on you after I finish slapping you around. Until you say you're sorry for calling me an American."

The guard seemed to have a moment of pause as his focus shifted from Burns to his gun to the pieces if his own weapon on the floor. Burns stretched and flexed and stood ready, hands open. The bigger man took a boxing pose and began throwing punches, shadow boxing in Burns' direction, but without advancing. Then, as if a bell had rung, the bigger man came at Burns fast, with his fists raised. Burns reached out and stopped him cold with a lightning fast, hard slap to his right ear that dropped the bigger man to one knee. "The *Osmanli Tokati*," Burns proudly proclaimed. "The Ottoman Slap. You probably have a concussion now."

"You slap to fight?" The guard was dazed but incredulous and rose up again rubbing his ear.

"Well, that was just to prove a point you know, because I said before I'd slap you around. It's a kind of figure of speech," Burns shrugged. "But I thought it might be fun to take it more literally. Anyway, I promise I won't slap you anymore." Burns crossed his heart and grinned.

The heavyweight advanced and threw a combination of punches that landed hard on Burns' shoulders and arms, with one blow glancing off his ribcage. Burns dropped his left shoulder and flexed his knees before driving his fist straight up to his opponent's chin.

"I'll just punch," said Burns, through gritted teeth.

The guard teetered and Burns quickly jumped back for fear of the big body falling on him. Much to Burns' disappointment, the brute didn't go down. *Fuck.* Bruised ribs, maybe a wrecked shoulder, and he could wreck his hands trying to knock this *Marble Man* out. Burns was seriously considering breaking his promise not to shoot when the dazed-but-not-confused Russian made the choice easy. The guard produced a knife and charged. Burns rolled off the attack, controlling the hand holding the blade as it passed his throat. The anger quickly took over and Burns drove a hard, straight kick to his opponent's knee. The guard's scream drowned out the cracking bones as he staggered to maintain upright on one leg.

"And kicking" Burns grunted. "Just punching and kicking," he smiled and crossed his heart. "Promise." He looked sincere as he crossed his heart again, for emphasis. He was hoping the guard had forgotten about the Beretta, which he stood closer to than Burns. The guard was preoccupied with a trickle of blood dripping from his open hand. He had apparently been cut and hadn't felt it as Burns had sent him tumbling to the floor. It was apparent that he was unnerved at the sight of his own blood as he dabbed at the side of his thick skull, looking for the cut. When he found it, he cursed in Russian.

"All right, big fella," said Burns. "It's the final showdown!" He charged straight at his opponent, faking a direct assault, then shifted his body left and right with a quick deke, as if he were skating around a defenceman on his way to score a goal. The guard reacted instinctively with a move that forced him onto his bad leg, the sharp pain eliciting another yell. Burns could have delivered a deathblow as he danced around the guard but opted for a kick to the still-intact left knee. The big man went down hard on both knees, the pain voiced itself in a growling roar, the wounded bear still threatening death. He drew himself up against the agony and held up his *rys*, the blade named for the Russian lynx, brandishing it with menace. Burns sprang past the guard and scooped up his gun with his right hand before the guard could react. He aimed for a headshot.

The guard remembered the gun too late. "Not fair fight," he whined, gesturing to his knife.

"Not fair?" Burns laughed. "Really?" Burns put two bullets in the guard, one in the head and one in the heart as the body sank to the floor.

"You're the one who pulled a knife, asshole."

Burns went back into the lavatory and collected Veda, who looked to be praying to heaven, eyes closed, from his perch on the toilet.

Veda was startled at first, then seemed relieved to see Burns. "Did you kill him?"

"Yeah, I killed him too," said Burns flatly. He motioned for Veda to follow as he headed for the door. He wondered where the second guard had come from until they reached the dock area where he saw the second golf car. He surmised Mr Fight Club had come from the hotel, perhaps for a shift change. He had left his car parked behind the one Burns had arrived in, making it impossible for either car to drive forward, or for the turntable to rotate. Burns knew the vehicle could probably go as fast in reverse as forward, so he hopped behind the wheel of the last car and called to Veda.

"Let's go."

He could see that Veda had become self-aware, and aware of his surroundings. He was pulling at the sweater Burns had thrown over him, trying to cover his genitals as he climbed into the front seat beside Burns.

"We'll get you a pair of coveralls and maybe a jacket upstairs," offered Burns.

"Upstairs?"

"Topside." Burns pointed up. "We're underground." He could tell Veda's world was slowly getting bigger again. He returned Veda's gaze. We're not in London anymore."

Veda smiled. "Yes, I know."

"Do you get carsick, Dr Veda?"

"No, I don't think so. I mean, I don't know."

Burns had been trained to operate a wide range of vehicles and crafts on land and sea as a soldier. Looking backwards was fine but sitting as a passenger or operator and seeing the world passing by in reverse at the outer edges of his field of vision had always made him nauseous. As the operator, the training was to use the mirror and stay facing forward. Burns remembered a simulated assault near the Adriatic Sea and how he had been reprimanded by the observing officer for turning around as he was manoeuvring a jeep in reverse. The evaluator had seen Burns' face as he fought down the bile but not mentioned it. A week later she agreed to allow Burns a second run.

Driving in reverse looking backward escaping a bomb blast in a tunnel would not lose Burns any points today, he reckoned.

He checked the lever that raised and lowered the centre wheel onto the rail and was at once amused and disappointed to discover the second guard had been driving with the car freewheeling. *My kinda guy*, he mused.

His watch read 1:26. Less than five minutes to detonation. He remembered the ride down had taken a little more than three minutes, with the brief stop along the way. He reasoned he would only have to go in reverse as far as the intersecting tunnel. There he could make a three-point turn and right the car to make a full speed getaway for the last few hundred metres. Burns grasped the wheel and turned his head and torso to focus on the distant black spot that would swell with light as he advanced up the hole. He threw the lever and felt the centre wheel engage as it came to rest on the track.

"Better safe than scraped!" He repeated his father's warning. Then he flipped the shifter into 'R' and stepped on the accelerator.

The backup signal buzzed and the car whirred a full two seconds as the electric motor engaged. It lurched backward but stayed firmly on its track as it reached its top speed. Burns grimaced and swore. Its top speed in reverse was about half of what the first car made on the way down. Either the governor on the motor was still engaged or the reverse drive was geared much lower. Or the battery is dying. He took one last look at the loading dock as they pulled away. The bodies were out of sight. He wondered if the first man to reach the end of the tunnel would miss Gagarin and the guard on their way to the lab, like Aitkens had done in London. Burns tried to knock back the sneering anger with a chuckle.

He checked his watch and confirmed his fear. At this rate of speed, he didn't have to wonder anymore if he would be near enough to hear the blast as it destroyed the viruses and the lab. He only wondered if he would see it coming, or feel it on the back of his neck.

"Where is this place? Veda asked, his voice too loud. "Where are we?"

Burns could see that Veda had reached another level on his way back to the present. The shock was fading.

"Reykjavik, Iceland. Near the airport." Said Burns. "Underground."

"Iceland," said Veda. Wow." He looked like he was daydreaming, not confused. "I've never been to Iceland."

"Maybe you'll see more of it next time," Burns offered.

Veda suddenly reached over and grabbed Burns' hand on the steering wheel and yelled, "Stop!"

Burns didn't react. He knew what was coming. He kept his focus on the dim light at the end of the tunnel and his foot on the accelerator.

"Kaia! They locked her in the vault!" Veda's cry echoed down the tunnel. Burns turned to face Veda and smiled, then he looked to the offending hand and back to Veda's gaping eyes.

Veda relaxed his grip quickly but not his voice. It wavered and faded from a wail to a whisper. "I have to save her. You can't... we can't..."

Burns hadn't thought about Kaia since the vault. He didn't know how much she meant to Veda, or how much of a picture he could paint for him.

"She's gone," said Burns. "I'm sorry."

He shrugged and turned back to the tunnel. "There's nothing in there for you."

Veda was silent. His expression of horror told Burns how grim he had made it sound.

"I didn't see her," he explained. "The vault was open." He held Veda's gaze and saw the deep loss, then shame filled the eyes and wash over Veda's face. He wanted to let Veda know that his girlfriend was not really his, and at least some of his work, if not all, had been destroyed. He wondered if the scientist would feel the guilt shift from killing one man to the disaster that his discovery could have unleashed on humanity. Or would he even realise? Burns had to let his contempt fizzle. He checked the impulse to lie and claim he hadn't seen anything in the vault. He would save that story for the debriefing, if it came to require plausible deniability.

The golf cart whirred, and its reverse warning signal continued to bray as they reached the first junction. Even if he was losing time, shutting off that wavering buzzer was Burns' first reason to pull the car off its track and swing into the mystery tunnel.

He executed the turn and heaved a sigh, satisfied to have silenced the droning signal and its echo in the tunnel. He was also satisfied he didn't puke. And that the car had accelerated quickly to its top speed, more than double what its speed was in reverse. And that Veda hadn't fallen out during the manoeuvre. In that order. Burns allowed himself a grin. Still almost five minutes to detonation, and less than a minute from the elevator. Burns assured himself that he wasn't going to burn to death or get crushed in a collapsing tunnel. He reckoned it was time to call in and confirm the arrival of Hilts' team at the spa.

But not before a couple of quick questions. Burns felt he had as much right to know as anybody.

"Look," he said. "I'm going to ask you a couple of questions. These are questions that the police and the Home Office and CIA and everybody else are going to ask you…"

"And the Health Minister," said Veda.

"Right," said Burns, stifling a laugh. Burns already knew the answer to his first question.

Veda answered before Burns could ask. "He stole my lab, the lab the Ministry has, has spent millions of pounds to…to…" he stammered and shook his head. "I was just getting started." Veda blinked at Burns. "How can I…" he trailed off and turned away. The car whirred past the tunnel leading to the spa. Burns didn't slow down as he glanced to his right to confirm the tunnel was empty.

How can you what? Burns wanted to ask. Start over again? Instead, he asked the first question as if he were speaking to a child.

"Do you know the man who brought you here?"

"I never met him before they—" Veda coughed. Burns could see him fighting his emotions. And memories. "Before here," he sniffed. "They brought me here. And Kaia," Veda sobbed.

Burns decided he would tell the man what he had seen. Someday. If he ever talked to him again. He only hoped a video never showed up on PornHub, or in Veda's email.

Burns could see the elevator shaft and the equipment cages in the distance.

"Do you know what he was planning to do?" Burns already had his own clear theory but he held onto the hope that Vladimir Konstantin Ivanov had shared his diabolical scheme with Dr Veda just before turning on the machine that would kill Veda in some slow torturous manner, like all good evil villains. Wait a minute, Burns mused. There was nothing slow about a C4 blast, except the cleaning up afterward. Burns reckoned Ivanov had originally wanted to keep and use Veda to further his goal of mass murder. Probably intended to soften Veda with a few days of torture before convincing him to work together. No doubt there was an extortion angle somewhere. But suddenly Veda and the other scientist had been deemed expendable. Burns couldn't complete the puzzle.

"He talked about the future," Veda offered. "But I don't remember what he said. I don't know his name."

Burns believed him. Veda still had a long way to go before he would wake up from the nightmare. Burns knew Veda would then have to decide how much he wanted to remember.

That was it, thought Burns. Rendition, reprogramming and compliance. Ivanov had snatched Dr Veda using a beautiful woman to get close to him. He even stole some of Veda's gear. Ivanov brought him to Iceland to work on the super vaccine, or more likely mega virus.

And then abandoned it all less than two days later?

Burns concluded that Ivanov must have been tipped off about the CIA's pending attack and was able to make a quick exit. Whether or not Ivanov made it out with his lethal weapons was their issue. Burns could leave that to them. He had done what he could to destroy whatever was left behind. He knew it would be naïve to assume that a psychopath would rush off without anything he truly needed for whatever he was cooking up. Nothing Burns had seen in the lab resembled any kind of weaponising equipment, there wasn't even the room for it, so maybe it wasn't his only facility.

But whatever was in the vials and jars left behind, even if they were just samples from previous trials, they weren't going to save anybody, or kill anyone either.

Burns checked his gun as the car neared the end of the tunnel, scanning the open space and the storage cages below the hangar. He slowed in the shadow, turning his eyes on the opening in the ceiling. The dimly lit hangar was a black hole, the lights on the ceiling distant planets. He pulled into the space next to elevator platform and slowed to a stop. He got out of the car and stepped around to take Veda's hand as he rose from his seat on ungainly legs. Burns kept a soft grip on Veda's arm as he led him onto the elevator platform. Veda leaned on Burns as the lift made a short jolt before rising smoothly to the upper floor. It took a few seconds for Burns to adjust his eyes to the darkness and suppress the fear reaction. Thankfully, the hangar was still deserted. He slipped his weapon in his pocket but held his grip on it. The lift came to a halt when it reached the level of the hangar floor. Burns swept his gaze around before he opened the safety gate and stepped off, inviting Veda to follow. They walked together toward the door.

Burns stopped at the rack near the exit and grabbed the smallest pair of coveralls hanging there. He handed them to Veda, who wordlessly climbed into the legs and pulled on the soiled grey work wear. Burns imagined the scientist had worn hazmat clothing often during his experiments, but here the acclaimed scientist looked like a kid dressing up in his father's work gear. Burns took a quick look out the window and opened the door. The two men stood silently, looking out at the deserted car park.

Burns figured it best if he checked in with Hilts before they stepped out into the cool night to wait in the car park. Burns checked his watch, deliberately, as if he was giving a signal to Veda.

"Time to check in," he said. He pulled out his phone and activated it. With a slide of his thumb on the touch screen, he considered the order of the two messages. He could send a text to DCI Wayne to request transport and streamline their passage at the airport. He would call Hilts. He hadn't decided how much he would say, but he had to make sure the cavalry didn't get in his way—or walk into an explosion.

The first message went to DCI Wayne, and was to the point:

En route w/dr to KEF. Request air transport. Will need help at check in

Without waiting for the reply, Burns dialled Hilts.

Hilts picked up on the first ring.

"So, you're at the hangar." Hilts' tone was almost the condescending parent. Burns knew Hilts was looking at a little dot on a map showing the location of Burns' phone.

"See anything yet?" Hilts asked.

"I've got my doctor," Burns answered. The response was a quiet sigh, impossible for Burns to discern if it was frustration or relief. Seconds passed. Burns glanced over at Veda, who was staring out at the empty car park. Burns gently pulled Veda away from the window and nodded for him to stay put in the shadow behind the door. He waved his phone and gesticulated, as if to say, "one moment please". Hilts seemed to be waiting for more intel, or at least Burns imagined so in the silence. Burns cut the quiet in two.

"I'm on my way out," he declared. "Any of your boys out this way yet?"

"That's why I asked if you'd seen anything." Hilts had changed his tone to his more natural, friendlier drawl. "There should be a small team onsite at your location any minute." Then he added with a laugh, "But don't worry. Ain't nobody gonna shoot you, or your Indian."

"I hope you told them I'm in here, Hilts," said Burns.

"Of course I told them," said Hilts. "But still, you oughtta tell 'em too. Y'know, let 'em know you're friendly, and all. Hang on."

Burns heard a short electronic tone as Hilts muted their conversation. The line remained silent for a few seconds. After another peep, Hilts returned. "They're securing the perimeter of the building."

"How many?"

"Why? You countin' ammo or something, Burns?" Hilts made the accusation sound like a joke, just like he would in the dressing room at intermission when one of his teammates wasn't pulling their weight. Burns let it pass.

"You told them," said Burns.

Hilts said, "Just ID yourself as friendly before you walk out the door."

"Right. Is that my safe word, friendly?" Burns looked at his watch.

"Exactly," Hilts answered.

"Fine," Burns grunted. "Fine."

"Stay on the line, will ya, Burnsy?"

"Roger that."

Burns opened the door slowly and shouted the magic word, then identified himself as "Charles Burns Plus One." He silently counted to three and said, "Coming out." He paused, then slowly pushed the door further, letting it swing to the wall where it landed with a metallic clang. Burns placed Veda back in the shadow of the doorframe and motioned for him to wait, gesturing "Me first" with his thumb as he stepped out.

He had seen the sniper laid out on the grass on the left flank as the first crack of light appeared when the door opened, so he concentrated his reflexes to engage from his right a full second before he heard the masked commando shout, "Freeze!" The harsh growl came loud into Burns' right ear. He turned slowly toward the command. It came from a large man in full black commando gear, replete with balaclava. The eyes were steely grey and threatened violence.

Burns turned his eyes past the gun and scanned the parking area and the open spaces between the nearest structures. He saw no other agents. He turned to the large man in black aiming a Beretta at his head, an arm's length away. Burns held his hands chest high, the left one empty and the right holding his phone.

"This is Hilts," Burns gestured to his phone.

"Who?"

"Your QB," said Burns. "Agent Hilts. Right here on the line. We were just talking about you, listen." He tapped the screen and smiled at the killer eyes that seemed slightly confused by the name. Burns smiled and angled his wrist, ever so slightly, to aim the phone toward the Beretta as he raised his voice.

"Hiltsy!" Burns called out. "You're on speaker," he said, sounding like a radio call-in host. "Say hello, please." No answer.

"You're on speaker," he repeated.

The phone was silent. Burns felt a knot in his stomach. Maybe Hilts was pissed because Burns had switched off his phone. Burns had been pissed too, and figured he still had a right to be.

Burns hadn't volunteered any information so far. Now seemed like a good time. He bit back on the anger welled up in his throat and called out, "Hilts!"

He drew the phone back, gambling that Hilts was still listening, and addressed everyone.

"Look, a bomb went off down there about eight minutes ago. There's a fire burning at the other end of a tunnel below the hangar." Burns paused, holding fast at the edge of full disclosure. "There might be more."

He knew he had plausible deniability. No one could prove he reset the timer in the vault to destroy the stolen deadly diseases, and any chance of their recovery.

The mask beside him growled, " Where's your Plus One?"

Burns ignored the question and asked one of his own, speaking to the phone. "You still there, Hilts?"

"I'm here."

Burns guessed Hilts wasn't the team's CO and had been talking to the other parties about the mission's status.

"What exactly is at the end of the tunnel, Burns?" Hilts asked. "What did you see?"

Burns looked at the two masked men in his field of vision. The sniper had risen from his prone position and advanced to less than 5 metres away, his rifle still trained on Burns. He reckoned the rest of the first team was completing their recon on the other sides of the hangar. Burns felt a jab when he pictured one of them reaching the airside door and entering the hangar. A moment later he spotted the third man to his left rounding the corner of the building. He swung his gaze and, as expected, the fourth soldier appeared at the opposite corner, coming from airside. All four men kept their weapons trained on Burns, but he felt no fear. He was glad to see them all outside the hangar. Despite his relief, Burns played up his anger to sound a little panicked.

"Could you at least get on your fucking radio and tell your boys to lower their weapons?"

"Yup, can do," said Hilts. "Hold on."

Burns listened in the pause. Agent Hilts was giving an order to someone. Burns presumed that Hilts had left his phone open so that Burns could hear him.

A moment later, he heard the Team Leader mumble "Roger that".

The four men lowered their weapons in unison and stood at-ease. Then Hilts went mute on the phone for several seconds and Burns watched as the men reacted to the orders coming directly to their ears. A second later they were in motion toward him. Each man took up his weapon, each pair of eyes looking past Burns to the door. Damn, thought Burns. They're going in.

"Wait!" Burns shouted, holding his phone in front of himself like it was a detonator. The men in black stopped advancing.

"I have to get my Plus One out," he said. Then he spoke in a cautionary tone to Hilts on the phone, but loud enough for the men, who were now all in range to hear.

"Look, I already told you there's a fire down there. I also disarmed two explosive devices," he said. He lowered his tone and directed the message to Hilts. Captain Bryce Hilts, Leader of men.

"But I can't guarantee you there aren't more," he said. "Your boys aren't dressed for it."

Burns had the eyes of all four men fixed on him, and he scrutinised their soldier's hearts. Two of them were young, their fear visible. Unwarranted, as far as Burns was concerned. Unless they knew about the charge he had set to go off. The other two, the first two he had seen, were at least as old as Burns was. All looked prepared to follow their orders like every good soldier. Until they change, as the old adage went. But he had given them pause.

"There are no armed combatants down there," Burns declared. It was an easy stretch. The men he had killed were armed, but no longer combatants.

"The tunnel is empty," he added, for Hilts' sake.

Burns could omit the presence of the corpses, justified by his own need-to-know principles. He looked at each of the men and held their eyes for a few seconds more. He put up a smile of camaraderie, as if he was on their side. He would be doing them a favour and speak to Hilts again on their behalf so they could all go home early.

"Maybe you oughtta call the fire department, or somebody," he offered.

Burns remembered his earlier idea that the smoke would draw the attention of the control tower at the airport. He looked at the sky in the direction of where the fire was burning underground and was disappointed by the lack of visible smoke. No alarms had been raised, no civilians were on the way yet. He held his next thought for a moment, then he shared it nonchalantly.

"Or just let it burn itself out. Up to you," Burns shrugged at the phone. "But I'd certainly keep these boys out of there." Burns nodded again for his new mates.

"What got blown up, Charles?"

Burns ignored Hilts' question. The tick-tock notification that signalled a message from DCI Wayne gave him the excuse.

"Sorry." Burns held up a finger. "One moment, please." read the message and frowned.

Catch a lift w/cousins

Then Burns heard an insect-like noise emanating from the left ear of the nearest man. The two younger soldiers' expressions changed. Grim determination was pressing down the fear, but Burns could still see it as they re-gripped their weapons. He could see the older men's eyes were fearful too, but not the unfocused fear of the younger men. The older two were looking at him as if he was a threat.

"Ok, hold up there, fellas," said Burns. "I just gotta get my guy out." Then, as a little joke to himself he added, "Less than a minute, promise. Okay?" He turned slowly in the doorway and calmly waved Veda nearer. "It's okay, Dr Veda. You can come out now."

Veda stepped into view, keeping his focus on Burns, as did the other four men. He made a broad gesture of muting his phone and putting it in his pocket then stepped up to the Team Leader to reason it out.

"Look, I'm not gonna stop you," Burns lied. "There's a plane parked in the hangar that's been there since your guy took off for warmer climes about two or three hours ago.

"Warmer climes?" asked the Team Leader. "Which direction?"

"Don't be an asshole," said Burns. He pointed and added, "South." He heard a flurry of murmuring voices on Hilts' end of the line and the soft chirp in the TL's ear, almost simultaneously.

"This is Iceland," Burns interjected. "Everywhere is a warmer clime."

Burns slid his thumb across the phone's mute button, opening the microphone to include Hilts. "Look," he told the Team Leader. "This is crazy. You know you shouldn't go in there. Not yet. Nobody should go in there without suits on." Burns straightened and stared at the TL, letting the man know he was passing judgment.

"You're not prepared."

"We have our orders. You can wait here," the Team Leader was cold, resolute. "Transport is on its way for you and your Plus One."

Burns followed the Team Leader's eyes to Veda, whose relief was stunted by the shock. Burns gave Veda a reassuring smile and nod. The smile was received and returned by chattering teeth as the shock escaped in shivers in the cool sub-Arctic night. Burns glanced at his watch. His internal clock had told him that his bomb had begun the final countdown. He knew the vault's blast would be almost completely localised inside its walls, with only minimal impact in the lab via the open door. And as long as the gas cylinders didn't get hot enough to explode, and the fuel tank… it was a gamble. He hadn't inspected the apparatus, but at least he had been careful enough to close all the valves, so he wouldn't have to worry about anything but the heat. He had to assume the jet fuel would only be enough to accelerate the burning of the subterranean structure to cinders. He hoped the air exchange would function well enough for the place to burn completely. But he also hadn't inspected the crates and boxes placed around the lab. If this was an exercise and I were evaluating me, thought Burns, I might be leaning toward fail. He allowed himself a laugh and a shrug.

Burns turned to the Team Leader and began again. "Ivanov is gone," he said. "I don't know what he took with him, but I bet you're after that, too." Burns held the man's eyes and knew in a moment how little the team knew. That was one reason why he got out of the armed response business.

He tightened his focus on the mini camera next to the Team Leader's eye and glared at his audience. Then he checked the phone to confirm Hilts was still connected. Burns resisted the urge to look at his watch in front of the men, knowing he had to make one last pitch to hold them back without tipping his hand. He used his dad's voice, starting with fatherly advice and ending with loud admonishment.

"But it might be wise to wait until the fire department or maybe a bomb squad can get here, because there's a fire burning out of control about a thousand metres down there."

Burns pointed. Then he looked. Still no smoke on the horizon to the south. Not for long, he mused.

"You heard from The Duke?" Hilts asked.

Detective Chief Inspector Wayne had been known as The Duke in the military, and later police circles, since his heroics in the Falklands, but Burns was surprised Hilts knew the nickname.

"The Duke is on the other line." Burns smiled. "About that ride home. I think I'll have to take you up on that, Agent Hilts. Can I call you that?" Burns teased. "Maybe you could ask one of your boys here to call me a cab."

"A car is on its way," Hilts declared. "Two minutes out."

"That sounds fine," Burns answered. "We'll just wait here in the car park then."

"Affirmative," Hilts replied. "Wait there. You'll ride back with the team after they finish recon."

Burns watched the men turn away from his gaze and toward the door. A sudden sense of failure hit him in the ribs like a needle, its contents burning as it spread through his body like a grass fire in August. Either his internal clock had failed, or he had failed to reset the bomb. Burns took Veda by the arm stepped through the men, who parted as they moved toward the hangar door. He checked his watch and drew his weapon after they passed.

"No," Burns raised his voice. "You really should not go in there!" Burns shouted at their backs and fired a warning shot. He gambled again, holding his gun aloft instead of preparing to return fire, and was relieved when the four soldiers turned without reflexively returning fire. The six men stood in motionless silence for several seconds, one still in shock, four of them expecting a statement of justification. One stalling.

Burns didn't need to explain. They all heard it. The thud-crack of the subterranean blast followed the report of Burns' sidearm just as the first echo subsided, like the call-and-answer of two sentries stationed in opposite corners of the kingdom. Burns had guessed that the fire in the vault would draw its breath from the tunnel, and would burn itself out in less than two or three hours. It didn't matter now. Burns hoped to be wheels-up and head-back sooner than that. As long as the compressed gas didn't blow, nobody would get hurt. He considered making one last plea to the team but decided his energy would better-spent wishing for a cloud of smoke to come pouring out of the tunnel.

"Okay," shrugged Burns. "Now you can go in, I suppose." Burns grinned.

"If you really feel like you have to."

The Team Leader had stepped away from the others to have a conversation on coms. Burns heard another "Roger that" before the leader turned back to his men and straightened to attention. He let his hand drift down from where it had been pressed against his earpiece and nodded silently to his men, a dispirited salute. A moment later they all lowered their weapons in unison, like a switch had been thrown and they had all been powered down simultaneously. Burns watched as the disappointment laid flat on the asphalt, the deactivated soldiers staring holes in it. His memory flashed through scenes from younger years. He knew both sides of the order to "stand down": the sigh of relief, and the hard swallow of failure. He turned away, facing the empty roadway, and spoke into his phone in a lowered tone.

"I hope you send two cars, Hilts."

Burns turned toward Veda and gestured to the car park. Veda stood facing Burns for a moment looking calm, and mostly clear. He pulled up the long, dangling sleeves of the coveralls and placed his palms together in Namaste. Burns acknowledged Veda's gesture of gratitude. Or are you expecting to be handcuffed? Burns smiled at his silent joke and stepped in beside Veda. They walked the few paces down the path and onto the open asphalt, stopping in the beam of the overhead lamp, and under the lens of the security camera. Burns gave it a cheesy smile and a wave before he turned back to see the four men still standing near the door.

"Thank fucking Christ," Burns muttered. Nobody else is going to die here tonight.

"Thank fucking Christ?" Veda blurted out. "What does that even mean?" Veda seemed suddenly incensed. "I mean, I can say fuck and, and fucking shit, but I mean why drag Him into it?"

"I, uh I dunno, I..." Burns stammered. "It's just an expression."

"An expression? What does that even mean?" Veda's tone was almost scolding as he continued, animated by outrage. "Thank Christ, okay. Even if you said 'Jesus Christ', without the thanks, but..." he stopped and collected himself. Burns watched as Veda regained control of his emotions. "I'm sorry," Veda shook his head. "It just doesn't sound..."

"Kosher, I know." Burns heard himself apologise with a joke. "And I'm sorry," he added.

Veda seemed relieved and laughed it off. "No, really. It's all right." Then he added, "But even 'thank Fuck' sounds better. But I don't know what that means either."

"You're right," Burns answered. "Who the fuck is Fuck, anyway?"

The two men shared a laugh, like two teenagers proud and embarrassed by their naughty discovery. The laughter was prolonged by the nervous release of emotion that lasted until a jet-black Hummer rounded the corner, eighty metres away. Veda's expression changed to hopeful anticipation, watching the oversized SUV as it approached, like a kid after school, waiting for his family car to round into view.

Burns frowned at his phone and spoke quietly. "Uh, Hilts?" he said. "Come back."

Burns didn't want to ride anywhere with the team whose mission he had just got scrubbed. It was never fun when it was his team, but CIA cowboys?

"You're in the next car, Burns," Hilts answered before the question came. "Just around the corner from you now."

Burns looked up the road for several seconds without speaking. Another big SUV appeared, the second of the two he had seen at the back of the rental yard. Burns caught sight of four faces inside as the Jeep passed under a streetlamp. A moment later a third vehicle appeared rounding the corner from the opposite direction. It was the little Ford he had left in the lot at the pizza restaurant, with two men inside.

"Cute," said Burns, as he eyed the cramped back seat.

"Conserving resources, utilising assets, my friend," Hilts replied. "Somebody has to return the car anyway. These gentlemen will take you to our transport."

The Team Leader and his men got into the first Hummer and drove off south, no doubt to locate the other end of the tunnel, followed closely by the second vehicle. Burns wondered if they would beat the airport fire brigade to the vent, and if they might find another way down to the lab. It didn't matter. His mission was almost complete.

"Perfect," Burns almost sang into his phone. "ETA London?"

"A-sap," said Hilts.

"See you back," Burns replied.

"See you on the plane."

Burns rang off and opened the rear door of the car. He leaned in, getting his face between the two men inside.

"Gentlemen!" Burns greeted the driver and passenger heartily. "Large Hawaiian, with shrimp and extra cheese?" He let the smile fall from his face and gave each a brief, stern inspection. They passed. Burns gave them a wink and clicked his tongue before he pulled himself out of the car and held the door for Veda, who climbed in and gingerly shuffled across the seat without looking at the two men in the front seat. Burns swung in and sank back into the upholstery, closing the door softly.

"Airport please," Burns sighed. "International Departures."

PART FIVE:
SUNDAY MORNING

Charles Burns had allowed his body to almost completely relax on the short ride through the industrial park to where the CIA aircraft waited. He grimaced as he recognised the plane. It was a C23 Sherpa, a small military cargo plane that had a range of about a thousand miles. And he knew the distance to London to be long enough for him to feel comfortable. As Burns got out of the car, he motioned for Veda to wait while he dialled up Hilts. He wrestled with the thoughts that had wound their way to the front of his mind, the serious doubts, the suspicion he had about the CIA, just as Hilts came on.

"Burnsy!" Hilts exclaimed. "What are you waitin' for?"

Burns was studying the two men at the foot of the gangway leading into the aft of the plane. They were agents, but wearing flight crew uniforms not commando gear. Only one had eyes on him and a look was exchanged, as two men who might work in the same factory but not know each other. He glanced at the man who got out of the passenger door on the opposite side of the car, and then down at the driver who was finger-drumming his patience on the wheel, as if he had nowhere to be anytime soon.

"Look, Hilts," Burns began, despite the survival instinct throbbing in his throat. He didn't want to start a fight. He had already visualised how it would end. He would have to wound or kill at least four men to escape if this was a trap.

A trap. Escape. Burns laughed to himself. He was really going to have to work on his trust issues.

"This plane," said Burns. "Are you sure it has the range to get us back to London?"

"She's got a big tank and a low payload, my friend," replied Hilts. "C'mon, get in. We got some catchin' up t'do." Hilts disconnected and Burns pocketed his phone. He stared at the Sherpa's darkened windows for a moment, wondering if Hilts was actually inside. He pulled the car door open and leaned in and smiled at Veda.

"We're good to go," said Burns. He offered his hand, Veda took it and pulled himself out of the car. His pulse was stable, and his eyes were clear. Burns released his grip and watched as a deep yawn slowly inflated the thin body, the limbs moving inside the baggy coveralls as Veda stretched and exhaled. Burns was reassured to see the hopeful look in Veda's eyes as they fixed on the plane that would take him home.

Burns made a point of catching the eyes of each agent as he led Veda into the plane. He was satisfied by what he saw, reactions ranging from intimidation to nothing more than mild curiosity—and no hostility. None followed as he and Veda walked to the open gate at the rear of the plane.

Burns watched Veda's eyes as the two men clasped wrists again. He felt himself mirroring the young scientist's expression. It was that familiar look of a man who had experienced life-threatening danger and lived to see the danger pass, to defeat it.

Burns took a firm grasp on the bulkhead with his other hand and lifted Veda up and inside. He used a little more force than was necessary and accidentally lifted Veda off his feet. Burns held him up for the moment it took Veda to regain his balance upon landing unsteadily next to Burns. Veda's face looked like he had just zoomed down that first short descent on a rollercoaster, the "teaser". Predictably, his face widened into the grin that usually lasted to the next precipice. Veda grinned and laughed, in little hiccups at first, until it sounded like a child singing a song it didn't know the words for. Veda's laughter got stuck in the refrain until his eyes met Burns' calming gaze.

"I think we can sit right over here," he said to Veda, then he added, "Right?" to the co-pilot who stood to the side of the gangway.

"No, mister..." said the co-pilot. He was waiting for Burns to identify himself.

"Burns," said Burns, pointing to himself. "Captain...?"

"Nope, I'm just mister," interjected the co-pilot. "Your friend can take a seat on that side over there. The medic will take a look at him when he gets back, but you're requested up front by..." The co-pilot dropped his tone to a loud whisper, as if what he said next could only be shared with Burns. "Agent Allen."

Burns covered his confusion with mock enthusiasm. "Agent Allen is here?" The co-pilot nodded in confirmation with a nervous smile. For a split-second, Burns' fear returned as he caught sight of a gurney, collapsed and stowed behind and below the four seats in the last row. Nicholas Veda was still in shock and dehydrated and could probably use an IV of fluids but Burns reckoned he didn't need any real medical attention until they got back to London. And he didn't want to let the Yanks get at his rescuee. Burns successfully pushed aside his suspicion of the Americans by reminding himself that Wayne had signed off on him taking Veda back with the CIA. He looked at the door that separated him from Agent Allen. He recalled the aircraft's dimensions and calculated the size of the room beyond the door, guessing it to be only a few steps from the forward hatch and the cockpit. He wondered if Agent Allen was Bryce Hilts, and how many other names the square-jawed hockey player from Texas had used. *File this one in the Never Saw That Coming file*, Burns mused.

"Come on up near the front with me, Doctor," Burns invited. Then with one last shot at the co-pilot he thumbed at Veda, presenting him as, "Mister Doctor."

The young officer lowered his gaze and swung his head forward in the direction of the passenger seating area, then casually looked aft, turning a blind eye to Burns' decision. Burns led Veda to the last seat on the port side where Veda gathered up the folds of the coveralls and sat easily. Veda automatically went for the two ends of the safety belt but Burns stopped him with a wave of his hand.

"You don't need to strap in just yet, Doctor Veda," Burns insisted. "Maybe I can get us an upgrade," Burns chuckled. He added calmly, "I'm just going up front to see how long until we take off and we get back to London, okay?"

Burns patted Veda's shoulder and strode forward without a second look. He stood at the door for a moment. Then he knocked three times before turning the handle and pulling the hatch open.

The room was empty. It was as he had guessed, a small anteroom before the cockpit, about nine metres square. Both the door to the cockpit and the forward hatch were closed and locked. What he hadn't guessed was that he would see Hilts' face on a monitor built into the communications console that comprised the starboard side of the small cabin. Burns released a rolling chair from where it was stowed on the bulkhead and mounted it like a horse. He rolled over to the screen to greet Hilts.

"Agent Allen Hilts?" Burns asked without expecting an answer. He went on, "You could have just called back. I have FaceTime," Burns chided. "Seeing you this big is a little too..." he pointed at the screen, drawing a large circle with his finger. "Life-like." He hung his elbows on the chair's back and grinned.

"Your legs burning?" Hilts asked, returning the smile. He looked like he was rubbing his legs below the camera's level. Burns guessed Hilts hadn't had any exercise since the game and was looking for a teammate to commiserate with.

"A bit," Burns lied. "I hope you're rubbing your quads and not something else, Big Guy."

Hilts chortled in choppy grunts, taking a moment to wipe the smile from his face. "What kind of intel can you give me?"

Burns perked up, feigning curiosity. "About what?"

"About the lab, aass-hole." Hilts made the word a song. "I mean, anything deadly? You talk to Detective Chief Inspector Wayne yet?"

"Yes," grinned Burns, refusing to acknowledge which question he had answered. He looked around for a few moments, pretending to be interested in the apparatus surrounding the monitor where Hilts' open-mouthed face awaited clarification. After a suitably uncomfortable pause Burns frowned for the camera. "Not recently."

Hilts was looking down at his hands, presumably sending a text message on his phone. He turned his face up to the monitor and smiled at Burns.

"He'll reach out a-sap," Hilts insisted.

"Copy that," Burns responded, grinning.

"So…"

Burns could see the impatience widening Hilts' eyes and was enjoying it before a flashing moment of guilt acknowledged his inability to be a "good team player".

Hilts inhaled deeply and held it until the frustration swelled in his throat and poured out. "So, yer gonna wait?"

Burns cleared his throat as he raised an eyebrow with a hint of reproach. "I dunno," he answered. He could take Hilts to task for not sharing enough from his side, or not. Just as he was about to continue, the text message from DCI Wayne came in:

Share anything helpful on the ride home. Transport will meet you at Stansted.

Burns quickly visualised the route from Essex to New Scotland Yard, a quick trip on a Sunday morning, unless they diverted to a hospital, which seemed likely.

Burns kept his focus down while holding back the smile of relief that crept at the corners of his mouth.

A second message gave further reassurance:

We're watching and listening.

No shit, thought Burns. He looked at Hilts. "What can I tell you," he shrugged. "It looked like it was still under construction. Not a '"Lights on, nobody home'" thing, more like the lights are on but nothing else is. Crates everywhere. Doctor Veda was being held and tortured in a wet room. I neutralised the guard." Burns hesitated, silently mocking his use of the word instead of saying killed. "Well, three guards," Burns admitted. He thought of young Gagarin. "And another..." Burns stopped short of labelling him hostile. He wondered if the bodies at the dock would be incinerated before investigators found them, or if it mattered.

"The bomb on the fuel tank exploded but I got my guy out before the fuel caught fire."

"Before it caught fire," Hilts repeated the words as if he was taking dictation.

"Yes," Burns asserted. "I got Doctor Veda out of his bondage and we stepped out of the jet fuel right before we caught fire." We took a service tunnel out to avoid the main thrust of the fire. That's where we ran into Guard Number Two. The fire wasn't out of control when we left the lab, but by the time I killed the second guard the smoke was getting deadly," Burns exaggerated. Then we got out, got into the golf cart and whoosh!" Burns smiled and opened his arms. "Here we are." He narrowed his smile. "Thankfully before we met your boys and the second bomb went off ...."

"Any weapons? Chemicals?" Hilts entreated. "Did you see anything BIO logical?"

"There was a vault," Burns admitted and went on slowly. "And glass cabinets, mostly empty, but some bottles and jars that could have been chemical or bio samples, yeah."

"Shit, Burns. And you just thought it'd be better to let it all burn?"

"Well yeah," Burns insisted. "But look. Bad ol' Vlad knew you were coming. Maybe he left before we even finished talking in DCI Wayne's office. The flight engineer told me they have two planes and the second one left not long after the one from Atlanta landed." Burns stopped.

The engineer?" Hilts asked. "Where'd you meet him, Burns?

"Yeah," Burns exhaled. "The other body in the tunnel was the company flight engineer." Burns gave Gagarin the posthumous title, offering it as a defence for the mostly innocent man. He knew it would also mean the young ex-cadet would be remembered, if only as a name in a report. A name that Burns would never forget, whether he wanted to or not.

"Gagarin," Burns tried not to grumble. "He's dead, with Guard Number One." He left it there. Burns caught his emotional response to change the subject, a split second later he remembered he had just cause. It was time to fill in some blanks for Hilts.

"I think I know what happened when you lost all your surveillance," Burns offered.

"And comms," Hilts confessed.

"That figures," Burns nodded. "I trust you've got what you need from Wayne about the attack on the Met."

"Yep, all over it, like a fat kid on a Smartie," Hilts declared. "Not me personally, y'unnerstand. We got people."

"Indeed," Burns agreed. He visualised the difference between how the CIA would be throwing money and resources at finding Ivanov, and what Chief Wayne had put together at the MCU2 to find Dr Veda. Burns was grateful to be where he was in all of it.

"So, what do you know, Charles?"

"I believe Ivanov may have left with a group of about twenty health-seekers from the spa and taken jet number two somewhere about three hours ago," Burns proclaimed. Then he added cynically, "about the time your surveillance was um, compromised."

Hilts looked excited, and relieved. "Okay, see, now that's intel! We're on the flight logs... now," he said. "Still."

"Reasonable to assume he's taken the stolen viruses or whatever with him," Burns suggested. "But that's something up the military's street."

"You bet," answered Hilts. "What else?"

Burns affected the look of a man searching his memory for the last remaining detail, despite having instant and total recall of the operation. "Bodies? Yes. Samples? Umm..." he studied Hilts and decided he could mention the other scientist whom he had found dead.

"And there was another corpse. Saw him on the floor in the same room as the gas cylinders. He was well-dead when I got there."

"I don't suppose you saw a name tag," said Hilts.

Burns was already sending the photo in a message to Hilts' phone. He heard it ping and watched as Hilts' eyes fell to look at his phone.

"That's him," Burns declared.

"Thanks." Hilts was silent as he uploaded the photo from his phone into the database.

Burns summed it up. "I think that's all the help I can give you, pardner." He smiled. "When do we leave?"

"When my team reports back, and the new team takes over. Military Intelligence, to coin a phrase, will be taking over later. Then we can all go home."

"I'm not waiting for those assholes," Burns grumbled. "We'll fly commercial."

"I'll get you out," Hilts was emphatic. "And when I go, you go, okay? Before."

"When you go, I go? Impressive, Agent Allen Hilts," Burns whistled. "Irony... What with you being somewhere else and all."

"I mean," said Hilts. His hard features slackened. "You know what I mean."

"Yes, sir!" Burns saluted the camera. *Before.* He knew it meant before the military gong show arrives.

"I'll get you home," said Hilts. "And your guy."

The look told Burns he was safe. Hilts was going to keep his end and make sure Veda remained in the care of British authorities. When Hilts had to hand over the operation to the military, Burns and Dr Veda would be gone. And if they asked, Burns was acting under orders of Chief Inspector John Wayne, not in any cooperative mission with the Americans. Burns gave a wistful grin and a raised eyebrow then lightly changed the subject again.

"So, you're telling me this plane has enough gas to get us back to London," he asked.

"She got here full and's goin' back almost empty, and she's been refuelled."

"How many men did she bring?"

"Don't worry, Burnsy," said Hilts. "There'll be a seat for you and your guy."

Burns knew it was set up for thirty passengers, in bench seats on opposite sides of the cabin. He had made several high-altitude jumps from one just like it. He remembered how tightly he gripped the strap handle and jostled with his mates as the aircraft rose to higher and higher altitudes on his first jump flight. He recalled the moment of fear that enthralled him, his breath condensing on his oxygen mask.

"And who are we waiting for?" Burns asked. He smiled, trying not to seem testy.

Hilts was suddenly distracted by his phone. He looked like it might be good news at first. Burns watched the enthusiasm wane as Hilts finished reading the message.

"The forward team located the other end of your tunnel," said Hilts, attempting a smile. He glanced down at the message, then added, "But not before the KEF fire department."

Burns smiled. He had heard the distant sirens as the airport fire brigade raced to the smoking vent. He relished the moment, imagining the scene between the Icelandic firefighters and the CIA assault team.

Hilts was despondent. Burns figured he had stuck his neck out to get the operation approved, and the target had managed to avoid capture. Failure. Hilts went on sharing the intel and Burns watched as the optimism went up in flames in Hilts' eyes.

"Apparently, there's a large underground tank of avgas or Jet A buried out there. Seems as though they're going to let it burn... no danger of explosion, they figure." Burns drifted away from Hilts' voice as his mind's eye visualised the conflagration destroying one of Vladimir Ivanov's laboratories. Another one. He came back to Hilts in mid-sentence, who was echoing the thoughts in Burns' head, but in a more downcast tone than the one Burns heard himself thinking.

"...air keeps flowing the fire should keep burning till the fuel's all gone... and everything else..."

Burns knew that to be true. He checked his watch, hoping enough time had passed for the fire to reach its maximum temperature. Low enough to not cause the gas cylinders to explode. Yet.

He shrugged it off and offered Hilts a silver lining. "Still nice that they're gonna wait it out though, eh?" Hilts wasn't as happy as Burns about the total destruction of the enemy's ability to make weapons. He had the sudden realisation his agenda and that of the airport fire brigade were in alignment, but from opposing ideals. "I mean, safety first, right?" He turned to the cockpit door and stared a moment. He shifted the conversation again. "Has this aircraft got oxygen for us?"

"No, you'll be flying low, with a flight time of about..."

"Six hours is my guess," said Burns.

"Uh-huh," Hilts grunted. "Giver take."

The two men lifted their eyes to look directly into the cameras mounted above their monitors.

"Look, I gotta get back to my guy," said Burns. "Thanks Hilts!" He smiled sincerely. "Hope you get yours."

"Whaddya ya mean?" Hilts looked offended.

"Your guy!" Burns laughed. "Hope you get your guy, too."

"We will," said Hilts. "We ain't all ex-Mounties like you, Burnsy, but we'll get him."

"I was never in the RCMP," Burns bit.

"I know. Just ridin' ya," teased Hilts.

"See you back."

"Right." Hilts turned his speech to his locker room tone. "Big game Friday night, Burnsy. Got us practice ice Tuesday night. Check your email."

Burns did, and laughed.

CU Next Tuesday

8pm

"Captain, my Captain," said Burns, saluting the camera.

"Big fuckin' game Friday."

They grinned at each other until Hilts ended the transmission.

Burns didn't relish the six-hour ride back to London but consoled himself with the fact that the plane had heat. He knew it would be chilly even if they flew low. He managed a laugh. At least they wouldn't have far to fall if she did run out of gas.

Burns stepped into the main cabin and closed the door. He stood still, facing the door for a moment as he centred his breathing, then he stretched his limbs and torso. He pulled at the door handle as he bent and stretched his legs and lower back, then slowly curled into himself down to touch the floor with his palms. He held the position and straightened his legs before bringing his body upright and shaking out his limbs. He turned to see an agent sitting next to Veda.

Burns felt a weird elation. He wasn't angry anymore. He had had many excuses, opportunities to feed anger from all directions since the mission began. Even Veda. Burns wasn't angry with the professor for his wacky save-the-world scheme. He couldn't have known when he set out in search of a cure that it might go wrong... Burns wasn't even angry with himself anymore for his earlier short-sightedness. But there was always kindling to be found and aggression lit, if he looked for it.

Vladimir Konstantin Ivanov.

Burns knew the aggression he felt toward the Russian former general was borne of fear. He had learned to embrace the fear and anger, and channel the energy into his actions. Psychopaths with catastrophic plans were always worthy of both. He had come to terms with his part in the operation and had completed his mission successfully. He was done, for now. What happened next would be up to somebody else.

But Burns did have those trust issues, as he had been told many times, in many ways by many people. Puffing himself up, he strolled toward the two men like a prize fighter approaching the ring to defend his title. Venting appropriately was always healthy, as far as he knew.

"Allo, Doc-tah," Burns winked at Veda then narrowed his eyes into a hard gaze at the young agent. He was speaking to the soft, brown, intimidated eyes of a rookie in the field.

"Ooo's your friend, then?" Burns studied Veda for a moment to gauge his comfort level with his new acquaintance. Uncomfortable but not threatened, he noted.

The agent took the initiative and offered the minimal "I'm Doctor Allen," in a toneless Midwestern accent.

Burns rose to the bait. "Oh, I see," he said, sarcastically playing up his 'London tough' accent. "An em-dee?" he mocked. "Doctor Allen, is it? Any relation to Agent Allen in there?" He nodded in the direction of the forward cabin. The agent offered a smile.

"And what kind of doctor might you be, workin' for the CIA an' all?" Burns was winding up. He could tell the agent felt it. What could be more fun than to mess with a psychologist's head?

"I have a PhD in criminal psychology," the young agent offered bravely. "I studied criminal psychology at—"

Burns cut him off. "Look, Doctor Class Of Last Week. Your Ivy League college is nothin' more than what got shat out by England's finest. England's universities have been producing scholars that changed the shape of the earth since before your Ivy League had a shrubbery, so don't go waving that shit under my nose, you hear?" He was sure he could see the words "I'm sorry" forming on the young agent's trembling lips.

Burns stepped closer and leaned in to physically impose himself on the agent. "Oi, wasn't you just standin' outside there, with the real CIA guys?" He watched as the uncertain eyes shifted focus from Burns and Veda to the exit and back, grappling with the urge to flee. Burns shifted to block the escape route. "Who the fuck told you you could speak to my friend? Didn't nobody tell you he's with me?" Eh?"

The young agent shifted his weight as his eyes bounced from Burns' hard stare and the open hatch.

"Right,' said Burns, and he took a sidestep back. "Go on then. Fack off!" The agent didn't hesitate to make a swift exit through the door, where Burns watched as the agent searched the faces of the men who were gathered outside a few metres away, smoking and chatting.

Just before the agent reached the trio of smokers Burns shouted, "Did he touch you, eh? This fuckin' doctor here?" he pretended to be talking to Veda but spoke loudly enough for the psychology major and the others to hear. Burns shot a steely glare at the young man, who had foolishly turned to face him, blankly staring and wondering why he felt guilty. Burns shot a finger and a stern look at the men surrounding the psychologist before he turned back to Veda and smiled calmly.

Veda shook his head 'no'. Burns thought Veda looked like he might be able to see that Burns had been playing, and that the game was over. He lowered his tone and stepped to the seat opposite Veda.

"Seriously, did he touch you, or give you anything?"

Veda looked like he had gone somewhere and had to come back before he answered, "No. Nothing." He looked toward the hatch, as if trying to remember whom they were talking about. "He asked me about my family," offered Veda.

"Your family is fine," said Burns. "They don't know anything about any of this, as far as we know."

Veda seemed unsure how to take the news. Burns figured Veda might need some help explaining any of this to his family. Suddenly Veda smiled, as if acknowledging Burns.

"I thought you were American, too."

"No sir, I'm Canadian, eh," Burns replied. He was struck by the thought that it might be the first time he wasn't offended by the supposition. More relief than pride. He was just glad that Veda's eyes were back in the present moment. "I spent a lot of time in the UK, and abroad, as a boy and a young…" He was going to say soldier. "Man. A younger man."

"You sounded like a football hooligan," said Veda.

"Well, thank you," said Burns with the false modesty of a West End actor on Opening Night. Burns could see his performance didn't land the way he had wanted it to do.

"I had a bad experience," Veda almost whispered, stung by a painful memory. "with some football hooligans when I was younger."

I'll bet you did. Burns wondered if he should apologise. Not a good idea right now, he reasoned. No, he wanted to close that window not open it.

"I do voices sometimes," he shrugged. "That's one I know works on a lot of Yanks, is all."

"Yes," said Veda and lightening more, "It was very convincing."

"Yeah," Burns chuckled softly and looked out the window opposite. He spotted a case of bottled water under the bench and reached over and pulled one out, cracked the seal and presented it to Veda. Then he grabbed a bottle for himself, opened it, raised it in a toast and drank.

"Just a few little sips," Burns insisted. He knew that Veda had had more than his fill when he was being waterboarded with a hood over his head. "Your body needs it." Burns knew that even if he been drowning him for hours earlier, a few sips would help to further take the edge of Veda's shock.

"Yes," said Veda in that same distant, flattened tone. Then he added sincerely, "Thank you. Thank you very much." He took the bottle and held it for a few moments, eyes closed. Burns knew enough to look away and let the man pray.

Burns gazed out the window. The spring sunrise was slowly warming the sky above the clouds at the horizon, appearing as much to the north as to the east, like he had witnessed at this time of year in Northern Canada and Finland. It would be a few hours before the band of light would be enough to shut off the streetlights. The sun would wake the sleeping city. Eventually, the warm band of light would be enough to continue the spring thaw and shrink the white, snowy mantle draped on the shoulders of the mountains in the distance.

Burns' reverie dissolved when the co-pilot appeared in the aft ramp and jumped in. He took one brief look at Burns and ignored Veda as he strode past and disappeared into the forward cabin. A few seconds later a voice creaked from the overhead speaker announcing simply, "Chocks away in two." A split second later the twin overhead engines kicked and sputtered to life.

The group of men outside had grown to ten and they began to make their way single file toward the plane. The first man moved to the centre of the port side bench and took a seat, leaving three spaces broadest between himself and Burns. The others followed, taking their places, alternating left and right. Burns, having a bit of fun, greeted each man with a Walmart Greeter's smile, surreptitiously sizing them up, if only out of habit. He was grateful to see that none of the men showed any outward hostility toward him. And their weapons were stowed. The soldiers had been told to let the mission go.

The two Team Leaders entered last and walked single file to the end nearest Burns and Veda, acknowledging each man as they passed. The first leader looked at Burns and threw him a 'thumbs up', holding it long enough to make it a question. Burns eyed Veda, long enough to make it look like an examination, and nodded. The two leaders exchanged a look and sat opposite each other. A moment later, they were both strapped in and slouching down into nap time. Whether it was experience or simple common sense they shared, Burns decided to like the Team Leaders. He bet himself they both knew the words to "The Gambler". And they were men who appreciated the value of sleep as much as he did.

The crew member he had locked eyes with outside was the last man in. He sealed the door and would have marched straight to the cockpit had Burns not stopped him with a quick grab on his elbow.

"Would you happen to have an extra jacket, for my friend?" he asked, but it didn't sound like a question. The crewman nodded and went aft to the cargo area and reappeared quickly with an airman's jumpsuit. He dropped it on the seat beside Veda, without a word, and headed for the cockpit.

"Thank you," Burns sang cheerily after the engineer. He picked up the better-insulated jumpsuit and helped Veda into it. Veda cozied into the oversized suit, looking like a kid in a sleeping bag. Burns watched as Veda fastened the buckle on his seat belt and the two nestled into their seats.

"All strapped in?" asked Burns. He leaned over and checked Veda's eyes once more. "Good," he smiled. "Shouldn't be long now."

Veda clapped his hands together softly and smiled, nodding slowly. He held the last nod for a slight bow to Burns, which he returned. Burns pulled at the sleeves of his own jacket and tucked in his hands then folded his arms into a pillow between his head and the bulkhead.

"Get some rest," he said. He laid his head back and closed his eyes.

"Kaia?" Veda suddenly blurted. "Dawson?"

"He's fine, recovering from being drugged," Burns answered.

"And Kaia?"

Burns considered what hope Veda might have if he told him that his best guess was that Kaia was still alive. But he had no idea where in the world she was, or who she was with. It wasn't his business to tell the young scientist that he had been played. Burns put the image of the seductive terrorist out of his mind before the anger could take hold. The engines roared overhead and the plane rolled to life.

"She isn't waiting for you back in London."

Burns had to shout over the din and failed to keep his tone sympathetic. The truth hit hard in the long pause as the two men turned their gaze outward at the horizon passing slowly by.

"I'm sorry but I forgot your name," Veda tried to crack the deafening silence, but the sound of the engines drowned him out.

"Charles Burns," he shouted back. "Metropolitan Police, Major Crimes Unit."

"I see," acknowledged Veda. "Thank you, Detective Burns."

Burns smiled. "I'm just a training officer," he shrugged modestly.

"I see," answered Veda, who didn't see.

"It's complicated," Burns shrugged.

"I see," Veda smiled, then asked, "Officer Burns, then?"

Burns laughed. The million-dollar question. His official title didn't matter. He imagined that his official transfer would be confirmed in short order, but for now...

He had successfully completed his mission, his first mission. It had been more soldiering and less detecting, and he had acted on his old instincts to achieve his mission's success. His body had responded. He was satisfied, not angry or afraid, for the moment. Maybe the scientist had put the world in danger. Maybe it was an accident. If Ivanov did manage to get something out of Veda, or Mary... Or both...

That's on the Americans. For now, it was head back and feet up until he was back at MCU2. His new unit. Debriefing would be quick, especially if Chief Wayne had been in on all the details all along. Burns wondered about the next step, if there was one, but only for a moment as the plane banked east and arched into the sunrise.

He pulled his left arm from under his head and laid it over his eyes, wishing he had one of his trusty black t-shirts to shield him from the sunlight.

"Just Burns," he answered, without raising his arm from his eyes.

AUTHOR'S NOTE:

This book is the first in the series. "Drowning" is also my first novel. I'm a self-publishing author, and I rely a lot on word of mouth to get my stories out there and in front of more readers. If you liked Book One: Drowning", and you know someone who might enjoy reading it, please forward my email (deantheraven@gmail.com) to them and I'll send them a free copy of the Ebook (limited offer!).

If you read "Drowning" and didn't like it, feel free to keep that to yourself. (Kidding.) Someone said, "There's no such thing as bad publicity", so there's that...
But maybe some of your friends might still enjoy the Something in the Water series, who knows? Feel free to pass this book on, with my regards.

Either way, it would be great if you could share your *honest review* of Book One: "Drowning" on Amazon, or anywhere people meet books.

With gratitude,
Dean

The following is a little Teaser, three scenes from "Blood" — the next book in the series. I don't recommend reading on if you haven't finished "Drowning", especially the first excerpt, which follows on from where Book One ends (and contains Spoilers).

Burns needed to stretch his legs. He glanced at the clock. He had been sitting too long. The tension had returned, a chill that started in his legs and stabbed at his core. It wasn't fatigue. He knew the agitation, the restlessness, wasn't his muscles reaction to the battle. Combat always cleared his mind and sharpened his senses. It was the frustration of sitting out that was twitching under his ribs. He didn't like to sit out. Especially when it gave him too much time to think.

The game was far from over.

He rose up tall and shrugged his shoulders, rolling his head from side to side. He stood spread-eagled and tried to twist the tension out of his body, turning his hips and torso side to side. Keeping his arms at his sides, he leaned his torso over to his right, then left, exaggerating the stretches for anyone who might be watching. Relaxed but ready.

Burns looked over at Hilts, who was sitting on the bench opposite, with the rest of the Ravens. They had forgotten about Burns sitting in the penalty box and were all watching the action on the ice.

He had let the frustration to boil over into anger. Again. It was in a scrum in front of the goal. Burns had come in from his wing to help the Ravens defenders battle the Saints forwards. A gangly Saint named Clarke, who usually stayed on the edge of the play, poked at the puck just as Smitty, the Ravens' goalkeeper, covered it with his catching glove. Burns gave his opponent just enough of a bump to send him arse over teakettle and into the goal behind Smitty. "Watch your fucking stick!" he shouted at Clarke's back.

The whistle blew, and when Clarke tried to extricate himself from the goal, Burns crosschecked him to the ice. The referee blew several short blasts on the whistle. Burns stood up and backed out of the crease, but he knew it was too late.

The referee pointed at him and made a 'T' with her hands, signaling an Unsportsmanlike Conduct penalty.

"Old time hockey," Burns said with a shrug, and a menacing smile for all the Saints players that had clustered around the front of the goal.

None of Clarke's teammates on the ice took exception to Burns' rough play, they all avoided his glare. Burns had his game face on, the snarling smile he had cultivated as a teenager playing competitive hockey in Calgary. He skated away from the cluster, looking innocent as he could when he passed the referee. Instead of going directly to the penalty box, he skated a slow loop toward the opponents' bench, silently challenging any player who returned his gaze.

One of the Saints, a team sponsored by one of the oldest Anglican churches in England, took the bait.

"Fuck you, Yank!"

Burns stopped gliding and took two quick strides to the boards to face his accuser. He leaned over the boards and glowered at the offending Saint.

"What did you call me?"

The referee blew the whistle, chirping wildly. Burns spun around to see the referee skating fast in his direction.

"We'll be having none of that tonight, Burns. That's two minutes." She signaled a misconduct penalty by placing her hands on her hips. "Two plus ten," she said.

The extended sentence had given him time to stew instead of cooling his temper. He had no way of knowing if Ivanov and whoever he was working with knew that Veda was safe back in England. He knew that the lab in Reykjavik would never produce a bioweapon. He had made sure of that. But Ivanov had escaped, and Burns wanted to find him. Find him and kill him. Ivanov had been responsible for countless deaths and had done enough evil before he kidnapped Veda to earn a guilty verdict. British and American intelligence had enough on Ivanov from his days in the old Soviet Army to charge him with war crimes. But he had never been charged with a crime. Burns wondered if Chief Inspector Wayne and MCU2 had gathered any more intel on Ivanov since that wild night last weekend. *Like, where is he?*

Burns sat down hard. *Unanswered questions.* He glanced at the clock and bounced back up when he saw there was less than a minute remaining is his sentence. His sudden movement jolted the timekeeper's attention away from the action on the ice. Burns directed the chubby volunteer's bespectacled eyes to the timer counting down the last few seconds of his penalty. He followed the timekeeper's gaze as it squinted at the heavy bolt on the gate and back up to the clock. He smiled sheepishly and rotated back to the action going on behind the Ravens' goal.

"Gotta wait for a whistle, Boss."

Burns' penalty expired, but he wasn't allowed back on the ice until play stopped. He whistled and shouted, "Hiltsy!" and pointed at the clock when the big defenceman glanced over at him. A few seconds later, Hilts got the puck and *accidentally* shot it into the Saints bench, causing the players to duck and a stoppage in play. Burns skated onto the ice and checked in with the Captain. He gave Hilts a nod of gratitude.

"Nice shot, Cap'n."

"No apologies necessary," Hilts smiled. He glanced over at the referee as they glided toward the face-off circle. "No harm, no foul." He put his hand on Burns' shoulder and leaned in for a two-man huddle and whispered, "Hey, can women have a Napoleon Complex?"

As they skated back to centre ice, Hilts grabbed Burns in a friendly headlock and leaned in to butt helmets. "One more," he said, loud enough for everyone around to hear. The big grin pursed into a whisper. "I gotta talk to you," he said. "After."

Burns saw the mischievous look in Hilts' eyes. He looked like a little kid with big a secret. Burns laughed and turned to another teammate, Danny Salloum, who played right wing when Burns wasn't on the ice.

"Take a break, Danny?" Burns asked.

Salloum nodded and looked up at the clock. He didn't need convincing.

"Better get us one, Burnsy."

Salloum gave Burns a stick tap on the shins and skated toward the bench. Burns spun round and skated backward, watching until his teammate turned to face him again. The body language, and the wide smile, told Burns there were no hard feelings.

"Roger that," Burns grinned.

He was thinking of two goals. One was the game-tying goal at the other end of the rink, easy to visualise scoring. He did it in the Ravens' last game. The memory was both visual and physical. He took Salloum's spot on the right side. He didn't really know the other two forwards, but that didn't matter. What he visualised happening didn't involve anyone but himself. He knew what he was going to do, and he wouldn't need any help. He'd put the puck in the top left corner of the net and shout "Yeah, Baby!" just like his favourite announcer.

He stood motionless, staring at the Saints' goaltender while his mind remapped the route to the target. The other goal was Vladimir Konstantin Ivanov, to "remove him from the battlefield". More specifically, to see Ivanov dead. He was a bad man who had done bad things and would continue if he wasn't stopped. Burns tried to meld the two targets, putting Ivanov's face in the goalie's mask. But the sharp, shrill referee's whistle vaporized the image of the Russian psychopath.

Ivanov was gone. Again. Burns almost missed the puck drop but was able to get his stick on it and sweep it away from the cluster, sending it back to Hilts. "Flipper!" he shouted.

Hilts flipped the puck over the crowd at centre ice. It landed inside the Saints' blue line, directly in front of a sprinting Burns. He beat the defender to the puck and spun him to the ice with an outside-inside move. The goalie's eyes were fearful as Burns bore down. He imagined staring down Ivanov, with deadly intent. But he couldn't picture a look of fear on the grim visage. The eyes were as dark as a shark's.

He fired a blistering shot that was in and out of the net before the frightened goalie reacted. "One down, one to go," he said.

■■■

The Security Service had spoken with Heathrow airport authority and the MCU2 team were granted permission to go around customs and security control. Two transports carried the team and their gear through a side gate and onto a taxiway. The oversized RAF Atlas waited on the tarmac. It was more than his six man team needed, but at least he wouldn't need to calculate the fuel and flight time. Burns spotted the fuel truck driving away on the other side of the aircraft as the transports came to a halt. He jumped out as the driver pulled the break.

"Step out and stand by, fellas," said Burns. He closed the door and waved at the ground crew, three men and one woman, all dressed in military fatigues. Then he walked to the rear of the transport and opened the doors. Kaake got out of his transport and did the same.

Burns smiled at the crew, enough to bend the dimple in his cheek.

"It's all yours," he said. He greeted them cordially and watched as they loaded the gear on board. Then he waved his team over.

Burns eyed each man, catching and holding each pair of eyes as they passed. He wanted to let them know he trusted them. *Just not how much.*

It was always hard for Burns to trust new teammates. On the ice, sure. Nobody's life is at stake. *Really.* But he had to know every soldier he went into battle with long enough, in training and off-base, to allow a mutual trust to build. Commanding Officers were no different. However, he was not always afforded the time or opportunity to judge the integrity of his superiors before he was ordered into action. The trust was not always mutual. Often, like tonight, not required.

Burns knew that he wasn't going to have to rely on his teammates for the mission to succeed. For his part of it, the plan was simple: *I go in first.*

He slept from the time the plane reached altitude until it began the descent into KEF.

■■

They drove in silence. The full moon lit the low fog hanging over the barren landscape. Burns cleared away the images of Ivanov's victims, past and future.

"Give one flash on your left turn indicator when you pass the driveway," said Burns. "For Aitkens."

Burns noted the Tesla parked in the lot, and the small tent pitched in the open pasture between the lot and the waterfall trail. He pointed as they passed. "You can camp anywhere in Iceland, unless there's a sign asking you not to," he explained.

Burns watched in the mirror as Aitkens signalled and turned into the lot. When he looked up again, he saw the hut. The lights were on.

■■

The 'ping' from his phone stirred him from another restless sleep. He hadn't slept properly since he made his hasty escape from Reykjavik. He knew it hadn't been a week, but the nights and days had seemed endless.

So, they still had this number. He had purposely refrained from using the phone to avoid being tracked.

Ivanov stared at the message.

He's gone, sir

He held his breath and pressed the button to dial the number. It rang once.

"He's gone, sir," the voice repeated the text.

"Gone," said Ivanov. "I know he's gone. Gone where?"

"We can't find him, General. His whereabouts are unknown. He has closed all contact."

And Kaia was with him, no doubt.

"What have you heard about the search?"

"Nothing, sir. I mean they are doing nothing. There is no search. They are saying it was an accident."

Ivanov squeezed flat the smile that wanted to celebrate. At least he still had friends in high places. For now.

"And Mary's Children?" he asked.

"We believe they all made it home, General."

"Thank you, comrade," said Ivanov. "You will contact me again when you find him, won't you?"

"Yes, my General. Of course."

Plan B was proceeding, at least. He stared at the two aluminium cases. Plan A wasn't dead yet.

CPSIA information can be obtained
at www.ICGtesting.com
Printed in the USA
LVHW021859180421
684845LV00012B/1296

9 798700 778350